WITHDRAWN

W9-AUZ-234

MERCY

JULIE GARWOOD

MERCY

WHEELER
PUBLISHING, INC.
ROCKLAND, MA

★ AN AMERICAN COMPANY ★

ASHEVILLE-BUNCOMBE LIBRARY SYSTEM

Copyright © 2001 by Julie Garwood
All rights reserved.

Published in Large Print by arrangement with Pocket Books, a division of Simon & Schuster, Inc., in the United States and Canada.

Wheeler Large Print Book Series.

Set in 16 pt Plantin.

Library of Congress Cataloging-in-Publication Data.

Garwood, Julie.
    Mercy / Julie Garwood.
        p. (large print) cm. (Wheeler large print book series)
    ISBN 1-58724-167-6 (hardcover)
    1. Lawyers—Louisiana—Fiction. 2. White collar crimes—Louisiana—Fiction. 3. Louisiana—Fiction. 4. Large type books. I. Title. II. Series

[PS3557.A8427 M47   2002]

2002016715
CIP

WHEELER LIBRARY SYSTEM

For my sister Mary Colette (Cookie) Benson
for your humor and your heart

I had Ambition, by which sin
    The Angels fell;
I climbed and, step by step, O Lord,
    Ascended into Hell.
              —W. H. Davies, *Ambition*

PROLOGUE

The girl was just plain amazing with a knife. She had a natural talent, a gift from God Almighty, or so her father, Big Daddy Jake Renard, told her when, at the tender age of five and a half, she gutted her first speckled trout with the precision and expertise of a professional. Her father was so proud, he picked her up, put her on his shoulders—with her little skinny knees on either side of his face—and carried her down to his favorite watering hole, The Swan. He plopped her down on the bar and gathered his friends around to watch her gut another fish he'd tucked into the back pocket of his worn-out overalls. Milo Mullen was so impressed he offered to buy the child for fifty dollars cash right then and there, and he boasted that he could make three times that amount in one week renting the little girl out to the local fish shacks on the bayou.

Knowing Milo was only trying to be complimentary, Big Daddy Jake didn't take offense. Besides, Milo bought him a drink and made a real nice toast to his talented daughter.

Jake had three children. Remy, the oldest, and John Paul, a year younger, weren't even teenagers yet, but he could already see they were going to be bigger than he was. The boys were pistols, slipping in and out of mischief every single day, and both as smart as whips. He was proud of his boys, but it was a fact that his little Michelle was the apple of

1

his eye. He never once held it against her that she damned near killed her mama getting herself born. His own sweet Ellie had what the doctors called a massive stroke inside her head right smack in the middle of that final push, and after her daughter was washed and wrapped in clean blankets, Ellie was taken from their marriage bed to the local hospital on the other side of St. Claire. A week later, when it was determined that she was never going to wake up, she was transferred by ambulance to a state institution. The doctor in charge of Ellie's care called the foul place a nursing home, but Big Daddy, seeing the stark, gray, stone building surrounded by an eight-foot iron fence, knew the doctor was lying to him. It wasn't a home at all. It was purgatory, plain and simple, a holding area here on earth where all the poor, lost souls did their penance before God welcomed them into heaven.

Jake cried the first time he went to see his wife, but he remained dry-eyed after that. Tears wouldn't make Ellie's condition any better or the terrible place she rested in any less bleak. The long hallway down the center of the building opened to room after room of seafoam green walls, institutional gray linoleum tile floors, and rickety old beds that squeaked every time the side rails were raised or lowered. Ellie was in a big square room with eleven other patients, some lucid, but most not, and there wasn't even enough space to pull up a chair next to her bed and sit a spell and talk to her.

Jake would have felt worse if his wife had known where she was resting, but her brain kept her in a state of perpetual sleep. What she didn't know couldn't upset her, he decided, and that fact gave him considerable peace of mind.

Every Sunday afternoon, once he had gotten out of bed and shaken off his aches and pains, he took Michelle to see her mama. The two of them, hand in hand, would stand at the foot of Ellie's bed and stare at her for a good ten or fifteen minutes, and then they would leave. Sometimes Michelle would pick a bouquet of wildflowers and tie them with twine and make a pretty bow. She'd leave them on her mama's pillow so she could smell their sweet fragrance. A couple of times she made a crown of daisies and put them on her mother's head. Her daddy told her the tiara made Mama look real pretty, like a princess.

Jake Renard's luck changed a couple of years later when he won sixty thousand dollars in a private numbers game. Since it wasn't legal and the government didn't know about it, Jake didn't have to pay taxes on his windfall. He considered using the money to move his wife to a more pleasant setting, but somewhere deep down inside his head he could hear Ellie's voice scolding him for being impractical, wanting to spend the money on something that would do no one any good. And so, instead, Jake decided to use a little of the cash to buy The Swan. He wanted his boys to have a future tending bar when they finished growing up, stopped chasing skirts, and settled down with wives and babies to support. The rest of the money he tucked away for his retirement.

When Michelle wasn't in school—Jake didn't figure she needed an education, but the state figured she did—he took her everywhere he went. On fishing days, she sat beside him and passed the time talking like a magpie or reading stories to him out of the books she made him take her to the library to get. While he took his afternoon nap, she set the table and her brothers prepared supper. She was quite the little homemaker. She kept an immaculate house, no small feat given the fact that her father and her brothers were admittedly slovenly. In the summer months she always had fresh flowers in mason jars on the tables.

In the evening, Michelle accompanied Big Daddy to The Swan for the late shift. Some nights the little girl fell asleep curled up like a tabby cat in the corner of the bar, and he'd have to carry her to the storage room in back, where he had a daybed set up for her. He treasured every minute he had with his daughter because he figured that, like many of the girls in the parish, she'd be pregnant and married by the time she turned eighteen.

It wasn't that he had low expectations for Michelle, but he was a realist, and all the pretty girls married young around Bowen, Louisiana. It was just the way things were, and Jake didn't figure his daughter would turn out any different. There wasn't much for the boys and girls to do in town except diddle with one another, and it was plain inevitable that the girls eventually found themselves in the family way.

Jake owned a quarter acre of land. He had built a one-bedroom cabin when he married Ellie, and he added on rooms as his family expanded. When the boys were old enough to help, he raised the roof and created a loft so that Michelle could have some privacy. The family lived deep in the swamp at the end of a winding dirt lane called Mercy Road. There were trees everywhere, some as old as a hundred years. In the backyard were two weeping willows nearly covered in moss that hung like crocheted scarves from the branches to the ground. When the mist rolled in from the bayou and the wind picked up and began to moan, the moss took on the eerie appearance of ghosts in the moonlight. On those nights, Michelle would scramble down from the loft and sneak into bed with Remy or John Paul.

From their house, the neighboring town of St. Claire was a quick twenty-minute walk away. There were treelined paved streets there, but it wasn't as pretty or as poor as Bowen. Jake's neighbors were used to poverty. They did the best they could to scratch a living out of the swampland and the water, and they scraped together an extra dollar every Wednesday night to play the numbers in hopes they would catch a windfall the way Jake Renard had.

Life took another surprising turn for the Renard family when Michelle entered the third grade at the Horatio Hebert Elementary School. She was assigned a brand-new teacher, Miss Jennifer Perine. During the fourth week of school, Miss Perine administered the standardized tests, received the results, and then sent an urgent request home with Michelle for a parent-teacher conference.

Jake had never gone to one of those before. He figured his daughter had gotten into a spot of trouble, maybe a little fistfight. She could be hot-tempered when pushed to the wall. Her brothers had taught her how to defend herself. She was little for her age, and they assumed she'd be an easy target for the bullies at school to pick on, so they made sure she knew how to fight, and fight dirty.

Jake reckoned he'd have to soothe the teacher's nerves. He put on his good Sunday clothes, added a splash of the Aqua Velva he only used on special occasions, and walked the mile and a half to the school.

Miss Perine turned out to be a pain in the ass, which Jake expected, but she was also pretty, and he hadn't expected that at all. He was immediately suspicious. Why would an attractive, young, single woman want to teach in the little gnat of a town of Bowen? With her fine looks and her shapely figure, she could get herself a job anywhere. And how come she wasn't married yet? She looked to be in her twenties, and in the parish that made her a spinster.

The teacher assured him she didn't have any bad news to impart. Quite the contrary.

She wanted to tell him what an exceptional child Michelle was. Jake's back stiffened. He interpreted her remarks to mean that his daughter wasn't quite right in the head. Everyone in the parish called Buddy Dupond an exceptional child, even after the police hauled him away and locked him up in a loony bin for setting fire to his parents' house. Buddy didn't mean any harm, and he wasn't out to kill anyone. He just had a fascination with fires. He'd set over twelve good ones—all in the swamp, where the damage didn't matter. He told his mama that he just plain loved fires. He liked the way they smelled, the way they glowed all orange and yellow and red in the dark, and most of all he liked the snap, crackle, and pop noise they made. Just like the cereal. The doctor who examined Buddy must have thought he was exceptional, all right. He gave him a fancy name. Pyromaniac.

It turned out that Miss Perine hadn't meant to insult Jake's little girl after all, and when he realized that fact, he relaxed. She told him that, after she had received the first set of tests back and read the results, she'd had Michelle tested by experts. Jake didn't know squat about IQs or how these experts could measure an eight-year-old's intelligence, but he wasn't surprised that his Michelle was—as he proudly told Miss Perine—as smart as a cookie.

It was imperative that he do right by the child. She told Jake that Michelle was already reading adult literature and that she was going to be skipping the equivalent of two full grades next Monday. Did he know that Michelle had an aptitude for science and math? Jake summed up all the educated talk to mean that his little girl was a natural-born genius.

Miss Perine told him that she believed she was a good teacher, but even so, she knew she wasn't going to be able to keep up with Michelle's educational needs. She wanted the little girl moved to a private school where her talents could be nurtured and she could set her own learning curve—whatever in tarnation that meant.

Jake stood, towering over the teacher as he shook her hand and thanked her for the nice things she had to say about Michelle. However, he added, he wasn't interested in sending his daughter away. She was just a little girl, after all, and it was too soon for her to leave her family.

Miss Perine coaxed him to hear her out. She offered him a glass of lemonade and pleaded with him to sit down again. Since she'd gone to the trouble of fixing refreshments—there was a little plate of cookies on the table too—he reckoned he had to be polite and listen.

The teacher started talking a mile a minute then, telling him all about the advantages his daughter would have with the proper schooling, and surely Jake didn't want to deprive her of the wonderful opportunities that would open for her. Miss Perine pulled a pink folder from her desk drawer and handed him a slick brochure with pictures so he could see what the school looked like. Michelle would love it there, she promised him. She would study hard, certainly, but there would also be time for fun.

Jake wanted the best for his daughter, and so he listened to every word Miss Perine had to say. The two of them were getting along just fine, sipping tart lemonade and chewing sweet peanut butter cookies while they chatted amicably about his girl, but damn if she didn't insult him by suggesting that he could apply for state assistance in paying the tuition, maybe even qualify for a grant he wouldn't have to pay back. Jake had to remind himself that the woman was new to Bowen and didn't know any better. Surely she hadn't meant any harm. Why, she was just trying to be helpful. But because she *was* new to the parish, she didn't have any notion how important a man's pride was in these parts. Take pride away from a man and you might as well run a knife through his heart.

Jake gritted his teeth as he politely explained he wasn't about to become a charity case, and he wasn't going to let anyone else pay for his daughter's education.

He was considered by some to be well-off because of his gambling windfall, but she didn't know anything about that, of course. Folks didn't talk about their illegal betting games with outsiders. Nevertheless, he still didn't much care for her making snap judgments about a family based on how they dressed or where they lived. If Jake decided to send his girl to that fancy school, he'd use

9

his retirement nest egg to pay the tuition, and when that money was all used up, then his sons could take on extra jobs to help with expenses.

But, before any decisions were going to be made, he thought he ought to discuss the matter with his wife. He talked to Ellie all the time, in his head anyway, and he liked to think she appreciated being included and that, in her magical way, she helped guide him with important family decisions.

He reckoned he ought to talk it out with Michelle too. She deserved to have a say in her future.

The following Sunday he took her fishing. They sat side by side on the dock with their fishing poles dangling in the murky water. His big knife was nestled in his leather pouch as a precaution against predators.

"Fish aren't biting, are they?" he remarked while he tried to figure a way to broach the subject of changing schools.

"Of course not, Daddy. I don't know why we're fishing this time of day. You're always telling me early morning is the best time to catch fish. How come you wanted to come fishing this late? It's going on to four already."

"I know what time it is, smarty-pants. I wanted to get you away from your brothers and have a talk with you about something... important."

"Why don't you just spit it out, then?" she asked.

"Don't you sass me."

"I'm not sassing you. Honest." She crossed her heart with her fingers.

She was as cute as a button, he thought, staring up at him with those big blue eyes. She needed her bangs trimmed again. They were hanging down, catching on her long lashes. He guessed he'd get the scissors out after supper.

"That Miss Perine's a real nice lady. She's pretty too."

She turned away from him and stared down at the water. "I don't know about that. She smells good, but she doesn't smile very much."

"Teaching is serious work," he explained. "That's probably why she doesn't do a lot of smiling. Do you get along with her?"

"I guess I do."

"We had a real nice visit about you the other night."

"That's what you wanted to talk to me about, isn't it? I just knew it."

"Hush now and hear me out. Miss Perine thinks you're an exceptional child."

Her eyes widened and she shook her head. "I don't set fires, Daddy. Honest."

"I know you don't," he replied. "She doesn't mean you're exceptional like Buddy Dupond. She means you're real smart."

"I don't like her."

She turned away again. He gave her a little nudge to get her to look up at him. "How come you don't like her? Is she making you work too hard? Is she putting too many demands on you?"

"I don't know what you mean, Daddy."

"Is the work too hard for you to do?"

She giggled as though he'd just made a joke. "Oh, no. It's awful easy, and sometimes I get bored because I get it all done too soon, and I have to sit there and wait until Miss Perine can find something else for me to do. Some of the kids are just now learning how to read, but I've been reading since I was little. Remember?"

He smiled. "I remember when you started in reading the paper to me while I shaved. You pretty much taught yourself."

"No, I didn't. You taught me the letters."

"But you put them together pretty much on your own. All I did was read to you. You picked it up quick. Took to it like a duck..."

"To water," she ended.

"That's right, sugar. Tell me why you don't like Miss Perine. Is it because you have to wait on her?"

"No."

"Well, then?"

"She wants to send me away," she blurted. Tears flooded her eyes, and her voice trembled. "Doesn't she, Daddy? She told me she wants to make you send me away to a different school where I won't know anybody."

"Now, you ought to know nobody's gonna make your daddy do anything he doesn't want to do, but this Miss Perine...well, now, she got me started in thinking."

"She's a busybody. Don't you pay her any mind."

Jake shook his head. His little girl had just turned one of his favorite sayings back on him. When her brothers teased her, he always told her not to pay them any mind.

"Your teacher says you've got a real high IQ."

"I didn't do it on purpose."

"There isn't anything wrong with being smart, but Miss Perine thinks we ought to figure a way to get you the best education we can. She thinks you can make something of yourself. I never considered it before, but I guess it isn't written in stone that you've got to get married and have babies lickety-split. Maybe this family has been setting our sights too low."

"Maybe so, Daddy."

He knew from her tone of voice that she was attempting to placate him.

"But I don't want anything to change," she added then.

"I know you don't," he said. "You know your mama would want us to do the right thing."

"Is Mama smart?"

"Oh, my, yes. She sure is."

"She got married and had babies lickety-split."

Lord, his girl was bright, all right. And how come it took a brand-new teacher to make him realize it?

"That's because I came along and swept her off her feet."

"'Cause you were irresistible. Right?"

"That's right."

"Maybe you ought to have a talk with Mama before you make up your mind about sending me away. She might know what you're supposed to do."

He was so shocked by what she'd just said, he jerked. "You know I like to talk things over with your mama?"

"Uh-huh."

"How could you know?"

She smiled up at him, her eyes shining. "'Cause sometimes you talk out loud. It's okay, Daddy. I like to talk things over with Mama too."

"All right, then. Tomorrow, when we go visit your mama, we'll both talk this over with her."

She started splashing her feet in the water. "I think she's gonna tell me I should stay home with you and Remy and John Paul."

"Now, listen here—"

"Daddy, tell me how you and Mama met. I know you've told me the story hundreds of times, but I never get tired of hearing it."

They had veered off the subject, and he knew his daughter had done it on purpose. "We aren't talking about your mama and me now. We're talking about you. I want to ask you an important question. Put your fishing pole down and pay attention."

She did as he said and waited with her hands folded in her lap. She was such a little lady, he thought to himself, and how in thunder had that happened living with three lumbering mules?

"If you could be anything in the world, anything at all, what do you suppose you'd be?" She was making a church steeple with her fingers. He tugged on her ponytail to get her attention. "You don't need to be embarrassed with your daddy. You can tell me."

"I'm not embarrassed."

"Your hair's getting red and so are your freckles."

She giggled. "My hair's already red, and my freckles can't change color."

"Are you gonna tell me or not?"

"You have to promise not to laugh."

"I'm not gonna laugh."

"Remy and John Paul would maybe laugh."

"Your brothers are idiots. They laugh at just about anything, but you know they love you and they'll work hard to see you get what you want."

"I know," she said.

"Are you gonna tell me or not? It sounds like you've already got some ideas about what you'd like to be."

"I do know," she admitted. She looked him right in the eyes to make sure he wasn't going to laugh and then whispered, "I'm going to be a doctor."

He hid his surprise and didn't say a word for a long minute while he chewed the notion over in his mind.

"Now, why do you suppose you want to be a doctor?" he asked, already warming to the idea.

"Because then maybe I could fix...something. I've been thinking about it for a long time, ever since I was little."

"You're still little," he said. "And doctors fix people, not things."

"I know that, Daddy," she said with such authority in her voice she made him smile.

"You got someone in mind you want to fix?"

Big Daddy put his arm around his daughter's shoulders and hauled her into his side. He already knew the answer, but he wanted to hear her say the words.

She brushed her bangs out of her eyes and slowly nodded. "I was thinking maybe I could fix Mama's head. Then she could come home."

CHAPTER ONE

PRESENT DAY, NEW ORLEANS

The first one was a mercy killing. She was dying a very, very slow death. Each day there was a new indignity, another inch of her once magnificent body destroyed by the debilitating disease. Poor, poor Catherine. Seven years ago she had been a beautiful bride with a trim, hourglass figure men lusted after and women envied, but now her body was fat and grossly bloated, and her once perfect alabaster skin was blotchy and sallow.

There were times when her husband, John, didn't recognize her anymore. He would remember what she used to look like and then see with startling clarity what she had become. Those wonderful sparkling green eyes that had so captivated him when he'd first met her were now glazed and milky from too many painkillers.

The monster was taking its time killing her, and for him there wasn't a moment's respite.

He dreaded going home at night. He always stopped on Royal Street to purchase a two-pound box of Godiva chocolates first. It was a ritual he had started months ago to prove to her that he still loved her in spite of her appearance. He could have had the chocolates delivered daily to the house, of course, but the errand stretched out the time before he had to face her again. The next morning the almost empty gold box would be in the porcelain trash can next to the king-size canopy bed. He would pretend not to notice she'd gorged herself on the sweets, and so would she.

John no longer condemned her for her gluttony. The chocolates gave her pleasure, he supposed, and there was precious little of that in her bleak, tragic existence these days.

Some nights, after purchasing the chocolates, he would return to his office and work until fatigue overcame him and he'd be forced to go home. As he maneuvered his BMW convertible up St. Charles to the Garden District of New Orleans, he'd inevitably start shaking as if he were suffering from hypothermia, but he wouldn't actually become physically ill until he entered the black-and-white foyer of his house. Gripping the box of chocolates in his hand, he'd place his Gucci briefcase on the hall table and stand there in front of the gilded mirror for a minute or two taking deep, calming breaths. They never soothed him, but he repeated the habit anyway night after night. His harsh breathing would mingle with the ticking of the grandfather clock on the wall adjacent to the mirror. The tick-tick-tick would remind him of the timer on a bomb. A bomb that was inside his head and about to explode.

Calling himself a coward, he would make himself go upstairs. His shoulders would tense and his stomach would twist into knots as he slowly climbed the circular staircase, his legs feeling as though they were encased in cement socks. By the time he reached the end of the long hallway, perspiration would dot his brow and he would feel cold and clammy.

He'd wipe his forehead with his handkerchief, plaster a phony smile on his face, and open the door, trying with all his might to mentally brace himself for the foul stench hanging in the air. The room smelled of iron pills, and the thick vanilla-scented air freshener the maids insisted on spraying into the stagnant air only made the stench worse. Some nights it was so bad, he had to hurry out of the room on a false errand before she heard him gag. He would go to any length to keep her from knowing how repulsed he was.

Other nights his stomach could handle it. He'd close his eyes while he leaned down and kissed her forehead, then he'd move away while he talked to her. He'd stand by the treadmill he'd bought for her a year after they were married. He couldn't remember if she had ever turned it on. A stethoscope and two identical, voluminous, floral silk bathrobes hung on its handlebars now, and its wide black vinyl belt wore a coat of dust. The maids never seemed to remember to clean it. Sometimes, when he couldn't bear to look at Catherine, he'd turn and stare out the arched Palladian windows at the softly lit English garden behind the house, enclosed like

19

all the other minuscule yards with a black wrought-iron fence.

The television would be blaring behind him. It was on twenty-four hours a day, turned to either the talk shows or the shopping network. She never thought to turn it down when he was talking to her, and he'd gotten to the point where he could ignore it. Although he'd learned to block the incessant chatter, he often found himself marveling over the deterioration of her brain. How could she watch such drivel hour after hour after hour? There had been a time, before the illness took over her life and her personality, when she had been an intellectual who could cut any adversary to the quick with one of her incredibly clever whiplash retorts. He remembered how she loved to debate politics—put a right-wing conservative at her impeccably appointed dinner table and there were guaranteed fireworks—but now all she wanted to talk about and worry about were her bowel functions. That—and food, of course. She was always eager to talk about her next meal.

He often thought back seven years to their wedding day and remembered how desperately he had wanted her. These days, he dreaded being in the same room with her—he slept in the guest quarters now—and the torment was like acid in his stomach, eating him alive.

Before she had taken to her bed out of necessity, she'd had the spacious suite decorated in pale green tones. The furniture was oversized Italian Renaissance, and there were statues of two favored Roman poets—Ovid and Virgil. The plaster busts squatted on white pedestals flanking the bay window. He had actually liked the room when the clever young interior designer had finished it, so much so that he'd hired her to redecorate his office, but now he despised the bedroom because it represented what was now missing in his life.

As much as he tried, he couldn't escape the constant reminders. A couple of weeks ago he'd met one of his partners at a trendy new bistro on Bienville for lunch, but as soon as he walked inside and saw the pale green walls, his stomach lurched and he had trouble catching his breath. For a few terror-filled minutes he was certain he was having a heart attack. He should have called 911 for help, but he didn't. Instead, he ran outside into the sunlight, taking deep, gasping breaths. The sun on his face helped, and he realized then that he was in the throes of a full-blown anxiety attack.

At times he was certain he was losing his mind.

Thank God for the support of his three closest friends. He met them for drinks every Friday afternoon to unwind, and how he lived for Fridays when he could unburden himself. They would listen and offer him solace and compassion.

What an ironic twist, that he should be the one out drinking with his buddies, while Catherine was the one wasting away in solitude. If the Fates were going to punish one of them for past sins, why her and not him?

21

Catherine had always been the upstanding, morally superior one in the marriage. She had never broken a law in her life, had never even gotten a parking ticket, and she would have been stunned if she'd known all that John and his friends had done.

They called themselves the Sowing Club. Cameron, at thirty-four, was the oldest in the group. Dallas and John were both thirty-three, and Preston, whom they had nick-named Pretty Boy because of his dark good looks, was the youngest at thirty-two. The four friends had gone to the same private school, and though they were in different classes, they had been drawn to each other because they had so much in common. They shared the same drive, the same goals, the same ambition. They also shared the same expensive tastes, and they didn't mind breaking the law to get what they wanted. They started down the criminal path in high school when they found out how easy it was to get away with petty larceny. They also discovered it wasn't very lucrative. On a lark, they committed their first felony when they were in college— robbery of a jewelry store in a nearby town— and they fenced the precious gems like pros. Then John, the most analytical in the group, decided the risks were too great for the return they were getting—even the best-laid plans could go wrong because of the elements of chance and surprise—and so they began committing more sophisticated white-collar crimes, using their education to foster connections.

Their first real windfall came from the Internet. Using their sleek laptops, they purchased worthless stocks under an alias, flooded the chat rooms with false data and rumors, and then, after the stocks had skyrocketed, sold their shares before the security regulators discovered what was going on. The return on that little venture was over five thousand percent.

Every dollar they extorted or stole was put in the Sowing Club account in the Cayman Islands. By the time the four of them had finished graduate school and taken positions in New Orleans, they had collected over four million dollars.

And that only whetted their appetites.

During one of their gatherings, Cameron told the others that if a psychiatrist ever examined them, he would discover that they were all sociopaths. John disagreed. A sociopath didn't consider anyone else's needs or desires. They, on the contrary, were committed to the club and to the pact that they had made to do whatever they had to do to get what they wanted. Their goal was eighty million dollars by the time the oldest turned forty. When Cameron celebrated his thirtieth birthday, they were already halfway there.

Nothing could stop them. Over the years, the bond between the friends had strengthened, and they would do anything, anything at all, to protect the others.

While each of them brought his own special talents to the club, Cameron and Preston and Dallas knew that John was the mastermind, and that without him they would never have gotten this far. They couldn't afford to lose him, and they became increasingly alarmed over his deteriorating state of mind.

John was in trouble, but they didn't know how to help. And so they simply listened as he poured his heart out. The topic of his beloved wife would inevitably come up, and John would fill them in on the latest horrific developments. None of them had seen Catherine in years because of the illness. That was her choice, not theirs, for she wanted them to remember her the way she had been, not the way she was now. They sent gifts and cards, of course. John was like a brother to them, and while they were genuinely sympathetic about his wife's condition, they were much more concerned about him. In their collective opinion, she was, after all, a lost cause. He wasn't. And they could see what he couldn't, that he was headed for disaster. They knew he was having trouble concentrating while at work—a dangerous tendency given his occupation—and he was also drinking too much.

John was getting roaring drunk now. Preston had invited him and the others over to his new penthouse apartment to celebrate the success of their latest venture. They sat at the dining room table in plush upholstered chairs, surrounded by a panoramic view of the Mississippi. It was late, almost midnight, and they could see the lights twinkling outside in the inky darkness. Every few minutes the sound of a foghorn would hum mournfully in the background.

The noise made John melancholy. "How long have we been friends?" He slurred the question. "Does anybody remember?"

"About a million years," Cameron said as he reached for the bottle of Chivas.

Dallas snorted with laughter. "Man, it seems that long, doesn't it?"

"Since high school," Preston said, "when we started the Sowing Club." He turned to John. "You used to intimidate the hell out of me. You were always so smooth and self-assured. You were more polished than the teachers."

"What'd you think of me?" Cameron wanted to know.

"Nervous," Preston answered. "You were always...edgy. You know what I mean? You still are," he added.

Dallas nodded. "You've always been the cautious one in the group."

"The worrier," Preston said. "Whereas Dallas and I have always been more..."

"Daring," Dallas suggested. "I never would have been friends with any of you guys if John hadn't brought us together."

"I saw what you didn't," John said then. "Talent and greed."

"Here, here," Cameron said as he raised his glass in a mock salute to the others.

"I think I was just sixteen when we started the Sowing Club," Dallas said.

"You were still a virgin, weren't you?" Cameron asked.

"Hell, no. I lost my virginity by the time I was nine."

The exaggeration made them laugh. "Okay, so maybe I was a little older," Dallas said.

"God, we were cocky little shits back then, weren't we? Thinking we were so clever with our secret club," Preston said.

"We *were* clever," Cameron pointed out. "And lucky. Do you realize the stupid risks we took?"

"Whenever we wanted to get drunk, we'd call for a meeting of the club," Dallas said. "We're lucky we haven't turned into alcoholics."

"Who says we haven't?" Cameron asked, and then laughed again.

John held up his glass. "A toast to the club and to the tidy profit we just made, thanks to Preston's oh-so-sweet insider information."

"Here, here," Cameron said as he clinked his glass against the others. "I still can't figure out how you got that information, though."

"How do you think I got it?" Preston asked. "I got her drunk, fucked her brains out, and after she passed out, I went through her computer files. All in a night's work."

"You boinked her?" Cameron howled.

" 'Boinked'? Who uses that word these days?" Preston asked.

"I want to know how you got it up. I've seen the woman. She's a pig," Dallas said.

"Hey, I did what I had to do. I just kept thinking about the eight hundred thousand we'd make, and I..."

26

"What?" Cameron asked.

"I closed my eyes, okay? I don't think I can do it again, though. One of you guys will have to take over. It pretty much...sucked," he admitted with a grin over his pun.

Cameron emptied his glass and reached for the bottle. "Well, too bad. You're stuck with the job as long as the women go crazy over those bulging muscles and that movie-star face of yours."

"In five more years we'll all be set for life. We can walk away, disappear if we have to, do whatever we want. Don't lose sight of the goal," Dallas said.

John shook his head. "I don't think I can hold on five more years. I *know* I can't."

"Hey, you've got to keep it together," Cameron said. "We've got too much to lose if you fall apart on us now. You hear me? You're the brains of this outfit. We're just..."

He couldn't come up with the right word. Preston suggested, "Coconspirators?"

"We are that," Dallas said. "But we've all done our part. John's not the only one with brains. I'm the one who brought Monk in, remember?"

"Oh, for God's sake, this isn't the time for an ego tantrum," Preston muttered. "You don't need to tell us how much you do, Dallas. We all know how hard you work. As a matter of fact, that's all you do. You've got nothing outside of your job and the Sowing Club. When's the last time you took a day off or went shopping? I'm guessing never. You wear

27

the same black or navy suit every day. You're still taking a brown bag for lunch—and I'll bet you even take the bag home to use again the next day. For that matter, when have you ever picked up a tab?"

"Are you saying I'm a cheapskate?" Dallas countered.

Before Preston could answer, Cameron interrupted. "Knock it off, you two. It doesn't matter which one of us is the smartest or works the hardest. We're all culpable. Do you know how many years we'd get if anyone ever found out what we've done?" Cameron asked.

"No one's going to find out anything." John was angry now. "They wouldn't know where to look. I made sure of that. There aren't any records except on my home computer disks, and no one's ever going to have access to those. There aren't any other records, no phone calls, no paper trail. Even if the police or the SEC gets curious, they wouldn't find a shred of evidence to pin on us. We're clean."

"Monk could lead the police to us." Cameron had never trusted the courier, or "hired help" as John called him, but they needed someone reliable, an implementor, and Monk fit the bill. He was every bit as greedy and corrupt as they were and had everything to lose if he didn't do what they wanted.

"He's worked for us long enough for you to start trusting him, Cameron," Preston said. "Besides, if he goes to the police, he'll take a much harder fall than we will."

"You got that right," John muttered. "Look, I know we said that we'd keep going until Cameron turned forty, but I'm telling you I can't last that long. Some days I think my mind... oh, hell, I don't know."

He got out of his chair and crossed to the window, his hands clasped behind his back as he stared at the lights. "Did I ever tell you guys how Catherine and I met? It was at the Contemporary Arts Center. We both wanted to buy the same painting, and somehow, during our heated argument, I fell in love. Man, the sparks between us...it was something to see. All these years later, and that spark's still there. Now she's dying and I can't do a damned thing to stop it."

Cameron glanced at Preston and Dallas, who both nodded, and then said, "We know how much you love Catherine."

"Don't make her a saint, John. She isn't perfect," Dallas said.

"Jeez, that was cold," Preston muttered.

"It's okay. I know Catherine isn't perfect. She has her quirks, just like we do. Who isn't a little compulsive about something?" he said. "It's just that she worries about being without, and so she has to have two of everything. She has two television sets, identical ones, sitting side by side on the table by her bed. She has one of them on day and night, but she worries it might break, so she makes sure she has a backup. She does the same thing when she's ordering something from a store or a catalog. Always buys two, but what's the harm

29

in that?" he asked. "She isn't hurting anyone, and she has so little joy these days. She puts up with me because she loves me." Bowing his head he whispered, "She's my entire life."

"Yes, we know," Cameron agreed. "But we're concerned about you."

John whirled around to confront them. His face was twisted with anger. "Hell, you're worried about yourselves. You think I'll do something to screw it all up, don't you?"

"The thought crossed our minds," Cameron admitted.

"John, we can't afford for you to go crazy on us," Preston said.

"I'm not going to go crazy."

"Yeah, okay," Dallas said. "Here's the way we're gonna play it. John will tell us if he needs help. Isn't that right?"

John nodded. "Yeah, sure."

His friends let the subject drop and spent the rest of the evening plotting their next project.

They continued to meet on Friday afternoons, but they kept silent about John's mounting depression. None of them knew what could be done about it, anyway.

Three months passed without a mention of Catherine. Then John broke down. He couldn't bear to watch Catherine suffer anymore, and he told them he was worried about money all the time now, which he thought was ludicrous given the fact that they had millions tucked away in the Sowing Club account. Millions they couldn't touch for five more years. He told them that insurance covered a pittance of the treatment Catherine needed, but not nearly enough, and if his wife continued to linger, her trust would eventually be gone and he would be financially ruined. Unless, of course, the others agreed to let him dip into the Sowing Club account.

Cameron protested. "You all know how *I'm* hurting for money, what with my divorce pending and all, but if we make a withdrawal now, without closing out the whole account, we could create a paper trail, and the IRS—"

John cut him off. "I know. It's too risky. Look, I shouldn't have brought it up. I'll figure out something," he said.

The following Friday afternoon, they met at their favorite bar, Dooley's. While it thundered and poured outside, and Jimmy Buffett sang about Margaritaville over the speakers, John leaned across the table and whispered his dark wish aloud.

He wanted to kill himself and end the torment.

His friends were appalled and outraged. They admonished him for even thinking such crazy thoughts, but it didn't take them long to see that their rebukes were not helping. On the contrary, they realized they were adding to his misery and his depression. Their harsh words quickly turned into solicitous ones. What could they do to help him?

Surely there was something.

They continued to talk, huddled around a table in the corner of the bar, putting their heads together to come up with a viable solution to their friend's untenable situation. Later, near midnight, after hours and hours of discussion, one of them was bold enough to suggest what all of them were thinking. The poor woman was already under a death sentence. If anyone should die, it should be his pathetic, long-suffering wife.

If only.

Later none of them would be able to remember who had voiced the proposal to kill her.

For the next three Friday afternoons, they discussed the possibility, but once the debate had ended and the vote had been taken, there was no going back. The decision, when it was finally made, was unanimous. There were no second thoughts, no nagging doubts on the part of any of the members of the club.

It was as absolute as dried blood on white carpet.

They didn't consider themselves monsters or admit that what they were doing was motivated by greed. No, they were simply white-collar over-achievers who worked hard and played harder. They were risk-takers, feared by outsiders because of the power they wielded. They were known as real ball breakers—a term they considered flattery. Yet, despite their arrogance and their audacity, none of them had the courage to call the plan what it really was—murder—and so they referred to it as "the event."

They did have balls of steel, considering that Dooley's was located just half a block away from the Eighth District station of the New Orleans Police Department. While they planned the felony, they were surrounded by detectives and policemen. A couple of Federal Bureau agents assigned to PID occasionally stopped by as well, as did the up-and-coming attorneys hoping to foster connections. The police and the courthouse lawyers considered Dooley's their personal watering hole, but then, so did the overworked and underappreciated interns and residents from both Charity Hospital and LSU. The groups rarely mingled.

The Sowing Club didn't take sides. They sat in the corner. Everyone knew who they were, though, and until the serious drinking got under way, they were constantly interrupted by greetings from coworkers and ass-kissers.

Oh, yes, they had gall and nerve, for in the midst of New Orleans's finest, they calmly talked about the mercy killing.

The discussion would never have gotten this far if they hadn't already had the connection they needed. Monk had killed for money, and he certainly wouldn't have any qualms about killing again. Dallas was the first to see the potential and to take advantage by saving Monk from the judicial system. Monk understood the debt he would have to repay. He promised Dallas that he would do anything, anything at all, as long as the risks were manageable and the price was right. Sentiment aside, their killer was, above all else, a businessman.

They all met to discuss the terms at one of Monk's favorite hangouts, Frankies, which was a dilapidated gray shack just off Interstate 10 on the other side of Metairie. The bar smelled of tobacco, peanut shells that customers dis-

33

carded on the warped floorboards, and spoiled fish. Monk swore that Frankie's had the best fried shrimp in the south.

He was late and made no apology for his tardiness. He took his seat, folded his hands on the tabletop, and immediately outlined his conditions before accepting their money. Monk was an educated man, which was one of the main reasons Dallas had saved him from a lethal injection. They wanted a smart man, and he fit the bill. He was also quite distinguished looking, very refined and shockingly polished considering he was a professional criminal. Until he was arrested for murder, Monk's sheet had been clean. After he and Dallas had struck the deal, he did a little bragging about his extensive résumé, which included arson, blackmail, extortion, and murder. The police didn't know about his background, of course, but they had enough evidence to convict on the murder—evidence that was deliberately misplaced.

The very first time the others met Monk was at Dallas's apartment, and he made an indelible impression upon them. They had expected to meet a thug, but instead they met a man they could almost imagine as one of them, a professional with high standards—until they looked closely into his eyes. They were as cold and as lifeless as an eel's. If it was true that the eyes were mirrors to the soul, then Monk had already given his to the devil.

After ordering a beer, he leaned back in the captain's chair and calmly demanded double the price Dallas had offered.

"You've got to be kidding," Preston said. "That's extortion."

"No, it's murder," Monk countered. "Bigger risk means bigger money."

"It isn't...murder," Cameron said. "This is a special case."

"What's so special about it?" Monk asked. "You want me to kill John's wife, don't you? Or was I mistaken?"

"No, but..."

"But what, Cameron? Does it bother you that I'm being blunt? I could use another word for murder if you want, but that won't change what you're hiring me to do." He shrugged and then said, "I want more money."

"We've already made you a very rich man," John pointed out.

"Yes, you have."

"Listen, asshole, we agreed on a price," Preston shouted, then looked over his shoulder to see if anyone had heard.

"Yes, we did," Monk replied. He seemed totally unaffected by the burst of anger. "But you didn't explain what you wanted done, did you? Imagine my surprise when I talked to Dallas and found out the details."

"What did Dallas tell you?" Cameron wanted to know.

"That there was a problem you all wanted eliminated. Now that I know what the problem is, I'm doubling the price. I think that's quite reasonable. The risk is more substantial."

Silence followed the statement. Then Cameron said, "I'm tapped out. Where are we going to come up with the rest of the money?"

"That's my problem, not yours," John said. He turned to Monk then. "I'll even throw in an additional ten thousand if you'll agree to wait until after the will is read to get paid."

Monk tilted his head. "An extra ten thousand. Sure, I'll wait. I know where to find you. Now give me the details. I know who you want killed, so why don't you tell me when, where, and how much you want her to suffer."

John was shaken. He cleared his throat, gulped down half a glass of beer, and whispered, "Oh, God, no. I don't want her to suffer. She's *been* suffering."

"She's terminally ill," Cameron explained.

John nodded. "There isn't any hope for her. I can't stand to see her in so much pain. It's...constant, never ending. I..." He was too emotionally distraught to continue.

Cameron quickly took over. "When John started talking crazy about killing himself, we knew we had to do something to help."

Monk motioned him to be quiet as the waitress walked toward them. She placed another round of beers on the table and told them she'd be back in a minute to take their dinner orders.

As soon as she walked away, Monk said, "Look, John. I didn't realize your wife was sick. I guess I sounded a little cold. Sorry about that."

"Sorry enough to cut your price down?" Preston asked.

"No, I'm not that sorry."

"So are you going to do it, or what?" John asked impatiently.

"It's intriguing," Monk said. "I would actually be doing a good deed, wouldn't I?"

He asked for the particulars about the wife's unfortunate condition and also wanted to know about the living situation inside the house. As John was answering his questions, Monk leaned forward and spread his hands in front of him. His fingernails were perfectly manicured, the pads smooth, callus free. He stared straight ahead, seemingly lost in thought, as if he were constructing the details of the job in his head.

After John finished describing the floor plan, the alarm system, and the maids' daily routine, he tensely waited for more questions.

"So, the maid goes home each night. What about the housekeeper?"

"Rosa...Rosa Vincetti is her name," John said. "She stays until ten every night, except for Mondays, when I'm usually home so she can leave by six."

"Any friends or relatives I need to be concerned about?"

John shook his head. "Catherine cut her friends off years ago. She doesn't like visitors. She's embarrassed about her...condition."

"What about relatives?"

"There's one uncle and a couple of cousins, but she's all but severed ties with them. Says they're white trash. The uncle calls once a month. She tries to be polite, but she doesn't stay on the phone long. It tires her."

"Does this uncle ever stop by uninvited?"

"No. She hasn't seen him in years. You don't have to worry about him."

"Then I won't," Monk said smoothly.

"I don't want her to suffer...I mean, when you actually...is that possible?"

"Of course it is," Monk said. "I have a compassionate nature. I'm not a monster. Believe it or not, I have strong values and unbendable ethics," he boasted, and none of the four men dared laugh at the contradiction. A hired killer with ethics? Insane, yes, yet they all sagely nodded agreement. If Monk had told them he could walk on water, they would have pretended to believe him.

When Monk finished discussing his virtues and got down to the business at hand, he told John he didn't believe in cruel or unnecessary pain, and even though he'd promised that there would be little suffering during "the event," he suggested, just as a precaution, that John increase the amount of painkillers his wife took before bed. Nothing else was to change. John was to set the alarm as he did every night before retiring, and then he was to go to his room and stay there. Monk guaranteed, with an assurance they all found obscenely comforting, that she would be dead by morning.

He was a man of his word. He killed her during the night. How he had gotten inside the house and out again without setting off the alarm was beyond John's comprehension. There were audio and motion detectors inside and video cameras surveying the outside, but the ethereal Monk had entered the premises without being seen or heard, and had quickly and efficiently dispatched the long-suffering woman into oblivion.

To prove that he had been there, he placed a rose on the pillow next to her, just as he had told John he would do, to erase any doubt as to who should receive credit and final payment for the kill. John removed the rose before he called for help.

John agreed to an autopsy so there wouldn't be any questions raised later. The pathology report indicated she had choked to death on chocolates. A clump of chocolate-covered caramel the size of a jawbreaker was found lodged in her esophagus. There were bruises around her neck, but it was assumed that they were self-inflicted as she attempted to dislodge the obstacle while she was suffocating. The death was ruled accidental; the file was officially closed, and the body was released for burial.

Because of her considerable bulk, it would have taken at least eight strong pallbearers to carry her coffin, which the funeral director delicately explained would have to be specially built. With a rather embarrassed and certainly pained expression, he told the widower in so many words that it simply wouldn't be possible to squeeze all of the deceased into one of their ready-made, polished mahogany, satin-lined coffins. He suggested that it would be more prudent to cremate the body, and the husband readily agreed.

The service was a private affair attended by a handful of John's relatives and a few close friends. Cameron came, but Preston and Dallas begged off. Catherine's housekeeper was there, and John could hear Rosa's wailing as he left the church. He saw her in the vestibule, clutching her rosary beads and glaring at him with her damn-you-to-hell-for-your-sins stare. John dismissed the nearly hysterical woman without a backward glance.

Two mourners from Catherine's side of the family also came, but they walked behind the others as the pitifully small group marched in procession toward the mausoleum. John kept glancing over his shoulder at the man and woman. He had the distinct feeling they were staring at him, but when he realized how nervous they were making him, he turned his back on them and bowed his head.

The heavens wept for Catherine and sang her eulogy. While the minister prayed over her, lightning cracked and snapped, and thunder bellowed. The torrential downpour didn't let up until the ash-filled urn was locked inside the vault.

Catherine was finally at peace, and her husband's torment was over. His friends expected him to grieve but at the same time feel relief that his wife wasn't suffering any longer. He had loved the woman with all his heart, hadn't he?

Despite others urging him to take some time off, the widower went back to work the day after the funeral. He insisted he needed to keep busy in order to take his mind off his anguish.

It was a bright, blue, cloudless day as he drove down St. Charles toward his office. The sun warmed his shoulders. The scent of honeysuckle hung heavily in the humid air. His favorite Mellencamp CD, *Hurts So Good,* blared through the speakers.

He pulled into his usual spot in the parking garage and took the elevator up to his suite of offices. When he opened the door bearing his name, his secretary hurried forward to offer her heartfelt condolences. He remarked to her that his wife would have loved such a glorious summer day, and she later told the others in the office that there had been tears in his eyes when he'd said Catherine's name.

As the days passed, he appeared to be battling his depression. During most of his hours at work he seemed withdrawn and distant, going through his routine as if in a daze. Other times, he seemed shockingly cheerful. His erratic behavior was a concern to his staff, but they dismissed it as the understandable remnants of his grief. The best thing they could give him now was space. John was not one to discuss his feelings, and they all knew what a private person he was.

What they didn't know was that John was also quite the busy boy.

Within a couple of weeks after "the event," he had thrown out every painful reminder of his wife, including the Italian Renaissance furniture she had so loved. He dismissed her loyal servants and hired a housekeeper who hadn't known Catherine. He had the two-story house painted from top to bottom in bright, bold colors, and he had the garden re-landscaped. He added the fountain he'd wanted, the one with the cherub spouting water out of its mouth. He'd wanted the fountain for months, but when he'd shown Catherine a picture of it in a catalog, she had decreed it too gaudy.

Everything was finished to his satisfaction. He'd chosen contemporary furniture because of the sleek, uncluttered lines. When it was delivered from the warehouse where he'd been storing it, the placement of each piece was personally overseen by the interior designer.

Then, when the last delivery truck had pulled away from the driveway, he and the oh-so-clever, beautiful young designer christened the new bed. They screwed the night away in the black-lacquered four-poster—just like he'd been promising her for over a year now.

CHAPTER TWO

Theo Buchanan couldn't seem to shake the virus. He knew he was running a fever because every bone in his body ached and he had chills. He refused to acknowledge that he was ill, though; he was just a little off-kilter, that was all. He could tough it out. Besides, he was sure he was over the worst of it. The godawful stitch in his side had subsided into a dull throbbing, and he was positive that meant he was on the mend. If it was the same bug that had infected most of the staff back in his Boston office, then it was one of those twenty-four-hour things, and he should be feeling as good as new by tomorrow morning. Except, the throbbing in his side had been going on for a couple of days now.

He decided to blame his brother Dylan for that ache. He'd really nailed him when they'd played football at a family gathering in the front yard at Nathan's Bay. Yeah, the pulled muscle was Dylan's fault, but Theo figured that if he continued to ignore it, the pain would eventually go away.

Damn, he was feeling like an old man these days, and he wasn't even thirty-three yet.

He didn't think he was contagious, and he had too much to do to go to bed and sweat the fever out of his body. He'd flown from Boston to New Orleans to speak at a law symposium on organized crime and to receive recognition he didn't believe he deserved for simply doing his job.

He slipped his gun into its holster. The thing was a nuisance, but he was required to wear it for the time being, or at least until the death threats he'd received while trying the mob case died down. He put on the jacket to his tuxedo, went into the bathroom of his hotel room, and leaned close to the framed vanity mirror to adjust his tie. He caught a glimpse of himself. He looked half-dead. His face was covered with sweat.

Tonight was the first of three black-tie affairs. Dinner was going to be prepared by five of the top chefs in the city, but the gourmet food was going to be wasted on him. The thought of swallowing anything, even water, made his stomach lurch. He hadn't eaten anything since yesterday afternoon.

He sure as certain wasn't up to pointless chitchat tonight. He tucked the room key into his pocket and was reaching for the door-knob when the phone rang.

It was his brother Nick calling to check in.

"What's going on?"

"I'm walking out the door," Theo answered. "Where are you calling from? Boston or Holy Oaks?"

"Boston," Nick answered. "I helped Laurant close the lake house, and then we drove back home together."

"Is she staying with you until the wedding?"

"Are you kidding? Tommy would send me straight to hell."

Theo laughed. "I guess having a priest for a future brother-in-law does put a crimp in your sex life."

"A couple of months and I'm gonna be a married man. Hard to believe, isn't it?"

"It's hard to believe any woman would have you."

"Laurant's nearsighted. I told her I was good-looking and she believed me. She's staying with Mom and Dad until we all head back to Iowa for the wedding. What are you doing tonight?"

"I've got a fund-raiser I have to go to," he answered. "So what do you want?"

"I just thought I'd call and say hello."

"No, you didn't. You want something. What is it? Come on, Nick. I'm gonna be late."

"Theo, you've got to learn to slow down. You can't keep running for the rest of your life. I know what you're doing. You think that if you bury yourself in work, you won't think about Rebecca. It's been four years since she died, but you—"

Theo cut him off. "I like my life, and I'm not in the mood to talk about Rebecca."

"You're a workaholic."

"Did you call to lecture me?"

"No, I called to see how you were doing."

"Uh-huh."

"You're in a beautiful city with beautiful women, incredible food—"

"So what do you want?"

Nick gave up. "Tommy and I want to take your sailboat out tomorrow."

"Father Tom's there?"

"Yeah. He drove back with Laurant and me," he explained.

"Let me get this straight. You and Tommy want to take my sailboat out, and neither of you knows how to sail?"

"What's your point?"

"What about my fishing boat? Why don't you take the *Mary Beth* out instead? She's sturdier."

"We don't want to fish. We want to sail."

Theo sighed. "Try not to sink her, okay? And don't let Laurant go with you guys. The family likes her. We don't want her to drown. I've got to hang up now."

"Wait. There's something else."

"What?"

"Laurant's been bugging me to call you."

"Is she there? Let me talk to her," he said. He sat down on the side of the bed and realized he was feeling better. Nick's fiancée had that effect on all the Buchanan brothers. She made everyone feel good.

"She isn't here. She went out with Jordan, and you know our sister. God only knows what time they'll get home. Anyway, I promised Laurant that I'd track you down and ask..."

"What?"

"She wanted me to ask you, but I figure I didn't need to," he said. "It's understood."

Theo held his patience. "What's understood?"

"You're gonna be my best man in the wedding."

"What about Noah?"

"He's in the wedding, of course, but I'm expecting you to be best man. I figured you already knew that, but Laurant thought I should ask you anyway."

"Yeah?"

"Yeah, what?"

Theo smiled. "Yeah, okay."

His brother was a man of few words. "Okay, good. Have you given your speech yet?"

"No, that's not until tomorrow night."

"When do you get your trophy?"

"It's a plaque, and I get it right before I give my speech."

"So if you blow it and put all those armed

46

officers to sleep, they can't take the trophy back, can they?"

"I'm hanging up."

"Hey, Theo? For once, stop thinking about work. See the sights. Get laid. You know, have a good time. Hey, I know...why don't you give Noah a call? He's on assignment in Biloxi for a few months. He could drive over to New Orleans, and the two of you could have some fun."

If anyone knew how to have fun, it was Noah Clayborne. The FBI agent had become a close friend of the family after working on several assignments with Nick and then later assisting Theo with his investigations as a federal attorney for the Justice Department. Noah was a good man, but he had a wicked sense of fun, and Theo wasn't sure he could survive a night out with Noah just now.

"Okay, maybe," he answered.

Theo hung up the phone, stood, and quickly doubled over from the pain that radiated through his right side. It had started in his belly, but it had moved down, and, damn, but it stung. The muscle he'd pulled felt like it was on fire.

A stupid football injury wasn't going to keep him down. Muttering to himself, he grabbed his cell phone from the charger, put it into his breast pocket with his reading glasses, and left the room. By the time he reached the lobby, the pain had receded and he was feeling almost human again. That, of course, only reinforced his own personal golden rule. Ignore the pain and it would go away. Besides, a Buchanan could tough out anything.

CHAPTER THREE

It was a night to remember. Michelle had never attended such an extravagant affair before, and as she stood on the steps overlooking the hotel ballroom, she felt like Alice about to fall through the looking glass into Wonderland.

There were flowers everywhere, beautiful spring flowers in sculptured urns on the marble floors and in crystal vases on all the white linen tablecloths. In the very center of the ballroom, beneath a magnificent crystal chandelier, was a cluster of giant hothouse magnolia trees in full bloom. Their heavenly fragrance filled the air.

Waiters glided smoothly through the crowd carrying silver trays with fluted champagne glasses while others rushed from table to table lighting long, white, tapered candles.

Mary Ann Winters, a friend since childhood days, stood by Michelle's side taking it all in.

"I'm out of my element here," Michelle whispered. "I feel like an awkward teenager."

"You don't look like one," Mary Ann said. "I might as well be invisible. I swear every man is staring at you."

"No, they're staring at my obscenely tight dress. How could anything look so plain and ordinary on a hanger and so—"

"So devastatingly sexy on you? It clings in all the right places. Face it, you've got a great figure."

"I should never have spent so much money on a dress."

"For heaven's sake, Michelle, it's an Armani. You got it for a song, I might add."

Michelle self-consciously brushed her hand down the side of the soft fabric. She thought about how much she'd paid for the dress and decided she would have to wear it at least twenty times to make it cost-effective. She wondered if other women did that—rationalized a frivolous expense to assuage the guilt. There were so many more important things she could have used the money for, and when, in heaven's name, was she ever going to have another opportunity to wear this beautiful dress again? Not in Bowen, she thought. Not in a million years.

"What was I thinking? I never should have let you talk me into buying this dress."

Mary Ann impatiently brushed a strand of white blond hair back over her shoulder. "Don't you dare start in complaining about the cost again. You never spend any money on yourself. I'll bet it's the first really gorgeous dress you've ever owned, isn't it? You're absolutely beautiful tonight. Promise me you'll stop worrying and enjoy yourself."

Michelle nodded. "You're right. I'll stop worrying."

"Good. Now let's go mingle. There's hors d'oeuvres and champagne out in the courtyard, and we've got to eat at least a thousand dollars' worth each. That's what I heard the tickets cost. I'll meet you there."

Her friend had just gone down the stairs when Dr. Cooper spotted Michelle and motioned for her to join him. He was the chief of surgery at Brethren Hospital, where she had been moonlighting the past month. Cooper was usually reserved, but the champagne had rid him of his inhibitions, and he was quite affectionate. And effervescent. He kept telling her how happy he was that she was using the tickets he'd given her and how pretty she looked all dressed up. Michelle thought that if Dr. Cooper got any happier, he was going to pass out in the soup.

While Dr. Cooper expostulated on the attributes of the crawfish, spraying spit every time he said the word "fish," she backed away to get out of the firing range. A few minutes later, Cooper's wife joined them with another older couple in tow. Michelle used the opportunity to sneak away.

She didn't want to get trapped sitting next to the Coopers during dinner. The only thing worse than a happy drunk was a flirtatious one, and Cooper was definitely headed in that direction. Since he and his wife were standing near the entrance to the courtyard and would see her if she went past, she walked around into the adjacent hallway with the bank of elevators, hoping there was a way to get to the courtyard from the opposite side.

And that's when she noticed him. He was leaning against a pillar, hunched over, tilted protectively to one side. The man was tall, broad-shouldered, well-built, like an athlete, she thought. But there was a sickly gray pallor to his complexion, and as she walked toward him, she saw him grimace and grab his stomach.

He was obviously in trouble. She touched his arm to get his attention just as the elevator doors opened. He staggered upright and looked down at her. His gray eyes were glazed with pain.

"Do you need help?"

He answered her by throwing up all over her.

She couldn't get out of the way because he'd grabbed hold of her arm. His knees buckled then, and she knew he was going to go down. She wrapped her arms around his waist and tried to ease him to the floor, but he lurched forward at the same time, taking her with him.

Theo's head was spinning. He landed on top of the woman. He heard her groan and desperately tried to find the strength to get up. He thought he might be dying, and he didn't think that would be such a bad thing if death would make the pain go away. It was unbearable now. His stomach rolled again, and another wave of intense agony cut through him. He wondered if this was what it felt like to be stabbed over and over again. He passed out then, and when he next opened his eyes, he was flat on his back and she was leaning over him.

He tried to bring her face into focus. She had pretty blue eyes, more violet than blue, he thought, and freckles on the bridge of her nose. Then, as suddenly as it had stopped, the fire started burning in his side again, so much worse than before.

A spasm wrenched his stomach, and he jerked. "Son of a bitch."

The woman was talking to him, but he couldn't understand what she was saying. And what the hell was she doing to him? Was she robbing him? Her hands were everywhere, tugging at his jacket, his tie, his shirt. She was trying to straighten out his legs. She was hurting him, damn it, and every time he tried to push her hands away, they came back to poke and prod some more.

Theo kept slipping in and out of consciousness. He felt a rocking motion and heard a siren blaring close to his head. Blue Eyes was still there too, pestering him. She was asking him questions again. Something about allergies. Did she want him to be allergic to something?

"Yeah, sure."

He felt her open his jacket, knew she could see the gun holstered above his hip. He was crazed with pain now, couldn't seem to think straight. He only knew he couldn't let her take his weapon.

She was a damned talkative mugger. He'd give her that. She looked like one of those J. Crew models. Sweet, he thought. No, she wasn't sweet. She kept hurting him.

"Look, lady, you can take my wallet, but you're not getting my gun. Got that?" He could barely get the words out through his gritted teeth.

Her hand pressed into his side. He reacted instinctively, knocking her back. He thought he might have connected with something soft because he heard her yell before he went under again.

Theo didn't know how long he was out, but when he opened his eyes, the bright lights made him squint. Where the hell was he? He couldn't summon up enough energy to move. He thought he might be on a table. It was hard, cold.

"Where am I?" His mouth was so dry, he slurred the question.

"You're in Brethren Hospital, Mr. Buchanan." The man's voice came from behind him, but Theo couldn't see him.

"Did they catch her?"

"Who?"

"J. Crew."

"He's loopy." A female voice he didn't recognize made the comment.

Theo suddenly realized he wasn't in any pain. He felt good, in fact. Real good. Like he could fly. Odd, though, he didn't have the strength to move his arms. A mask was placed over his mouth and nose. He turned his head to get away from it.

"Are you getting sleepy, Mr. Buchanan?"

He turned his head again and saw her. Blue Eyes. She looked like an angel, all golden. Wait a minute. What the hell was she doing here? Wait...

"Mike, are you going to be able to see what you're doing? That eye looks bad."

"It's fine."

"How'd it happen?" the voice behind Theo's head asked.

"He clipped me."

"The patient decked you?"

"That's right." She was staring into Theo's eyes when she answered. She had a green mask on, but he knew she was smiling.

He was in such a happy daze now and so sleepy he was having trouble keeping his eyes open. Conversation swirled around him, but none of it made any sense.

A woman's voice. "Where did you find *him*, Dr. Renard?"

"At a party."

Another woman leaned over him. "Hubba, hubba."

"Was it love at first sight?"

"You decide. He threw up all over me and ruined my new dress."

Someone laughed. "Sounds like love to me. I'll bet he's married. All the good-looking men are married. This one's sure built. Did you check out the goods, Annie?"

"I hope our patient is sleeping."

"Not yet," a male voice said. "But he isn't going to remember anything."

"Where's the assist?"

"Scrubbing."

There seemed to be a party going on. Theo thought there were at least twenty or thirty people in the room with him. Why was it so damned cold? And who was making all the clatter? He was thirsty. His mouth felt like it was full of cotton. Maybe he ought to go get a drink. Yeah, that's what he would do.

"Where's Dr. Cooper?"

"Probably passed out in the dessert by now." Blue Eyes answered the question. Theo loved the sound of her voice. It was so damned sexy.

"So you saw Cooper at the party?"

"Uh-huh," Blue Eyes answered. "He wasn't on call tonight. He works hard. It was nice to see him having a good time. Mary Ann's probably having a great time too."

"You." Theo struggled to get the word out. Still, he'd gotten her attention because when he opened his eyes, she was leaning over him, blocking out the glaring light above him.

"It's time for you to go to sleep, Mr. Buchanan."

"He's fighting it."

"What..." Theo began.

"Yes?"

"What do you want from me?"

The man hiding behind him answered. "Mike wants your appendix, Mr. Buchanan."

It sounded good to him. He was always happy to accommodate a beautiful woman. "Okay," he whispered. "It's in my wallet."

"We're ready."

"It's about time," the man said.

"Who do you want to hear tonight, Dr. Renard?"

"Need you ask, Annie?"

A groan went around the room. Then a click. Theo heard the chair squeak behind him, then the stranger's voice telling him to take deep breaths. Theo finally figured out who the man behind him was. Damn if it wasn't Willie Nelson, and he was singing to him, something about Blue Eyes cryin' in the rain.

It was one hell of a party.

CHAPTER FOUR

Theo slept through recovery. When he awoke the following morning, he was in a hospital bed. The side rails were up, and he was hooked to an IV. He closed his eyes and tried to clear his mind. What the hell had happened to him? He couldn't remember.

It was past ten o'clock when he opened his eyes again. She was there, standing beside the bed, pulling the sheets up around his waist. Blue Eyes. He hadn't imagined her after all.

She looked different today. She was still dressed in surgical scrubs, but her hair wasn't hidden underneath a cap. It was down around her shoulders, and the color was a deep, rich auburn.

She was much prettier than he remembered.

She noticed he was awake. "Good morning. How are you feeling? Still a little drowsy?"

He struggled to sit up. She reached for the controls and pushed a button. The head of the bed slowly rose. Theo felt a tugging in his side and a mild stinging sensation.

"Tell me when."

"That's good," he said. "Thanks."

She picked up his chart and started writing while he blatantly stared at her. He felt vulnerable and awkward sitting in bed in a hospital gown. He couldn't think of anything clever to say to her. For the first time in his life he wanted to be charming, but he didn't have the faintest idea how to go about it. He was a die-hard workaholic, and there simply hadn't been room for social graces in his life. In the last four years—since his wife's death—he had become blunt, abrasive, and to the point because it saved time, and Theo, these days anyway, was always in a hurry to get things done. This sudden turnabout surprised him. He actually wanted to be charming. Go figure, as his youngest brother, Zack, would say. Still, Theo thought he could manage it. Yeah. Charming was definitely doable.

"Do you remember what happened last night?" she asked, glancing up from her notes.

"I had surgery."

"Yes. Your appendix was removed. Another fifteen minutes and you definitely would have ruptured."

"I remember bits and pieces. What happened to your eye?"

She smiled as she started writing in his chart again. "I didn't duck fast enough."

"Who are you?"

"Dr. Renard."

"Mike?"

"Excuse me?"

"Someone called you Mike."

Michelle closed the folder, put the lid back on her ink pen, and tucked it into her pocket. She gave him her full attention. The surgical nurses were right. Theo Buchanan was gorgeous...and sexy as hell. But none of that should matter. She was his physician, nothing more, nothing less, yet she couldn't help reacting to him as any woman naturally would react to such a fit specimen. His hair was sticking up and he needed a shave, but he was still sexy. There wasn't anything wrong with her noticing that...unless, of course, he noticed her noticing.

"You just asked me a question, didn't you?" She drew a blank.

He could tell he'd rattled her, but he didn't know why. "I heard someone call you Mike."

She nodded. "Yes. The staff calls me Mike. It's short for Michelle."

"Michelle's a pretty name."

"Thank you."

It was all coming back to Theo now. He was at a party, and there was this beautiful woman in a slinky black evening gown. She was breathtaking. He remembered that. She had killer blue eyes and Willie Nelson was with her. He was singing. No, that couldn't be right. Obviously, his head hadn't quite cleared yet.

"You were talking to me...after the surgery," he said.

"In recovery. Yes," she agreed. "But you were doing most of the talking." She was smiling again.

"Yeah? What did I say?"

"Mostly gibberish," she said.

"You took my gun. Where is it?"

"Locked up in the hospital safe with your other personal possessions. Dr. Cooper will make sure you get them back before you leave. He's going to be taking over your care. You'll meet him in a little while when he makes his rounds."

"Why?"

"Why what, Mr. Buchanan?"

"Theo," he corrected. "My name's Theo."

"Yes, I know. Your brother told me you go by that nickname."

"Which brother?"

"How many do you have?"

"Five," he answered. "And two sisters. So who'd you talk to?"

"Nick," she answered. "You gave me his phone number and asked me to call him. He was concerned and made me promise to call him again after the surgery. As soon as you were wheeled into recovery, I called and assured him that you were going to be fine. He wanted to come," she added, "but he sounded relieved when I told him it wasn't necessary."

Theo nodded. "Nick hates flying," he explained. "When did I give you his phone number? I don't remember."

"When you were in pre-op. You were very talkative, once we gave you something to get rid of the pain, and by the way, the answer's no. I won't marry you."

He smiled, sure she was joking. "I don't

remember being in pre-op. I remember the pain, though. It hurt like a son of a..."

"I'm sure it did."

"You did the surgery, didn't you? I didn't imagine that?"

"Yes, I did the surgery."

She was backing out of the room. He didn't want her to leave just yet. He wanted to find out more about her. Hell, he wished he were more adept at small talk.

"Wait."

She stopped. "Yes?"

"Water...could I have a glass of water?"

She went to the bedside table, poured a tiny bit of water into a glass, and handed it to him. "Just a sip," she said. "If you get nauseated and throw up, you'll mess up my stitches."

"Okay," he said. He took a drink and handed the glass back to her. "You don't look old enough to be a surgeon." Stupid, he thought, but it was the best he could come up with at the moment.

"I hear that a lot."

"You look like you should be in college." That statement, he decided, was worse than stupid.

She couldn't resist. "High school, actually. They let me operate for extra credit."

"Dr. Renard? May I interrupt?" A male aide was standing in the hallway, shifting a large cardboard box under his arm.

"Yes, Bobby?"

"Dr. Cooper filled this box with medical supplies from his office for your clinic," the young man said. "What do you want me to do with it? Dr. Cooper left it at the nurses' station, but they wanted it moved. It was in the way."

"Would you mind taking it down to my locker?"

"It's too big, Dr. Renard. It won't fit. It isn't heavy, though. I could carry it out to your car."

"My father has the car," she said. She glanced around, then looked at Theo. "Would you mind if Bobby left my box here? My father will carry it down to the car for me just as soon as he arrives."

"I don't mind," Theo said.

"I won't be seeing you again. I'm going home today, but don't worry. You're in good hands. Dr. Cooper's chief of surgery here at Brethren, and he'll take good care of you."

"Where's home?"

"In the swamp."

"Are you kidding?"

"No," she said. She smiled again, and he noticed the little dimple in her left cheek. "Home is a little town that's pretty much surrounded by swamp, and I can't wait to get back there."

"Homesick?"

"Yes, I am," she admitted. "I'm a small-town girl at heart. It isn't a very glamorous life, and that's what I like about it."

"You like living in the swamp." It was a statement not a question, but she responded anyway.

"You sound shocked."

"No, just surprised."

"You're from a big, sprawling city, so you'd probably hate it."

"Why do you say that?"

She shrugged. "You seem too...sophisticated."

He didn't know if that was a compliment or a criticism. "Sometimes you can't go home. I think I read that in a book once. Besides, you look like a New Orleans kind of woman to me."

"I love New Orleans. It's a wonderful place to come for dinner."

"But it won't ever be home."

"No."

"So, are you the town doctor?"

"One of several," she said. "I'm opening a clinic there. It's not very fancy, but there's a real need. So many of the people don't have the resources to get regular medical care."

"Sounds like they're very lucky to have you."

She shook her head. "Oh, no, I'm the lucky one." Then she laughed. "That sounded saintly, didn't it? I am the lucky one, though. The people are wonderful—at least I think they are—and they give me far more than I can give them." When she spoke, her whole face lit up. "You know what I'm going to like best?"

"What's that?"

"No games. For the most part, they're honest, ordinary people trying to scrape a living together. They don't waste a lot of time on foolishness."

"So, everyone loves everyone else?" He scoffed at the notion.

"No, of course not," she replied. "But I'll know my enemies. They won't sneak up behind me and blindside me. It isn't their style." She smiled again. "They'll get right in my face, and I'm going to like that. Like I said, no games. After the residency I just finished, that's going to be a refreshing change."

"You won't miss the big beautiful office and all the trappings?"

"Not really. There are rewards other than money. Oh sure, it would be great to have all the supplies and equipment we need, but we'll make do. I've spent a lot of years getting ready for this...besides, I made a promise."

He kept asking her questions to keep her talking. He was interested in hearing about her town but not nearly as much as he was fascinated with her expressions. There was such passion and joy in her voice, and her eyes sparkled as she talked about her family and friends and the good she hoped she could do.

She reminded him of how he had felt about life when he had first started practicing the law, before he'd become so cynical. He, too, had wanted to change the world, to make it a better place. Rebecca had ended all that. Looking back, he realized he had failed miserably.

"I've worn you out, going on and on about my hometown. I'll let you rest now," she said.

"When can I get out of here?"

"That's Dr. Cooper's call, but if it were up to me, I'd keep you another night. You had

63

quite a nasty infection. You need to take it easy for a couple of weeks, and don't forget to take your antibiotics. Good luck, Theo."

And then she was gone, and he'd lost the only chance he had to find out more about her. He didn't even know where her home was. He fell asleep trying to figure out a way to see her again.

CHAPTER FIVE

The room was filled with flowers when Theo woke up from his morning nap. He heard whispering in the hallway, opened his eyes, and saw a nurse talking to an older man. She was pointing to the box the aide had left.

The man looked like a retired linebacker, Theo thought. Or maybe a boxer. If he was Dr. Renard's father, she'd gotten her good looks from her mother's side of the family.

"I don't want to disturb you," the man said, his voice thick with a Cajun accent. "I'd just like to pick up this box Dr. Cooper fixed up for my daughter and be on my way."

"Come in," Theo said. "You're Dr. Renard's father, aren't you?"

"That's right. My name's Jake. Jake Renard." He walked over to the side of the bed and shook Theo's hand. Theo didn't have to introduce himself. Jake knew who he was. "My girl told me all about you."

"She did?" He couldn't hide his surprise.

Jake nodded. "You must have been real quick, son, because my Mike knows how to take care of herself."

Theo didn't know what the man was talking about. "I was 'quick'?"

"When you clipped her," he explained. "Where'd you think she got that shiner?"

"I did that?" He was incredulous. He had no memory of it, and she hadn't said anything about it. "Are you sure?"

"I'm sure. I figured you didn't mean to hit her. She told me you were in considerable pain at the time. You were lucky she noticed you." He leaned against the bed rail and folded his arms across his chest. "Now, my daughter doesn't usually talk about her patients, but I knew she had gone to a fancy party wearing a brand-new dress she didn't want to spend money on, and when I asked her if she had a good time, she told me about you. She had only just gotten there when she had to turn around and go back to the hospital. She didn't get to have a single bite of food."

"I should apologize to her."

"You tore her dress. You should probably tell her you're sorry about that too."

"I tore her dress?"

"Just after you threw up on her." Jake chuckled, then shook his head. "Ruined that brand-new four-hundred-dollar dress."

Theo groaned. He did remember doing that.

"You look like you need to get some rest. If you see my daughter, will you tell her I'm waiting down in the lobby? It was sure nice to meet you."

65

"Why don't you wait here?" Theo suggested. "I've slept as much as I'm going to," he added. "When your daughter comes looking for you, I can tell her thank you."

"I guess I could sit a spell. I don't want to wear you out, though."

"You won't."

Jake dragged a chair to the side of the bed and sat down. "Where's home, son? From your accent, I'd have to guess the east coast."

"Boston."

"Never been there," Jake admitted. "Are you married?"

"I was."

"Divorced?"

"No, my wife died."

His tone of voice suggested that Jake not pursue that line of questioning.

"What about your parents? They still around?"

"Yes, they are," he answered. "I come from a big family. There's eight of us, six boys and two girls. My father's a judge. He keeps trying to retire but hasn't quite figured out how to do it yet."

"I don't believe I've ever known a judge," Jake said. "My wife, Ellie, wanted a big family, and if we'd been blessed, I probably would have figured out a way to feed them all. I was willing to do my part, but we had to stop with three. Two boys and a girl to round the family out."

"Where exactly is home, sir? Your daughter was talking about her clinic, but she never mentioned the name of the town."

"Call me Jake," he insisted. "Bowen, Louisiana, is home, but I don't expect you've ever heard of it. The town's not big enough to be a speck on a map. Bowen's tiny, all right, but it's the prettiest stretch of land in all Louisiana. Some afternoons when the sun's going down and the breeze picks up, the moss starts in swaying and the light bounces off the bayou just so, and the bullfrogs and the gators start in singing to each other...well, son, I think to myself that I must be living in paradise. It's that pretty. The closest town is St. Claire, and that's where folks do their Saturday shopping, so we're not completely isolated. There's a hospital there on the north side. It's old, but adequate," he added.

"Do your sons live in Bowen?"

"Remy, my oldest, is out in Colorado. He's a fireman and still not married," he added. "He comes home every now and again. John Paul, the middle one, left the marines and moved back to Bowen a couple of years ago; he's not married either. Too busy, I imagine. He lives in a nice little cabin he built deep in the swamp, and when he isn't working the bar for me, he's a carpenter. Last year we opened a brand-new high school, and John Paul helped build it. Daniel Boone is what it's called. Named after a local celebrity."

"You don't mean it's named after the Daniel Boone who helped settle Kentucky...the frontiersman...is that what you're saying?"

"That's the one, all right."

"You're saying Boone lived in Bowen?"

Jake shook his head. "No, son, we can't boast that, but legend has it that Daniel roamed the area hunting and fishing. Of course, that was way back in the 1700s before Bowen was even a town. Still, we like to think that Daniel fished our waters and stayed a spell."

Theo managed not to laugh. It appeared that the people in Bowen were hard-pressed for local heroes.

"Where does the name Bowen come from?"

"It comes from the word *Bowie,* like in the knife."

"For Jim Bowie? Did he stop by too?"

"We like to think he did."

"You're putting me on."

"No, I'm not," Jake insisted. "Of course, Jim didn't show up at the same time Daniel did. He came years later, in the 1800s," he said.

"Are you sure you aren't getting Daniel Boone mixed up with Davy Crockett?"

"I sure hope not. The school's already got the lettering on it in stone."

"Is there proof that Boone was in Bowen?"

"None to speak of," Jake admitted with a twinkle in his eye. "But we believe it to be true. Now, as I was telling you, the Bowen kids used to have to bus over to the fancy high school in St. Claire, but it just got too cramped. It was past time we had our own. We've even got a football team. We were all real excited about that last year...until we saw them play. Lord, they're a sorry lot at best. I never missed a game though, and I won't miss this year either because, now that my daughter is home, she'll be going with me. Mike agreed to be the team's physician, which means she's got to sit on the sidelines and fix them up when they get hurt. We all know they're going to get trounced again, but I figure I ought to be supportive of their efforts by showing up and cheering them on. We didn't win a single game last year. We've got some real big boys, but they don't know what to do when they get the ball. They don't know how to hit either. You like to watch football, Theo?"

"Sure," he said.

"You ever play?"

"Yes, I did," he answered. "High school, and college until I trashed my knee."

"What position? You're tall and thick through the shoulders. I'd guess quarterback."

Theo nodded. "That's right. It seems like a long time ago."

Jake had a speculative gleam in his eyes. "You ever think about coaching?"

Theo laughed. "No, I haven't."

"Mike might be able to fix up your knee for you."

"You must be very proud of your daughter, coming back home to open a clinic."

"Of course I'm proud of her," he said. "I'm not going to let her work herself to the bone, though. There are other doctors in St. Claire, and they'll be taking call for one another so each of them can have some time off now and again."

"Why is she doing surgery here in Brethren?"

"To make some extra money. They call it moonlighting, but she's finished now and won't be coming back. Do you like to fish?"

"I used to, but the last few years, there just hasn't been any time for it," he admitted. "I remember, though, there's nothing like that feeling of peace that comes over a man when he's—"

"Holding a fishing pole in one hand and a cold beer in the other?"

"Yeah, that's right. Nothing like it in the world."

They started discussing their favorite lures and bait, and then did a good deal of bragging about the fish they'd caught. Jake was impressed. He didn't think anyone understood or loved fishing as much as he did, but he had to admit that from the way Theo talked, he had met his match.

"I'm telling you, you ought to come up to Bowen. We've got the best fishing in the state, and I mean to prove it to you. We'll pass a good time out on my dock."

"I may take you up on the offer sometime," he said.

"What do you do for a living?" Jake asked.

"I'm an attorney."

"How come the chief of police is sending you flowers?" he asked. He looked sheepish as he added, "They were sitting on the counter at the nurses' station before they brought them on in here, and I read the card."

"I came to New Orleans to give a speech," he said, leaving out the fact that he was being honored by the local authorities. "I work for the Justice Department."

"Doing what exactly?"

"I was assigned to a special task force," he said. He realized he was still being evasive and added, "The area was organized crime. I just finished up."

"Did you get your man?"

Theo smiled. "Yeah, I did."

"Are you out of a job now?"

"No," he answered. "Justice wants me to stay on. I'm not sure what I'm going to do."

Jake continued with his questions. Theo thought he would have made a great prosecutor. He had a sharp mind and a quick wit.

"You ever think about going into private practice?" Jake asked.

"Sometimes."

"There aren't any good attorneys in Bowen. We got two over in St. Claire, but they'll rob you blind. Folks don't think much of them."

While Jake talked about his town, Theo kept trying to think of a subtle way to bring the subject back to Michelle.

"Is your daughter married?" So much for subtle.

"I was wondering when you were going to get around to asking me about Mike. The answer's no, she isn't married. She hasn't had time. Of course, the men in Bowen and St. Claire are all trying to get her attention, but she's been too busy setting up her clinic to pay them any mind. She's still young," he added. "And smart. Lord, is my girl smart. She finished college before she was twenty, then started in on her medical training. She had to go out of state to do her residency, but she came home to visit every chance she got. She's mindful of family," he added with a nod. "And she's pretty too, isn't she?"

"Yes, she is."

"I figured you'd notice."

Jake stood up and put the chair back against the wall. "It was nice passing the time with you, but I should go now. You get some sleep, and I'll carry that box to the car. Dr. Cooper gave my daughter some old surgical equipment, and when she asked me to come and fetch it, she was smiling like it was Christmas morning. If you ever make your way to Bowen, you be sure and come by The Swan. That's my bar," he explained. "Drinks on the house."

He was at the door when Theo stopped him. "If I don't see your daughter before she leaves, please tell her thank you for me, and also tell her how sorry I am about the dress."

"I'll be sure and tell her."

"Maybe our paths will cross again someday."

Jake nodded. "Maybe so."

CHAPTER SIX

John's friends never saw it coming. Two weeks to the day after Catherine's funeral, Cameron happened to run into the grieving widower at Commander's Palace, a four-star restaurant located in the Garden District. Cameron was sitting in one of the dining rooms waiting for his attorney to join him to discuss the never-ending and thoroughly nauseating topic of his divorce settlement. His wife was determined to destroy him financially and to publicly humiliate him in the process, and from the way things were going, it looked as though she would succeed.

John was having dinner with a young woman in the next room. The blond looked vaguely familiar. Her head was bent down, and she was diligently writing in her Day-Timer.

Cameron couldn't remember where he'd seen the woman before, but he was pleased to see his friend out for the evening, even if it was business. John's moods had been so volatile since his wife's death. One minute he was overjoyed, almost euphoric, and the next, he was wallowing in self-pity and depression.

The blond lifted her head, and Cameron got a good look at her face. She was quite pretty. He still couldn't place her. He decided to interrupt the couple to say hello. He ordered a double scotch neat as fortification to get through the ordeal ahead of him with his attorney, then started winding his way through the tables into the next dining room.

Had he not dropped his pen, he never would have known the truth. He bent down to scoop it up, and that was when he saw John put his hand on the blond's thigh under the white linen tablecloth. Her legs spread, and she shifted ever so slightly until she was leaning into his hand, which was now moving upward under her dress.

Cameron was so shocked by the intimacy he almost lost his balance. He quickly caught himself and stood. Neither John nor the woman noticed him. She had turned her head and was staring off into space, her eyes half-closed in obvious bliss.

Cameron couldn't believe what he was seeing, but that instant of disbelief swiftly turned into confusion.

He suddenly remembered who the blond was, though he couldn't recall her name. She was the insipid female who called herself an interior decorator. Cameron had met her in John's office. Oh, yes, it was all coming back to him now. She didn't have taste or talent. She had turned his friend's office into a bordello parlor by painting the beautiful walnut-paneled walls a deep, garish mustard yellow.

She obviously had talent in another area though. The way John was all but licking his lips as he greedily stared at her pouting mouth indicated she was real talented in the bedroom. Cameron continued to stand near the doorway, staring at his friend's back while the truth settled in his mind.

The son of a bitch had duped them all.

Incredulous, and at the same time overwhelmed with anger, Cameron turned and walked back to his table. He tried to convince himself that he was jumping to the wrong conclusions. He had known John for years and trusted him completely.

Until now. Damn it, what had John done to them? White-collar crime was one thing; murder was quite another. The club had never gone this far before, and what made it all the more chilling was that they had convinced themselves that they were actually doing a good deed. Tell that to a jury of their peers and watch them laugh.

Dear God, had Catherine really been terminal? Had she been dying a slow, agonizing death? Or had John simply been lying to them to get them to do his dirty work?

No, not possible. John wouldn't have lied about his wife. He'd loved her, damn it.

Cameron was sick to his stomach. He didn't know what to think, but he did know it would be wrong to condemn his friend without knowing all the facts. Then it occurred to him that the affair, if that was what this was, could have begun after Catherine's death. He latched onto the idea. Yes, of course. John had known the decorator before his wife's death. The blond had been hired by Catherine to redecorate her bedroom. But so what if he had known her? After his wife died, John was grieving and lonely, and the young woman was available. Hell, she probably pounced on his vulnerability right after the funeral.

A nagging doubt remained. If this was innocent, then why hadn't John told his friends about her? Why was he hiding it?

Maybe because his wife's ashes hadn't even had time to cool off yet. Yeah, that was it. John knew it wouldn't look good to get involved with another woman so soon after Catherine's death. People would certainly think it was odd and start talking and speculating, and the club sure as hell didn't want that to happen. John was smart enough to know he should keep a low profile.

Cameron had almost convinced himself that what he had seen was pretty harmless, but he still felt compelled to make certain. He didn't let John see him. He paid his bar tab and slipped out of the restaurant. He had the valet bring around the used Ford sedan he was forced to drive these days—his soon-to-be ex-wife had already confiscated his cherished Jaguar, damn the slut. He drove to the next block, ducked down in the seat, and turned to watch for the couple to come outside. While he waited, he called his attorney on his cell phone to cancel dinner.

The two of them came outside twenty minutes later. They stood at the curb, facing each other about five feet apart, acting stiff and formal, as though they were little more than strangers, John with his hands stuffed in his pants pockets, the blond clutching her purse and her Day-Timer. When her car arrived, she tucked her purse under her arm and shook John's hand. The valet held the door of her cherry red Honda open, and she got inside and drove away without a backward glance.

To the casual observer, the scene was very businesslike.

A minute later John's gray BMW convertible arrived. He took his time removing his suit jacket, folding it just so before carefully placing it on the passenger's seat. The well-fitted suit was Valentino, the only designer John ever wore. A wave of bitterness washed over Cameron. Six months ago he, too, had had a closet full of Joseph Abboud and Calvin Klein and Valentino suits, but then his wife, in a drunken rage, had grabbed a butcher knife and shredded the clothes into rags. That little tantrum had destroyed over fifty thousand dollars' worth of garments.

God, how he longed to get even. Some nights he lay in bed and fantasized about all sorts of ways to kill her. The most important element in the daydream was pain. He wanted the bitch to suffer as she was dying. His favorite scenario was smashing her face through a glass window and watching the whore slowly bleed to death. In his fantasy a shard of glass barely nicked her artery.

Oh, yes, he wanted her to suffer the way she was making him suffer, to get even with her for stealing his life from him. She'd frozen all of his assets until the divorce settlement was reached, but he already knew what the outcome would be. She was going to take it all.

She didn't know about the Sowing Club or the assets they had hidden. No one did. Her attorney wouldn't be able to find the money either, even if he had been looking. The millions of dollars were in an offshore account, and none of it could be traced back to him.

But for now, it didn't matter that he had money hidden. He couldn't touch any of it until he turned forty. That was the deal the four friends had made, and he knew the others wouldn't let him borrow from the fund. It was too risky, and so, for the next five years, he was going to have to bite the bullet and live like a pauper.

John was the lucky devil. Now that Catherine was dead, he had what was left of her trust fund, which he didn't have to share with anyone.

Cameron was filled with envy as he watched his friend put on his Saints' ball cap. He knew John only wore the thing to hide his bald spot. He was going to be completely bald by the time he was fifty, like all the men in his family, no matter what precautions he took. But what did that matter? He'd still look real good to women. Women would put up with any flaw if there was money involved.

Cameron dismissed this latest bout of self-pity with a shake of his head. Feeling sorry for himself wasn't going to change anything. Besides, he could hold on for a few more years. Concentrate on the future, he told himself. Soon he would be able to retire as a multimillionaire and move to the south of France, and there wouldn't be a damned thing his ex could do about it.

John slid onto the soft leather seat. Then he loosened his tie, adjusted the rearview mirror, and drove away.

Should he follow him? Cameron threaded his fingers through his hair in frustration. He knew he wasn't being fair to John and that it was wrong for him to become so easily spooked by what was surely innocent. John had loved his wife, and if a cure had been possible, Cameron knew that his friend would have spent every dollar he had to save Catherine.

Yet, the nagging uncertainty wouldn't go away, and so he did follow him. He figured that if he could just sit down with him and talk, they would be able to clear up this...misunderstanding. John would tell him this suspicion was simply a reaction to the horrible guilt he was feeling over what they had done in the name of mercy.

Cameron thought about turning the car around and going home, but he didn't do it. He had to be sure. Had to know. He took a shortcut through the Garden District and arrived at John's house before he did. The beautiful Victorian home was on a coveted corner lot. There were two enormous, ancient oak trees and a magnolia casting black shadows on the front yard. Cameron pulled onto the side street adjacent to the electronically gated driveway. He turned the lights off, then the motor, and sat there, well-concealed under a leafy branch that blocked out the streetlight. The house was dark. When John arrived, Cameron reached for the door handle, then froze.

"Shit," he whispered.

She was there, waiting. As the iron gate was opening, he spotted her standing on the sidewalk by the side of the house. The garage door lifted then, and Cameron saw her red Honda parked inside.

As soon as John parked his car and walked out of the garage, she ran to him, her large round breasts bouncing like silicone balls underneath the tight fabric of her dress. The bereaved widower couldn't wait to get her inside the house. They tore at each other like street dogs in heat. Her black dress was unzipped and down around her waist in a matter of seconds, and his hand was latched onto one of her breasts as they stumbled to the door. His grunts of pleasure blended with her shrill laughter.

"That son of a bitch," Cameron muttered. "That stupid son of a bitch."

He had seen enough. He drove home to his rented one-bedroom apartment in the untrendy section of the warehouse district and paced for hours, stewing and fuming and worrying. A bottle of scotch fueled his anger.

Around two in the morning, a couple of drunks got into a fistfight outside of his window. Cameron watched the spectacle with disgusted curiosity. One of them had a knife, and Cameron hoped he'd stab the other one just to shut him up. Someone must have called the police. They arrived, sirens blaring, minutes later.

There were two officers in the patrol car. They quickly disarmed the drunk with the knife and then slammed both men up against a stone wall. Blood, iridescent under the garish streetlight, poured from a gash in the side of one drunk's head as he crashed unconscious to the pavement.

The policeman who'd used the unnecessary force shouted a crude blasphemy as he rolled the unconscious man over onto his stomach and then knelt on his back and secured the handcuffs. Then he dragged him to the car. The other drunk meekly waited his turn, and within another minute or two, both were locked in the back of the car on their way to the city jail.

Cameron gulped a long swallow of scotch and wiped the perspiration from his brow with the back of his hand. The scene under his window had freaked him, especially the handcuffs. He couldn't handle being cuffed. He couldn't go to prison, wouldn't. He'd kill himself first...if he had the courage. He had always been a little claustrophobic, but the condition had worsened over the years. He couldn't be inside a windowless room these days without feeling tightness in his chest. He'd stopped using elevators, preferring to walk up seven flights of stairs rather than spend thirty or forty seconds inside a metal elevator box, squeezed in like a dead sardine with the other office dwellers.

Dear God, why hadn't he thought about his claustrophobia before he agreed to this lunacy?

He knew the answer and was drunk enough to admit it. Greed. Fucking greed. John was the motivator, the planner, the man with the vision...and the money connections. With the fervor of a southern evangelist, he'd promised he could make them all rich. Hell, he already had. But he had also played them for the greedy fools he knew they were. When he started talking about killing himself, he knew

81

they'd all panic. They couldn't lose John, and they would do anything to keep him happy.

And that was exactly what the bastard had counted on.

Bleary-eyed from drink, Cameron finished the bottle of scotch and went to bed. The following morning, Sunday, he battled a hangover until noon. Then, when he was clearheaded, he came up with a plan. He needed absolute proof for Preston and Dallas to see, and once they realized how John had manipulated them, Cameron would demand that they split the profits in the Sowing Club now and go their separate ways. He wasn't about to wait five more years to collect his share. After what John had done, all Cameron could think about was running away before they got caught.

Cameron had a few connections of his own, and there were a couple of calls he needed to make. He had five working days before the confrontation he planned on Friday. Five days to nail the son of a bitch.

He didn't tell anyone what he was doing. Friday rolled around, and he arrived at Dooley's late, around six-thirty in the evening. He made his way to their table and took the seat across from John. The waiter had spotted him and brought him his usual drink before Cameron had taken off his suit jacket and loosened his tie.

"You look like hell," Preston said in his customary blunt way. Of the four, he was the health nut and made it clear at every opportunity that he didn't approve of Cameron's lifestyle. Built like an Olympic weightlifter, Preston was obsessive about working out five nights a week at a posh health club. In his opinion, any man who didn't have steely upper arms and a stomach you could bounce a quarter off of was a weakling, and men with beer guts were to be pitied.

"I've put in some long hours at work this week. I'm tired, that's all."

"You've got to start taking care of yourself before it's too late," Preston said. "Come with me to the club and start lifting weights and running the track. And lay off the booze, for Christ's sake. It's killing your liver."

"Since when did you become my mother?"

Dallas, a die-hard peacemaker, couldn't stand discord, no matter how minor. "Preston's just concerned about you. We both know you've been under a lot of stress lately with the divorce and all. We just don't want you to get sick. Preston and I depend on you and John."

"Preston's right," John said. He swirled his swizzle stick in the amber liquid as he added, "You do look bad."

"I'm fine," he muttered. "Now enough about me."

"Yeah, sure," Preston said, offended by the censure in Cameron's voice.

Cameron gulped down his drink and then motioned for the waiter to bring him another. "Anything new happen this week?" he asked.

"It's been dull for me." Preston shrugged. "But I guess in our business that's good. Right, Dallas?"

"Right. It's been pretty dull for me too."

"What about you, John? Anything new going on with you?" Cameron asked mildly.

John shrugged. "I'm hanging in there, taking it a day at a time."

He sounded pathetic. Cameron thought John's performance was a bit overdone, but Preston and Dallas bought it and were sympathetic.

"It will get easier," Preston promised. Since he had absolutely no experience with losing anyone he cared about, he couldn't possibly know if John's life would get easier or not, but he felt he should give his friend some sort of encouragement. "With time," he added lamely.

"That's right. You just need some time," Dallas said.

"How long has it been since Catherine died?" Cameron asked.

John raised an eyebrow. "You know how long it's been." He stood, removed his suit jacket and carefully folded it, then draped it over the back of the chair. "I'm going to go get some Beer Nuts."

"Yeah, bring some pretzels too," Preston said. He waited until John had walked away before turning on Cameron. "Did you have to bring Catherine's name up now?"

John told the waitress what he wanted and was walking back to the table when he heard

Dallas say, "John was just starting to relax. Give the guy a break."

"You don't need to coddle me," John said as he dragged his chair out and sat down. "I haven't kept count of the hours and minutes my wife has been gone," he said. "Some nights it seems like only yesterday."

"It's been almost a month." Cameron studied his friend as he made the comment. He picked up his glass and saluted John. "I think you ought to start dating. I really do."

"Are you crazy?" Dallas whispered. "It's way too soon."

Preston vehemently nodded. "People will talk if he starts dating this soon, and talk leads to speculation. We don't want that. Don't you agree, Dallas?"

"Hell, yes, I agree. I can't believe you suggested it, Cam."

John leaned back in his chair. His shoulders slumped ever so slightly and his expression looked pained. "I couldn't do it, not yet anyway. Maybe never. I can't imagine being with another woman. I loved Catherine, and the thought of replacing her makes me sick to my stomach. You know how I felt about my wife."

Cameron gripped his hands together in his lap to keep himself from reaching across the table and grabbing the lying bastard by the throat.

"Yeah, I guess you're right. I was being insensitive." He reached down into his open briefcase and pulled out a thick manila file folder. Pushing his drink aside, he carefully placed it in the center of the table.

"What's that?" Dallas wanted to know.

"Another investment opportunity?" Preston guessed.

Cameron stared at John as he dropped his bomb. "Lots of notes and figures," he said. "And..."

"And what?" John asked.

"Catherine's medical records."

John was reaching for the folder. When Cameron announced what was inside, John reacted as though a rattlesnake had just landed on his hand. He jerked back and then came up halfway out of his chair. The shock was quickly replaced by anger. "What the hell are you doing with my wife's medical records?" he demanded.

John's face was so red he looked as if he was about to have a stroke. Cameron began to hope that he would and that it would be massive and debilitating. The prick should suffer as much and as long as possible.

"You son of a bitch," Cameron hissed. "I saw you Saturday night with the blond. I couldn't figure out why you hadn't told us about her, and so I decided to do a little investigative work on my own."

"You didn't trust me?" John was genuinely outraged.

"No, I didn't."

Turning to Preston and Dallas, Cameron said, "Guess what? Good old Catherine wasn't dying. John just wanted to get rid of her.

Isn't that right, John? You played us for fools, and, damn, we were that. We believed every word you told us. You knew Monk wouldn't kill her unless we all agreed. That was the deal when we hired him. He works for the club, and you didn't have the guts to kill her yourself. You wanted to involve us, didn't you?"

Dallas whispered, "I don't believe it."

Preston was too stunned to speak. He stared at the file folder as he asked, "Is Cameron right or wrong? Catherine was terminal, wasn't she? You told us it was her heart, a congenital defect..." He stopped and turned helplessly to Cameron. Then he whispered, "My God."

John's lips were pinched together. His eyes blazed with fury, his gaze fully directed on Cameron. "What gave you the right to spy on me?"

Cameron laughed harshly. "You arrogant ass. You've got the balls to be outraged that I spied on you and your little Barbie doll?" Glancing at Dallas, whose complexion was rapidly turning green, he asked, "Want to hear something else really funny? You'll get a kick out of this news. I know I did."

Dallas picked up the folder and asked, "What?" John lunged to grab the file, but Dallas was quicker.

"Catherine introduced this woman, Lindsey, to John. She hired the bitch to redecorate her bedroom. Isn't that right, John? The affair started almost immediately after you met her, didn't it? But you had already decided to kill your wife."

"I don't think it's a good idea to talk about this here," Preston said with a worried glance around the bar to see if anyone was watching them.

"Of course we should talk about this here," Cameron said. "This is, after all, where we planned the mercy killing."

"Cam, you've got it all wrong," John said. He looked earnest now, sincere. "I've only had one date with Lindsey, and it wasn't really even a date. It was a business meeting."

Eager to believe John was telling the truth, Preston vigorously nodded. "If he says it was business, then that's what it was."

"Bullshit. He's lying. I followed him home. I saw Lindsey's car parked in his garage, and she was there waiting for him. They were all over each other. She's living with you now, isn't she, John? And you're hiding it from everyone, especially the three of us." Cameron began to rub his temples. He'd had a pounding, relentless headache off and on for the past week, ever since he discovered John's nasty little secret. "Don't bother to answer. I've got all the facts right here," he said, pointing to the folder Dallas had just opened. "Did you know Lindsey thinks you're going to marry her? I got that bit of information from her mother. She's already planning the wedding."

"You talked to Lindsey's mother? All that alcohol has gotten to you, Cameron. It's made you delusional...paranoid."

"You pompous ass," he scoffed.

"Lower your voice," Preston pleaded. His brow was covered with perspiration, and he wiped it away with the bar napkin. Fear made his throat dry.

"Shall we discuss Catherine's little trust fund that John was so worried would run out?"

"What about it?" Preston asked. "Was there any left?"

"Oh, yes," Cameron drawled. "About four million dollars."

"Three million, nine hundred seventy-eight thousand to be exact," Dallas read from the folder.

"Dear God...this can't be happening," Preston said. "He told us...He told us he took her to Mayo, and they couldn't do anything for her. Remember, Cameron? He told us..."

"He lied. He lied about everything, and we were so damned trusting we believed him. Think about it, Preston. When was the last time any of us saw her? A couple of years ago? It was right before she went to Mayo, wasn't it? We all saw how bad she looked. Then when she got back, John said she didn't want to see anyone. And so we respected her wishes. For two years, it was John who told us how her condition was deteriorating and how much she was suffering. All that time, he was lying."

They all stared at John, waiting for him to explain.

John lifted his hands, palms up in mock surrender, and smiled. "I guess the game's over," he said.

Stunned silence followed the announcement.

"You admit it?" Preston asked.

"Yeah, I guess I do," he said. "It's kind of a relief, really, not to have to sneak around you guys any longer. Cameron's right. I've been planning this for a long time. Over four years," he boasted. "Did I ever love Catherine? Maybe, in the beginning, before she turned into an obsessive, demanding pig. It's funny how love can turn into hate so quickly. Then again, I might not have loved her at all. It could have been her trust fund. I did love the money."

Dallas dropped a glass. It landed with a thud on the carpet. "What have you done to us?" The question came out in a choked whisper.

"I did what I had to do," John defended. "And I don't have any regrets. Well, no, that isn't exactly true. I regret inviting Lindsey to move in. I mean, I've loved every minute I've had her. She'll do anything in bed, anything at all that I ask, and she so wants to please me. She's getting clingy, though, and I'm sure as hell not going to get tied down again."

"You son of a bitch," Cameron snarled.

"Yes, I am that," John agreed smoothly. "Want to know the best part, besides the pig's trust fund? It was so damned easy."

"You murdered her." Dallas closed the folder.

John shifted in his chair. "No, that's not exactly true. *I* didn't murder her. *We* did."

"I think I'm going to be sick," Dallas stammered, and then bolted for the bathroom.

John seemed amused by the reaction. He motioned to the waiter to bring another round of drinks.

They sat stiffly together, like strangers now, each lost in his own thoughts. After the waiter had placed fresh drinks on the table and left, John said, "I bet you'd like to kill me with your bare hands, wouldn't you, Cameron?"

"I'd sure as hell like to," Preston said.

John shook his head. "You're a hothead, Preston. Always have been. And with your muscle-building regime, you could break every bone in my body. *But,*" he added, "if it weren't for me, you'd already be in prison. You don't think things through. You don't have what it takes. I guess you just don't have a calculating mind. We've had to push you into every financial decision. And we had to pressure you into agreeing with us to pay Monk to kill Catherine." He paused. "Cameron, on the other hand, does have what it takes."

Cameron inwardly cringed. "I knew you didn't have much of a conscience, but I never figured you'd screw us. We're all you've got, John. Without us, you're...nothing."

"We were friends and I trusted you," Preston said.

"We're still friends," John argued. "Nothing's changed."

"The hell it hasn't," Cameron shot back.

John was completely unruffled. "You'll get past it," he promised. "Especially when you remember how much money I've made for you."

Cameron propped his elbows on the table and stared into John's eyes. "I want my cut now."

"It's out of the question."

"I say we dissolve the club. We each take our share and go our separate ways."

"Absolutely not," John said. "You know the rules. None of us touches a dime for five more years."

Dallas came back to the table and sat down. "What did I miss?"

Preston, who now looked as though *he* was going to be sick, answered, "Cameron wants to dissolve the club and split the assets now."

"No way," Dallas said, appalled. "You make a withdrawal, and it can be traced by the IRS. It's out of the question."

"He can't touch the money unless we all go with him to the bank, remember? We all have to sign before we're given access. That's how we set it up," John reminded them.

"You're a real bastard, John."

"Yeah, so you said. Face it, Cameron. You aren't angry because I lied to you. You're pissed off because your life's miserable right now. I know you better than you know your-self. I know what you're thinking."

"Yeah? Enlighten me."

"You think I didn't have it all that bad. Right?"

"Yes," Cameron admitted. "That's exactly what I'm thinking."

John's voice was calm as he said, "But you didn't have the courage to do more than whine. I did. It's as simple as that." He turned to Dallas. "You know, you'd never have asked Monk to kill Catherine if I hadn't lied."

"But, John, if you wanted out, why didn't you just divorce her?" Dallas asked.

"The money," he answered. "I wanted every dollar she had. By God, I deserved it for putting up with her. She was a controlling bitch," he added, and for the first time there was bitterness and hatred in his voice. "Unlike Cameron, I didn't mask my misery with booze. I planned. You have no idea how sickening she was. Her weight had gotten out of hand. She was a hypochondriac. All she thought about and talked about was her health. She did have a heart murmur, but it was no big deal. She was thrilled when she found that out. It gave her a reason to become even more slovenly. She took to her bed and stayed there, being waited on hand and foot by her maids and by me. I kept hoping her heart would blow up, and, honest to God, I tried to kill her with the ton of chocolates I brought home every night, but it was taking too long. Granted, I could have screwed around on her every night and she wouldn't have known. In fact, I did screw around and she didn't find out. Like I said, the woman was too lazy to get out of bed, much less leave her bedroom. I couldn't stand coming home to her. Looking at her made me want to puke."

"Are we supposed to feel sorry for you now?" Cameron asked.

"No," he answered. "But as for crossing the line, we did that a long time ago."

"We never murdered anyone."

"So what? We'd still get twenty, maybe thirty years for all the crimes we have committed."

"But they were white-collar crimes," Preston stammered.

"Is that going to be your defense against the IRS?" John asked. "Think they'll just slap your hands?"

"We never killed."

"Well, now we have," John snapped, irritated with Preston's whiny attitude. Focusing on Cameron now, he said, "I'll tell you this. It was easy...easy enough to do again. You know what I'm saying? We could wait a little while, maybe six months or so, and then talk to Monk again about your situation."

Dallas's mouth dropped open. "Are you out of your mind?"

Cameron cocked his head. He was already thinking about it. "I'd love for Monk to pay a visit to my wife. It would be worth every penny I had."

"It's possible," John said smoothly.

"If you don't stop talking like that, I'm out," Preston threatened.

"It's too late for you to get out," John countered.

"There's no such thing as a perfect murder," Dallas said.

"Catherine's was pretty damned perfect," John said. "I can tell you're thinking about it, aren't you, Cam?"

"Yeah," he admitted. "I am."

Preston suddenly wanted to wipe the smug look off of John's face. "You've become a monster," he said. "If anyone finds out about Catherine..."

"Relax," John said. "We're in the clear. Now stop worrying. No one's ever going to find out."

CHAPTER SEVEN

Catherine had the last laugh. The controlling bitch had ordered her attorney, Phillip Benchley, to wait six weeks to the day after her death to read her last will and testament. John was furious about the delay, but he knew he couldn't do anything about it. Even in death the woman continued to try to manipulate him.

Catherine had hired Phillip before she'd married John. He was a partner in the prestigious firm of Benchley, Tarrance, and Paulson. Benchley knew which side of the bread was buttered. The old fart had catered to Catherine's every whim. She must have changed her will at least three times that John knew of while they were married, but the last time he went through her papers to make sure he was still the primary beneficiary was six months ago. After that, he'd done his best to monitor her phone calls and visitors to make certain she didn't have the opportunity to talk to her kiss-ass attorney again.

Since her death, John's bills had been piling up, most of them now past due, and Monk was breathing down his neck, waiting for his money. To placate him, John had had to up the bonus to twenty thousand.

John fumed while he waited in Benchley's plush corner office. It was outrageous that the attorney was keeping him waiting.

John checked the time again. Three-forty-five. He was supposed to meet his friends at Dooley's to celebrate. He knew they were probably just now leaving their offices.

The door opened behind him. John didn't bother to turn around. He wasn't going to be the first to speak either, no matter how childish that made him appear.

"Good afternoon." Benchley's voice was cold, damn near glacial.

"You've kept me waiting forty minutes," John snapped. "Let's get this done."

Benchley didn't apologize. He took his seat behind his desk and placed a thick folder on the blotter. He was a little man with frizzy gray hair. He slowly opened the file.

The door opened again, and two young men John assumed were junior associates walked over to stand behind Benchley. Before John could ask what they were doing, Benchley gave him a clipped one-word explanation. "Witnesses."

The second Benchley broke the seal and began to read, John relaxed. Fifteen minutes later he was shaking with rage.

"When was the will changed?" He had to force himself not to yell.

"Four months ago," Benchley explained.

"Why wasn't I notified?"

"I'm Catherine's attorney, sir, if you will remember. I had no reason to inform you of your wife's change of heart. You did sign the prenuptial, and you have no claim to her trust fund. I've made a copy of the will for you to take with you. Catherine's instructions," he added smoothly.

"I'll contest it. Don't think I won't. She thinks she can leave me a hundred dollars and leave the rest to a goddamn bird sanctuary, and I won't contest it?"

"That isn't quite accurate," Benchley said. "There is a four-hundred-thousand-dollar gift to the Renard family, to be divided equally among her uncle Jake Renard and her three cousins, Remy, John Paul, and Michelle."

"I don't believe it," he railed. "Catherine hated those people. She thought they were white trash."

"She must have had a change of heart," Benchley said. Tapping the papers with his fingertips, he added, "It's all here in the will. Each of her relatives will receive one hundred thousand dollars. And there was one other special request. Catherine was quite fond of her caretaker, as I'm sure you're aware."

"Of course she liked her. The woman catered to her every whim and made no bones about hating me. Catherine was amused by that."

"Yes, well," Benchley continued, "she left Rosa Vincetti one hundred fifty thousand dollars as well."

John was infuriated over that news. He

wished now he'd had Monk kill her too. He hated the holier-than-thou witch with her hawkish eyes. How he had relished firing her. Now she, too, was getting a piece of his money.

"Every dime belongs to me," he shouted. "I'll fight this and win, you pompous ass."

Benchley appeared unruffled by the tantrum. "Do what you will. However...Catherine thought you might want to fight her wishes, and so she gave me this sealed envelope to hand deliver to you. I have no idea what's inside. But Catherine assured me that after you've read it, you will decide against a legal battle."

John signed for the package and snatched it from Benchley. Venom all but spewed from his mouth when he said, "I don't understand why my wife would do this to me."

"Perhaps the letter will explain."

"Give me a copy of the damned will," he muttered. "And I assure you, nothing Catherine had to say in her letter is going to change my mind. I'm litigating."

He slammed out of the office. The rage was boiling inside his head. Then he remembered all the bills and Monk. What the hell was he going to do about that?

"Goddamn bitch," he mumbled as he got into his car.

It was dark inside the garage. John turned the overhead light on and tore open the envelope. There were six pages in all, but Catherine's letter was the first page. John lifted the paper to see what other surprises she'd saved.

Incredulous at what he was seeing, he flipped back to the first page and frantically began to read.

"My God, my God," he muttered over and over again.

CHAPTER EIGHT

John was frantic. He broke every law imaginable as he sped up St. Charles, weaving in and out of traffic like a drunk driver at seventy miles an hour.

Catherine's obscene letter was clenched in his hand. He kept slamming his knuckles into the leather dashboard, wishing it were her face he was smashing. That bitch! That conniving bitch!

He couldn't believe what she had done to him, wouldn't believe it. It was all a bluff. Yeah, that was it. Even in death, she was still trying to manipulate and control him. She couldn't possibly have gotten around all the safeguards he'd built into his computer. She hadn't been that smart, damn it.

By the time he pulled into his driveway, he had almost convinced himself that it was all a hoax. He misjudged the distance and hit the garage door when he slammed on the brakes. Cursing, he jumped out of the car and ran to the side door and only then realized he'd left the motor running.

He cursed again. Stay cool, he told himself. Just stay cool. The bitch was still trying to get under his skin, unnerve him. That was all. But he had to be sure. He ran through the empty house, knocking over a dining room chair in his haste. When he reached the library, he kicked the door shut behind him and lunged over the desk to turn the computer on, then sat down in the padded chair.

"Come on, come on, come on," he muttered, drumming his fingertips on the desktop while he waited for the computer to boot up. The second the icon appeared, he slipped in the disk and typed the password.

Scrolling down the documents, he counted the lines as Catherine had instructed in her letter, and there on line sixteen, right smack in the middle of the transaction made over a year ago, five words had been inserted. *Thou shalt not commit adultery.* John roared like a wounded animal. "You fat bitch," he screamed. Stunned, he fell back in his chair.

His cell phone began ringing, but he ignored it. Cameron or Preston or Dallas was calling to find out what was keeping him. Or maybe it was Monk calling to find out when and where to meet him to collect his money.

What in God's name was he going to tell Monk? John rubbed his temples while he thought about the problem. Dallas was the solution, he decided. He would let Dallas handle Monk. After all, Monk didn't belch without Dallas's permission, and he would surely agree to wait for payment if he were told to.

But what would John tell the group? Lying wasn't going to get him out of his nightmare, and the longer he waited, the worse it would get. He had to tell them, and soon, before it was too late.

He desperately needed a drink. He crossed the room to the bar, spotted the empty silver ice bucket, and knocked it to the floor. When Catherine had been alive, she had made sure the bucket was always full of ice, no matter what time, day or night. Such a stupid little detail, but suddenly important to him. She ran the house from her bed, just as she tried to run him ragged with her whining and her demands.

He poured a full glass of whiskey and carried it back to the desk. Leaning against the side, he drank it down, hoping it would steady his nerves for the ordeal ahead of him.

The phone rang again, but this time he answered it.

It was Preston. "Where are you? We've been waiting to celebrate your windfall. Get your butt over here." Music and laughter clattered in the background.

John took a breath. His heart felt as though it were going to explode. "There isn't any windfall."

"What?"

"We've got a problem."

"John, I can barely hear you. Did you say you didn't get the windfall yet?"

"Are the others there with you?"

"Yes," Preston answered, his voice cautious now. "We even ordered you a drink and—"

"Listen to me," he said. "We've got a serious problem."

"What kind of a problem do *we* have?"

"It's not something I want to talk about over the phone."

"Where are you?"

"At home."

"You want us to come over there? Is this problem something we need to talk about right away?"

"Yes, it is."

"What the—"

"It's bad," he shouted. "Just get over here."

John hung up before any more questions were asked. He refilled his glass at the bar, then returned to his desk. He sat staring at the glowing monitor screen as darkness descended.

Cameron and Preston rode together and arrived at his doorstep fifteen minutes later. Dallas was right behind them.

John showed them into the library, hit the light switch, and pointed to the letter he'd unwadded and left on the desk blotter. "Read it and weep," he muttered. He was well on his way to getting drunk.

Cameron picked up the paper and silently read it. When he was finished, he tossed the letter back on the desk and went for John's throat. Preston blocked him.

"Are you crazy?" Cameron shouted as his face turned red. "You let your wife have access to our records? My God..."

"Calm down, Cameron," Preston demanded as he pulled him back.

"You read the letter, and then tell me to calm down," Cameron shouted back.

Dallas got out of the chair, reached for the letter, and read it aloud to Preston.

Dear John,

Long good-byes are tiresome, and so my farewell is going to be short and sweet.

It was my heart, wasn't it? Forgive me for being trite and saying I told you so, but it was as I suspected all along. I died of heart failure, didn't I? Do you believe at last? I wasn't such a hypochondriac, after all.

By now you must be reeling from the shock of finding out that I have changed my will and have left you nothing. I know you well, John, and right now you're determined to contest it, aren't you? Perhaps you'll claim that I was out of my mind or too critically ill to know what I was doing. I suggest, however, that by the time you finish reading this, you will have decided to go away quietly and hide. One thing I am certain of is this—you won't contest.

You're also thinking about all the expenses you've incurred since my death. I've requested that the will not be read for six weeks from the date of my passing because I know that you will go on a little spending frenzy, and so I want you to be left high and dry. I want you to have to hide from your creditors too.

Why have I treated you so cruelly? Retribution, John. Did you truly believe I would let you have one dollar to spend on your whore? Oh, yes, I know about her. I know all about the others too.

Are you fuming, my darling? Get ready for more. I've saved the best surprise for last. I wasn't such a "stupid cow." That's right, I've heard you on the phone with your whore, calling me such names. I was crushed and angry at first, and so disillusioned, I cried for a week. Then I decided to get even. I began looking through your office for evidence of your affairs. I was obsessed with knowing how much of my money you had spent on your sluts. When you would leave for your office, I would get my "fat ass" out of bed and go downstairs to your library. It took quite a long time, but I was finally able to come up with your password and get into your secret little files. Oh, John, I never realized how twisted and corrupt you and your Sowing Club friends are. What will the authorities say about all of your illegal investments? I made copies of every single file, and just to make certain that you will know I'm telling you the truth, do hurry home and pull up the file labeled "Acquisitions." Scroll down to line sixteen. I've inserted a little message in one of your latest transactions, just to let you know I've been there.

Are you worried? Terrified? I, on the other hand, am gloating. Imagine my joy in knowing that after I'm gone, you will spend the rest of your life rotting in prison. The day you get this, the printouts are going out to someone who will do the right thing.

You shouldn't have betrayed me, John.

Catherine

CHAPTER NINE

Michelle had just finished the paperwork to dismiss one of Dr. Landusky's patients and was sitting in his cubicle on the surgical floor of St. Claire Community Hospital, trying to summon up enough strength to finish dictating her charts. Nine were completed, and she only had two more to go. Most of the patients belonged to Landusky. She'd been taking calls for him for the past two weeks while he went on a whirlwind tour of Europe, but he would be back at work tomorrow, and Michelle would officially start her first vacation in so many years she couldn't remember the last one.

She couldn't go anywhere, though, until the charts were finished. And the mail. My God, there was a stack of unopened mail she'd carried from her cubicle to Landusky's, and she vowed she wouldn't stop until she had sorted through it all. Exhausted, she looked at her watch and groaned. She'd been on her feet since four-fifteen this morning. A ruptured spleen from a motorcycle accident had gotten her out of bed an hour earlier than usual—and it was now five o'clock in the evening. She propped her elbows on the stack of charts she'd already dictated, rested her cheeks in the palms of her hands, and closed her eyes.

She was sound asleep thirty seconds later. Michelle had learned, while doing her residency, the benefits of catnaps. She had conditioned herself to sleep anywhere, anytime.

"Dr. Mike?"

She jerked awake. "Yes?"

"You need some caffeine," a nurse remarked as she walked past. "You want me to get you something to drink? You look wiped out."

Michelle didn't hide her irritation. "Megan, you woke me up to tell me I looked tired?"

The nurse was a young, pretty woman, fresh out of school. She had been working at the hospital less than a week, but already she knew everyone's name. She had just received notice that she'd passed her state boards. Nothing was going to bother her today, not even a surgeon glaring at her.

"I don't know how you can sleep like that. You were chatting on the phone just a minute ago, and then boom, you're drooling on your charts and snoring."

Michelle shook her head. "I don't drool, and I don't snore."

"I'm going down to the cafeteria," Megan said. "Do you want me to get you something?"

"No, thanks. I'm on my way out the door. I've just got to finish going through the mail and I'm done."

An aide interrupted. "Dr. Mike?"

"Yes?"

"There's a delivery for you down in ER," she said. "I think you have to sign for it. It looks important," she added. "I hope you're not getting sued."

"Dr. Mike hasn't been here long enough to get sued," Megan interjected.

"The messenger said the package is from a law firm in New Orleans, and he won't leave until he hands it over to you and gets your signature. What do you want me to tell him?"

"I'll be right there."

Michelle picked up the completed charts and put them in the out box. She left the two she still had to dictate on top of the stack of mail, then took the stairs down to the emergency room. The messenger was nowhere in sight. The staff secretary spotted her and hurried over to hand her a large manila envelope. "Here's your package, Doctor. I knew you were busy, so I told the messenger I had the authority to sign your name for deliveries."

"Thanks, Elena."

She turned to go back up to the surgical floor, but Elena stopped her. "Don't thank me yet, Doctor. There was a bad wreck on Sunset, and the paramedics are bringing in a vanload of kids. They're two minutes out. We're going to need your help."

Michelle carried the large envelope with her into the doctors' lounge to get a Diet Coke. Then she returned to the nurses' station, sat down, and popped the lid on the beverage. She needed the caffeine to get her second wind, she decided. She put the can down and reached for the envelope just as the door opened and a paramedic shouted for assistance.

"We've got a bleeder."

Michelle hit the ground running, the envelope all but forgotten.

CHAPTER TEN

No man is an island, and Leon Bruno Jones wasn't the exception. The Count, as he was called by his associates because his eyeteeth were noticeably longer than his other front teeth, resembled a vampire when he smiled. Leon looked as though he could suck the blood out of his victim, and if the extortion numbers in his duplicate set of books were accurate, he had taken more than blood.

Leon had a very large circle of friends, and all of them hated Theo Buchanan. Without

Theo's investigation, Leon wouldn't have turned state's evidence and he wouldn't have testified before a Boston grand jury, bringing down one of the most powerful organized crime rings in the country.

Theo had returned to Boston a few days after his surgery. Even though Leon's case had ended and a half dozen high-level mob bosses were now behind bars, Theo still had a ton of reports to file and a mountain of documents to record. His superiors in the Justice Department suggested that he maintain a low profile. Theo had received death threats before, and though he certainly didn't take them lightly, he also didn't allow them to interfere with his work. For the next couple of weeks he spent long, exhausting days at the office.

Finally, when the last paper had been filed and his staff had given their final reports, Theo closed the door to his office and headed home. He was worn-out, mentally and physically. The pressure of the job had gotten to him, and he wondered if, after all was said and done, his efforts actually made much difference. He was too tired to think about it. He needed a good night's sleep. No, he needed a month of good nights. Then maybe he could see things a little more clearly and decide where he should go from here. Would he take the job of heading up a new crime study that the Justice Department had offered, or would he return to his private law practice and spend his days in meetings and negotiations? Either way, he would be jumping right back on the treadmill. Was his family right? Was he trying to escape life by working nonstop?

The department heads had urged him to stay out of sight for a little while, at least until Leon's family simmered down some. Time away from it all actually sounded good to Theo right now. Visions of a fishing line rippling the serene waters of a Louisiana bayou popped into his head. Before he'd left New Orleans, he'd promised to return to give the speech he'd missed, and he guessed now was as good a time as any. After the speech, he could take a little trip and check out the fishing hole that Jake Renard had bragged about. Yes, a little time to chill out was just what he needed. There was another reason he was anxious to return to Louisiana, however...and it had nothing to do with fishing.

Three and a half weeks post surgery, Theo was back in New Orleans standing at the podium in the Royal Orleans ballroom waiting for the applause to die down so he could give his long overdue speech to the law enforcement officers who had come once again from all over the state to hear what he had to say. Suddenly, there she was, inside his head, messing with his thoughts. She had the most wonderful smile, like bottled sunshine. She also had a killer body, no doubt about that. He remembered how, lying in that hospital bed, he hadn't been able to take his eyes off her. Any normal man would have reacted the way he had. He had been sick at the time, but he hadn't been unconscious.

He was trying to remember the conversation he had had with her when he suddenly realized the applause had ended. Everyone in the ballroom was staring expectantly up at him, waiting for him to begin, and for the first time in his life, he was unnerved. He couldn't remember a single word of his prepared speech, or even the topic. He glanced down at the podium where he had placed the program, read the title and a brief description of the talk he was supposed to give, and ended up winging it. Because he kept his remarks short, his trapped audience loved him. Overworked and overstressed, they had been given a one-night reprieve to eat and drink and celebrate. The sooner he finished boring the badges off of them with platitudes about putting their lives on the line every day, the happier they would be. His thirty-minute presentation ended in just under ten minutes. Their response was so enthusiastic, he actually laughed. They gave him a standing ovation.

Later, on his walk back to his hotel, he thought about his bizarre behavior and concluded that he was acting like a boy who had just discovered sex. He felt like he'd traded places with his youngest brother, Zachary. These days Zack couldn't speak two full sentences without the words "girl," "hot," and "sex" in them.

Theo didn't know what had come over him, but he figured it would all go away as soon as he went fishing. He loved to fish. When he was out on his boat, the *Mary Beth,* he completely relaxed. It was almost as good as sex.

Tuesday morning, before he headed to Bowen, Theo had a breakfast meeting with a couple of New Orleans police captains, and then he stopped by Dr. Cooper's office. The doctor worked him in just so he could give him hell about not keeping his appointment after the surgery. After he finished his lecture about how important his time was, he checked Theo's incision. "It's healed nicely," he announced. "But you could have gotten into trouble if there had been any complications. You shouldn't have flown back to Boston so soon after surgery. It was a stupid thing to do."

Cooper sat down on the stool next to the examination table. "To be honest, I didn't expect any complications. Mike did an excellent job. She always does," he said. "She's as good with a knife as I am, and that's high praise indeed. She's one of the best cutters in the country," he added with a nod. "You were very fortunate she saw you were in trouble. I offered her a place on my team, even hinted at a partnership. She's that gifted," he stressed. "When she turned me down, I encouraged her to go on and get a subspecialty under her belt, but she wasn't interested. She's too stubborn to see she's wasting her talent."

"How so?" Theo asked as he rebuttoned his shirt.

"Doing family practice out in the boonies," Cooper said. "Mike will be doing a little cutting, but not much. It's a waste, all right."

112

"The people of Bowen might not see it that way."

"Oh, they need another doctor, no doubt about that, but…"

"But what?"

Cooper was fiddling with the lid of the cotton swabs. He abruptly closed it and stood. "Bowen isn't the sweet little town she made it out to be," he said. "I talked to her this morning about a bowel resection she'd sent me, and she told me her clinic was vandalized. Turned upside down."

"When did it happen?"

"Last night. The police are investigating, but so far, Mike told me there aren't any leads. You know what I think?"

"What's that?"

"Kids did it, looking for drugs. When they didn't find what they wanted, they tore up the place."

"Maybe," Theo said.

"Mike doesn't keep hard drugs in her clinic. None of us do. Patients who need that kind of medicine should be in a hospital. It's a real shame," he added. "She worked hard to get that clinic ready, and she was so happy and excited to be going back home again." He paused to shake his head. "I worry about her. I mean to say…if it wasn't vandalism, then maybe someone doesn't want her back in Bowen."

"I'm headed to Bowen to go fishing with her father," Theo said.

"You could do me a favor then," he said. "I've got another box of supplies I was going to take to her, but you could take them for me, and while you're there, you could look into this vandalism. Maybe I'm overreacting, but..."

"But what?"

"She's scared. She didn't say so, but I could tell. I got this feeling while I was talking to her that there was something else she wasn't telling me. Mike doesn't get scared easily, but she sounded upset when she was talking to me."

Theo left the doctor's office a few minutes later carrying a large cardboard box of medical supplies. He had already checked out of the hotel, and his suitcase and fishing gear were packed in the car he'd rented.

The sky was pristine blue, and it was sunny and warm, a perfect day for a drive in the country.

CHAPTER ELEVEN

It was early afternoon, and Cameron, Preston, and John were all chomping at the bit for Dallas to arrive. They had been waiting in John's library for over an hour and were becoming more and more anxious.

Dallas was late as usual.

"Where the hell have you been?" Cameron demanded the second Dallas walked into the library, looking as tired and haggard as the others. "We've been waiting for hours."

114

"I've been running my ass off," Dallas snapped. "And I'm not in the mood for attitude, Cameron, so knock it off."

"Do we pack up and leave the country?" Preston asked. "Are the police going to knock on our doors?"

"Jesus, don't talk like that." Cameron broke out in a cold sweat.

"I don't think we're going to have to pack our clothes just yet," Dallas said.

"You got the copies of our files back?" Preston asked eagerly.

"No," Dallas answered. "I didn't get them...yet. I found out what courier service the law firm uses and went there. Fortunately, they hadn't mailed the receipt back to the firm yet, and I got a copy. I called Monk immediately, and he headed out right away. Catherine sent the information to a relative, a Dr. Michelle Renard in Bowen, Louisiana."

"I don't get it. Why would Catherine wait till she was dead to send it to a relative and not just turn it over to the Feds the minute she found out?" Cameron asked.

John answered. "I know exactly what she was doing. Catherine was a fanatic about marriage being forever, and she wasn't going to let me go. She would have used what she discovered to make me behave. The last couple of months, she must have thought I was coming around. I was being so sickeningly nice to the woman. But Catherine was vindictive. No matter how nice I was to her, she was going to send me to prison after she died. Still, I never would have guessed that she would have sent the file to the family she'd practically disowned."

"Did the doctor sign for the package?" Preston asked.

"Yes."

"Son of a bitch. We're screwed."

"Quit interrupting and let me finish," Dallas said. "I talked to the man who delivered the package. He told me he went to Renard's home first. She wasn't there, and so he headed over to the hospital. He said she signed for the package in the emergency room."

"Why do we care where she was when she signed for it?" John asked.

"I was getting to that," Dallas replied. "The messenger remembered that, when he was pulling out of the parking lot, he almost ran into an ambulance as it came flying by. He said another ambulance was right behind the first, and while he waited, he saw the medics unload four boys. He remembers seeing a lot of blood on their clothes."

"So?" Preston prodded.

"So, my guess is that Dr. Renard was pretty busy last night."

"We're supposed to hang tight because you guess the doctor didn't have time to read the files and call the police?" Cameron asked.

"Will you shut up?" Dallas snapped. "As soon as Monk got to Bowen, he drove over to the St. Claire hospital. Sure enough, Dr. Renard had been in surgery. Monk told one of the aides that he wanted to talk to the doctor about a financial opportunity and asked her if he should wait. The aide told him that Renard had two back-to-back surgeries and wouldn't be done for several more hours."

"What else?" John asked. He was sitting behind his desk, drumming his fingers on the blotter. Dallas resisted the urge to stop him.

"The slip showed she signed for the delivery at exactly five-fifteen," Dallas said, checking a notepad. "I checked with the ambulance service, and the time of arrival at the hospital was five-twenty. So..."

"She couldn't have had time to do anything about the package," Preston said.

Dallas continued. "While Renard was in surgery, Monk put a tap on the phone line to her house. When he got back to the hospital, there had been a shift change in the ER. He took advantage of the opportunity to slip into the doctors' lounge and search Renard's locker. He even had an aide helping him. He told her a package had accidentally been sent to the wrong person."

"And she bought it?"

"Monk can be charming when he wants to," Dallas said. "And she was young. They didn't find anything, but she gave him all kinds of information about Dr. Renard."

"Maybe Renard took the package to surgery," John suggested.

"I doubt that," Dallas said. "The aide said she went up with a patient."

"Then what did Monk do?"

"He waited. It was late when Renard left the hospital, and he followed her. She made one stop on the way home. She went by a clinic, and she had some papers in her hands when she went inside. Monk would have searched her car then, but she'd left the motor running, which indicated she wasn't going to be there long."

"Did she have the papers when she came back out?"

"None that he could see," Dallas answered. "But she was carrying a backpack. Anyway, he followed her home, waited until he was sure she was asleep, then broke in and searched the house. He found the backpack in the laundry room and went through it first."

"It wasn't there." John made the statement.

Dallas nodded.

Cameron began to pace. "She had to have taken it to her clinic. Maybe she was thinking she'd deal with it today."

"Monk went back and checked the clinic. It wasn't there either. He assured me he searched everything. Only problem was, he broke a lock on her desk and decided he had to trash the place so it would look like kids had been there."

"Where the hell is the package?" John was furious now and wasn't trying to hide it. "I can't believe the bitch sent it to her cousin. She hated her relatives."

"I don't know where it is," Dallas said. "But it occurred to me..."

"What?" Preston urged.

"She can't possibly know what she has."

CHAPTER TWELVE

St. Claire, Louisiana, was easy for Theo to find. Bowen was impossible. There weren't any signs pointing the way, and as Jake had indicated, the little town wasn't on a map. Loath to admit that he was lost and needed directions—a genetic flaw passed down to the males in the family, according to his sisters, Jordan and Sydney—Theo drove around in circles until he was almost out of gas and had to stop. When he went inside the filling station to pay, he broke down and asked the attendant if he happened to know where Bowen was located.

The freckle-faced, slightly cross-eyed teenager nodded enthusiastically. "I sure do know where Bowen is. Are you new in town?" Before Theo could answer, the boy asked another question. "Are you looking for the new high school? It's over on Clement Street. Hey, I bet you are." He paused to give Theo the once-over, then squinted up at him and nodded. "I know why you're here."

"You do?"

"Sure I do. You're interviewing for the coaching job, aren't you? Yeah, that's it, isn't it? You're answering the ad, aren't you? We heard someone was maybe interested, and it's you, right? It wasn't a rumor after all. We really need help 'cause Mr. Freeland—he's the music teacher, but I guess you already know that—doesn't know squat about football. So are you going to take the job?"

"No, I'm not."

"Why not? You haven't even seen the place yet. I don't think it's right to make up your mind before you even see the place."

Theo's patience was wearing thin. "I'm not a football coach."

The teenager wasn't buying it. "You look like you ought to be a coach. You got the shoulders, like maybe you used to play some football when you were young."

When he was young? Just how old did the kid think he was? "Look, all I want is directions—"

The teenager cut him off. "Oh, I get it," he said, nodding enthusiastically.

"Get what?" Theo asked in spite of his better judgment.

"It's a secret, isn't it? I mean, until the position is filled, it's like a secret. You know, when the principal announces his choice at the big rally in a couple of weeks. By the way, Coach, my name's Jerome Kelly, but everyone calls me Kevin on account of that's my middle name." He reached across the counter to shake Theo's hand. "It sure is nice to meet you."

Theo clenched his jaw. "I'm just trying to find Bowen. Are you going to tell me where it is or not?"

Kevin put his hands up in a conciliatory gesture. "Okay. You don't need to get mad at me. But it is a secret, right?"

Theo decided to agree just to get the boy off the subject. "Yeah, right. It's a secret. Now, where's Bowen?"

Kevin was grinning from ear to ear. "You see that?" he asked, pointing to the street in front of the station.

"What?"

"That street."

"Sure I see it."

Kevin nodded again. "That's Elm Street, but there aren't any elms on it. I'm a kicker."

"You're a what?"

"A kicker. Mr. Freeland says that ought to be my position on the team. I can kick a football forty yards without breaking a sweat."

"Is that right?"

"I could be your punt returner too. I'm that fast."

"Listen, Kevin, I'm not the new football coach."

"Yeah, I know, and I won't tell anybody until it's officially announced. You can count on me, Coach."

"Where's Bowen?" His voice now had a real bite in it.

"I was just getting to that," he said. "Now, if you drive on this side of Elm Street, the east side," he qualified as he pointed out the window again, "then you're in St. Claire. If you don't know which way is east and which way is west—I sometimes have trouble with that— you'll know you're in St. Claire if you see sidewalks. Bowen doesn't have any sidewalks."

Theo gritted his teeth. "And where exactly *is* Bowen?"

"I'm telling you," he promised. "Now, if you cross Elm Street, like if you were walking...?"

Theo really hated this kid. "Yeah?"

"There you are."

"Where?"

"In Bowen. Get it? One side of Elm Street is St. Claire, and the other side is Bowen. It's as simple as that. I sure hope you'll give me a shot at kicker. I'd be a real asset to the team."

Theo counted out the bills for the gas and asked, "Have you ever heard of a bar called The Swan?"

"Sure," he said. "Everyone knows The Swan. It's a big old place tucked in the swamp, clear on the other side of Bowen. It's got a big swan on top. You can't miss it once you find it."

"So tell me how to find it."

Kevin came through this time with directions. When he was finished describing the convoluted route, he said, "You know the people in St. Claire like to think of Bowen as their suburb, but that really pisses off the people of Bowen. Oh...sorry. I probably shouldn't say 'pisses off' in front of faculty."

Theo pocketed his change, thanked Kevin for his help, and headed back to the car. Kevin chased after him. "Sir, what's your name?"

"Theo Buchanan."

"Don't forget," he called out.

"Forget what?"

"That I should be your kicker."

Theo grinned. "I won't forget."

Kevin waited until the car had pulled out

onto Elm, then raced back inside to call his friends. He wanted to be the first to tell the secret news about Coach Buchanan.

Ten minutes later Theo was driving down yet another seemingly endless unmarked gravel road. On either side were lush foliage and cypress trees with grayish green moss dripping from each branch. It was hot outside and terribly humid, but it was so beautiful and peaceful Theo rolled down the window to take in the sweet, earthy scents.

He could see murky water beyond the trees as he continued on the road at a snail's pace. He wanted to stop the car and simply sit there and take it all in. What a great place to do some exploring on foot, he thought. That thought led to another. Didn't alligators live in the swamp? Hell, yes, they did. Forget hiking anywhere.

What was he doing here? Why had he come all this way just to go fishing? Because she was here, he admitted, and he was suddenly feeling foolish. He considered turning the car around and going back to New Orleans. Yeah, that's what he should do. If he hurried, he could catch a late flight and be back in Boston by midnight. Wasn't that where he belonged? If he wanted to fish, he could take his boat out on the ocean and do some serious "catch a whale" kind of fishing.

He was nuts, that's what he was. He was just plain nuts. He knew what he should do, and yet he kept driving.

The road curved again, and suddenly there it was, The Swan, straight ahead at the end of the lane. The second he saw the building, he burst into laughter. Honest to God, he'd never seen anything like it. The building had gray corrugated sides and a pitched metal roof. It looked more like a big old barn, and a bit off-kilter at that, but the charm was definitely in the huge swan perched on top of the roof. Only, it wasn't a swan at all. It was a hot pink flamingo, and one wing was hanging precariously by a thin metal wire.

There was an old battered Ford pickup parked in the gravel lot. Theo parked his car next to it, got out, and removed his suit jacket. He was rolling up the sleeves of his blue dress shirt and walking to the entrance before he remembered he'd worn the suit jacket to conceal the gun and holster clipped to his belt. It was too hot and muggy to put his jacket back on. He decided not to worry about the gun being noticeable. Michelle already knew he carried a weapon. Besides, he was too busy trying to figure out what he was going to say to Jake when he asked him why he was there. He wondered if the old man would appreciate hearing the truth. I've become obsessed with your daughter. Oh, yeah, the truth would set him free, all right, and no doubt get him punched in the nose.

The door was half open. Theo pushed it wider and walked inside. He spotted Jake Renard behind the bar, a dishcloth in his hand, wiping down the varnished wooden counter. Theo removed his sunglasses, tucked them into his shirt pocket next to his reading glasses, and nodded to the man. He hoped Jake would remember him and was trying to figure out what to say to him if he didn't. What was the other reason he'd driven to Bowen? Fishing. Yeah, that was it. He wanted to go fishing.

Jake did remember him. The second he spotted Theo, he let out a hoot like a country singer about to break into song. Then he grinned from ear to ear, dropped the dishcloth, wiped his hands on his overalls, and came rushing around the counter.

"Well, I'll be," he said. "Well, I'll be."

"How are you doing, Jake?"

"Just fine, Theo. I'm doing just fine. You come to fish?"

"Yes, sir, I did."

Jake shook Theo's hand, pumping it enthusiastically. "I sure am happy to see you. I was telling Ellie just the other night that we'd be running into one another again, and here you are, plain as day."

Theo knew who Ellie was. Jake had mentioned his wife when he had visited with him in the hospital.

"How is your wife?" he asked politely.

Jake looked startled but quickly recovered, then said, "My wife passed on, God rest her soul, a good while back."

"I'm sorry to hear that," Theo said, growing more confused. "If you don't mind my asking, who is Ellie?"

"My wife."

"Oh, then you remarried."

"No, I never had the urge to marry again after my Ellie died. I didn't think I could ever find

125

anyone who could measure up to her." He paused to smile. "I just knew you'd show up on your own. I thought about calling you, but I knew Mike would have my hide if I did, and besides, I figured you'd find a way to come out to Bowen."

Theo didn't know what to make of the old man's comments. Then Jake said, "I knew once I put the notion of fishing in your head, you'd figure out a way to take a couple of days off. A true fisherman can't ever say no, no matter how long it's been since he's held a fishing pole in his hand. Isn't that the way of it?"

"Yes, sir," he said.

"If you turn out to be a natural-born fisherman—and I've got a feeling you are—then I may have to pair myself with you in the tournament coming on next weekend. I've always partnered up with my friend Walter, but Mike had to yank his gallbladder out yesterday, and he isn't going to be in any shape to pull his weight. He's already told me to find someone else. You'll still be here, won't you?"

"I hadn't thought about how long I'd stay in Bowen."

"Then it's settled. You'll stay on."

Theo laughed. "What kind of tournament are you talking about?"

"Oh, it's a big affair around here," he said. "Once a year, all the fishermen come from miles around to compete. Everyone puts in fifty dollars cash," he added. "It adds up to quite a hefty prize, and I've been wanting to beat old Lester Burns and his brother Charlie for the past five years. They've taken the ribbon and the cash prize every single year since we started the tournament. They've got the fancy equipment, which gives them the advantage. The rules aren't complicated," he added. "You just catch your quota, and the judge weighs them out in front of the crowd at the end of the day. Afterwards there's a party with good Cajun food right here at The Swan. Say, what do you think of my place?" he asked. He made a sweeping gesture with his arm. "It's nice, isn't it?"

Theo looked around with interest. The sun streaming in through the open windows beat down on the hardwood floors. Tables had been placed against the wall, their chairs stacked on top. There was a bucket with a mop propped against the corner of the bar, and to the left was a jukebox. Overhead fans made a clicking sound as the blades slowly circled. The room was surprisingly cool given the temperature outside.

"It's very nice," he remarked.

"We do a heck of a business come the weekend," Jake said. "Yes, sir, it sure is good to see you, son. Michelle's going to be pleased too. She's mentioned you more than once."

For some reason that bit of news was inordinately nice to hear. "How's she doing? I saw Dr. Cooper and he told me her clinic was vandalized."

"They tried to destroy the place is what they did," he said. "No rhyme or reason to it. They didn't take anything, just turned it upside down. Poor Mike hasn't had time to do more than look over the wreck. She saw the clinic this morning. Just as soon as she got home and changed her clothes, she got called back for another surgery. She hasn't had a minute to sort out the mess and tell her brother and me what she wants us to do to help clean it all up. I'm telling you, she's been run ragged. I expect her to keel over any second now."

"I'm doing just fine, Daddy."

Theo turned at the sound of her voice, and there she was, standing in the doorway, smiling at the two men. She was dressed in a pair of khaki shorts and a burgundy-and-white rugby shirt that was spotted with paint.

He tried not to stare at her legs, but, damn, it took work. They were incredible. Long, shapely...amazing.

"What are you doing in Bowen, Mr. Buchanan?" Michelle asked, hoping to heaven her voice was calm. Finding him in her father's bar had shaken her, and when he turned and smiled at her, she thought her knees were going to buckle. Her heart started fluttering, and she was pretty sure she was blushing. And why not? As the nurses in the OR had said, Theo Buchanan was drop-dead gorgeous.

"Is that any way to treat a guest, asking questions like that?" her father said.

She couldn't get past the shock of finding Theo there. "Did you call him and ask him for his help?" she asked her father with an accusing scowl.

"No, young lady, I did not. Now, stop giving me that glare and remember your manners. When Theo was resting up in the hospital, I invited him to come fishing with me."

"Daddy, you invite everyone you meet to come fish with you," she said.

She turned back to Theo. "You really came to fish?"

"Actually, I—"

Jake interrupted. "I just told you he did, and you know what I just decided? I'm gonna let Theo partner with me in the tournament next weekend."

"How are you feeling?" she asked Theo, retreating to the comfortable, safe role of physician. "Any complications?"

"I'm as good as new thanks to you. That's one of the reasons I drove out here...besides fishing. I wanted to pay you for the dress I ruined, but mostly I wanted to say thank you. You saved my life."

"Isn't that nice to hear, Mike?" Jake was beaming like a neon road sign. "It's why you went into medicine, isn't it? To save lives?"

"Yes, Daddy," she said.

"Are you hungry, Theo?" Jake asked. "It's past noon, and I'll bet you haven't had lunch yet. I've got some gumbo simmering in the pot. Come and sit at the bar and pass the time while I finish up. Mike, why don't you get Theo a nice cold beer."

"Water will be fine," he said.

He followed Michelle to the bar, noticing that her lopsided ponytail bounced with each step she took. Just how young was she? God, maybe he was going through a midlife crisis. Yes, that was it. Michelle made him feel young again. Except that he was only thirty-two. Wasn't that a little early for a midlife anything?

Jake placed a big bowl of thick gumbo in front of Theo and handed him a napkin and a spoon. "Be mindful," he warned. "It's hot."

Theo thought he meant that the gumbo needed to cool for a minute. He stirred it and took a big bite. He swallowed. Two seconds later his eyes were tearing, his nose was running, and he was coughing and trying to catch his breath at the same time. He felt as if he'd just swallowed molten lava. He grabbed the glass of water and gulped it down.

"I think you made it too hot this time," Michelle said. "How much of your special hot sauce did you add?"

Jake handed Theo another glass of water and watched him try to drink it while he was still coughing. "I just added one bottle," he said. "It seemed a little bland to me when I sampled it. I was fixing to add some more."

Michelle shook her head. "He comes here to say thank you, and you try to kill him."

Theo still couldn't talk. Jake had reached across the counter and was vigorously pounding him between his shoulder blades. Theo would have told him to stop, but he was pretty sure his vocal cords had just been cremated.

Michelle handed him a crust of French bread. "Eat this," she ordered. "It will help."

"I'll bet you're ready for that cold beer now, aren't you?" Jake asked as soon as Theo swallowed the bread.

Theo nodded, and after he had taken a long drink of the Michelob that Jake had handed him, he turned to Michelle and said, "I saw Dr. Cooper this morning."

"I thought you were doing all right," she said. She'd gone behind the counter and was stacking glasses.

"I am," he answered. "But I didn't keep the first appointment. I flew home to Boston a few days after the surgery, but they rescheduled my speech, so I came back. Better late than never," he added.

"You must have felt half dead by the time you got home," she said. "Playing the tough man can kill you."

He nodded. "It about did," he admitted. "Anyway, Cooper told me about the vandalism at your clinic."

"Do you see, Mike? I didn't call him," Jake asserted emphatically. "I suggested calling you," he admitted to Theo, "because you're the only FBI man I've ever met."

"I work as an attorney in the Justice Department," he corrected.

"Still, the FBI is part of the Justice Department, isn't it?"

"Yes," he said, "but—"

Jake wouldn't let him explain. "Which is why I wanted to call you. I thought maybe you could look into the matter, but Mike wouldn't hear of it. You know what else those boys did to her clinic? They sprayed those pretty white walls with black paint. Words I'm not going to repeat. They tore up her files too, and con-

131

taminated her supplies. Michelle's got to start all over again. Don't you, honey?"

"It will all work out. The timing's good anyway. I've got the next two weeks off to get the clinic cleaned up. That's plenty of time."

"But that was supposed to be your vacation time. You were going to rest up and do some fishing." He turned back to Theo. "My daughter has always been an optimist. She gets that from me. Now, Theo, what do you think we ought to do about this situation?"

"You did call the police, didn't you?" he asked Michelle.

She looked exasperated. "Yes, I did. Ben Nelson, the chief of police in St. Claire, took the report. He's investigating, and like my father, he thinks it was kids looking for drugs. Hopefully, word will get out that I don't keep any there, and this will be an isolated incident."

"I'm not sure I can do anything constructive..."

Jake disagreed. "You work for the government, and you carry a gun. I figure those folks in Justice wouldn't give you a weapon unless they had trained you to use it."

"Daddy, you sound like you want him to shoot someone."

"I'm just saying he's an expert. Ben Nelson is a fine chief of police. We're lucky to have him," he said. "But two heads are better than one. Isn't that right, Theo?"

"I doubt that the chief would want me to interfere in his investigation."

132

"You wouldn't be interfering, and I think he'd be happy for your assistance."

"For heaven's sake, Daddy. It was just vandalism. Ben will catch the kids. Give him time."

"Mike, honey," Jake said, "why don't you go get me a glass of cold milk from the refrigerator." The minute she was out of earshot, he turned back to Theo, leaned closer, and lowered his voice. "Pride's going to be my daughter's downfall," he said. "She's stubborn and so independent she thinks she can take on the world by herself, but she's got enough on her plate being a doctor. Maybe it was vandalism. Maybe it wasn't. But since you're going to be passing time with us for a few days, I think you ought to look into this situation. Besides, she saved your life—you said so yourself—and you owe it to my daughter to watch out for her while you're here." He glanced over his shoulder before whispering, "I'm thinking it might be a good idea if you stayed at her house." He saw Michelle walk out of the kitchen and quickly added, "Don't let her know I said anything to you." As Michelle was handing her father the glass, Jake said emphatically so that both could hear, "Yes, sir, I think Ben could use another opinion. I've had my say and that's the last you'll hear about the subject."

Michelle grinned. "For how long?"

"Don't you sass your daddy. I just thought Theo might like to help out."

"I'd be happy to take a look at the clinic," Theo offered.

"Good. Mike can take you there now, and then tonight you can stay at my place...or with Mike," Jake said with a conspiratorial glance at Theo. "We've both got extra bedrooms. I won't hear of you staying at some motel. You're my partner in the tournament, so you're also my guest, and you can eat all your meals free here at The Swan."

"No, that's all right."

He said it so quickly Michelle laughed. "I don't think Theo likes your gumbo."

She gave him that smile again. That incredible smile. What the hell was he getting into? This fishing trip was getting complicated. "I forgot," he said. "Cooper sent another box of supplies for you. It's in the trunk of the car."

"That was nice of him."

"He's wooing her is what he's doing."

"He's a married man, Daddy."

"He's wooing you to join his practice and move to the big city. That's what I meant."

A knock sounded at the door interrupting the conversation. They all turned as the door opened wider and a teenage boy stuck his head inside. The kid was huge. He had a buzz haircut and looked as if he weighed over two hundred fifty pounds.

"Mr. Renard?" His voice cracked when he called out Jake's name. "Since you're not officially open for business, would it be all right if I came inside?"

Jake recognized the boy. His name was Elliott and he was the oldest of Daryl Waterson's brood. Daryl and Cherry had eight strapping boys, all healthy and fit, but the family was in a bad way financially, ever since an unfortunate shredder accident at the mill. The older boys were working part-time jobs to help feed the family until Daryl could get back on his feet.

"Elliott, you know my rules. No one underage steps foot inside The Swan anytime, day or night. You don't want me to lose my liquor license, do you?"

"No, sir, I sure don't."

"You looking for work?"

"No, sir. I got a good job over in St. Claire with the packing company unloading boxes on weekends. We were all just wondering how long—"

"Who exactly is *we?*" Jake demanded.

"Some of the guys."

"Are they all underage too?"

"Yes, sir, I guess they are, and the girls too, but they—"

"Shut the door after you, son. You're letting the flies in. You be sure to give my best to your folks, and tell Daryl I'll be over Sunday to pass the time with him."

Elliott looked confused. "Yes, sir, I will, but—"

"Get going now."

"Daddy, don't you think you ought to find out what they want to see you about?" Michelle asked.

Theo started for the door. "Maybe one of them knows something about the vandalism at your clinic," he said. "We ought to talk to them."

"Maybe I was too hasty," Jake admitted. "Is somebody sick or hurt, Elliott? Mike, maybe you ought to have a look."

Elliott was frantically shaking his head. "It's nothing like that," he said. "I mean no one's hurt." He turned around, leaned out the door, and shouted, "Hey, you guys, he wears a gun. Is that cool or what?"

The teenager whirled around again just as Michelle walked forward. He glanced at her legs and quickly looked away. "No, ma'am, I mean, no, Dr. Mike, no one needs to see you. I mean we all like looking at you...no, that's not what I mean. I'm just saying no one's sick or nothing. Honest."

Elliott had turned three shades of red. Staying coherent in the presence of a beautiful woman was obviously beyond him. Theo had great empathy for the kid.

"Do you know something about the vandalism?" she asked.

"No, ma'am, I don't, and I did ask around just like your dad told my dad to tell me to do. No one knows anything, and it's kind of odd 'cause usually if kids do something like that, they like to brag. You know what I mean? Only no one's bragging. Nobody I talked to knows anything. Honest."

"Then why are you here, Elliott?"

He couldn't quite bring himself to stop staring at Michelle, but he was able to point at Theo. "Uh...we were all just hoping...uh, that is, if he doesn't mind...uh, maybe Coach Buchanan could come outside now and meet some of the team."

Michelle was sure she hadn't heard correctly. "What did you just say?"

"Maybe Coach Buchanan could come out and meet some of the team."

She blinked. *"Coach Buchanan?"*

Theo was at a loss for words. Where in God's name would Elliott get the idea...Then it clicked and he started laughing. "There was this kid—"

Elliott interrupted his explanation when he shouted outside, "Coach is coming out. Everybody get ready."

Jake was nudging Theo between his shoulder blades. "Might as well step outside, son, and find out what all the ruckus is about."

"This is all a misunderstanding," he said as Michelle walked to the door. Theo followed her and was about to explain, but the second he stepped out into the sunlight, a resounding cheer went up. He looked around in amazement. The parking lot was filled with cars and pickups and kids, at least forty of them, and every single one was shouting and whistling.

Four young, perky, blond-haired girls moved forward in unison. They were all wearing the same outfit, white shorts and red T-shirt. One of them had a pair of red-and-white pompoms, and she led the others in a cheer.

"Give me a *B*, " she shouted, and was aptly rewarded with a screeching, *"B!"* "Give me a *U*, give me a *K*, give me an *A*, give me an *N*, give me an *A*, give me an *N*. What's that spell?"

"Beats me," Theo said dryly.

"Bukanan!" the crowd roared.

Michelle burst into laughter. Theo put his hands up, trying to quiet the mob. "I'm not your coach," he shouted. "Listen to me. It's all a misunderstanding. This kid—"

It was hopeless. No one paid any attention to his protest. The exuberant teenagers came running toward him, all shouting at the same time.

How in thunder had this gotten so out of hand? He felt Jake put his hand on his shoulder, and he glanced back at him.

The old man was smiling broadly. "Welcome to Bowen, son."

CHAPTER THIRTEEN

He tried to clear up the misunderstanding, but the boys, obviously high on testosterone, wouldn't let Theo get a word in as they surrounded him, each shouting to be heard over the others. They wanted Coach to know what their special talents were and what positions they wanted to play. One boy called Moose shoved his way to the front of the crowd and told Theo he thought he would make a good linebacker. From the kid's size, Theo thought he could probably handle the entire line.

He kept trying to quiet them down so he could explain, but they were too excited to listen. In the background, the cheerleaders were doing back flips across the parking lot.

Michelle wasn't much help. She couldn't seem to stop laughing. Then one boy thought he might like to get a closer look at Theo's gun. Theo's reaction was swift, instinctive. He grabbed the kid by the wrist and pushed. The boy landed on his knees.

"Cool reflexes, Coach." Moose nodded as he shouted his approval.

"You kids back away," Jake shouted. "Let Coach and Mike get to his car. Go on now. Move out of the way. They've got to get over to Mike's clinic so Coach can start investigating."

Calling Theo "Coach" was only making the matter worse, and from the grin on Jake's face, Theo knew he was doing it on purpose.

Michelle took Theo's hand and led the way through the throng while Theo continued to try to get the kids to listen to him. The pair wound their way around the vans and pickups to where he'd parked his rental car. He opened the passenger door for Michelle and was immediately surrounded again by the high schoolers. Theo was a tall man, but some of the boys towered over him. He couldn't help but think that, with the right training and motivation, they could be one hell of a team.

He gave up trying to explain and simply nodded as he walked around to the driver's side and got in.

"Yeah, right, center," he said as he pulled the door closed and hit the lock button.

"Center what?" she asked.

"That kid with the earring wants to play center."

She was biting her lower lip to keep from laughing, but as they were leaving the parking lot, Theo was subjected to yet another cheer, and Michelle lost it.

"Give me a *B!*"

"You know what those kids need?" he asked.

"Let me guess. A football coach."

"No, they need an English teacher, someone who can teach them how to spell."

"They're just very happy you're here," she said. She wiped the tears away from her eyes and let out a sigh.

"Listen," he said, "all I did was stop for gas, and this kid mistook me for the coach."

"They're going to be very disappointed you've led them on. Oh, my, I haven't laughed like that in a long time."

"Glad I could help," he said dryly. "Tell me something. How come no one in this town will listen to me?"

"They're too busy trying to impress you. Are you going to let Andy Ferraud quarterback this year?"

"Very funny."

"He's got a good arm."

He stopped the car at the intersection and turned to her. "I came to fish."

After a few seconds Michelle realized the car wasn't moving. He had obviously stopped to wait for her to give him directions, and there she sat, like a lump, staring at him.

"Turn left here," she instructed. "My clinic's a few blocks down this road. If you keep going, you'll run into my house. It's about a block further along the curve. It's a little two-bedroom house actually. Nothing fancy. I'm rambling, aren't I? It's odd," she added. "I think you make me nervous."

"Why is that odd?"

"*I* should make you nervous. After all..."

"What?"

"I've seen you naked."

"And you were, of course, naturally impressed."

"Your appendix impressed me."

"Whatever it takes to make a beautiful woman notice me," he said as he steered the car to the left.

"There's my clinic."

It would have been hard to miss. The clinic was the only building on the gravel road. Theo pulled into the black tarred lot on the side of the building and parked the car near a giant sycamore tree. The branches of the tree draped across the roof. It was a disaster waiting to happen.

"You should get someone to trim those branches for you. A good lightning storm and you could lose your roof."

"I know. It's on my to-do list."

Her clinic was a small, rectangular, stone building that had been freshly painted white. The front door was black, and above the doorknob in the center was a black plaque with Michelle's name in gold letters. There were two overturned potted geraniums in cement planters flanking the stone walkway. Both of the planters had been smashed.

Michelle led him to the back entrance of the building. There were trash bags ripped apart, and the metal garbage container had been overturned. The backyard resembled a dump site.

"I just finished painting the door, and look what they did to it."

Across the white enameled door, the word "bitch" had been spray-painted—spelled correctly, Theo noticed.

She pointed to a discarded spray can on the ground. "They got the paint from the supply closet."

He glanced at the back lot again, then backed out of the way so Michelle could get her key into the lock to let him inside. She brushed against him as she walked past into the back hall and flipped on the lights.

There were three examination rooms, and all of them appeared to be intact. Aside from the spray paint on the walls, the exam tables and the cabinets had been left alone. The doors were open and the supplies had been overturned, but it didn't appear that much had been tampered with.

Her office was another matter altogether. Theo whistled when he saw it. The room looked as if a cyclone had hit it. Her desk had been turned on its side, the drawers ripped out and smashed in, and there were papers everywhere.

"I meant it when I said I hadn't had time to start cleaning up," she warned. "I took one look and called Ben."

Theo was looking at an old sofa across the room. One of the vandals had taken a knife to it. The burgundy leather had been shredded, and the stuffing was sticking out like puffed wheat. It looked like someone had worked himself into a rage in this room.

"Look what those creeps did to my door. I always keep my office closed, but I never lock the door. All they had to do was turn the knob. They went to a lot of trouble kicking it in."

"Maybe they had just figured out you didn't have any hard drugs around."

"And went crazy?"

"Possibly."

She started down the hallway. "Wait until you see the front. It's worse."

Theo continued to stand in the office doorway staring at the wreckage.

"What are you doing?"

"Figuring out the pattern."

"What pattern?"

He shook his head. "How come your brother and your dad haven't started cleaning up the place? Jake told me he offered, but you wouldn't let him touch anything. Why not?"

"I'm going to have to put the files back together first or at least be here when they do it so I can supervise. The information in the patient files is confidential, and I need to make sure all the reports get back in the right folders."

"I thought you were just opening this clinic."

"I am."

"Then where did all the patient files come from?"

"They're Dr. Robinson's files. He left Bowen two months ago and sent all his patient files to me. I found out about it after the fact," she said. "I knew he hated Bowen, but he really left his patients in the lurch. He told my dad that life was too short to work in a, and I quote, 'Godforsaken shanty town.' "

"With that attitude, his patients must have loved him," he said.

"No, they didn't like him much, and they only went to him for medical help when they were desperate. They knew how he felt about our town...and about them, or rather, us. You ready to see the front office?"

"Sure." He followed her down the hall and around the corner to the nurses' station behind the reception area. A glass partition that separated the space was shattered, and most of the jagged glass was still on the floor. There was a broken window next to the file cabinets. He slowly crossed the room to get a closer look at it. Then he looked at the floor below and nodded.

"Be careful where you step," she warned.

Though it didn't seem possible, the nurses' station was much worse. The countertop had been torn out of the wall and was on the floor on top of a mound of torn files and papers. The fabric on the chairs in the reception room had also been cut. They were all too badly damaged to be repaired.

Theo was glancing from the reception room to the nurses' station when Michelle interrupted his concentration.

"Thank God I'm starting a vacation."

"It's going to take more than two weeks to get this place in shape again."

She disagreed. "Two of my friends are going to drive up from New Orleans. It shouldn't take us more than one long day to get files in order. They're both nurses and will know what goes where. Once the paperwork is put away, John Paul and Daddy can help me paint. I've got enough time," she added. "But not the money to replace the furniture, not yet anyway." She picked up one of the chairs and put it against the wall, then bent to shove the white cotton stuffing back inside. "I guess duct tape will work for now."

"I'd be happy to loan you some money."

It was definitely the wrong thing to say. She shot upright like a rocket, and the look on her face told him he'd shocked and insulted her.

She didn't give him time to figure out a way to do damage control. "I don't want your money. In Bowen, we take care of our own. We don't expect outsiders to save the day."

"That's pride talking. I was only trying to—"

"Help a little lady in distress? I don't mean to sound rude, but you are an outsider, and you don't understand how important it is for us to be able to manage the clinic ourselves."

"You saved my life, and I only wanted to..." Her frown stopped him. "You're right.

145

I don't understand, but I'm not going to press you. I'll even apologize. I didn't mean to insult you."

Her expression softened. "Look, I know you meant well, but this isn't your problem. It's mine, and I'll deal with it."

He put his hands up. "Fine," he said. "You deal with it. So tell me, what did the chief of police say? Does he have any idea who did this?"

"Not yet," she said. "Even if he does catch the kids who did this, I still won't be compensated. No one around here has any money. Surely you noticed the absence of mansions on your drive into town. Most of the families have to work two jobs just to make ends meet."

He nodded toward the reception room. "This looks pretty bad."

"It's a setback, but I'll recover."

"What about insurance?"

"It will ease the pain, but it won't cover everything. I had to spend a fortune for malpractice insurance, and there wasn't much left over. To save money, I took a huge deductible." Without pausing for air, she switched topics. "Do you need help carrying in that box?"

"No."

"You can put it in the back hall and be on your way. Fish won't be biting this late in the afternoon, but you could get settled at Dad's."

She was trying to get rid of him and wasn't being at all subtle about it. She obviously didn't know what she was up against. Theo was every bit as stubborn as she was, and he had already decided he wasn't going anywhere.

"I think I'll stay with you...if you don't mind."

"Why?"

"You've got to be a better cook."

"These days, I don't have much time to cook."

"See? You're already better. Come on. I'll unload that box, and then we can drive over to your place. I want to see your house, unpack, and get out of this suit."

He tried to leave, but she blocked him. "Why?"

"Why what?"

They were standing toe to toe. He towered over her, but she didn't appear to be the least intimidated. "Why do you want to stay with me? Dad has more room."

"Yeah, but you're prettier, and he did offer me a choice. His place or yours. I'm choosing yours. Small-town hospitality and all that...it would be rude to turn me down."

"You mean southern hospitality, but you still haven't told me—"

He interrupted her. "Let me get settled in your house, grab a cold drink, and then I'll tell you what I think about this mess."

Theo went to the car, got the box out of the trunk, and put it on the floor in the back hall, then waited for her to turn the lights off.

"I should stay and start cleaning," she said halfheartedly.

"When will your friends be coming?"

"The day after tomorrow."

He nodded. "How about if I have a friend of mine go through the place first?"

"Why?"

"To tell me if I'm right or wrong. Take tonight off, Michelle. Then we'll get your brother and your dad to help. It won't take us any time at all."

"You came here to fish."

"Yeah, and I will fish. Now can we go get a cold drink?"

She nodded, pulled the door closed behind them, and headed for the car.

"Cooper told me you sounded scared on the phone."

"I was scared...so scared I've been jumping at shadows." She stopped to smile. "My imagination's playing tricks on me."

"How so?"

"I thought someone was in my house last night...while I was sleeping. I heard a noise and I got up and went through the whole house, but there wasn't anyone hiding in a corner or under my bed. It could have been John Paul. He drops by at odd times."

"It wasn't your brother, though?"

"I can't be certain. He might have left before I called out to him. It was probably just a bad dream, or the house was making a settling noise. I even thought someone might have been at my desk. It's in the library just off the living room," she explained.

"Why do you think that?"

"The phone is always in the upper right-hand

corner of my desk...it's kind of an obsession of mine to keep the center of my desk clear so I can work, but when I went downstairs this morning, the first thing I noticed was the phone. It had been moved."

"Anything else?"

"I've had this creepy feeling that someone's been following me." She shook her head at the absurd idea. "How paranoid is that?"

CHAPTER FOURTEEN

Theo didn't tell her she was paranoid, and he didn't laugh. Unfortunately, his expression on the way to her house wasn't giving her any hints as to what was going through his mind.

"Is that it?" he asked, nodding at the house on the curve of the road.

"Yes," she said, temporarily distracted. "I have the only house on the entire block."

He grinned. "FYI. Your house is on a dirt road, not a block."

"By Bowen's standards, this is a block."

The setting was incredibly beautiful. There were at least a dozen big trees surrounding her lot. The wood-framed house had a wide columned porch and three dormers jutting from the roof. There was water about a hundred yards beyond. As he pulled into the drive, he could see more trees growing crookedly out of the bayou.

"Do you get many snakes around here?"

"Some."

"In the house?"

"No."

He sighed with relief. "I hate snakes."

"I don't know too many people who like them."

He nodded and then followed her up the sidewalk to the front steps. Michelle had a thing for flowers, he noticed. There were flowers in the window planters on either side of the door and more around the porch in big clay pots with ivy spilling over.

She unlocked the front door and led the way inside. Theo put his bag down in the entry next to an old chest and glanced around. By all appearances the house had been painstakingly restored. The hardwood floors and moldings were beautifully finished to a soft luster, and the walls were painted a pale buttery yellow. Theo detected the aroma of fresh varnish. He propped his fishing pole against a wall and closed the door behind him. When he locked the deadbolt, he saw how flimsy it was. He opened the door again, squatted down, and examined the lock closely, looking for signs of tampering. There weren't any visible scratches, but she needed to replace it very soon.

He stepped into the foyer. To the left was a small dining room furnished with a dark mahogany table and chairs and a beautifully crafted sideboard on the wall facing the windows. The color was in the rug. It was a deep, bright red with splashes of yellow and black.

To the right of the entrance was the living room. An overstuffed beige sofa faced two easy chairs in front of the stone hearth. A trunk sat on another colorful rug in front of the sofa, and on top of the makeshift coffee table were stacks of books. At the back of the living room were French doors, and he could see the desk beyond.

"The house is really a big square," she said. "You can walk from the dining room into the kitchen and breakfast room, cross the back hall into my office, and then walk through those French doors into the living room. There aren't any dead ends in this house and I like that."

"Where are the bedrooms?"

"The stairs are in the back hallway next to the laundry, and I've got two bedrooms upstairs. They're big, but the floors and the walls still need to be refinished. I'm taking it a room at a time. We'll have to share the bathroom if you don't mind," she added. "Or you can use the bath on this floor, but there's a washer and dryer in there. When I'm finished remodeling, there will be two separate rooms."

Michelle's house was furnished simply, yet everything was tasteful and uncluttered, a reflection, he decided, of the woman who lived there.

"Is that a Maitland-Smith?" he asked as he walked into the dining room to get a closer look at the table.

"You know furniture manufacturers?"

"Yeah, I do," he said. "I appreciate fine workmanship. So is it?"

"No, it isn't a Maitland-Smith. It's a John Paul."

He didn't recognize the name for a second or two; then he realized she was telling him her brother had made the furniture.

"No way your brother did this."

"Yes, he did."

"Michelle, this is a work of art."

He gently stroked the tabletop as though it were a baby's forehead. Michelle watched him, pleased that he appreciated her brother's work.

The mahogany wood felt as smooth as polished marble. "Incredible," Theo whispered. "Look at these great lines."

He squatted down to look underneath. The legs were ornately carved, and the scrollwork was amazing. It was perfect. Every line was perfect.

"Who taught him how to do this?"

"He's self-taught."

"No way."

She laughed. "My brother's a perfectionist in some things. He's certainly talented, isn't he?"

Theo wasn't finished examining the set. He stood and picked up one of the chairs. Then he turned it upside down and whistled. "Not a nail or screw in sight. Man, oh, man, what I would give to be able to do work like this. With the right care, this chair will last for centuries."

"You do carpentry?" She didn't know why, but the thought of Theo doing anything manual surprised her. It seemed contradictory to what she knew about him.

He glanced at her and saw her surprise. "What?"

"You don't seem the type to work with your hands."

"Yeah? What type do I seem?"

She shrugged. "Wall Street...custom-made suits...servants. You know, big-city boy."

He raised an eyebrow. "You're wrong. I do some of my best work with my hands." Flashing her a grin, he added, "Want some references?"

The sexual innuendo wasn't lost on her. "Do I have to lock my bedroom door tonight?"

His expression immediately sombered. "No, I would never intrude on your privacy. Besides..."

"Yes?"

He winked at her. "If I play my cards right, you'll come to me."

"Are you this brazen with all the women you meet, Mr. Buchanan?"

He laughed. "I don't know what it is, Michelle. You seem to bring out the devil in me."

She rolled her eyes.

"Honest," he said, "I really do like working with my hands. I like building things...or at least I used to. I'll admit, I'm not any good yet."

"What have you made?"

"My last project was a two-story birdhouse. I built it four years ago, but it was a failure.

The birds won't go near it. I'm starving, Michelle. How about I take you out to dinner."

"I'd rather stay in tonight," she said. "If that's all right with you. You are my houseguest..."

"Like it or not?"

"Actually, it's kind of nice, having a Justice Department attorney under my roof. Maybe you'll keep the wolves at bay."

"You're still going to lock your bedroom door, though, aren't you?"

It was strange to banter with a good-looking man. And fun, Michelle thought. There really hadn't been much time for any of that while she was in medical school, and then residency, where all she could think about was getting a nap. Banter was definitely not part of her curriculum.

"The truth is I don't have a lock on my door," she told him. "Come with me. I'll show you where you'll be sleeping, and you can change clothes while I rummage through the refrigerator."

Theo grabbed his bag and followed her through the dining room into the kitchen. It was a bright, cheerful, country kitchen and twice the size of the dining room. In the breakfast nook were an old oak table and four paint-splattered folding chairs. There were three double-hung windows above the old enamel sink, overlooking the screened porch and the back lot. Her yard was long and narrow, and in the distance he could see a dock jutting into the murky water beyond. An aluminum outboard boat was tethered to one of the posts.

"Do you fish off that dock?"

"Sometimes," she said. "But I like my dad's dock better. I catch more fish there."

There were three doors off the back hallway. One led to the screened porch, another opened to a freshly painted bathroom, and the third led to the garage. "There's another bathroom at the top of the stairs. Your bedroom is on the left."

Theo didn't immediately go upstairs. He dropped his bag on the steps, checked the back door lock, shaking his head because it was so weak a ten-year-old could have gotten it open. Then he looked at the windows on the first floor. When he returned to the kitchen, he said, "Anyone could have climbed in your windows. Not one of them was locked."

"I know," she admitted. "I'll keep them locked from now on."

"I'm not trying to frighten you," he said, "but as far as the vandalism—"

"Would you mind waiting until after we eat? It's been a stressful day."

She turned around and went to the refrigerator. She could hear the stairs squeak as Theo went up. The old iron bed in the guest room had a lumpy mattress, and she knew his feet were going to hang over the rail. She also knew he'd never say a word about any discomfort because he was a gentleman.

She loved his Boston accent. The thought popped into her mind as she was stacking vegetables on the counter, and she immediately pushed it aside. Yes, Boston. A world away. Then she sighed. Theo had come to fish and to return a favor, she decided. He would help sort out this mess she'd gotten into, and then he would go back to Boston.

"End of story."

"What did you say?"

She flinched. "I was talking to myself."

He was wearing a pair of old, faded jeans and a gray T-shirt that had definitely seen better days. His white tennis shoes were also gray, and there was a hole in one of the toes. She thought he looked incredibly sexy.

"What's so funny?"

"You. I expected pressed and creased jeans, I guess," she said. "I'm kidding," she quickly added when she saw his frown. "You fit right in...except for that gun."

"I'll be happy when I can give this sucker back. I don't like guns, but the authorities back in Boston have asked me to wear it until the furor over my last case dies down."

"Have you ever had to shoot anyone?"

"No, but I haven't given up hope," he said with a sly grin. "May I have that apple?"

He took a bite out of it before she gave him permission. "Damn, I'm hungry. What are you fixing?"

"Grilled fish with vegetables and rice. Is that okay?"

"I don't know. It sounds a little too healthy for me. I like junk food."

"Too bad. You're eating healthy in my house."

"After dinner, how about we sit down and talk about what's going on in your life."

"Like what?"

"Like who in this town wants to screw with you," he said. "Sorry, I should have said, 'who has a grudge.' "

"I've heard worse," she said. "I used to have quite a mouth myself," she boasted. "When I was a little girl. I picked up the colorful language from my brothers. Daddy said I could make a grown man blush, but he nipped that in the bud."

"How? Soap in your mouth?"

"Oh, no, nothing like that." She turned on the faucet and began to wash the green onions. "He just told me that every time I used a bad word, my mother cried."

"So he used guilt."

"Exactly."

"Your dad talks about her as though..."

"She's waiting at home for him."

"Yes."

She nodded. "Daddy likes to talk things over with her."

"How'd she die?"

"She had a massive stroke while she was in labor with me. She never recovered, and she eventually died."

The phone rang, interrupting the conversation. Michelle wiped her hands on a towel and answered. Her father was calling from The Swan. She could hear glasses clinking.

Theo leaned against the counter and finished his apple while he waited for Michelle to tell him what she wanted him to do to help with dinner. His stomach growled in anticipation, and he looked around the kitchen for something to snack on. The woman didn't keep any junk food around. How could she drink a cold beer without a handful of potato chips? That seemed almost criminal to him.

"Do you mind?" he asked, pointing to the cabinets.

She waved him ahead, and he immediately started searching the shelves for something more to eat. Jake was doing most of the talking on the phone. Every minute or two Michelle would try to get a word in.

"But, Daddy...we were just fixing...yes, Daddy. I understand. All right. I'll go right over...Why does Theo have to go with me? Honestly, Daddy, the man came here to fish...No, I wasn't arguing. Yes, sir. I'll call you as soon as we get back." Then she laughed, and it was such a joyful sound, Theo smiled in reaction. "No, Daddy, I don't think Theo wants any more of your gumbo."

After she hung up the phone, she put the fish back in the refrigerator. "Sorry, but dinner's going to have to wait a little while. Daryl Waterson is having trouble with his hand, and Daddy told him I'd drive over there and look at it. Daryl's probably just bandaged it too tight again. I'd insist that you stay here and relax, or start dinner for me, but my car's at The Swan and Daddy thinks you ought to go with me. Do you mind?"

Since he didn't have any intention of letting Michelle out of his sight until they had had a talk about her situation, he didn't mind at all.

"No problem," he said. "Daryl's the big kid's dad? The teenager who came into the bar looking for me? What was his name?"

"Elliott," she said. "And yes, Daryl's his dad."

"Maybe we could drive through a McDonald's on the way. Get some french fries and a Big Mac."

"Do you just not care about your arteries?"

It was the way she asked the question that made him laugh. She'd sounded so appalled. "Sure I do. So how about it?"

"There aren't any McDonald's in Bowen."

He ran upstairs to get his car keys while she went into her office to get her medical bag. Theo beat her to the front door and waited.

"You've got your house key?" he asked.

She patted her pocket. "Got it."

"I locked your back door. You left it open." He sounded as though he was accusing her of a crime.

"I sometimes forget to turn it. We don't worry about locking our doors in Bowen."

"Was your clinic locked up tight?"

"Yes, it was."

"From now on," he said as he pulled the front door closed behind them and made sure it was locked, "every door is secured. Okay?"

"Yes, okay," she said as she put her medical bag on his backseat.

Theo was backing out of the driveway when he glanced at her and said, "Think we could stop for—"

"No."

"You don't know what I want."

159

"Yes, I do. French fries, greasy burger—"

"Potato chips," he said.

"Too much sodium."

While she directed him down one unmarked road after another, he argued with her about nutrition. "Don't you ever lighten up?"

"I'm a doctor, so I guess the answer is no."

"Doctors aren't allowed to eat anything that tastes good?"

"I had no idea my houseguest was going to be such a whiner. Daddy likes junk food. You could move in with him."

She was afraid she sounded belligerent. Theo gave her the opening to prove she wasn't a complete stuffed shirt or a prude when he asked, "What do people do around here for fun?"

She shrugged. "Oh, pretty simple things...go to the movies, swap fishing stories over a pitcher of beer at The Swan, have potluck dinners at the VFW hall, visit neighbors to compare tomato crops...and then, of course, there's the perennial favorite...sex."

"What?" he asked, sure he hadn't heard her correctly.

"Sex," she repeated innocently. "They have sex. Lots and lots of sex."

He laughed. "I knew I was gonna like this place."

CHAPTER FIFTEEN

There's Daryl's house at the end of the road," Michelle said.

Theo would have parked by the curb, but there wasn't one. There wasn't a driveway either, and so he pulled up on the grassy slope and parked the car next to a battered old Chevy van. The two-story frame house was in desperate need of repair. The bowed steps looked as though they were about to cave in.

Daryl's wife, Cherry, was watching for them behind the screen door. As soon as they got out of the car, she came out on the porch and waved to them.

"Good of you to come by, Dr. Mike. Daryl's hand is giving him fits. He doesn't like to complain, but I can tell he's in considerable pain."

Theo took Michelle's medical bag and followed her. She introduced him. After Cherry wiped her hands on her apron, she shook his hand. She was a rather plain woman with a weathered complexion, around the age of forty, Theo guessed, but when she smiled, she was quite lovely. The nickname, Cherry, obviously was due to her bright red hair.

"I've heard all about you from our oldest boy, Elliott. I don't think I've ever seen him so excited," Cherry said. "You certainly did impress him," she added with a nod. "Come on inside. I was just fixing to set the table for supper. Oh, before I forget to tell you, Mr. Freeland might be passing by to say his hello. He rang up about twenty minutes ago."

"Mr. Freeland?" The name seemed familiar to Theo, but he couldn't remember where he'd heard it before.

"The music teacher at the high school," Michelle said.

Cherry led the way through the living room and dining area. The furniture was sparse and worn-out. The kitchen was small and crowded with a long oak table and ten chairs, none of which seemed to match.

Daryl was waiting for them. He was seated at the head of the table feeding a banana to the baby in the high chair next to him. The little boy had more of the banana on his face and hands than in his mouth. The baby spotted his mother and broke out in a toothless grin. Then he saw Michelle and immediately clouded up. His lower lip trembled.

She kept her distance. "No shots today, Henry," she promised.

The toddler burst into tears. Cherry patted the baby's hand and soothed him with a handful of Cheerios she placed on his tray.

"Every time Henry sees me, I hurt him," Michelle said. "When I can afford it, I'm going to hire a nurse and let her give the shots."

"Don't you mind Henry. He'll figure out you aren't here to mess with him in a minute or two," Cherry said.

Daryl stood and put his hand out to shake Theo's as Michelle made the introductions.

The man's left hand and arm were bandaged to the elbow.

"Why don't you sit down next to Dr. Mike by that stack of papers," Cherry suggested to Theo, "while she has a look at Daryl's hand."

Daryl wasn't too subtle as he shoved the papers closer to Theo. "Big Daddy Jake thought you might find these papers of mine interesting...you being a lawyer and all."

Theo knew a setup when he saw one. He nodded and sat down. Michelle knew what was going on as well, but she went through the motions of looking at Daryl's hand.

After checking the color of his fingers, she asked, "Are you changing the bandage every day?"

"Yes," he said, his gaze fully directed on Theo. "Cherry changes it for me."

"We've got enough of the gauze you gave us to last another week," Cherry said. She, too, was watching Theo closely and was nervously twisting her apron in her hands.

Theo wasn't sure what was expected of him. Michelle decided to fill him in.

"Daryl worked for the Carson Brothers' sugar mill."

"After the accident they let me go. Laid me off permanently is what they did," he explained as he rubbed his chin.

"Did the accident happen while you were at work?" Theo asked.

"Yes, it did," he answered.

"Daryl put in twenty-two years at that mill," Cherry interjected.

"That's right," her husband said. "I started the day I turned seventeen."

Theo did the math and was shocked when he realized Daryl was only thirty-nine or forty years old. The man looked ten years older. He was as worn-out as his house. His hair was streaked with gray, he had deep calluses on his right hand, and his shoulders were stooped.

"Tell me about the accident."

"Before or after you look through those papers?" Daryl asked.

"Before."

"All right. I'll make it simple. I was operating a shredder, which is a big machine you just can't do without in a sugar mill, and I told Jim Carson it wasn't working right and he needed to shut it down and get it fixed, but he wouldn't listen to me. He's hard up for money, and I understand that, of course. Still, I wish he had listened. Anyway, I was doing my job, and all of a sudden the belt snapped and the whole darn thing came down on me. Crushed every bone in my hand, didn't it, Mike?"

"Just about," she agreed.

She was standing over him and thought she might be making him nervous, and so she pulled up a chair and sat down between him and Theo.

"Did you do the surgery?" Theo asked Michelle.

"No, I didn't," she answered.

"Dr. Mike sweet-talked a hand surgeon in New Orleans into fixing me up," Daryl said.

164

"He did a good job too, didn't he, Daryl?" Cherry added.

"He sure did. Because of him, I'm going to keep all my fingers. I can already move them."

"It's a miracle is what it is," Cherry said.

"Jim Carson came to see me in the hospital. It wasn't a social call," he added. "He told me it was carelessness on my part because I knew that machine wasn't working right, and I went ahead and used it. He called me a slacker and let me go."

"Is there a union at this mill?"

"Oh, no, the Carson brothers would close the mill down before they'd let a union in there. They complain they don't make enough money as it is to make ends meet and make payroll, and if they had to put up with employees trying to tell them what to do, well then, they'd just fold up."

"They're always threatening to retire and close the mill if anyone makes trouble for them," Cherry said. She let go of her apron and went to the sink to wet a cloth to wash her baby's face.

"Have you got a pen?" Theo asked Michelle. "I want to make a couple of notes."

She opened her medical bag and sorted through her instruments. The baby, Theo noticed, was watching Michelle with what could only be described as a comically wary expression.

"Henry doesn't trust you," Theo said, grinning. The baby turned to Theo and smiled. Drool dripped down his chin.

While his mother tried to wash the banana off his fingers, Michelle handed Theo a notepad and a pen. He put on his glasses and began writing.

"What about worker's compensation?" Theo asked.

"Jim told me their insurance rates would go up if I put in a claim and that I didn't qualify anyway, since the accident was my fault."

"Daryl's worrying about the other folks at the mill," Cherry said. "If Jim Carson shuts it down, everyone will be out of work."

Theo nodded, then picked up the papers Daryl had collected and began to read. The conversation immediately stopped, and Daryl and Cherry waited expectantly. The only noise in the kitchen was the baby slurping on his fist.

It didn't take Theo long to finish. "Did you sign any papers about your termination?" he asked.

"No," Daryl answered.

"Don't forget to tell Theo about the lawyer," Cherry reminded her husband.

"I was just getting to that," Daryl said. "Jim sent over Frank Tripp to talk to me."

"Everyone calls him Maggot," Cherry said. She had moved to the stove and was stirring the stew she'd prepared for supper. "We call him Maggot to his face," she added. "We don't go behind his back. We want him to know what we think of him."

"Now, calm down, Cherry, and let me tell it," Daryl said softly. "Frank's a lawyer over in

St. Claire, and if I weren't sitting in my house, I'd have to spit after saying his name. He's a common thug is what he is, and so is his partner, Bob Greene. They've got a partnership together, and they work on a monthly...what's that word I'm searching for, Cherry honey?"

"Commission?"

"Retainer," Theo said.

"Yes, that's the word. Anyway, like I was saying, they get a monthly retainer from the Carsons, and it's their job to take care of any problems that come around, problems like me."

"That sounds like a sweet deal," Michelle said softly.

"We were wondering..." Cherry began, and then nodded to Daryl. "Speak up, honey. Tell him what's on your mind like Big Daddy told you to do."

"All right. Cherry and I were wondering if there might be something you could do about this, since you happen to be a lawyer yourself. We'll pay you for your time, of course. We don't take charity."

"But we don't want to get you into any trouble," Cherry said.

"How would you be getting me into trouble?" Theo asked, thoroughly perplexed.

"Since you haven't officially resigned from the Justice Department yet and signed the coaching contract at the school, Big Daddy explained you can't take money."

"Because you get paid by the Justice Department," Cherry said. "Is that true? Or was Big Daddy just speculating?"

"If there is a fee, I need to know the amount so I can start figuring how I'm going to come up with the money," Daryl said.

"There won't be any fee," Theo said.

"Then what Big Daddy said was true?"

"Yes," he lied.

"Is there anything you can do about the Carsons?" Cherry asked again. Her voice was hopeful, but her face showed her worry.

"Without making the Carsons mad enough to shut the mill down," Daryl reminded him. "Big Daddy spoke highly of your abilities..."

"He did, did he?" Theo wanted to laugh. He couldn't imagine what Jake could have said about him. Jake certainly didn't know what Theo's abilities were. Theo and the older man had discussed fishing and little else.

"Yes, sir, he did, and he thought you could have a little chat with Jim Carson on my behalf. You know, get him to be reasonable. They take so much out of our pay for medical each month, and then they don't let us use it in an emergency. That doesn't seem right to me."

"It isn't right," Theo agreed.

"Maybe you could talk to Jim's brother, Gary. He's older, and Jim does whatever Gary tells him to do. Gary runs the place," Cherry said.

Theo nodded again. "I'm not familiar with Louisiana law," he began, and immediately noted that Daryl's expression went from hopeful to resigned. "Which means I need to do some research, talk to some friends who can give me some advice," he added, and was pleased to see Daryl nodding and smiling again. "So here's what I propose we do. I'll do the research, figure out a course of action, and then you and I will sit down together and I'll give you your options. In the meantime, I don't think it's a good idea to tell anyone about this conversation. I don't want the Carsons or their attorneys to know I'm looking into this. Agreed?"

"Yes," Daryl said. "I won't say a word to anybody."

"What about Big Daddy Jake?" Cherry asked. "He already knows we're talking to you."

"He won't tell anyone," Daryl said to his wife.

A child shouted for his mother, disrupting the conversation. "Mama, Mr. Freeland's waiting on the porch. Can he come on in?"

Then another little boy around the age of five or six came running into the kitchen. His face was covered with freckles and he had his mother's curly hair.

"John Patrick, bring Mr. Freeland into the kitchen."

The little boy wasn't paying his mother any attention. He had squeezed up next to Michelle and had latched onto her arm.

"We should get out of your way," Theo said as he pushed his chair back. "I've read through these papers, Daryl. You can keep them here."

"You can't leave," Cherry said. "Mr. Freeland came all this way to meet...I mean, it wouldn't be right for you to leave without meeting him."

"Since he just happened to be in the neighborhood," Daryl said. His gaze was directed at the tabletop, but Theo didn't have to look him in the eyes to know he was lying.

"Does Mr. Freeland happen to have a legal problem?" he asked Michelle.

She smiled, then promptly changed the subject. "John Patrick," she said to the hovering child. "This is my friend, Theo Buchanan. He came all the way from Boston just to go fishing."

John Patrick nodded. "I know who he is already. Everybody knows. Dr. Mike, can you tell your brother he's got to come around again? And will you tell John Paul to hurry 'cause I left my kickball in the backyard and I need it. Okay?"

"Is Lois back?" she asked.

"The boy seems to think she is," Daryl said. "He's going to get an ulcer fretting about her."

"We haven't seen Lois in over a month now, but John Patrick's still worried about her showing up unexpectedly. He won't get his ball out of the yard until your brother comes by again, and he won't let any of us go out there and fetch the ball for him either. I have to hang my clothes out to dry in the side yard just to calm him. Our John Patrick's a worrier," Cherry added for Theo's benefit, as if that would explain the child's bizarre behavior.

"John Patrick's named after Dr. Mike's brother, John Paul," Daryl interjected.

170

"So will you tell him?" the boy pleaded.

Michelle put her arm around the child. "Just as soon as I see him, I'll tell him you'd like him to come back over. Now, you've got to stop worrying, John Patrick."

"Okay," the child whispered. "The man sitting here..."

"Theo?"

John Patrick nodded.

"What about him?" Michelle asked.

"Could I ask him something?"

"You can ask me anything you want," Theo said.

John Patrick straightened and turned to Theo. Though Theo didn't have much experience dealing with children, he thought he could hold his own with a six-year-old.

"What do you want to know?"

The boy wasn't shy. He leaned into Theo's leg, stared him right in the eye, and said, "My daddy says Big Daddy Jake says you've got a gun. Do you?"

The question surprised him. "Yes, I do have a gun, but I'm not going to be keeping it much longer. I'm going to give the gun back," he told the child. "I don't like guns."

"But you've got it now?"

"Yes, I do."

The kid's fascination was a concern, and Theo thought he should probably give a short lecture about the dangers and how guns weren't playthings. He was trying to figure out how to put it all on a six-year-old's level, but apparently John Patrick had already moved on.

171

"So could you go outside?"

"You want me to go out into your backyard?"

John Patrick solemnly nodded. Theo glanced at Michelle and caught the twinkle in her eye.

"Okay?" the boy asked.

"Yeah, okay," Theo agreed. "And what do you want me to do when I get out there?"

"Could you shoot Lois for me?"

He knew the kid was going to ask that question, but it still shocked the hell out of him. He was speechless.

"No, Theo isn't going to shoot Lois for you," his father said in exasperation. "You don't want Dr. Mike's boyfriend to get into trouble with the law, do you?"

"No, Daddy, I don't."

"It's just as well," Michelle said. She patted the little boy as though she were consoling him. "If Theo shot Lois, he'd just make her mad."

"She's mean when she's mad," the kid told Theo.

The screen door banged once, then again and again in the background. "Go and wash up for supper," Cherry told John Patrick.

The little boy gave Theo a look of disappointment and then went to the sink.

"He's kind of a bloodthirsty little boy, isn't he?" he whispered to Michelle.

"He's a sweetheart," she replied.

"If I were Lois, I'd run for the woods."

The screen door banged again, and suddenly the floor under Theo's feet began to vibrate. It sounded like a herd of buffalo was running through the living room. Then a slew of boys of various ages and sizes came lumbering into the kitchen. Theo lost count after five.

Mr. Freeland was the last to enter the crowded kitchen. Elliott had to squeeze against the refrigerator to let the man in.

Freeland could have been mistaken for one of the boy's friends, except he was dressed in a shirt and tie. He was just a little over five feet tall and rail thin. He wore thick horn-rimmed glasses that slid down the bridge of his nose. He pushed them up with his index finger.

"Mr. Freeland's the music teacher over at the high school," Daryl explained.

"Nice to meet you, Mr. Freeland."

There were two of Daryl's boys behind Theo's chair, making it impossible for him to stand. He reached around to shake Freeland's hand.

"Please call me Conrad," he insisted. "Cherry, Daryl," he added with a nod to each of them. Then he turned to Michelle and nodded again. "Mike."

"Conrad," Cherry said, nodding back. "How's Billie doing?"

"Billie's my wife," Conrad explained to Theo. "And she's doing just fine. The baby's only getting us up once a night now, so we're both getting more sleep. Billie sends her regards."

"Boys, move out of the way and let Mr. Freeland sit down beside Theo so they can talk," Cherry said.

There was a good deal of shuffling in the kitchen as the children took their places at the table. Theo moved closer to Michelle to give Conrad room.

"I can't stay but a minute," Conrad said as he pulled the chair out and sat. "Billie's got supper waiting for me." Turning his full attention to Theo, he said, "Daryl and Cherry understand the importance of an education for their eight boys. They'd like to see all of them go to college."

Theo nodded. He wasn't sure what more he was supposed to say.

"Now, Elliott has a four point in school. He's going to try to get an academic scholarship, but those are hard to come by," Conrad said. "He's a hard worker and a very smart boy."

"Thank you, Conrad," Daryl said, as though he and not his son had just been given the compliment.

"We're thinking Elliott could maybe get a full scholarship...with your help."

"And how can I help?" Theo asked, bewildered.

"By getting him a football scholarship."

Theo blinked. "Excuse me?"

"Elliott has what it takes to make the cut," Conrad said. "He could be good, real good, with the proper...guidance."

Everyone started talking at once then. "The St. Claire team was undefeated last year," Cherry told Theo just as Daryl remarked, "It sounds like an impossible goal, but you could do it. Big Daddy Jake spoke so highly of you."

"And your connections," Conrad supplied.

Theo turned to Michelle. "Why did I know your dad was behind this?"

She shrugged, then smiled. "Daddy likes you."

"Big Daddy was thinking that if they could see our boy shine on that field, well then, they'd make him an offer and pay his college expenses," Daryl explained.

Theo put a hand up. "Hold on a minute..."

They ignored his protest. "They're always looking for good linebackers," Conrad said.

"That's right, they are," Daryl agreed. "But Big Daddy thinks that because Elliott is so fast, he could maybe run with the ball too."

Michelle nudged Theo to get his attention. "The scouts do go to the St. Claire games to see the talent."

Then Conrad nudged him to get him to turn to him. "Why don't we get started?"

"Started?" Theo asked as he rubbed his temples. He was developing one hell of a headache. "Doing what?"

Conrad pulled out some folded papers from his back pocket and put them on the table. Then he reached into his shirt pocket, pulled out a smaller piece of paper and a stubby yellow pencil, and looked expectantly at Theo.

"Where did you attend college?"

"Excuse me?"

Conrad patiently repeated the question.

"Michigan," Theo answered. "Why do you want to know..."

"That's a big school, isn't it?" Cherry asked.

"Yes," Conrad answered.

"I imagine it's a fine school too," Daryl remarked.

Theo glanced around the table and noticed the others, including the children, were staring at him. Everyone seemed to know what was going on. Everyone but him.

"Did Big Daddy suggest that you talk to me about schools?" he asked. Good God, now he was calling the old man Daddy.

No one answered his question. Then Conrad asked, "And you played football, didn't you?"

"Yeah, I did."

"And then you went on to law school."

It was a statement, not a question, but Theo still responded. "That's right."

"Did you stay on in Michigan to get the law degree?"

What in thunder was going on? "No," he answered. "I got my MBA and law back east."

"What's an MBA?" Cherry asked.

Michelle answered. "A master's in business administration," she said.

"And law too. Don't that beat all." Daryl sounded in awe.

"Yeah, well, lots of people get—"

Conrad interrupted him. "Where exactly did you get these degrees?"

"Yale."

"Oh, my, that's a fine school," Cherry said.

Conrad nodded. "I imagine your grades were impressive. I'm right, aren't I?" he asked as he furiously wrote on his paper.

It all clicked, and Theo couldn't figure out why he'd been so slow on the uptake. The guy was interviewing him for a position at the high school.

Theo decided he was going to have to have a little talk with Jake as soon as possible. Set him straight.

"I bet you've still got your old playbooks too, don't you?" Conrad asked him then.

" 'Playbooks'?"

"Football playbooks," Michelle explained.

She was smiling sweetly, and she was thoroughly enjoying his discomfort and confusion. He decided he needed to have a private talk with her too.

"Okay, this has gone far enough." His voice held a firm, no-nonsense tone. "There's been a misunderstanding that I need to clear up right now. You see, I stopped for gas on my way to Bowen. And this kid—"

It was as far as he got. Michelle wouldn't let him continue. She put her hand on top of his and said, "You did keep your old playbooks, didn't you?"

"Why would you think that?"

"It's a guy thing."

"Yeah, well, as a matter of fact I did keep a couple of them. But," he hastily added, "they're packed away with all my other junk in the attic."

"Couldn't you have one of your brothers send them to you? You could ask him to overnight them."

"And then what?"

"You could go to the next practice with me and look the team over."

Elliott pressed forward. "We sure would appreciate it."

Everyone started talking again about the team, everyone but little John Patrick. The boy was trying to get to Theo's gun. He kept pushing the kid's hand away. He felt as though he'd just been dropped into the middle of a foreign land where no one understood a word he said.

"I'm not a football coach!" he yelled. When everyone quieted down, he nodded emphatically. "That's right. You heard me. I'm not a football coach."

He'd finally taken control, and he felt inordinately pleased with himself as he sat back in his chair and waited for the truth to sink in.

The announcement didn't faze them. "These boys are mighty eager to learn," Conrad pressed. "But I'm not going to pressure you, Theo. No, sir, I'm not. We don't do things like that in Bowen. Do we, Daryl? We're laid back."

"Yes, we're laid back," he agreed.

Conrad tore off a piece of paper, bent over the table, and wrote something down. Then he folded the paper and looked at Theo again.

"The principal of our school is in Memphis, but I talked to him long distance before I drove over here." He pushed the folded paper toward Theo. "We both think you'll be happy with this."

He stood and nodded to Cherry. "I can't keep Billie waiting any longer, and I sure thank you for letting me interrupt your supper hour. Theo, I look forward to seeing you at our practice tomorrow. Mike knows the where and when."

He handed Theo the legal-sized papers he'd placed next to the folded note, shook his hand as he told him it was a pleasure talking with him, and then worked his way through the boys to the door. He paused at the doorway. "You wouldn't happen to have a teacher's certificate, would you, Theo?"

"No."

"I didn't think so, but I thought I should ask. It's all right. You needn't worry. The board of education will work with us on this, you being a special circumstance and all. Good night, everybody."

Theo didn't rush after Freeland to set him straight. He decided he could wait until practice the next day to explain things. Without the chaos that surrounded him in the small kitchen, calmer heads would prevail.

"Mama, when are we gonna eat?" John Patrick asked.

"I'm putting it on the table right this minute."

"We should be going," Theo said to Michelle.

"You'll stay to supper?" Cherry asked. "We've got plenty."

He shook his head. "Ordinarily I'd take you up on your offer, but the fact is my stomach isn't up to a meal just yet. I ate some of Jake's gumbo, and it was a little too spicy for me. My stomach's giving me fits."

It was a lie, but Michelle thought he'd told it well. Cherry was nodding in sympathy. Daryl looked a little suspicious.

"We always have enough to feed our guests."

"He's from the big city, Daryl," Michelle reminded him as though that explained everything.

"I forgot about that," he said. "I guess Jake's gumbo would upset your stomach if you weren't used to hot food."

"I could make you a cup of my special tea," Cherry offered. "It should settle you down in no time at all."

"I sure would appreciate that."

Daryl nodded. "Fix him up then, Cherry. Mike, do you mind changing this bandage for me while you're here?"

And so Theo drank hot, bitter tea in a hot, muggy kitchen while Michelle rebandaged Daryl's hand and Cherry fed her children. John Patrick insisted on moving his plate next to Theo, and by the time the child finished eating, Theo's stomach was growling. It took extreme discipline not to grab one of the homemade biscuits out of the kid's hand.

They left the family after Theo had finished his third cup of tea. John Patrick took hold of Theo's hand and officially walked him onto the front porch. The little boy tugged on Theo's shirt and said, "Tomorrow's my birthday. Are you gonna get me a present?"

"That depends," Theo replied. "You have anything specific in mind?"

"Maybe you could come back with a bigger

gun." He let go of Theo's hand and looked over his shoulder. "Don't tell Mama I asked you for a present."

Michelle had already gone down the steps and was waiting for Theo by the car.

"That kid," Theo remarked as he backed the car onto the road. "I've got a feeling we'll be reading about him in about fifteen years."

"He's an angel."

"He's bloodthirsty," he countered. "I don't get it. He's got at least four older brothers... right?"

"Yes?"

"So how come they don't tell this Lois to leave him the hell alone? I used to look out for my younger brothers and sisters. I wouldn't let anyone mess with them. That's what big brothers are supposed to do."

"Do you still look out for them?"

"Do your brothers still look out for you?"

"They try," she said. "Fortunately, Remy is in Colorado, so he can't interfere in my life too much these days, and John Paul has always been a bit reclusive. Of course, he still shows up at the most unexpected times. I think Daddy sends out an SOS every once in a while."

John Patrick was frantically waving to them. Michelle rolled down her window and waved back to the little boy.

Theo put the car in drive and headed toward Bowen. Glancing back at the child, he shook his head and said, "I'm telling you, that kid's just not normal."

She laughed. "He's a perfectly normal little boy."

"Lois isn't a neighbor, is she?"

"So you noticed there aren't any other houses on this stretch. No wonder you work for the Justice Department. You're very observant."

"Hey, I'm on vacation," he countered. "I'm allowed to be a little slow. So tell me, what exactly is Lois? A possum? No, I bet it's a raccoon. God, it's not a snake, is it? They can dig holes and—"

"Lois is an alligator."

He slammed on the brakes and damn near wrecked the car, narrowly missing a big oak when he swerved off the road. Even though he knew alligators lived in the swamp—hell, he read *National Geographic* like everyone else, and he occasionally watched the Discovery Channel when he had insomnia—it still had never occurred to him that there would be any so close to a house.

And who in his right mind named an alligator Lois? "Are you telling me there's a full-fledged, live alligator living in that kid's backyard?"

The expression on Theo's face was priceless. He looked as though he'd just found out there really was a bogeyman.

"That's exactly what I'm telling you. The females are very territorial. Lois has decided their backyard belongs to her. She chases anyone who goes out there...or at least she did, until my brother moved her. And, by the way, I would appreciate it if you didn't mention this to Ben Nelson. Alligators are protected, and my brother could get into trouble."

"Do you people name all your alligators?"

"Just some."

He rubbed his forehead. "Jeez," he whispered. "You ready to go back to Boston?"

"Not before I go fishing. So tell me, how do I get back to your place?"

She gave him directions, and before he knew it, they were in St. Claire, where there were actually sidewalks. When he turned the corner at an honest to goodness traffic light, he could see the golden arches looming in the distance.

"Ah," he sighed. "Civilization."

"I'm still going to cook a healthy dinner when we get home," she said. "But I figured..."

"What?"

"You deserved a treat."

"Yeah? Why?"

"Because you were starving when you were sitting in that kitchen drinking hot tea...because you didn't grab the biscuit in John Patrick's hand that you were eyeing like a hungry wolf...and because..."

"What?"

"You let Daddy take advantage."

CHAPTER SIXTEEN

A whole day had passed since the package had been delivered. Cameron waited again with the others in John's library for Dallas to arrive to give them Monk's report.

The waiting was making him crazy. Dear God, how had he arrived at this place? What had happened to him? He had had such dreams, such hopes when he'd started out. Where had it all gone wrong?

Now he felt as though he were trapped in a ghoulish game of beat the clock. Every hour that passed was an hour closer to the iron bars slamming shut on him. When he closed his eyes, he could hear the sound of the door locking him in.

"We can't just sit on our hands and do nothing," Cameron said. "It's been a day now. The clock's ticking. We've got to do something and do it fast."

Preston agreed. "I say we drive to Bowen tonight."

"And what do you propose we do when we get there?" John asked.

"Anything is better than sitting here waiting for the police to come and get us," Preston argued. "The longer we wait—"

Cameron cut him off. "I'm through waiting. If I have to take matters into my own hands, then that's what I'm going to do."

John slammed his fist down on the desk. "The hell you are," he roared. "We're in this together, and you aren't going to do anything unless we all agree. Do I make myself clear?"

"Since when did you become our leader?" Cameron muttered. Shaken by John's fury, he tried to regain the upper hand. "I don't remember voting for you," he blustered.

"I made all of you a fortune," John said. "And that makes me leader."

"This isn't getting us anywhere," Preston said. "Everyone just calm down and try to be reasonable. Maybe Dallas will have some good news for us."

"That's another thing," Cameron said. "How come Monk won't report to any of us? Why does he have to go through Dallas? He's getting his money from all four of us, and we should be able to get hold of him any time we want. Hell, I don't even know Monk's cell phone number."

"I think Cameron's right. Why can't we talk directly to Monk?"

"The two of you are obsessing over a minor detail," John said. "Dallas brought Monk in, remember? Maybe our killer doesn't like meeting with the four of us because he doesn't trust us."

"Bull," Preston said. "Dallas just likes running him. It's a stupid power play if you ask me."

John was irritated. "I don't give a damn who he gives his report to as long as he gets the job done."

Dallas was standing in the doorway listening to the conversation. "You want Monk's phone number? Two-two-three—one-six-nine-

nine. Happy now, Cameron? What about you, Preston? Want to know his home address? Even I don't know that, but I could put a tail on him and find out...if you want that information too."

"Tell me you've got good news," Preston said, ignoring the sarcasm.

"If you're asking me if Monk has the package, the answer's no."

"He still hasn't found the damn papers?" Cameron asked incredulously.

"The package has to be in the hospital," Preston said. "It's the only place Monk hasn't been able to search thoroughly."

"Then get him back in there," Cameron demanded.

"I told Monk to stay on Renard," Dallas said. "He can't be two places at once, and besides, he already looked through her locker at the hospital. Remember what I told you, Cameron? He even had an aide helping look around the ER. He can't just waltz in there and start opening drawers. Use your head."

"I don't like assumptions." John made the statement as he rocked back and forth in his swivel chair behind the desk. "I'm not convinced Michelle Renard didn't take that package with her when she left the hospital. Just how thorough do you think Monk was when he went through her house and her clinic? Maybe he was in a hurry..."

"Bull," Dallas said. "He's a professional, and he did his job. Why wouldn't he be thorough? He's going to make a hell of a lot of money the second he hands over the package. He wants to find the files as much as we do."

Turning to John, Preston said, "God damn your wife. She put us in a hell of a situation here."

"Get real. We killed her, remember?" Dallas said.

Cameron buried his face in his hands and leaned forward on his elbows. "John, you're the one who got us into this nightmare, you son of a bitch."

John remained calm. "What's done is done. We have to think about the future."

Cameron shouted back. "What future? If we don't get those papers, it's over."

CHAPTER SEVENTEEN

There were six messages on Theo's cell phone. He went to Michelle's library to listen and make notes while she started dinner. When he was finished, he called Noah Clayborne and asked him to drive over from Biloxi.

"Is dinner ready? I'm hungry," he asked when he came into the kitchen.

"No, dinner isn't ready," she said. "This isn't a bed-and-breakfast. You're going to help." She picked up the knife and began chopping celery and carrots. He leaned against the sink watching her.

"Damn, you're good."

"That's what all the boys say."

"You're like a robot with that knife. Quick, precise...impressive."

"You do know how to turn a girl's head."

He grabbed one of the carrots and popped it into his mouth. "What do you want me to do? I'm starving."

"That double cheeseburger didn't do the trick?"

"That was just an appetizer."

"You could light the grill for me. There are some matches in the drawer to your right."

"Is the grill in the backyard?" He was looking suspiciously out the back window, squinting to see into the twilight through the screened-in porch.

"Of course it's in the backyard. What's the matter?"

"Do I have to worry about another Lois out there?"

"No," she assured him. And then, as her daddy would say, the devil got hold of her and she couldn't resist adding, "Of course, Elvis could be in the neighborhood. You might want to take the broom out with you, just in case."

He stopped in his tracks. "Elvis?"

She tore a sheet of aluminum foil and was piling vegetables in the center. "Our local celebrity. Last time anyone reported seeing him, he swore Elvis was sixteen feet long."

"You named an alligator Elvis? What's the matter with you people?"

"We don't name all of them," she defended. "Just the impressive ones."

"You're joking about Elvis. Right?"

She smiled sweetly. "Sort of."

"It's *sort of* damned cruel to torment a man who has an obvious phobia about alligators, Mike."

"I would prefer it if you called me Michelle."

"I would prefer it if you didn't joke about alligators."

"Okay. Deal."

"So how come I can't call you Mike? Everyone else does."

She was carefully folding the edges of the foil when she answered. "I don't want you to think of me as a...Mike."

"Why not?"

"It isn't very feminine. How many men do you know who would want to get involved with a woman named Mike?"

"What?"

"Never mind."

"I don't want to 'never mind.' Are you saying you want to get involved—"

She interrupted him. "No, that isn't what I'm saying. Just don't call me Mike. Now, go light the grill, and stop looking at me as though you think I've lost my mind. If you get scared, scream and I'll come out with a broom and save you."

"Men don't scream, and you, Michelle, have a sick sense of humor." He glanced out the window again and then said, "Ah, hell. Alligators come out at night, don't they? I'm the one who's lost his mind. What am I doing in this..." He was going to say godforsaken place but caught himself in time. "...wilderness."

She'd guessed where he'd been headed, though. The glint in her eyes told him so.

"I don't know. You tell me. What are you doing here?"

"I came to fish, remember? I didn't figure on alligators getting in my way."

"So far, none have," she pointed out. "And you didn't come here just to fish."

"You're right."

"And?"

He shrugged. "Maybe I'm looking for something. Okay?" Now he sounded antagonistic.

She turned back to the sink. "Tell me what it is. I'll help you find it."

He went outside without answering her. She couldn't understand where the sudden tension had come from. One minute they were joking, and the next Theo had turned dead serious. On the surface he was a laid-back, take-everything-in-stride kind of man. *Still waters*...she thought. There was a good deal more to Theo Buchanan than his good looks.

She decided to lighten up. If he wanted to tell her what his agenda was, then he would. She wasn't going to nag him like a fishwife.

It was such a lovely, sultry evening that they ate dinner at the wrought-iron table on the porch. The conversation was superficial and strained, but it didn't interfere with Theo's appetite. He ate like her father, with unbridled gusto. When he was finished, there wasn't a single leftover.

"If I ate like you do, I'd have to widen the doorways," she said.

He leaned back in the chair and closed his eyes. "It's so peaceful here, listening to the sounds of the bullfrogs and crickets."

She didn't want to give him an upset stomach by getting him all riled up again, so she didn't mention that the sounds in the distance were coming from the alligators. Since she'd grown up in the swamp, she didn't even notice it. She had a feeling city boy would freak out, though.

He insisted on doing the dishes. Since she didn't have a dishwasher, he had to do them by hand. She put the seasonings away while he washed the silverware, then grabbed a towel and started drying.

"How come you aren't married?" he asked.

"I haven't had time."

"Are you seeing anyone now?"

"No."

Good, he thought. He had no intention of hanging around Bowen, but while he was here, he didn't want any other man getting in his way. And that made him a heartless son of a bitch, he thought.

"What are you thinking?" she asked. "You've got the most ferocious look on your face."

I'm a selfish bastard. That's what I'm thinking. "I'm wondering why you don't have men chasing you. One look and any man would know..."

"Know what?"

He grinned. "You've got the goods."

She rolled her eyes. "What a romantic way to give a girl a compliment."

"Hey, I'm from Boston, remember? Men are

raised to be blunt. Are there any men around here you're interested in?"

"Why do you want to know?"

"Just curious."

"I think Ben Nelson would like to get something going, but I'm not going to encourage him. Ben's nice, but there isn't any chemistry between us. You know what I mean?"

"Sure I do. Like the chemistry between us."

"Excuse me?"

"You heard me." He handed her a plate to dry, noticed it was still streaked with soap bubbles, and snatched it back to rinse again. "You've been wanting to jump my bones since the minute I walked into your dad's bar."

He'd hit that nail on the head, but she wasn't about to admit it. "Jump your bones? I think not."

"I'm simply calling it like it is."

"And how did you come up with that notion?"

"I saw it in your eyes."

"You couldn't have."

"I couldn't?"

She smiled. "You were too busy looking at my legs."

He didn't appear the least chagrined. "They're fine-looking legs."

"I'll admit there is a certain physical attraction, but that's perfectly healthy."

"Is this a lead-in to a lecture about hormones?"

"That depends on how long I'm going to have to stand here and wait for you to finish washing that bowl. You don't do a lot of dishes, do you?"

"Your point?"

"You're taking forever."

"I'm slow and easy with everything I do."

It wasn't what he said but how he said it that made her heartbeat escalate. Was he slow and easy in bed? Oh, Lord, wouldn't that be something?

"You were married, weren't you?" She blurted out the question.

"Yes, I was. I wasn't very good at it."

"Your wife died."

"That's right."

She reached up and put another dish away in the cabinet. "That's what Daddy told me. How did she die?"

He handed her a salad bowl. "Why do you want to know?"

"I'm curious," she admitted. "If you think I'm being too intrusive, I won't ask any more questions."

"No, it's okay. She died in a car crash."

"Oh, Theo, I'm sorry. How long ago did the accident happen?"

"It wasn't an accident."

There was absolutely no inflection in his voice. He might as well have been talking about a leaky faucet.

"No?"

He sighed. "No, it wasn't an accident. You know what? This is the first time since it happened four years ago that I've said it out loud."

She could tell by his demeanor that he wanted her to change the subject, but she wouldn't accommodate him. It wasn't morbid curiosity on her part. If it had taken him four years to be able to admit the truth, then maybe it was time he got it all out.

"It was a suicide?"

"Yes and no."

He handed her another bowl. "I don't think she meant to kill herself. At least not that way. My wife was taking the slow route."

"Meaning?"

"Alcohol and drugs."

She didn't say anything but waited until he continued.

"She mixed alcohol with all the pills and God knows what else already in her system. It was a lethal combination. At least that's what the autopsy report indicated. She was out of control behind the wheel. She drove the car over a bridge into the bay. A hell of a way to end it, wouldn't you say?" He didn't wait for an answer. "I doubt she even knew what was happening to her, and I thank God she didn't take anyone else with her."

It took extreme discipline not to show any outward reaction to what he had just told her. Theo was a proud man, and she knew that if she showed any compassion or sympathy, he would close up on her, and she didn't want that to happen.

"Your friends and your family...do any of them know what really happened?"

"No," he said. "I'm pretty sure Nick guessed

194

something was wrong, but he never said anything."

"Maybe he was waiting for you to talk to him."

"Yeah, maybe."

She didn't know how far she should push. Leaning against the sink, she carefully folded the wet towel and asked, "Do you blame yourself?"

He shrugged, as though the question weren't important. "I've come to terms with what happened. It sure convinced me I wasn't cut out for marriage. I put everything in front of it. I should have been paying more attention to her, though. I was so busy at work, putting in twenty-hour days, and I didn't notice what was going on at home. Hell, I knew she drank, but I didn't realize it had become a problem. I think that's called 'burying your head in the sand.'"

"She made the choice. I know I sound unsympathetic, but you didn't pour the pills or the alcohol down her throat. She did."

"Marriage is a partnership," he said. "I didn't hold up my end of the agreement. She was...fragile. Yeah, fragile. She needed help, but I was too blind to see it. Maybe I didn't want to see it."

"I think it's healthy that you're finally able to talk about what happened. Now maybe you can get rid of it."

"Get rid of what?"

"The anger and the hurt and the guilt."

"Don't turn shrink on me." He handed her a spatula to put away, then drained the sink.

"There, I'm finished," he said. "Do you have any more questions, or can we move on?"

She wanted to ask him if he had loved his wife, but she didn't dare. She had pushed him as far as he was willing to go. "Okay, we'll move on. Dinner's over."

"Yeah?"

"I asked you to be patient until after dinner. Now I'd like you to tell me what you think about my clinic."

"I'm going to," he promised. "I'll be right back." He left the kitchen and headed upstairs.

"What are you doing?" she called up the stairs.

"I'm gonna get my laptop and set it up in your library," he called back. "I've got to check my e-mail." He paused at the top of the stairs and looked down at her. "Hopefully, I'll have some answers. Then we'll talk."

Michelle went back into the kitchen and washed the countertops. When she was finished, she turned the light off and went upstairs. She stood in the doorway of her guest room. "I'm going to take a shower. It's been a long day."

He was bent over the bed, unlocking his attaché case. He'd already unpacked his duffel bag. His clothes were folded on her dresser.

The room was a mess. There were boxes piled high in front of the windows facing the backyard. She hadn't bothered to dust or vacuum the area rug, and she was pretty sure there were cobwebs in all the corners.

"I've been using this room for storage,"

she said. "And that old bed is going to give your back fits."

"You think so?"

"You're longer than the bed," she pointed out. "And the mattress is lumpy."

"Don't worry about it. I can sleep anywhere."

"I'm still feeling guilty. I guess you could have my bed. It's king-sized."

"Yeah?"

He stood and gave her *the look*. She recognized it instantly. She'd seen enough late-night movies and had been around enough men on the prowl to recognize it. Theo made *the look* sexier than Mel Gibson did, and God only knew, she'd always been a sucker for Mel.

"Stop it." She laughed after she gave the order. "Just stop it right now."

He raised an eyebrow. Oh, God, now he was doing Cary Grant.

"Stop what?" he asked innocently.

What could she say? Stop looking at me as though I just asked you to get naked and have hot, mind-altering sex with me?

"Never mind," she said. "So do you want to?"

"Sleep in your bed? What an invitation."

"Excuse me?"

"You want to share your bed?"

Oh, boy, did she want to. How long had it been since she'd been involved with a man? She couldn't remember. Probably because it had ended in disaster and she had deliberately blocked the memory.

Slow and easy. Oh, boy.

Her throat felt like it was closing up on her. "I don't think that would be a good idea."

He took a step toward her. "How come?"

If she were thirty years older, she would have thought she was having a hot flash. Her entire body felt as though it was on fire, and she was having difficulty catching her breath. Her endorphins were going crazy too. She was feeling light-headed. If he took another step toward her, she knew she'd start hyperventilating. And wouldn't that be a wonderful turn-on. Men weren't the only ones who needed to take a cold shower to squelch their sexual appetites. She felt like she needed to dive headfirst into her freezer.

She blamed him for her scattered thoughts. He was the one giving her *the look*, after all.

He was slowly walking forward, obviously giving her time to make up her mind. Her feet were rooted to the floor and her stomach started tingling. "It would complicate things."

"How?"

"We'd have sex, and then—"

"Great sex," he corrected. "We'd have great sex."

He had her thinking about it, and the look in his eyes told her he was thinking about it too. She nodded, tried to swallow, but her throat was too dry. Her pulse was racing. Probably a hundred sixty beats per minute. Irregular too. Great, she thought, a gorgeous man flirts with her and she goes into ventricular fibrillation. If he took another step, she thought she just might drop dead. Wouldn't that be something? The pathology report would show cause of death was cardiac arrest.

He stopped a foot away from her. He gently stroked her cheek with his fingers and then nudged her under her chin, forcing her to look up at him. She felt awkward and unsure, until she saw the laughter in his eyes.

"So what are you thinking?" he asked.

As if he didn't know. "That you're making me nuts. Theo, you might as well understand before this goes any further..."

"Yes?" he asked softly. His hand had moved to her neck, his touch warm.

"What?"

"You said I need to understand something."

He was rubbing the back of her neck now. She got goose bumps.

"Yes, you do." She nodded. "No, I mean...oh." *Breathe,* she told herself. *Take a deep breath and try to locate your brain.* "Okay, here's the way it is. I'm not cut out for a casual fling. I have to have a...solid connection with a man before I go to bed with him. I don't believe in recreational sex." She forced a smile in hopes of lightening the moment and added, "I'm a dinosaur."

"Did I mention I like dinosaurs?"

Oh, boy, she inwardly sighed. *Oh, boy.*

His fingers gently played with the hair at the nape of her neck. "Your hair is so soft," he whispered. "The color's like fire."

"I get the red hair and freckles from my

199

mother," she answered, grasping for a rational thought.

"Did I mention I like women with freckles? I get this overwhelming urge to kiss every one of them."

"I've got freckles all over my body."

"We'll get to those."

She felt light-headed again. "It isn't going to happen."

"We'll see."

Lord, he was cocky. He really needed to work on that flaw, and she meant to tell him so when her head cleared. Right now, she was too busy trying to stand on her feet. The man aroused her simply by touching her. Every nerve ending in her body responded to him.

When she realized she wanted to tear his clothes off, she pulled back. She gently pushed his arm away. Her legs felt like Jell-O, but she managed to turn and walk to her bedroom. As she was shutting the door behind her, she made the mistake of looking at him. He was leaning against the doorframe smiling at her.

She wasn't going to let him know how potent his touch was. Mr. Big City Boy needed to be taught a lesson. He wouldn't get his way.

"You mess with me and you pay the consequences," she said. "You can take a cold shower after I do." How telling was that? Too late, she realized what she'd given away. "I'm taking a cold shower because I'm hot," she explained, and then realized she'd only made it worse.

"Michelle?" he drawled out.

"Yes?"

"I haven't begun to mess with you."

She shut the door and leaned against it. "Oh, boy," she whispered.

CHAPTER EIGHTEEN

Michelle was counting all the reasons she shouldn't and wouldn't get involved with Theo. She'd gotten up to number twenty when he knocked on the bathroom door.

"I haven't taken my shower yet."

"Yeah, I know. I was just wondering if you wanted me to hook up your computer for you?"

"You found it?"

She opened the door a crack and peeped out, holding her cotton robe together across her breasts.

"It was hard to miss. I tripped over one of the boxes when I put my clothes on the washer. So do you want me to or not?"

"Hook up my computer? Sure," she said.

She shut the door in his face and started counting all over again. When she got to number twenty-three—she'd have to change the sheets—she realized she was getting desperate and went back to the number one reason. The man would break her heart.

She stepped into the bathtub and turned the shower on full blast. The icy cold water made her grimace. She adjusted the temperature and let the warm water soothe her.

By the time she rinsed the shampoo from her hair, she'd worked herself back up into a fit of indignation. Mess with her indeed. She wasn't so easily manipulated, she thought as she combed the tangles out of her hair and then turned on the blow dryer.

He'd probably be a demanding lover...

"Hell," she whispered. Slow and easy. Would she ever get those words out of her mind? It was like a song that kept replaying in her head.

She brushed her teeth, then put moisturizer on her face and stared at herself in the mirror. "Admit it," she whispered. "You want to sleep with him."

She shook her head. No, that wasn't true. She wanted to have sex with him. And what was wrong with that? Absolutely nothing. She was merely fantasizing, and fantasy was a perfectly healthy function of the human psyche.

Acting upon the fantasy was another matter altogether. Reason number one...that heart-breaking thing..."Been there, done that," she whispered.

Oh, no, she wasn't going to get involved with Theo Buchanan. And so she didn't put on one of the short nightgowns that she usually wore to bed. She got her long blue silk pajamas out of her bottom drawer instead. She buttoned every button, including the top one. The mandarin collar rubbed the sensitive skin underneath her chin. She reached for the matching blue slippers, but rejected those and found an old pair of thick white terry-cloth slip-ons under her bed. She brushed her hair to get it out of her eyes, dabbed on a little colorless, moisturizing lip gloss, then hunted through her closet and dug out her heavy white flannel robe. The hem dragged on the floor. The robe had buttons and she secured every one of them. It also had a belt. She double knotted it.

Then she looked at herself in the mirror. Good, she thought. She looked like a nun.

Theo was in the library. He'd unloaded the computer equipment and had it up and running by the time she came downstairs. He was reading something on the monitor. He glanced over the top of his horn-rimmed glasses at her when she entered the room, and his gaze froze. In a flash he noticed every little detail about her—how the blue pajamas matched the color of her eyes; how her hair, down around her shoulders, shimmered like russet gold in the soft light; how, without an ounce of makeup, she looked beautiful.

She was dressed for bed...as long as the bed was in Antarctica. Michelle was a physician, but she sure didn't know anything about how a man's mind worked. All those clothes...they just made him fantasize about what was underneath.

His imagination went to work, and he pictured her stripping off each layer before slipping between the covers. Ah, hell, don't think about it, he warned himself. For the love of God, don't think about the soft, warm skin underneath all that fabric.

Michelle walked over to the desk. Feeling extremely self-conscious because of the way he was staring at her, she fiddled with the knot in her belt and asked, "So? What do you think?"

"Theo?" she asked when he didn't immediately answer. He had a funny smile on his face now and was staring at her feet.

"What's the matter?"

"Are you expecting a snowstorm tonight?"

Her hand went to her throat. "I was chilly."

He laughed.

"I *was*," she insisted. "I get cold when the air conditioner is on. I turned it down so you would be comfortable."

"Uh-huh."

Now she felt stupid because he wasn't buying her lie.

"Cute bunny slippers."

"Thank you," she said. "If you're finished mocking me, answer my question. What do you think...about my computer?"

"It's ancient."

"Will you stop staring at my slippers?"

Exasperated, she leaned against the side of the desk and removed the slippers. Theo laughed again when he saw that she was wearing socks.

"*Now* what's so funny?" she demanded.

"I was just wondering if you were wearing long underwear too."

"I don't own any long underwear," she countered. "Now, will you answer my question. Does my computer work or not?"

"Where did you get this thing?"

"My brother Remy gave it to me. He picked it up secondhand the last time he was home. I haven't had time to set it up. I've only been in the house a couple of weeks. John Paul wanted to put another coat of varnish on the floors, and if you knew my brother, you'd understand he does things on his own schedule. I've been using the computer at the hospital. I know this one is outdated, but eventually, when I can afford it, I'll get a newer one."

Theo angled the screen near the corner of the desk, adjusted the keypad the way he thought she'd want it, then leaned back in the soft leather chair. "So, whoever is following you...he isn't some brokenhearted guy you dumped?"

"We've been over that."

"We're going over it again."

She didn't argue. "No, I haven't been involved with anyone. Besides that, I'm a physician. I don't break hearts. I—"

"Yeah, I know. You fix them."

"No, I refer them."

His laptop was on the opposite side of the desk. It was a slick, expensive piece of equipment. As she was examining it, a big red *E* floated across the screen. It was followed by a single beep.

"You've got mail."

He reached over, touched a key, and saw who had sent him the message. She read the name before he hit the key and the screen went blank.

She wasn't sure if he was waiting until later to read the message because he knew it wasn't important or because he didn't want her to read it.

"Who's Noah?"

"A friend."

"I read the name," she explained even though he hadn't asked. "You were talking to him on the phone earlier."

"Yes; he called. He must have been waiting by his computer, because I just sent him a message a couple of minutes ago, while you were in the shower, and he already responded."

"If you want to read the message now, I'll go in the other room."

"No, that's okay. You can read it with me. You won't understand it, though."

"Too technical?"

Before she could take issue, he said, "Too Noah. If you knew him, you'd understand. The guy's got a warped sense of humor."

"You make that sound like a compliment."

"It is," he said. "In his line of work, it helps to be a little warped."

Theo hit a button and waited. Michelle leaned over his shoulder so she could read the message. It was convoluted, and didn't make any sense to her.

"Is it in code?"

"No," he answered gruffly. Damn, he wished she'd move back. He could smell the clean scent of her shampoo, feel the heat from her soft body.

He tensed in reaction. He pictured himself pulling her onto his lap and kissing the breath out of her. Then he expanded the fantasy until he was thinking about all the other things he wanted to do with her and to her. He'd start with her toes and work his way up until he had every button undone and he was—

"Who's Mary Beth?"

"Excuse me?"

"Noah said he never thanked you for letting him use Mary Beth the last time he was in Boston. You boys share your women?"

"*Mary Beth* is a fishing boat. I invited Noah to drive to Bowen to go fishing. I told him about the tournament, and he wants me to sign him up. He's going crazy in Biloxi. He's doing a training program, and he hates it." He turned back to the monitor, removed his glasses, and set them on the desk. He was having trouble concentrating now. It was all he could do to restrain himself from grabbing her. What the hell was the matter with him? Michelle was a complication he didn't need now. She wasn't the love-her-and-then-leave-her type of woman, and he wouldn't be staying around.

He knew he wasn't making any sense. He had come to Bowen because of her, and yet...

She poked him in the shoulder to get his attention. "Who's Priest?"

"Father Tom Madden," he answered. "He's like a brother," he added. "When he was just starting grade school, he moved in with our family. He's Nick's age, and the two of them are best friends. They went to Penn State together. Nick's going to marry Tommy's little sister."

"Why does Noah call him Priest?"

"Because, and I'm quoting Noah now, 'It pisses him off.' That's why he does it. Tommy lets him get away with anything."

"Why's that?"

"Because Noah almost died saving Tommy's life. He drives Tommy crazy, but they've actually become good friends. The three of them go fishing every once in a while," he said.

She nodded, then asked, "That last line Noah wrote...what does he mean, 'regarding the other, no problem'?"

"It means he knows I'm out of my element here, and so he's going to check out a couple of things for me."

"Your answer is as ambiguous as his message."

She walked away from the desk and opened the French doors connecting the library to the living room. There were medical journals strewn along her sofa. She picked them up, stacked them on an end table, and sat down with a sigh.

She lifted her hair up so her neck would get some air. God, she was hot. The heavy robe was suffocating her. She picked up one of the journals and was going to fan her face, then realized how telling that would be and put the magazine down.

Theo leaned back in his chair and peered around the half-open door. "Are you okay? You look a little flushed."

The man didn't miss anything. "I'm just tired."

"How long have you been up?"

"Since four or five."

He finished typing into his computer. "I'll leave this on," he said. Then he stood, stretched, and rolled his shoulders.

He reminded her of a big old tomcat. "How come you packed your laptop? Going to check your e-mail while you're fishing?"

"It's like my cell phone. I never leave home without it. Do you want something to drink?"

"No thanks, but you help yourself."

Theo went into the kitchen, grabbed a Diet Coke out of the refrigerator, then searched through her pantry. He found an unopened box of low-fat, low-sodium Triscuits and carried the box with him back to the living room.

He sat down in the big, overstuffed easy chair, kicked his shoes off, and swung his feet up on the matching ottoman. Placing his drink on a cardboard box next to the chair, he held up the Triscuits and said, "Want some of these?"

"I just brushed my teeth. Do you ever fill up?"

"Not on stuff like this."

He opened the box and began to munch on the crackers. "I've got some friends making calls and a couple of my interns doing some research for me. It isn't a tough assignment, so hopefully, they'll e-mail me tonight and have everything ready to go tomorrow."

"Justice Department work while you're on vacation?"

"Sugar mill work."

She perked up. "Oh? Do you think you might be able to help Daryl and his family?"

"I'm going to try. What do you know about the Carson brothers?"

"Not much," she admitted. "You should talk to Daddy. He's known the brothers for years. He can answer your questions. This is a small community, so information is pretty easy to get. Everybody keeps up on what everybody else is doing."

"And yet, no one knows anything about the break-in at the clinic," he remarked. "I've given it some thought, and I don't believe kids trashed it."

"Then what do you think?"

"It was a one-man operation. I could be wrong, but I don't think I am. There was a pattern."

"I don't understand. What do you mean by 'a pattern'?"

"There was order to the chaos. He came in through the back door—"

"But the window in the reception area was broken."

"He broke it while he was inside. That was easy to figure out. The glass fragments prove it."

"What else?"

"I don't do this kind of thing for a living," he said. "I prosecute. But if they were kids looking for drugs, as your dad and your friend Ben Nelson believe, then how come the examination rooms were barely touched?"

"The glass and the locks were broken in the medicine cabinets."

"Yes, but the needles and the prescription

pads were still there. And what about the files, Michelle? Why would someone take the time to go through boxes of files?"

"Maybe they were just throwing things left and right."

"This didn't look like a simple case of vandalism to me. Kids who set out to vandalize... they bring along their own fun equipment."

"Like what?"

"Spray paint," he said. "The guy who did this used your paint to mess up the rooms. Makes me think he didn't come prepared to tear things up. And the trash bags in the yard looked like someone had gone through them. There wasn't a scratch on the lock on your back door, which tells me that he had the right tools and knew how to use them."

"As in a professional?"

He didn't answer. "Noah's going to be here tomorrow. If you don't mind, I'd like you to leave the clinic the way it is until he's finished looking around."

"Just tomorrow?"

"Yes."

"Okay," she agreed. Her friends weren't coming to help until the day after. She could wait until then. "What does Noah do for a living?"

He didn't give her a specific answer but said, "He's FBI," and left it at that.

"FBI?" She couldn't hide her alarm. "Then you must think—"

He interrupted her. "Don't jump to conclusions. Noah's a family friend, and I thought it would be a good idea to let him look at the clinic. Get his opinion. Besides, he's over in Biloxi, and he loves to fish. A day or two in Bowen will be a vacation for him."

"I will appreciate his help...and yours too, but I wonder if maybe we aren't making a mountain out of what could have been just a random act."

"You don't really believe that, do you?"

She rubbed her temples. "No, I guess I don't. I don't think Ben believes kids did it either," she admitted. "He walked around the clinic with me, and we both noticed there weren't any footprints outside the window. The grass was still soggy. It had rained hard the night before. There should have been footprints."

"So why did you argue with me about how he got in?"

She shrugged. "I guess I just wanted it to be easy and make sense. Do you know the first thought I had when I saw my office?"

"What's that?"

"Someone really hates me. It scared me," she said. "I've been racking my brain trying to come up with a name, but honestly, I haven't been back in town long enough to make enemies. Give me a couple of months, and I'm sure I'll have a list as long as my arm."

"I doubt that," he said. "The man was definitely out of control in your office. Noah will have some ideas for us."

He popped another Triscuit in his mouth. Without some squirty cheese or peanut butter, the crackers tasted like sawdust to him, but he kept eating them anyway.

"Men like Noah catch criminals, and you put them away."

"Something like that."

"At least you don't have to worry about people shooting at you."

"That's right." His quick agreement was a lie, of course. Hell, he'd been shot at, kicked, bitten, punched, and spit on while he was doing his job. He'd even had a contract taken out on him—twice now that he recalled—and when he went after Leon's family, he received daily threats.

"I have a theory," she said.

"Let's hear it." He was digging into the bottom of the box, searching for one last piece of sawdust he could eat.

"One of Dr. Robinson's patients was trying to steal his file."

"What would his reason be?"

"I don't know. I thought that if he had some contagious disease or some diagnosis he didn't want his insurance company or his family to know about, then maybe he might want to steal his file. I know I'm reaching, but that's the only theory I can come up with as to why the files were all torn apart."

"Did Robinson give you a list of his patients?"

"Yes, he did. There was a printout in a manila envelope taped to one of the boxes. He didn't have a big practice considering the length of time he worked here. From what I've heard, Dr. Robinson needed to take a couple of sensitivity classes. He offended his patients."

"Which is why he didn't have a big practice."

"That's right."

"After Noah goes through the clinic and tells us what he thinks, you're going to have to match the files with the list of names to see if anyone's chart is missing."

"Assuming that list wasn't destroyed."

Theo nodded. "I also think you should call Robinson and ask him if there were any difficult patients. You'll know what to ask."

"Yes, all right. He probably has a copy of the patient list anyway if we need it."

He noticed she was rubbing the back of her neck. "Are you getting a headache?"

"Sort of."

"Maybe I can 'sort of' fix it."

He got up and joined her on the sofa. Then he put a pillow on the floor between his bare feet and told her to sit there while he worked the kinks out.

The offer was irresistible. She got settled between his knees and stretched her legs. He put his hands on her shoulders, then pulled back.

"Take your robe off."

She unbuttoned the robe, untied the belt, and slipped the robe off.

"Now take your pajama top off."

"Nice try."

He grinned. "Okay, then unbutton the top buttons."

She had to undo three buttons so his hands could get to her skin. Too late, she realized what she was doing. His big, warm hands were touching her bare skin, and, oh, Lordy, did it feel wonderful.

"Your skin's soft."

She closed her eyes. She should make him stop, she thought. How crazy was this? Theo was the reason she was feeling so tense, and now he was making it blissfully worse. Oh, yes, she should definitely make him stop. She turned her head to the side instead so he could rub the knot on the column of her neck.

"You know what I thought when I first met you?"

"That I was irresistible?" she teased. "So irresistible you had to throw up on me?"

"You're never going to let me live that down, are you?"

"Probably not."

"I was out of my mind with pain then," he reminded her. "And that's not what I was talking about anyway. After the surgery, when you came into my room and you were telling me about Bowen and your clinic and the people who live here...you know what I was thinking then?"

"That you wish I'd stop talking and let you get some sleep?"

He tugged on her hair. "I'm being serious here. I'm gonna tell you why I really came to Bowen."

His tone of voice indicated he wasn't teasing. "I'm sorry. What were you thinking?"

"That I wanted what you had," he said.

"Oh?"

"I saw something inside of you I had when I first started out, but somewhere along the

215

way, I lost it. That never bothered me until I met you. You made me want to find it again...if that's possible."

"What was it you saw?"

"Passion."

She didn't understand. "Passion for my work?"

"Passion to make a difference."

She paused for a moment. "I don't want to change the world, Theo. I'm only hoping I can make a difference in a little corner of it." She got up on her knees and turned around to face him. "You don't think you make a difference?" she asked, astonished.

"Yeah, sure I do," he said very matter-of-factly. "I've just lost my enthusiasm for the job, I guess. I'm not sure what's wrong with me. The men I put away...they're like rodents. Every one I lock up, three more take his place. It's frustrating."

"I think you're experiencing burnout. You've been working long hours since your wife died. You don't allow yourself time to play."

"How do you know that?"

"You told me you loved building things with your hands, but you also said you haven't had time for the hobby in four years. In other words, since your wife died."

She could tell he wanted to interrupt her, and so she hastened to add, "And fishing too. You told me you used to love to fish, but the way you said it was as though you were talking about a past life. You've been punishing yourself long enough, Theo. You have to let it go."

His immediate reaction was to tell her he hadn't come to Bowen to get analyzed and that she should leave him the hell alone. She'd hit too close to the bone...but she'd only told him what he already knew. For the past four years he'd been running as fast as he could so he wouldn't have time to think about his failure to save his wife. The guilt had been eating at him for a long time. It had taken his energy, his enthusiasm, and his passion.

"You need to kick back and let life pass you by for a couple of weeks."

"Doctor's orders?"

"Yes," she said. "You'll feel rejuvenated. I promise."

She was worried about him. He could see it in her eyes. Lord, she was sweet. And what was he going to do about that? He was beginning to like her a hell of a lot more than he'd anticipated.

"And if you decide to go back to Boston, you'll have a new attitude."

"*If* I go back?"

"I meant *when* you go back," she corrected.

He didn't want to think about Boston or work or his future or anything else for that matter, and that was so unlike him. He was a planner, always had been for as long as he could remember, but now he didn't want to plan anything. He wanted to do exactly what Michelle had suggested. Kick back and let the world pass him by.

"It's funny," he remarked.

"What is?"

"You...me. It's like fate threw us together."

She smiled. "You're a contradiction, Theo. A lawyer with a romantic side. Who would have thought that was possible?"

Theo decided to lighten the mood. Michelle was so easy and fun to tease and gave as good as she got. He liked embarrassing her. The esteemed doctor could blush with the best of them.

"You know what else I thought when I met you?" he asked with a playful grin.

"No, what?" she asked suspiciously.

"You were sexy. Real sexy."

"Oh." The word came out with a sigh.

" 'Oh,' what?"

Oh, boy. "The baggy green surgical scrubs, right? The outfit's a real turn-on."

"That cute little mask hid your best feature."

"My freckles?"

"No, your mouth."

Oh, boy. Oh, boy. Theo certainly knew how to flirt. He could make her squirm and pant at the same time.

She smiled sweetly. "You haven't seen my best feature yet."

He raised an eyebrow in that wonderful Cary Grant way she loved. "Yeah?" he drawled. "Now you've got me curious. You're not going to tell me what your best feature is, are you?"

"No."

"You want me to spend half the night thinking about it?"

She hoped he would. She hoped he'd squirm a little too, just the way she did every time he looked at her. She knew she wasn't going to get much rest tonight. Why should she be the only one sleep-deprived? Tit for tat, she thought. She was suddenly feeling quite pleased with herself. Theo might have been the master at sexual banter, but she was finally feeling as though she was holding her own. She wasn't such a neophyte after all.

You mess with me and you pay the consequences.

"You want to fool around?" he asked.

She laughed. "No."

"If you're sure..."

"I'm sure."

"Then maybe you'd better button your top."

She glanced down at her chest and let out a loud groan. The silk pajama top was completely undone. Damn those silk buttons. They never stayed put. Her breasts were covered, though just barely. Mortified, she frantically rebuttoned.

Her face was bright pink when she looked at him. "Why didn't you say something?"

"Are you kidding? Why would I want to do that? I liked it. And don't look at me that way. I didn't unbutton the thing. I'm an innocent bystander."

She sat back on her heels while she put her robe on. "I'm going to bed. Thanks for the massage. It helped."

He leaned forward, cupped the sides of her face and kissed her. Her mouth was so soft and warm and sweet. She tasted like peppermint.

He took his time coaching a response, trying not to rush her.

There hadn't been time to prepare. She hadn't realized he was going to kiss her until his lips were touching hers. She didn't resist. She should have, but she didn't. Her lips parted, and then he deepened the kiss and she went limp.

She was his for the taking and both of them knew it.

He abruptly pulled back. "Sweet dreams."

"What?"

"Good night."

"Oh. Yes, I'm going to bed."

There was a definite twinkle in his eyes. He knew what he'd just done to her. She'd all but melted in front of him. Lord, what would happen if they made love? She'd probably have a complete mental breakdown.

How could he turn it on and off so quickly and efficiently? Experience and discipline, she decided as she stood and walked out of the room. Years and years of experience and discipline. She, on the other hand, apparently had the discipline of a rabbit. One kiss and she was ready to have his babies.

God, she was disgusting. And did he have to be such a great kisser? She shoved her hair out of her face. Mr. Big City was going to eat her alive if she didn't get a handle on her emotions. She wasn't an innocent. She'd been in a relationship before, and at the time, she'd believed she was going to marry the man. He hadn't kissed the way Theo had, though, and he hadn't made her feel so alive and desirable.

The big jerk. Michelle tripped on the hem of her robe going up the stairs. As soon as she reached her bedroom, she threw the robe on a chair. Then she got into bed. She stayed there about five seconds, got up again, and went downstairs.

Theo was back at the desk, typing on his laptop.

"Listen, you." She came close to shouting.

"Yes?" he asked, his hands poised over the keyboard.

"I just want you to know..."

"What?"

"I'm a damned good surgeon. While you were out getting all that experience...screwing around, and I use that word specifically..."

"Yes?" he asked, a hint of a smile playing at the corners of his mouth.

She poked herself in the chest. "I was busy learning how to use a scalpel. I just wanted you to know..."

"Know what?" he asked when she abruptly stopped.

Her mind went blank. Several seconds passed in silence. Her shoulders slumped and she said, "I don't know."

Without another word, she left the room.

Could she have made a bigger fool of herself? "I doubt that," she whispered as she got into bed. She felt like David going to meet Goliath and forgetting to bring his slingshot. Letting out a loud groan, she rolled onto her stomach, pulled the pillow over her head, and closed her eyes.

He was making her nuts.

CHAPTER NINETEEN

Monk hated surveillance. He stood in the shadows of a weeping willow watching Dr. Renard's house, waiting to make certain she had gone to bed so he could return to his motel room and catch a few hours' sleep. He would have to listen to all the taped telephone calls first, of course. He rubbed his thigh as though to console himself because he'd torn his best pair of khakis climbing the telephone pole when he'd placed the tap.

While he stood there, hour upon hour, waiting and watching, he thought about past assignments. He liked to go over each minute detail. He wasn't being ghoulish, and he certainly wasn't getting any perverse pleasure thinking about his victims. No, his goal was to review his performance and then analyze it. What mistakes had he made? What could he do to improve himself?

He'd learned something from each job he'd taken. The wife in Biloxi kept a loaded gun under her pillow. If her husband knew about it, he'd failed to mention it to Monk. He had almost gotten his head blown off, but fortunately he'd been able to wrestle the gun away from her. Then he'd used it to kill her instead of wasting valuable seconds trying to suffocate her. Expect the unexpected. That was the first lesson.

And then there was the teenager in Metairie. Monk's performance that night had been less than perfect, and looking back, he realized he had been lucky that no one had walked in on him. He'd stáyed much too long. He should have left the second the job was finished, but he watched a movie on television instead. What made that all the more remarkable was the fact that Monk never watched television. He felt he was far too intelligent to stare at the trash the networks put out to numb the already numb minds of beer-guzzling couch potatoes.

This movie had been different. And vastly amusing. The film had just begun playing when he'd broken into the victim's bedroom. He still remembered every detail from that night. The pink-and-white-striped wallpaper with the tiny pink rosebuds, the assortment of stuffed animals on the client's bed, the pink frilly curtains. She had been the youngest client he had ever taken on, but that fact hadn't bothered him much at all. A job, after all, was simply that. A job. All he cared about was getting it done and getting it done right.

The music from the video, he recalled, had been blaring. The client had been awake, half-stoned on a joint she'd just smoked. The air smelled sweet, heavy. She was dressed in a short blue T-shirt, her back against pillows and the headboard of the pink canopy bed, a super-sized bag of Doritos in her lap. She mindlessly stared at the screen, unaware of his presence. He'd murdered the teenage girl with the acne-ravaged face and the oily brown hair as a special favor—and for twenty-five thousand—so that good old Dad could collect on a three-hundred-thousand-dollar policy he'd taken out on his only child six months before. The policy had a double indemnity clause, which meant that if the cause of death was proven to be accidental, Dad would receive double the face value. Monk had gone to great lengths to make the murder look accidental so that he would receive double his fee. The father had been most appreciative of his work, of course, and although it hadn't been necessary to explain why he wanted his daughter murdered—the money was all Monk was interested in—he confessed that he was desperate to get the loan sharks off his back and was only doing what he had to do.

Ah, fatherly love. Nothing like it in the world.

While he was killing her, he listened to the dialogue from the movie, and within a minute or two, he was captivated. He shoved the deceased's feet out of his way, sat down on the foot of the bed, and watched the movie until the last credits came on, all the while munching on Doritos.

He had just stood up to leave when he heard the garage door opening. He'd gotten away in the nick of time, but now, thinking about the foolish risk he'd taken, he realized how fortunate he'd been. What lesson had he learned from that experience? Get in and get out as quickly as possible.

Monk believed he'd vastly improved since those early murders. He'd dispatched Catherine without any problems at all.

He glanced up at the doctor's bedroom window again. She was staying up much later than he'd expected, but then, she was entertaining a man. When Monk had followed her to The Swan, he'd spotted the man in the crowd of loud, crass teenagers. He'd only gotten a brief look at his face and shoulders. The adolescents completely surrounded him as they shouted to get his attention. They were calling him Coach.

Expect the unexpected. He'd called Dallas, read the license plate number on the rental car, and asked for a thorough background check.

The light finally went out in her bedroom. Monk waited another half hour to make certain she had gone to bed before he quietly made his way down the side of the gravel road to where he'd hidden his vehicle. He drove back to the motel in St. Claire, listened to the tape he had made of her phone calls, disappointed there was nothing significant there, set his alarm clock, and finally went to bed.

CHAPTER TWENTY

There were definite perks to carrying government credentials and knowing people in high places. By ten o'clock in the morning, Theo had all the information he needed on the Carson brothers. What he had learned about the con artists pissed the hell out of him. He also had the writs and the filings ready, thanks to his eager interns and a guaranteed-on-time courier service.

What Theo planned to do wasn't all that conventional and could possibly be thrown out in a court of law, but he wasn't concerned about that now. He hoped to have Daryl's problem with the sugar mill resolved before the brothers wised up, and from what he had learned about the two attorneys the brothers kept on a monthly retainer, they were little league players who wouldn't figure out they had been manipulated until after the fact.

Theo also had another advantage that he'd never used until today. As a member of the Justice Department, he could strike as much fear into the hearts of small-time criminals as the IRS.

He was whistling while he fixed breakfast. Michelle walked into the kitchen just as he was putting the utensils on the table.

She looked good enough to eat. Dressed in tight, faded blue jeans that emphasized her long legs and a snug white T-shirt that ended just above her navel, she looked sexier to him than she had the night before, and he hadn't thought that was possible. Heaven help him, the woman just kept getting better and better.

He handed her a glass of juice. "Want to have some fun?"

Those weren't the first words she expected to hear. "What kind of fun?" she asked cautiously.

"Sugar mill fun."

She couldn't believe she was actually a little disappointed. "Oh. Yes...yes, of course. May I help?"

"Sure you can, but eat your breakfast first. I've got it all ready for you. I like cooking," he added enthusiastically, as though he'd only just realized that fact. "It relaxes me."

She glanced at the table and laughed. "Opening a box of cereal and getting the milk out of the fridge isn't cooking."

"I made coffee too," he boasted.

"Which, translated, means you pushed the button. I got it ready last night."

He pulled out a chair for her, got a whiff of her perfume, and wanted to get closer. He moved back instead and leaned against the sink. "You look nice today."

She tugged on the hem of her T-shirt. "You don't think this top is a little tight?"

"Why do you think I said you look nice?"

"Every time I put it on, I take it off and find something else to wear. It's the latest fashion," she added defensively. "My friend Mary Ann gave it to me, and she told me my belly button is supposed to show."

He pulled his faded navy blue T-shirt up until his navel was showing. "If it's in fashion, I'm in."

"I'll change," she said, prying her attention away from his hard, flat stomach. The man was disgustingly fit, which was a miracle considering the amount of junk food he ate.

"I like what you're wearing," he protested.

"I'm changing," she said again. Then she shook her head. "It's difficult...trying to get comfortable in my skin these days."

"What do you mean?"

"I spent so many years trying not to look like a girl."

He thought she was joking and laughed.

"It's true," she said. "When I was in medical school, I did everything I could to downplay the obvious fact that I was a woman."

Astonished, he asked, "Why would you do that?"

"The head of one department was extremely prejudiced against female doctors and did everything he could to make our lives miserable. He was such a creep," she added. "He and his buddies would go out drinking with the male students, but only after he had loaded the female students down with research assignments and extra work. I didn't care about that, but I didn't like having to jump through twice as many hoops as the male students. Complaining would have made the situation worse. The only alternative for a female student was to drop out, which was exactly what the head of the department wanted."

She suddenly smiled. "One night, while some of the other women and I were getting zonkered on margaritas, we figured it all out."

"What'd you figure out?"

"The department head was afraid of us. Keep in mind we were exhausted and tipsy."

"Did you come up with a reason for why he was afraid of you?"

"Our minds. He knew the truth."

"What truth?"

"Women have vastly superior minds." She laughed as she added, "Fear and insecurity were at the root of the prejudice. I remember, at the time the revelation was stunning to us. It wasn't true, but we were too drunk to know or care. I realize now of course that it was all nonsense, we aren't any less or any more capable than male doctors, but being able to laugh and feel smug helped us get through the really tough times."

"Was your residency as difficult?"

"No, it was completely different. We were all treated equally horrible twenty hours a day, seven days a week. It didn't matter that I was a woman. All I needed to know was how to run. It was grueling," she admitted. "I learned how to catch fifteen minutes of sleep standing up. I was fortunate to train under a gifted surgeon. He was obnoxious," she said, "but he and I got along. I pretty much lived in scrubs, and fashion wasn't part of the curriculum."

"My doctor's a female."

"No kidding."

"Yes. She took my appendix out."

"I'm not your doctor. If that were the case, I'd put you on a low-sodium, low-fat diet."

"Did I mention I don't like my doctor and that I never follow her advice? As for clothes, it doesn't matter what you wear, Michelle. Men are still going to stare at you. I just hope the Carson brothers aren't gawking out the window at you while I'm trying my best to terrorize them."

"You're going to use terror tactics? Cool."

"I thought you'd approve."

"What do you mean, looking out the window at me? Can't I go inside with you?"

"Sorry. You don't get to watch the brothers sweat."

"Why not?"

"Because I don't want you to hear what I'm going to say. You never know. You might have to testify against me in court one day."

"Exactly what are you planning to do?"

He grabbed the sugar bowl from the lazy Susan on the counter and sat down across from her. "Wait and see," he said. Then he reached for the box of cereal and poured a huge helping of cornflakes. "I like Frosted Flakes better," he remarked as he started dumping sugar on top.

She got nauseated watching him. "I've got a five-pound bag of sugar in the pantry. Why don't you get it down, grab a spoon, and dig in."

"Sweetheart, sarcasm first thing in the morning isn't appreciated. Want some coffee?"

"I made that for you," she said. "I usually drink a Diet Coke for breakfast."

He laughed. "And you're criticizing my eating habits?"

She got a cold can out of the refrigerator, popped the lid, and took a long swallow. "Did I hear the doorbell this morning?"

"I had some papers messengered to me from New Orleans. It's kind of amazing the driver found your house. My directions were iffy."

"You have offices in New Orleans?"

"I've got friends there," he said. "After I talked to Daryl, I called some people in Boston. Since I'm not familiar with Louisiana law or workman's comp, I had to use some of my connections."

"It seems to me that if an employee were injured while on the job, then he's entitled to workman's compensation."

"There are exceptions."

"Like what?"

"If the employee did anything to cause the accident, like come to work drunk, he could be denied workman's comp."

"Or if he used a machine he knew was broken?"

"That's the argument the Carsons will use."

"But you're prepared for that."

"Yes."

"Why are you moving so quickly?"

"Because I don't want to leave Daryl hanging. I'm not going to be here long, and I want to try to get his problem fixed before I go back home. I promised him."

She lowered her head and watched her cornflakes get soggy. She had known all along that Theo was going to leave. Of course, she did. And that was the reason she was trying not to become attached. There was only one little wrinkle in her plan. As loath as she was to admit it, she wanted to grab hold of him and never let go.

The big jerk. This was all his fault. If he hadn't kissed her, she wouldn't be feeling miserable now.

"Is something wrong?" he asked.

"No. Why do you ask?"

"You've got that look on your face...like you want to kick someone."

"I was just thinking."

"About what?"

She pushed the uneaten cereal out of her way, leaned back in her chair, and folded her arms. "Nonspecific viruses." There was a thread of belligerence in her voice.

"That's the last thing in the world I would have guessed you were thinking about. Viruses. Go figure."

"Nonspecific viruses," she corrected.

"My mistake. So tell me. What exactly were you thinking about nonspecific viruses?"

"They're insidious...and destructive, the way they attack the body. One minute you're feeling just fine and dandy, and the next, your throat is scratchy and sore and your body begins to ache everywhere. Then your glands get so swollen you have trouble swallowing. When you think you couldn't possibly feel any worse, you start coughing, and before you know it, you've got all sorts of secondary complications."

232

He stared at her for several seconds and then asked, "And you were thinking about this because...?"

You're leaving, you big jerk. She lifted her shoulders. "I'm a physician. I think about such things."

"Are you feeling okay?"

"Yes, but who knows how I'll feel in five minutes. It's cruel...these viruses. They strike just like that." She snapped her fingers and nodded.

"But if they aren't the deadly kind of virus, then eventually they run their course and go away. Right?"

"Oh, yes, they go away, all right," she snapped.

Theo said what he was thinking. "What the hell's wrong with you?"

"I feel a virus coming on."

"You just said you were feeling fine," he pointed out.

"I don't want to talk about this any longer. Sick people depress me."

"Michelle?"

"Yes?"

"You're a doctor. I'm going out on a limb here, but don't you treat sick people all day long?"

She suddenly realized how childishly she was behaving and tried to come up with an excuse for her moment of madness. "I'm not a morning person."

"Don't you do most of your surgeries early in the morning?"

"Yes, I do, but the patients are already under. They don't care what kind of a mood I'm in. Did you sleep well?" she asked, deliberately changing the subject.

"Yes. What about you?"

"Yes. It was nice not having the phone jar me awake. Have you heard from your friend Noah, yet?"

"No."

"He'll need to stop by here to get the key to the clinic so he can look around. We'll have to wait for him."

"Noah won't need a key."

"How will he get in?"

"He'll break and enter, but don't worry. He won't really break anything. He prides himself on being quick and quiet."

"Are you supposed to meet him at a set time and place?"

"No," he said. "But I'm not worried. Noah will find me. What's on your schedule today?"

"Since you don't want me to start cleaning up the clinic until Noah's gone through the place, I've got a free day. I do need to get hold of Dr. Robinson and find out about his difficult patients," she said. "And the only other thing I have to do is drag you to football practice at three. You did promise Mr. Freeland that you'd stop by, and since I'm the team physician—and I use the term loosely—I have to be there."

"They need a doctor during practice?" he asked, grinning.

"Oh, yes," she said. "The boys do a lot of damage to one another banging heads and other body parts. It doesn't seem to matter that they wear helmets and pads. I had a dislocated shoulder last week and a badly sprained knee two days ago. The boys are really awful, but don't tell anyone I said so. Speaking of Mr. Freeland," she continued, "he wrote down a number on that paper he handed you. Did you look at it, and were you duly impressed?"

"Yes, I read the number. I can't really say I was impressed."

"Amused, then?"

He nodded. "I make more in a week than he offered for the year."

"It's not a rich district."

"I understand."

"And I'm sure he assumed you'd be making money working as a lawyer too."

"Uh-huh."

"Are you going to change into your suit before we go to the mill?"

"What's wrong with what I'm wearing?"

"Levi's? Is that proper attire when you want to intimidate someone?"

"It isn't what you wear that counts. It's all in the attitude. When can you be ready to leave?"

"Give me ten minutes."

She stacked the dishes in the sink and then hurried upstairs to change her shirt to a less revealing one while Theo collected his papers.

As he was backing the car out of the drive, he said, "First stop is Second and Victor. I know it's in St. Claire, but you'll have to give me exact directions."

"It's easy. It's right behind McDonald's."

"Good. I can get some fries to hold me over until lunch."

"Your blood must be as thick as Crisco."

"No, it isn't. I've got low cholesterol and lots of the good stuff."

Michelle directed him through the streets of St. Claire.

"Turn left here," she instructed. "Why are we going to Second and Victor?"

"Fencing. Ah, there it is." He pulled into the lot adjacent to the St. Claire Fencing Company, parked the car but left the motor running, and got out. "I already called the order in, so this won't take long. I just need to pay." He hit the power lock and then shut the door.

She waited with the air conditioner running full speed. It was hot and muggy outside, and the weatherman had predicted an eighty percent chance for an afternoon thunder-shower. She lifted her hair and fanned her neck. She still hadn't readjusted to the humidity in Bowen. Or the pace of life. She was used to running, and now she was going to have to learn how to slow down again.

It took ten minutes for Theo to complete the transaction. Michelle was dying to know why he wanted to buy a fence, but she wasn't going to ask any more questions. If he wanted her to know, he'd tell her in his own good time.

She lasted until Theo had parked the car in front of the St. Claire Bank and Trust, which was exactly three blocks away from the fencing company.

"Did you buy a fence?"

"Uh-huh."

"What kind did you get?"

He was going through the stack of papers in the files he had tucked in the console between them. "Wrought iron," he said. He pulled out two official-looking documents, then got out of the car and came around to open her door for her.

"That's awfully expensive."

"It was worth the price."

"And?"

"And what?"

"And why did you buy it?"

"Call it a consolation prize," he said, "because I'm not going to get a bigger gun."

He knew she didn't understand. She'd already gone to the car when little John Patrick had told him about his birthday.

"There are fencing companies back in Boston."

"Yes, there are."

It suddenly dawned on her. "Does this have anything to do with Lois?"

"Lois who?"

She gave up. "You're not going to tell me?"

"That's right. I'm the strong, silent type."

"I hate the strong, silent types. They're all type A personalities. Heart attacks waiting to happen."

He pulled the door open. "Sweetheart, don't you ever think about anything but medicine?"

If he only knew. Since she'd met him, the only thing she'd been able to think about was going to bed with him. But she wasn't going to admit it. "Sure I do," she said. "Want to know what I'm thinking right now?"

"Are you getting cranky again?"

She laughed. "When was I cranky?"

Theo motioned to the guard, then stepped back so Michelle could go inside first. He knew his weapon would set the alarm off. He flashed his government ID at the elderly man and waited for him to hit the release button. The gun was concealed in an ankle strap he'd had sent to him with the papers.

The guard waved Theo inside. "How can I help you, Officer?"

Theo didn't correct the misassumption. "I have an appointment with the president of the bank. Could you direct me to his office?"

The guard nodded enthusiastically. "Sure I can. Mr. Wallbash is in the back. You can see him sitting behind his desk on the other side of the glass wall."

"Thank you."

Theo caught up with Michelle, pointed to a chair in the lobby outside of the president's office, and said, "Maybe you should wait here. I may have to use a dirty word in there."

"What would that word be?"

He leaned down close to her ear and whispered, *"Audit."*

"Excuse me, ma'am. Aren't you Big Daddy Jake's girl?" The guard was hurrying toward Michelle.

She whispered, "Good luck," to Theo and then turned to the old man. "Yes, I am," she said.

"Then you're the doctor, aren't you?"

He introduced himself and shook her hand. "I heard about what happened down at your clinic. My wife, Alice, and I were just saying how nice it was going to be to have Jake's girl looking out for us. We both need a good doctor. Alice has trouble with her bunions and her corns. She can't put on her Sunday shoes 'cause it hurts so much, and I've got to do something about my bursitis. Some days I can't raise my right arm at all. When do you think you'll be seeing patients?"

"Hopefully, in a couple of weeks."

"We can wait until then," he said. "We've put up with our aches and pains this long. This part-time job of mine helps me keep my mind off my ailments," he added. "I fill in for the regular guard two days a week. I guess you could say I keep banker's hours." He laughed at his own joke and then said, "Will you look at that? Mr. Wallbash looks like he's gonna have himself a heart attack. His face is as red as a chili pepper, and he's sweating like a pig. He sure doesn't like what the officer is telling him."

Michelle agreed. Wallbash did look ill. He shuffled through the papers Theo had placed on his desk, then looked up long enough to glare at Theo.

She couldn't see Theo's face because his back was to her, but whatever he was saying as he leaned over the desk was having quite an impact on Wallbash. The president put both hands up as though he were being robbed and nodded vigorously.

She thought she knew why. Theo must have used the magic word.

He wasn't inside the president's office all that long, and he didn't shake the man's hand when he was leaving. Wallbash was busy mopping the sweat from his brow. Theo paused in the doorway, and whatever he said in parting made the color drain from Wallbash's face.

Theo's expression was ferocious as he crossed the lobby to her. He noticed her watching him, winked, then grabbed hold of her hand, nodded to the guard, and kept right on going, dragging her along in his wake.

She waited until they were in the car to find out what had happened. "Well?"

"Wallbash isn't happy, but he'll cooperate. He damn well better," he added in a voice that made her take notice.

"Now what?"

"One more stop and then we can eat lunch. Tell me how to get to the sugar mill."

She gave him directions and then asked him to tell her what he'd done. "Wallbash looked like he was going to have a tantrum."

"The Carson brothers have done their banking at the St. Claire Bank and Trust since the company began. They're one of the bank's largest depositors, and that ought to tell you something about the sweet deal those sons of bitches have going. Wallbash and Gary Carson are friends. According to Wallbash, he's a real nice guy."

"What about his brother?"

"Jim Carson's a hothead. I think Wallbash is a little afraid of him. Jim's the one who went to the hospital to fire Daryl. They play it that way on purpose because it gets them what they want."

"Like good cop, bad cop?"

"More like bad and worse. You know, I'll take a hothead over a sneaky little weasel manipulator any day of the week. If I'm lucky today, both brothers will be at the mill and I'll get to watch them do their routine."

"But what was the purpose of visiting the bank?"

"I froze their accounts."

She burst into laughter. "That can't be legal."

"Sure it is," he countered. "Wallbash has the papers, all signed and legal. He has to cooperate, or I'll nail his..."

He stopped himself in time. She ended the sentence for him. "His backside to the wall?"

"Yeah."

"Why do you keep looking at your watch?"

"Timing is everything," he said. "My appointment with Gary Carson is at twelve-thirty."

"You made an appointment?"

"Sure."

"Did you tell him what you wanted to see him about?"

"And ruin the surprise? Of course I didn't tell him the truth. I told his secretary I wanted to do some business with the mill."

"Turn left at the next corner," she instructed. "And follow this road for a couple of miles.

The mill's out in the country," she added. "So Carson thinks he's getting a new account."

"That's right."

"Wallbash will probably call him and tell him about your visit."

"He'll call him at exactly one o'clock and not a minute before, or I'll have auditors tearing that bank apart before he can blink. He'll wait."

"Would you really do that?"

He didn't answer her. She studied his profile for several minutes and then said, "When you want something, you don't let anything get in your way, do you?"

"That's right, I don't. You might want to keep that in mind."

"You always win?"

He looked at her. "What do you think?"

It was subtle, the way he had changed the subject. They both knew they were talking about getting his way with her now. Then she remembered what he had said to her before he'd even unpacked the night before. He wouldn't have to go to her bed. She would come to him. When hell freezes over, she thought. She turned to look out her window. Then another thought occurred to her, and she said, "What about payroll? If you froze their accounts, how will the men get paid?"

"The court will appoint someone to write the checks."

"What if the brothers shut down the mill out of spite?"

"They're making too much money to shut down, and besides, I'm not going to let them."

"You can do that?"

"Sure I can. If they don't cooperate, when I'm finished with them, the employees will own the company."

Theo could see the mill in the distance. There were smokestacks jutting out of round silos nestled in between two huge concrete-block buildings. All were connected.

The closer he got, the bleaker the place looked. It had a dirty gray façade and dirty windows, but it didn't look as if it was in bad shape. He parked in the gravel lot, got out, and looked around.

"Mr. Buchanan?"

He turned at the sound of the voice. "Connelly?"

A tall, thin man wearing a business suit approached the car. "Yes, sir."

"Everything in order?"

Connelly lifted his briefcase. "Yes, sir, it is. I just got word. He's filed."

Theo leaned into the open car door and said to Michelle, "Do you mind waiting here?"

"Okay," she answered, "but if I hear gunshots, I'm going to come running."

He turned to Connelly, introduced him to Michelle, and then said, "When I come out, you go in. I want you to wait outside the door."

Theo left the motor running. Removing her seat belt, Michelle pushed the seat back and turned on the radio. Willie Nelson was singing. She took it as a good omen. Maybe Theo wouldn't run into any trouble after all.

Three songs and nine commercials later, Theo came outside. He was smiling as Connelly passed him on his way inside. Theo double-timed it to the car, slid into the seat, and put the car in drive before he shut his door. She barely had time to click her seat belt closed before he was speeding down the drive.

"Are we making a fast getaway?"

"I'm hungry."

"But you're watching the rearview mirror," she remarked as she turned in her seat to look out the back window.

"Just being cautious. Never know who might have a shotgun under his desk."

"It went that well?"

"Actually, it did go well. Gary Carson's a real nice guy. Couldn't have been more understanding and pleasant. Wants to do the right thing. I can't tell you how many times he said that. Of course, he qualified it with the veiled threat that he'd have to close the mill because, and I quote, 'We're just scraping by.' "

"And how did you respond?"

He flashed her a grin. "I laughed."

"So you were tactful."

He laughed. "Sure."

"You're really getting a kick out of this, aren't you?"

He seemed surprised by the question and then said, "Yes, I am. It feels good helping Daryl. Feels real good."

"Because you can see the difference you're making."

"Yes. Of course, this case is easy. I should have it settled before the weekend."

"You really think you can get the problem fixed in a couple of days?"

"Yes, I do. Unless the brothers have some cash stashed away I don't know about and think they can hold out. But even then, it won't matter. They've broken so many laws, I could put both of them behind bars. OSHA would have a field day in that plant."

"Did the hothead go for your throat?"

"No," he said.

She grinned. "You sound disappointed."

"I am," he admitted. "I wanted to see their routine. Jim Carson's in New Orleans for the day, but he's supposed to be back in Bowen around six. Gary mentioned he was going to wait to tell his brother face-to-face instead of calling him on his cell phone, probably so he can get him foaming at the mouth before he sics him on me. My guess is that I'll be hearing from Jim about five minutes after Gary imparts the news."

"Did you happen to tell Gary where you were going to be tonight?"

He grinned. "I might have mentioned that I'd be at The Swan."

She sighed. "You may get to shoot someone after all."

CHAPTER TWENTY-ONE

The new high school football stadium was impressive. The football team, on the other hand, was anything but. They were, in Theo's estimation, unbelievably bad.

The boys wanted to show off for him. They did have talent; they just didn't know what to do with it. Conrad Freeland had to scream at the top of his lungs to be heard over the boys' shouting matches. He used his whistle so often the kids pretty much ignored the sound. Practice was chaotic and deafening.

Conrad finally got the first string to cooperate long enough to line up. They then began running back and forth across the beautifully manicured field like chickens with their heads cut off.

Theo and Michelle stood next to the music teacher on the fifty-yard line watching. Beaming with pride, Conrad turned to Theo and asked, "What do you think of your boys?"

Theo ignored the "your boys" reference—he wasn't about to claim ownership of this motley crew—and said, "Why don't you run some plays, and Michelle and I will sit in the stands and watch. It's been a few years," he warned, "but maybe I can give you some suggestions."

Conrad looked confused. Nodding toward the field, he said, "That was the play."

"Excuse me?"

"You just saw the play."

"*The* play? You only have one..." He was trying not to smile, because he didn't want Conrad to think he wasn't taking practice seriously.

The music teacher nervously tugged on his collar. He was dressed for a music recital in an immaculately pressed long-sleeve white dress shirt, pin-striped tie, and a navy blazer. The clouds were heavy with rain, and it was so sticky and hot that Theo thought Conrad had to be suffocating.

Michelle nudged him. "It's a nice play, isn't it?"

He didn't answer. Then Conrad said, "We've only perfected that one play you just saw. We call it the stinger."

"I see," he remarked for lack of anything better to say that wasn't a blatant lie.

"Good, isn't it?"

Michelle nudged Theo again. He ignored her and turned to Conrad. He didn't want to hurt the man's feelings. It was obvious he had worked hard to get the undisciplined boys to cooperate, but Theo wasn't going to start lying to him either, and so he simply said, "Interesting."

"You've got to understand my position and the background of the team," Conrad said, his voice earnest now. "Last year was our first year with a football team, and the coach...well, he just up and left in the middle of the season. Of course, he didn't win any games. The boys don't know what to do out there. I don't know what I'm doing either," he admitted. "Give me a flute, and I'll teach you how to play

247

it, but this," he added with a wave of his hand, "is beyond me. It's why we desperately need playbooks. I really have tried to do a good job."

"I'm sure you have," Theo agreed, trying to think of something positive to say.

"I even went searching on the computer. I can give you the history of football, but I can't tell you how to play the game. I couldn't make head nor tail out of all the drawings I found on the Internet. Lots of circles and arrows that didn't make any sense to me."

He removed the whistle from around his neck and offered it to Theo. "See what you can do, Coach."

"I'm not..." Conrad had already jogged toward the watercooler. "...the coach," Theo ended.

Michelle leaned into his side. "They're really awful, aren't they?" she whispered.

"Oh, yes," he agreed.

She smiled. "I'll go sit in the bleachers until you're finished."

Okay, he thought. One practice. He'd talk to the boys, tell them he'd send Freeland some playbooks and maybe a couple of films they could watch too, and that's it. Then he was out of here. Yeah, that was *his* game plan.

Putting two fingers into his mouth, he whistled to get the boys' attention and then motioned them over to him.

They ran like lumbering overweight foals. One kid fell down, got up, ran a couple more yards, and tripped over his own feet again. Theo hoped he wasn't going out for the position of running back. They squeezed in around him as they pressed him with questions. Theo didn't say a word. He simply held up one hand and waited. The noise finally died down.

In a low voice, he told them to remove their helmets and sit down on the grass in front of him. They actually obeyed. When they dropped to the ground, Theo swore he felt the earth move underneath him. Then Elliott Waterson shouted, "Where's your gun, Coach?" And the noise started all over again.

Theo didn't say a word. He simply stood there with his arms folded across his chest, waiting for them to catch on. It didn't take long. Within a minute it was quiet again.

In a near whisper, he said, "Elliott, my gun is in a safe place, but I swear, the next kid who interrupts me while I'm talking is going to get clobbered. Understood?" He was forcing the boys to sit still and strain to hear what he had to say. "Now, here's what we're going to do."

Michelle sat on the hard bleachers watching the transformation. She was astonished at how easily Theo had taken control of the boys. The team sat with their legs folded underneath them, their helmets in their laps. Every eye was on Theo, and the boys seemed to be hanging on his every word. Conrad looked impressed. He had walked back to Theo's side and was nodding every now and then.

"Excuse me, ma'am?"

Michelle turned at the sound of the voice and saw a tall, slightly overweight, dark-haired man standing just outside the tunnel that led to the locker rooms. He looked vaguely familiar to her.

"Yes?"

He walked forward. The stranger was dressed in khaki shorts and a matching short-sleeve khaki shirt with the word "Speedy" sewn above the breast pocket. There was a name tag dangling from the clip below the pocket. He carried a Speedy Messenger package—she recognized the label—but he was too far away for her to read his name.

"I'm looking for a Dr. Michelle Renard. Would you happen to know where I can find her?"

"I'm Dr. Renard."

The messenger beamed. "Thank heavens. I've been all over this town searching for you."

He tucked the package under his arm and hurried up the metal stairs.

"Do you have something for me?"

"No, Doctor. What I've got is a problem, but I'm hoping you'll help me solve it before Eddie gets himself canned."

"Excuse me?"

The messenger smiled. "Eddie's the new guy with our company, and he screwed up big time," he said. "My name's Frank, by the way." He extended his hand to shake hers. His palm was damp, his grip weak.

"How did your friend screw up?" she asked.

"He delivered the right packages to the wrong people," he said. "But he really needs the job because his wife is expecting, and if Eddie gets fired for messing up, he'll lose his insurance. Eddie's only nineteen," he added. "And I feel responsible because I'm the man who trained him, so I'm using my day off to try to fix this before the boss finds out about it."

"That's very nice of you," she said. "How can I help?"

"You see, Eddie picked up a package from a law firm in New Orleans on Monday, and he should have filled out the label and put it on the package right then and there at the receptionist's desk, but Eddie didn't do that. He took it back to the company van. Now, he'd already picked up another package from Belzer Labs, and he hadn't put the label on that package either. He figured he'd sit in the air-conditioned van and fill out both labels, but he stuck them on the wrong packages. The only way I found out about the screwup was when a secretary from another law firm called to say she had gotten the wrong package. When she opened hers, she found a bunch of literature about a new drug the company was going to be selling. Fortunately for Eddie, I was the one who happened to answer the phone. If that secretary had talked to the boss, I hate to think what would have happened. Speedy Messenger Service prides itself on being fast and reliable, and I swear that this is the first mix-up we've had in over three years. Anyway," he added as he shifted from foot to foot, "I was hoping you could give me the package you got by mistake, and I'll deliver it to the law firm today."

Michelle shook her head. "I'd like to help you, but I don't remember receiving any special deliveries. When and where was it delivered? Do you know?"

"Eddie took it to the hospital."

His hands, she noticed, shook as he flipped through the pages of his notebook. He was nervous and couldn't quite look her in the eyes. She thought that was odd but then decided he was embarrassed because of the mix-up.

"I already went over there, hoping I'd find you, and one of the nurses was kind enough to look at the weekly log. She said there was an accident late that afternoon and that you were in surgery when Eddie made the delivery, but that doesn't make any sense, since you signed for it."

"Oh, yes, I remember the accident. I was on the surgical floor, up to my elbows in charts I had to finish before I could leave. I did get a call from ER telling me there was a package for me. I don't remember getting it, though."

"Maybe it will jog your memory if I tell you that you signed for it."

"I did?" She certainly didn't remember doing that.

Frustration crept into his voice when he said, "Yes, Doctor, you did. We always keep a copy of the receipt in our offices and mail the original back to the sender, and I'm telling you," he added, his anxiety not quite masking his anger, "your signature is as clear as can be."

"It won't do you any good to get angry," she said. "And if you could read my handwriting, then I definitely didn't sign for it. No one can read my writing. I do think I know what must have happened," she added. "The staff secretary down in ER signed my name. That's pretty much standard procedure."

She racked her brain, trying to remember the sequence. Exhausted from being up most of the night before, she had made up her mind not to leave on vacation until every one of her charts had been dictated. "I did go down to get the package."

"Where?" he asked urgently with a hasty look over his shoulder at the football team. "Did you go to admitting or to the emergency room?"

"ER," she answered. "And that's when the paramedics arrived." She shrugged then. "I went right back up to surgery and did two cases back-to-back."

"So you never opened the package, did you?" He was smiling and sounded relieved.

"No, I didn't open it," she said. "I certainly would have remembered doing that, especially if there were papers from a law firm."

"You can understand how anxious the attorneys are to get those papers. They were going to another law firm. It's all confidential stuff. I could drive over to the hospital right this minute and get the package from that secretary, couldn't I? What's her name?"

253

"Elena Miller, but she won't give it to you unless I tell her it's okay."

"Could you call her now? Eddie already picked up the package meant for you and is on his way here now. I sure would like to get this finished today. I've got my phone with me."

He moved closer so he could hand her the phone. Michelle could smell his aftershave. He'd used a heavy hand, but it didn't mask the odor of sweat.

He was acting like a nervous twit. No wonder he was sweating. He kept looking over his shoulder at the field, as though he expected one of the boys to hurl a football at him. She dialed the hospital, asked for Elena, and was put on hold.

"He has them mesmerized, doesn't he?" she remarked as she waited for the secretary to pick up.

"What?"

"The coach. He has those players hanging on his every word. I noticed you were watching them."

"Oh...yes, yes, he does."

Elena Miller picked up a phone in the emergency room, and in her usual harried voice snapped, "Miller here."

"Hi, Elena. It's Dr. Renard. Am I interrupting you in the middle of something important?"

"I'm always in the middle of something important, Doctor, and you forgot to finish your charts. You left two," she said. "And you left your mail untouched. Your 'in' box is brimming over, Doctor. Now, aren't you glad you called? What can I do for you?"

"I did finish my charts," she argued. "Every last one of them, so if Murphy thinks he's going to put me on report, you tell him I'll have his hide."

"Relax, Doctor. Murphy's on vacation too. What can I do for you?" she repeated.

Michelle explained about the mix-up with the packages. "Do you remember signing for a package that was delivered around five o'clock Monday?"

"Right this minute, I can't even remember what I ate for supper last night. I do remember Monday was one of those hellacious days in the ER. We had a rush of accidents, and then there was that real bad one out on the highway. There were at least twenty mothers and fathers jamming the halls while the doctors worked on their kids. I certainly don't remember signing for anything, but it doesn't matter if I remember or not. If I signed for it, then I put a yellow sticky on your locker telling you I had a package for you. I would have put it inside your locker, but you still haven't given me your combination."

"Sorry about that," she said. "I keep forgetting. Do you have any idea where the package is now?"

"I'll look around. It's either in my desk or on top of your locker. What do you want me to do when I locate it?"

"Give it to the man from Speedy Messenger Service. He'll be there soon."

"Yes, all right. I'll be here until six tonight, but not a minute later. Tonight's bridge night at the church, and I have to be there by six-thirty to help set up. It's my turn to be hostess."

"I'm sure he'll get there before then. Thanks, Elena."

As she pushed the "end" button and handed the phone back to Frank, she noticed Theo was walking across the field toward them. Frank seemed to be watching Theo too. He kept his eye on him when he asked Michelle, "What did she tell you? Does she have the package?"

"Relax. Eddie's going to keep his job. Elena will be at the hospital until six, and she'll be happy to make the exchange."

He didn't say thank you. In fact, his exit was quite abrupt. Pulling the brim of his ball cap down low on his brow, he ran down the steps. His head was turned away from the field. As he was disappearing into the tunnel, she shouted, "You're welcome."

He didn't hear her. Desperate to get away before anyone else got a good look at his face, he ran as fast as he could through the locker rooms and outside, across the parking lot. He was panting from the effort. He fell against the car door, doubled over, and tried to catch his breath while he grabbed at the door handle. He heard a sound behind him and whirled around in a half crouch.

His eyes widened. "What the hell are you doing, sneaking up on me like that? Are you following me?"

"What do you think *you're* doing?"

"I'm doing what needs to be done," he argued. "No one else was getting anywhere. The doctor won't ever see me again. Besides, the risk was worth it. I know where the package is. I'm on my way to pick it up right now."

"You were told not to interact with the subject. That point was made perfectly clear to you. Now the doctor knows what you look like. You've made a stupid mistake, and the others aren't going to like it."

CHAPTER TWENTY-TWO

Theo was quiet on the ride back to Michelle's house. They were both hot and sticky and wanted to shower before he took her to dinner at The Swan. He had offered to take her somewhere else a little more fancy, but she had promised her father that she would help tend bar if he needed her. Wednesday was a busy night for her father's bar, and because the fishing competition was coming up on Saturday, it would surely be crowded.

"Couldn't your brother help your dad?" he asked.

"John Paul hasn't surfaced in the last week."

"Does your brother disappear a lot?"

"When my father needs him, he's there."

"But how does he know your father needs him? Does he call him?"

She smiled. "John Paul doesn't have a phone, and he wouldn't answer it if he did. He usually shows up on Friday morning to see what Daddy needs him to do. John Paul's never worked the bar during the weeknights."

"What if your dad got into trouble? What if he got sick or something?"

"John Paul would know something was wrong."

"ESP?"

"He just would know."

"Your brother sounds strange."

"He isn't strange," she said defensively. "He's just different."

"What about your other brother?"

"Remy? What about him?"

"Is he different?"

"By your standards, no, he isn't different."

Neither one of them said another word for several minutes. Michelle broke the silence when she noticed he was frowning.

"What are you thinking about?"

"The kid who kept tripping out on the field today."

"What about him?"

"He was wearing his brother's shoes."

"And you're trying to figure out what you can do about it."

"The team needs new equipment," he remarked. "Conrad's going to talk to the coach over in St. Claire about letting our team use their weight room. None of them should go out on that field until they're conditioned for it. You know what I mean?"

"They need to build up their muscles and their stamina."

"Exactly. Otherwise they could get hurt."

"You called them 'our team.' "

"No, I didn't."

"Yes, you did. I heard it as clear as a bell."

He changed the subject. "What did that messenger want? I saw you talking to him on my way to the watercooler."

"There was a mix-up at the hospital. I sent him to the ER staff secretary. She'll straighten it all out."

He nodded, then changed the subject once again. "How much money do you think the cash prize will amount to for the fishing tournament?"

"I don't know how many will enter this year, but if I were to guess, I'd say two men in a boat, fifty dollars each...and last year they had over seventy entries..."

"So, if we say eighty people sign up this year, that's four thousand."

"That's a lot of money around here."

"Four thousand dollars could buy a lot of shoes."

"Sounds like you've got a plan."

"Yeah, well, the key to the plan is to win."

She laughed. "No kidding. What about my dad?"

"What about him?" he asked as he pulled into her drive and parked the car.

"Two thousand dollars will belong to him."

"He'll donate it. Your dad's a softy." He followed her to the front door. "But like I said, the key to the grand plan is to win the tournament."

"It's killing you that you can't just go out and buy the team what they need, isn't it?"

She'd hit the nail on the head. "Yes," he admitted. "But I know I can't do that. Their parents would get their backs up. I'd be stomping on their pride. Right?"

"Yes, you would. You'll go broke if you keep buying little boys expensive fences and shoes and football pads for the team and heaven knows what else."

"No kid should have to worry about an alligator in his backyard."

She turned at the door, put her hands on his shoulders, and kissed him.

"What was that for?" he asked when she sauntered away.

She looked back, gave him a quick smile, and said, "Why did I kiss you? That's an easy one. I kissed you because I think you're sweet."

He reacted as though she'd just insulted him. "There is nothing sweet about me."

"Oh? You were worried about embarrassing that boy wearing his brother's shoes, weren't you?"

"I never said I was worried."

She smiled. "No, but you were, weren't you?"

"Yeah, but—"

"You're...sweet."

"I make a lot of money, Michelle, and it sure as certain isn't because I'm sweet."

He was slowly advancing, and with each step he took toward her, she took a step back.

"I don't care how much money you make. You've got everybody fooled back in Boston, don't you? They probably think you're a killer prosecutor."

"I am a killer prosecutor and proud of it."

"You were concerned about John Patrick, and that's why you purchased the fence. You know what that makes you?"

"Don't say it," he warned.

"Sweet."

He shook his head. "No. I know why you really kissed me, babe. Be honest."

He caught her around the waist as she was backing into the library. She was laughing as he pulled her up against him. His chest was like a brick wall. A warm brick wall.

He leaned down until his mouth hovered just an inch or two above hers. "Want me to tell you why you kissed me?"

"I'm waiting in breathless anticipation."

"It's simple. You want me."

He expected a protest, but wasn't the least disappointed when she said, "When you're right, you're right."

"You know what else?"

"What's that?" She leaned back so she could look at him.

"You're dying to get your hands on me." He pulled her closer.

She wrapped her arms around his waist and hooked her thumbs in his waistband.

"I did get my hands on you. You really

need to work on that ego. I've noticed you don't have any self-confidence around women. It's sad really...but..."

"But what?" he asked, rubbing his jaw against the side of her face as he waited for the zinger.

"You're still sweet," she whispered into his ear, then took his earlobe between her teeth and tugged.

He groaned. "I'll show you sweet."

Tilting her head back, his mouth came down on top of hers, and he kissed her with a passionate hunger. The kiss was wet, hot, wild, and thoroughly arousing.

Then it got better. The expression "putty in his hand" came to mind as she clung to him and allowed him to rob her of every logical thought. The kiss went on and on, and the taste of him was so wonderful, she kept trying to get closer and closer.

His touch was sinfully carnal, and she never wanted him to stop. He stroked her arms, her back, her neck as he worked his magic, and she was caught up in such an erotic spell that the only thought she could hold on to now was a chant. *Don't stop. Don't stop.*

"Don't."

She said it out loud a second after he'd pulled back.

They were both shaking. "Don't what?" he whispered gruffly.

He was panting. She was arrogantly happy because she knew she was the reason for his distress, but then she realized she was doing the same thing.

"Don't what?" he repeated as he leaned down and kissed her once again. A light, gentle caress that left her wanting more.

"I don't know."

"This is getting out of hand."

Her forehead was pressed against his chest. She bumped his chin when she nodded.

"And speaking of hands..."

"Yes?"

He kissed the top of her head. "You probably should move yours."

"What?"

"Your hands." His voice was gritty.

A gasp. Then, "Oh, God."

It took about five seconds to extricate herself from his jeans. Her face was burning as she turned and walked out of the room. She could hear him laughing as she climbed the stairs.

She grabbed her robe, went into the bathroom, and stripped out of her clothes. After she turned the shower on full blast, she stepped into the tub and all but ripped the shower curtain apart as she pulled it closed.

"Reason number one," she muttered, "he'll break my heart."

CHAPTER TWENTY-THREE

It was a quarter to seven when Theo and Michelle reached The Swan, and the place was hopping. Old vans and rusted-out pickups sporting rifle racks and bumper stickers almost filled the parking lot. *I'd rather be fishing* seemed to be the bumper sticker of choice, but the one that caught Theo's eye had the word *Gator-Aid* painted in bright fluorescent letters. When he looked closer, he noticed the picture of an alligator with a Band-Aid. He didn't know what that was supposed to mean.

He also noticed there weren't any brand-new vehicles in the lot. If there was any doubt that it was a poor area, the proof was all around him. Some of the pickups looked as though they belonged in a junkyard. But if he'd learned anything while in Bowen, it was that people made do with what they had.

"What are you thinking about?" she asked him as she led the way around a dented gray van.

"How hard it is to scrape a living here," he answered. "But you know what? I haven't heard any complaints."

"No, you wouldn't. They're too proud."

"Did I mention you look pretty tonight?" he asked.

"In this old thing?"

This "old thing" was a short V-necked blue-and-white-checked sundress that she'd spent twenty minutes deciding upon. She'd spent another twenty minutes working on her hair. She wore it down around her shoulders, and it curved softly around her face. She'd worked hard curling it to make it look as though she hadn't. Then she'd added some blush to highlight her cheekbones, and brushed on a tiny bit of lipstick and gloss. When she realized she was becoming compulsive about her appearance—she'd changed in and out of the sundress three times—and that all the primping was for him, she stopped.

"When someone gives you a compliment, you're supposed to say thank you. You look pretty tonight," he repeated, "in that 'old thing.' "

"You like making fun of me, don't you?"

"Uh-huh."

He'd lied when he'd told her she looked pretty, but he couldn't put into words how he'd felt when she'd come downstairs. *Dynamite* came to mind. *Breathtaking* was another adjective he could have used, but the one word that kept repeating in his head he was too embarrassed to say. *Exquisite.*

She would have had a field day with that compliment, he thought. And what was the matter with him? He was silently waxing poetic. Now, where had that come from?

"It's a sin to make fun of anyone."

Theo opened the door for her, then blocked her entrance while he read the hand-printed sign on the wall. "No wonder it's so crowded tonight. It's all-the-beer-you-can-drink night."

She smiled. "It's always all-the-beer-you-can-drink, as long as you pay for each glass and you don't drive. The locals know about it."

"Something smells good. Let's eat. God, I hope it's not spicy."

"Since it's Wednesday, you can have fried catfish and french fries, which I'm sure your arteries will love..."

"Or?"

"French fries and fried catfish."

"I'll have that."

As they zigzagged their way to the bar, Theo was stopped more often than she was. Several men and women wanted to shake his hand or pat his shoulder as he passed by, and all of them, so it seemed, wanted to talk football.

The only person who stopped her was a man who wanted to discuss his hemorrhoids.

Her father was at the far end of the bar by the storage room, huddled with Conrad Freeland and Artie Reeves. Jake was frowning and nodding at whatever Conrad was telling him and Artie, and he didn't notice her coming toward him.

Armand, the cook, was working in the kitchen, while his brother, Myron, tended bar.

"Daddy's rooked Myron into helping him," she said. "I guess I'm off the hook for a little while."

"Your dad's waving to us."

When they finally reached her father, he lifted the countertop and hurried over to Michelle. She noticed Artie and Conrad were both frowning at her.

"Theo, why don't you go pour yourself a beer and sit at the bar while I have a word in private with my daughter."

The look her father gave her told her she'd done something to displease him. She followed him into the storage room and then asked, "Is something wrong, Daddy?"

"He's gonna leave, Mike, that's what's wrong. The boys and I were talking, and we decided we just can't let that happen. This town needs Theo Buchanan. Surely you can see that. Most of the folks here tonight came out specifically because they want to talk to him."

"They want free legal advice?"

"Some do," he admitted. "And then there's that sugar mill business and the football season is coming on."

"Daddy, what do you expect me to do? The man lives in Boston. He can't commute."

"Well, of course he can't." He grinned over the foolish notion of flying back and forth to Bowen.

"Well, then?"

"We think you could change his mind if you worked at it."

"How?" she asked. Exasperated, she put her hands on her hips and waited. Knowing how her father's larcenous mind worked, she knew whatever suggestion he came up with was going to be a doozy. She braced herself to hear what it was.

"Put the welcome mat out."

"What does that mean?"

"Conrad and I came up with a good plan, and Artie thinks it might work. Now, Conrad told me that Theo happened to mention you wanted him to stay at my place."

"Yes, I did."

"How hospitable was that, Mike?"

She didn't know how he'd managed it, but he'd put her on the defensive.

"I'm being nice to him now. Honest."

"Have you made him your gumbo?"

"No, but—"

"Good," he said. "Conrad's wife is going to sneak on over to your house with a pot full of her gumbo tomorrow morning, and you can pass it off as your own."

"That's dishonest," she pointed out. And then it dawned on her what her father wasn't saying. "Wait a minute. I thought you liked my gumbo."

He'd moved on. "What about your lemon pound cake? You didn't happen to make that yet, did you?"

"No." She took a step toward him. "I'm warning you, Daddy. If you say 'good,' I'm never going to invite you over for supper again."

"Honey, now isn't the time to be sensitive. We've got a crisis on our hands, and we've only got a couple of days to change his mind."

"Nothing any of us do will matter."

"Not with that attitude, it won't. Get with the program, and don't be so negative."

Her father was so enthusiastic that she felt terrible trying to rain on his parade. "It's just that—"

He started talking at the same time. "Marilyn just left."

"Artie's wife?"

"That's right. She makes a real tasty chocolate cake, and she's on her way home to bake one tonight. It should be in your kitchen by noon tomorrow."

She didn't know if she should be insulted or amused. "And Theo's going to think I whipped that up? Exactly when would I have had time to bake him a cake? I've been with the man all day, and tomorrow morning I'm supposed to go to the clinic and start sorting through files."

"No, you don't understand what we're trying to do. Marilyn's going to leave a nice happy-you're-here card so he'll get the idea how friendly everyone is. Karen Crawford's smoking a brisket and fixing her potato salad, and of course, she'll have a nice card all written up. Daryl's wife doesn't want to be left out. She's bringing over a pot of green beans fresh from her garden."

"With a nice card," she remarked as she folded her arms and frowned at her father.

"That's right."

"Then why am I supposed to pretend I made the gumbo?"

"Because I won't have Theo thinking you can't cook."

"I *can* cook."

"You took him to McDonald's." It wasn't a comment; it was an accusation.

Michelle's appreciation for small-town openness suddenly dwindled. Someone had obviously been spreading the word. Suddenly the big, bad, impersonal city didn't sound quite so horrible.

"He *wanted* to go there," she argued. "He likes McDonald's...and so do I. They have great salads."

"We're all trying to be friendly."

She laughed. When Daddy and Conrad and Artie put their heads together, they came up with some of the most outrageous ideas. At least this one wouldn't land them in jail.

"And you want me to be friendly too."

"That's right. You know what I'm talking about. Make him feel at home, like he belongs here. Take him out and show him the sights."

"What sights?"

"Michelle, are you going to cooperate or not?"

He was getting testy. He only called her Michelle when he was frustrated with her. She started laughing again, which she knew he didn't appreciate at all, but she couldn't help it. The conversation was crazy.

"Okay," she said. "Since this means so much to you and Conrad and Artie, I'll cooperate."

"It means a lot to the men and women who work at the sugar mill and the boys on the football team too. You should have heard what Conrad told us about practice today. He said Theo had those boys all revved up and ready to go. He also said that Theo knows a whole lot more about football than he does."

"Everyone knows more about football than Conrad does."

"Theo knows how to organize the boys. He gained their respect just like that." He snapped his fingers and nodded. "I've got a whole lot of reasons why I want him to stay, but you know the one reason that tops all the others?"

"No, Daddy. What's that?" She had already made up her mind that if he said he hoped Theo would marry her and take her off his hands, she would walk out of the bar.

"He went out and bought a fence as a birthday present for Daryl's boy. You don't meet too many thoughtful men like Theo these days. And think about the money that fence must have set him back."

"I'll do my part, but please don't get your hopes up. Theo's going to go home, and nothing any of us do will change that."

"There's that negativity again. We've got to give it our best try, don't we? This town needs a good, honest lawyer, and Theo Buchanan fits the bill."

She nodded. "All right. How about tomorrow I make my étouffée?"

He looked appalled. "Oh, no, honey, don't do that. Serve him up Billie's gumbo. Remember the way to a man's heart is through his stomach."

"But you love my étouffée." Her shoulders slumped then. "You don't love it?"

He patted her shoulder. "You're my daughter and I love you. I had to tell you I like it."

"Do you know how long it takes to make that dish? All day," she told him before he could offer a guess. "You could have mentioned you didn't care for it before now."

"We didn't want to hurt your feelings, you being so tenderhearted and sensitive."

"Honestly, Daddy, you could have...Wait a minute. 'We'?"

"Your brothers and me. They love you too, honey. You're a fine cook with plain dishes, and your biscuits are still light and fluffy, but we need to dazzle the man now. Like I was telling you, the way to a man's heart..."

"Yes, I know...is through his stomach. That's hogwash, by the way."

"Oh? How do you think your mama nabbed me?"

When was she going to learn she could never win an argument with her father, no matter what she said? Finally admitting defeat, she said, "Her world famous bundt cake."

"That's right."

"I don't want to nab Theo the way Mama nabbed you."

"I know that. It's the town that wants to nab him."

"Okay, I'll do my part. I promise. Now, let me see if I've got this straight. Doing my part means I don't cook at all, I lie about the gumbo and tell Theo I made it, and, oh, yes, I'm sup-posed to be friendly. Do you want me to put a chocolate mint on his pillow tonight?"

Wrapping his arms around her, he gave her a big bear hug. "That might be overkill. Now, go sit, and I'll bring out supper for you and Theo."

Michelle didn't have another quiet minute for the next three hours. After she and Theo had eaten, she put on an apron and got to work cleaning the tables and helping carry out pitchers of cold beer. Theo was stuck sitting at the bar between two men clutching papers in their hands. A line had formed behind him. Daddy was leaning over the counter making the introductions.

More free legal advice, she thought. Myron had disappeared over an hour ago, and since her father was busy trying to manipulate Theo, she took over tending the bar.

By ten-thirty the kitchen was officially closed and cleaned, and the crowd had thinned out. There were only about a dozen people inside the bar when she removed her apron and went to the jukebox. She put in a quarter she'd taken from the cash register, punched B-12, and then sat down at a corner table she'd just cleared. She leaned her elbow on the table and propped her chin in the palm of her hand.

Her gaze kept going back to Theo. The big jerk looked so serious and adorable in his gray T-shirt and jeans. Did he have to be so sexy? And why couldn't she find something wrong with him so she could obsess about that and get over him. All she could think about was having sex with him. Oh, God, did that mean she was turning into a slut? The sex would be amazing. *Stop thinking about it. Think about something else.*

Another thought popped into her head that was even more depressing. Great. When he left—and he would leave—the town was going to blame her. Oh, they wouldn't say anything, but they'd all think it was her fault. She hadn't been friendly enough.

She wondered how they would all feel if they knew just how friendly she wanted to be. *Admit it, damn it. You're feeling sorry for yourself because he will go back to Boston and his oh-so-sophisticated life there, and you want him to stay in Bowen. Forever.*

Well, hell, how had that happened? How could she have been so stupid? Hadn't counting up all the reasons why she shouldn't fall for him meant anything? Evidently not. She'd been too naïve to pay attention to her own cautions. She was a strong woman, so why hadn't she been able to protect herself from him? Did she love him? Oh, Lord, what if she did?

Not possible, she decided. Love couldn't happen this quickly...could it?

Michelle was so busy worrying she didn't notice him coming toward her.

"You look like you lost your best friend. Come on. Dance with me."

Go away and let me wallow in self-pity. "Okay."

Theo dug a quarter out of his pocket, dropped it in the jukebox, told her to choose, and she promptly punched A-1.

The music started, but it wasn't until he had taken her into his arms that she realized that she'd made a big mistake. The last thing she needed now, in her vulnerable, feeling-sorry-for-herself state, was to be touched by him.

"You're as stiff as a board. Relax," he whispered against her ear.

"I am relaxed."

He gently shoved her head down and pulled her closer until their bodies were pressed together. Oh, boy. Big, big mistake. Too late now, she thought as she snuggled against him and curled her fingers around his neck. "I love this song."

"It sounds familiar, but that doesn't make any sense. I don't usually listen to country western music."

"It's Willie Nelson singing 'Blue Eyes Cryin' in the Rain.' "

He was nuzzling her cheek, driving her to distraction. "It's a nice song. I like it," he said.

She tried to pull back; he wouldn't let her. "It's a sad song," she said, cringing over how antagonistic she sounded.

They swayed slowly to the rhythm of the music.

"It's an old story," she explained.

"What's that?"

He kissed the sensitive spot just below her ear, giving her goose bumps. She trembled. He had to know what he was doing to her. Oh, God, she really was putty in his hands.

"It's about a woman who falls in love with a man and then he leaves her and she's..."

"Let me guess...crying in the rain?"

She could hear the laughter in his voice. His hand was gently stroking her back.

"How come he leaves her?"

"Because he's a big jerk." Too late she realized she'd said the thought out loud. She quickly added, "It's just a song. I'm only guessing. Maybe she actually left him, and she's so happy to be rid of him she's crying in the rain."

"Uh-huh."

She moved closer, her fingers softly rubbing the back of his neck in tiny circles.

"You should probably stop doing that."

"You don't like it?" She ran her fingertips through his hair as she asked the question.

"Yes, I do like it. That's why I want you to stop."

"Oh." So she could make him nuts too. That wonderful realization made her feel a little reckless.

"So, you probably don't want me to do this," she whispered, and kissed the pulse at the base of his neck.

"Michelle, I'm warning you. Two can play this game."

"What game?" she asked innocently, and then she kissed his neck again, tickling him with her tongue. She felt a bit daring. Daddy was in the kitchen, and no one was paying them any attention. Besides, Theo's big body pretty much concealed hers. That made her even more reckless, and she pressed even closer to him. "If you don't like what I'm doing…"

The challenge didn't go unanswered. "You're bad," he told her.

She sighed. "Thank you."

"You know what I like?"

"What's that?" A breathless whisper.

"I like the way you smell. When I get close to you, your scent drives me crazy and makes me think about all sorts of things I'd like to do."

She closed her eyes. *Don't ask. For the love of God, don't ask.* "What kinds of things?"

Until that moment, she had foolishly believed she'd been holding her own against a master. She had been the one to start the erotic conversation, and she knew from the way he was holding her that she'd definitely shaken him.

But then he began whispering in her ear, and she realized she was in way over her head. In a low, husky voice he told her exactly what he'd like to do to her. In his fantasies, she was, of course, the star, and every part of her body, including her toes, were featured players. The man had an active imagination, and he certainly wasn't shy about sharing. Michelle had no one to blame but herself. She *had* asked. But that didn't matter. By the time he finished describing several creative ways he would make love to her, the blood was roaring in her ears, her bones felt as if they'd turned into mush, and she had melted against him.

The song ended. He kissed her cheek, straightened, and let go of her. "Thanks for the dance. You want a beer or something? You look kind of flushed."

Kind of flushed? She felt as if it was a hundred fifty degrees inside the bar. When she looked into his eyes, she could tell that he knew exactly what he had just done to her.

"It's kind of stuffy in here. I think I'm gonna go outside and get some fresh air," he casually announced.

She watched him walk away. He had just pushed the door open and stepped outside when she went running after him.

"That's it."

She caught up with him outside, standing in the moonlight. She poked him between his shoulder blades and said it again, much louder this time. "That's it. You win."

He turned around. "Excuse me?"

She was so angry she poked him in the chest. "I said you win."

"Okay," he said calmly. "What did I win?"

"You know what I'm talking about, but since we're alone, why don't I spell it out? This game we've been playing. You win. I honestly thought I was holding my own, but obviously I was wrong. I'm just not good at it. Okay? So you win."

"What exactly do I win?"

"Sex."

He raised an eyebrow. "What?"

"You heard me. We're going to have sex, Theo Buchanan. Oops, I mean we're going to have great sex. Got that?"

A devilish smile crossed Theo's face, and then he seemed to stare off into space. Was he already thinking about making love, or couldn't he pay attention long enough to listen to her concede?

"Michelle, honey—"

"You're not paying attention, are you? I want to have sex with you. The bad kind," she qualified. "You know what I'm talking about. The hot, steamy, tear-our-clothes-off, mind-blowing, scream-out-loud sex. Like in the old song 'All Night Long,' that's you and me, babe. All night long. You name the time and the place, and I'm there."

She'd apparently rendered him speechless. That had to be a first. Maybe she wasn't so bad at this stuff after all. Theo just stared at her with that lopsided grin in place. She suddenly felt as cocky as a rooster getting ready to crow.

She folded her arms across her waist and demanded, "So? What have you got to say to that?"

He took a step toward her. "Michelle, I'd like you to meet an old friend of mine, Noah Clayborne. Noah, this is Michelle Renard."

He was bluffing. He *had* to be bluffing. She gave a tiny shake of her head. He nodded. She shook her head again, whispered, "Oh, God," and closed her eyes. This couldn't be happening.

She didn't want to turn around. She wanted to vanish into thin air. How long had he been standing there? Her face began to burn. She swallowed, then forced herself to turn.

He was there, all right. Tall, blond, amazing blue eyes, and a killer smile.

"It's nice to meet you," she stammered. Her voice sounded like she had laryngitis.

Until she'd turned, she hadn't thought it could get any worse. She was wrong about that. Her father was standing in the doorway, just a few feet away from Noah, and he was definitely close enough to have overheard what she'd said to Theo. Maybe he hadn't heard, though. Maybe he'd just gotten there. She gathered her courage and glanced at him. Daddy looked thunderstruck.

Michelle came up with a quick game plan. She would simply pretend it hadn't happened.

"Did you just get here?" she asked nonchalantly.

"Uh-huh," Noah drawled. "So, Theo, are all the pretty ladies in Bowen this friendly?"

The door slammed shut behind her father as he rushed forward. Now he appeared mortified. "When I said 'put out the welcome mat,' I thought you understood what I meant. There's friendly and then there's *real* friendly, and I raised you to know the difference."

"Daddy, Theo was flirting, and I was simply calling his bluff."

"I wasn't bluffing." Theo shrugged.

Her foot came down hard on top of his exactly one second later.

"Yes, you were," she said. "Honest, Daddy, I was just...teasing."

"We'll be talking about this later, young lady," Jake said as he turned and walked back inside.

Then Noah piped in. "Theo was flirting? You're kidding about that, aren't you?"

"He *was* flirting."

"We're talking about the guy standing behind you. Theo Buchanan?"

"Yes."

"It's hard to believe. I don't think he knows how to flirt."

"Oh, he's really good at it. Honest," she insisted.

"Yeah? It must be you, then. I was telling Jake that this is the first time in over five years that

I've seen Theo wearing anything but a suit and a tie. He's always been a workaholic for as long as I've known him. Maybe you bring out the *bad*," he said, drawing the word out, "in him."

She took a step back and bumped into Theo. She wasn't thinking about running, but she didn't like knowing he blocked her exit. "Could we please change the subject?" she asked.

Noah took pity on her. "Sure we can. Theo told me you're a doctor."

"Yes, that's right." Good, she was back on safe ground. Maybe Noah had some kind of medical problem and wanted her advice. God, she hoped so.

"What kind of a doctor are you?"

"She's a surgeon," Theo answered.

Noah grinned. "Aren't you kind of young to be playing with knives?"

"She operated on me."

Noah shrugged. Then he moved forward. "Dance with me. We'll find a nice Willie Nelson song and get to know each other."

He draped his arm around her shoulder and led her back inside. Theo stood there frowning as he watched the familiarity. Noah was a blatant womanizer. He'd made more conquests than Genghis Khan, and Theo didn't like seeing him work his charms on Michelle one bit.

She perked up. "You like Willie Nelson?"

"Sure I do. Everyone likes Willie."

She glanced back at Theo. "Your friend has good taste."

Then Noah drew her attention. "Could I ask you a question?"

She was so thankful she'd gotten past her embarrassment, she said, "You may ask me anything."

"I was just wondering..."

"Yes?"

"Is there any other kind of sex besides the *bad* kind?"

CHAPTER TWENTY-FOUR

Cameron knew he had screwed up, but he wasn't going to admit it. He leaned against the paneled wall of John's library, his head bowed, as Dallas and Preston and John took turns tearing into him.

"How long do you think it will take the doctor to remember she saw you at Catherine's funeral?" Preston asked as he jumped up from his chair. Slamming his powerful fist into the palm of his other hand, he paced back and forth across the room.

"She won't remember," Cameron muttered. "I was never anywhere near her at the funeral. Besides, I was sick of waiting, and I think the risk was worth it."

Dallas exploded. "How could it be worth the risk, you ass? You didn't get the package, and now you've got people looking for it. You're a mess, Cameron. It's the booze. It's fried your brain."

Preston stopped in front of him. "Now you've put us all in jeopardy," he shouted.

"Screw you," Cameron shouted back.

"Calm down," John ordered. "Dallas, get Monk on the phone. You need to read him that report."

Monk was sitting in his SUV waiting for the doctor and her lover to come out of The Swan. His vehicle was well concealed between two vans at the back of the parking lot. There were four cars in the next row in front of him. It was hot and muggy, but he didn't turn on the air conditioner. All four windows were down, and he was being eaten alive by mosquitoes. Compared to standing in the brush watching the doctor's house with bugs crawling up his legs, this watch was luxurious.

He was thinking about calling to tell Dallas about the latest developments, but just as he decided to wait until he got back to the motel, his cell phone began to vibrate.

"Yes?"

"Buchanan's a U.S. attorney."

Monk's head snapped up. "Repeat, please."

"The son of a bitch works for the Justice Department."

Expect the unexpected. Monk took a breath and waited as Dallas read the report. What the hell had the Sowing Club gotten him into? He could hear voices in the background.

"Where are you?" Monk asked.

"At John's house. We're all here."

"Who's shouting?"

"Preston."

He heard another voice yelling. He thought it might be Cameron. Monk was disgusted.

They were acting like rats turning on one another for a scrap of meat. If there hadn't been so much money involved, Monk would have walked away from this mess. Cameron had already become a loose cannon, and from the argument he was listening to now, he knew it wouldn't be long before the others began to disintegrate.

"I can't believe you didn't immediately run the report," Monk said. "You've wasted valuable hours."

"You told me he was a football coach...No, you're right. I won't make excuses or blame you. I should have run the report much earlier."

Monk was somewhat placated by Dallas's taking accountability.

"When can you kill him?" Dallas asked.

"Let me think," Monk said. "I don't like to be rushed. These things take time to plan, and I refuse to go off half-cocked. Spontaneity leads to mistakes. But if your report is accurate—"

"It is," Dallas rushed out.

"Then perhaps he's in Bowen simply because of her. Men will do crazy things for—"

Dallas interrupted him again. "A piece of ass? You think that after he gave that speech in New Orleans, he drove all that way just to get laid?"

"You haven't seen her," Monk said. "She's quite...lovely. Beautiful, in fact."

"Okay, so what you're saying is that this Justice guy is in town just to see her. Right? I mean, it does make sense, doesn't it? She does his surgery, saves his life, so he falls for her, and since he has to return to New Orleans anyway, he figures he might as well drive out to Bowen and screw her."

Monk puckered his lips in disapproval of Dallas's vulgar vocabulary. "Have you reevaluated, then?"

"Hold on," Dallas said. "John's saying something."

Monk patiently waited. He heard Preston arguing, shook his head, and reminded himself once again how much money was at stake.

"The doctor's got to be killed before she remembers where she's seen Cameron before," Dallas said. "Buchanan has had death threats, so John thinks we could make it look like a hit on him."

"And the doctor just happened to be with him and got in the way?"

"Exactly," Dallas said. "We're coming to Bowen tomorrow. You stay on the doctor until I call you. And watch for that package."

"Of course," he said smoothly. "And, Dallas, just so you know, I'll be reading those files before I hand them over."

"You're still concerned your name is there? It isn't. I read the damn thing twice. When this is over, you're going to be set for life. You know that, don't you, Monk?"

"Yes," he said. "I am curious about how much money is in that account, however. If it's as sizable as I imagine, I do believe I'm entitled to a percent. Call it profit sharing, if you like, but since I'm taking all the risks..."

Dallas responded to the greedy bastard's demand by hanging up on him.

CHAPTER TWENTY-FIVE

Theo certainly wasn't jealous. Teenage boys got jealous, and he was way beyond that stage in his life. He was getting irritated, though. Michelle was laughing and having a good old time dancing with Noah. Theo sat at the bar making notes while a man explained his problem. The guy had purchased a used car that had a thirty-day guarantee. The man paid cash, drove the car off the lot, but two blocks later the muffler fell off and the radiator exploded. Since he hadn't owned the vehicle for thirty minutes, he had it towed back to the lot and demanded his money back. The owner of the lot explained that the guarantee of satisfaction only covered the tires and the engine. He also suggested that, next time he purchased a car, he read the fine print before signing.

Michelle laughed again, drawing Theo's attention. He loved the sound of her voice, and from the way Noah was smiling at her, Theo figured he was enchanted too.

Once again turning back to the man sitting next to him, he tried to concentrate. When he glanced over at the couple for about the hundredth time, Noah had pulled up his T-shirt and was showing Michelle the ugly scar on his chest.

He muttered, "Enough," dropped his pen on the counter, and went over to put an end to the dance.

"You trying to impress Michelle with all your bullet holes?"

"I already impressed her with my wit and charm," Noah said.

She shook her head. "You were very lucky. That bullet should have killed you."

"I *was* lucky," he agreed. "God was looking out for me, I guess," he said. Then he laughed. "I was in church when I got hit."

She was sure he was joking. "Did you fall asleep during the sermon and make the minister mad?"

"Something like that."

"Daddy will want to hear that story," she said. "Where is he?"

"He's in the kitchen making sandwiches," Theo answered.

"You can't still be hungry after the catfish."

"He offered, said he was making one for himself. He's making one for Noah too."

Thinking to help her father, she went around the bar and headed to the kitchen. She heard Noah say, "By the way, Theo, you might want to look at the sign-up sheet for the fishing deal Saturday. The sheet's tacked to the wall over there."

"Why do I need to look at it?"

"You've been bumped."

"No way." Theo refused to believe him...until he looked. His name had been crossed off, and Noah's was written above it.

Michelle hurried into the kitchen. Her father handed her a paper plate filled with a double-decker turkey sandwich swimming in mayo and a huge mound of greasy french fries. He carried an identical plate out and set it on the counter.

"If Theo stays another couple of weeks, he'll have to have a bypass," she said. "You're killing the man with kindness."

"Turkey's not bad for you. You said so yourself."

"A jar of mayonnaise on it makes it bad," she said. "And there's a gallon of oil in those fries."

"That's what makes them good." Turning his back on her, he called, "All right, boys, here's your snack. I made the sandwiches without any of my hot barbecue sauce, Theo, just in case you were worried."

Noah and Theo were looking over the list. She nudged her father and whispered, "Did you trade Theo for Noah as your partner in the tournament?"

He looked guilty as sin. "Honey, I had to."

Incredulous, she asked, "Why?" She didn't give him time to answer. "How friendly was that, making a promise and then breaking it?"

"I was being practical."

"What does that mean?"

She followed him back into the kitchen. "Wrap up my sandwich for me, Mike, so I can take it home with me."

She got the foil out and did as he asked. "You still haven't answered me," she reminded him.

Jake leaned against the island and folded his arms. "The way I see it, we stand a better chance of winning if there's four of us trying for the prize instead of just two, and Noah was going to sweet-talk you into partnering with him. I didn't figure Theo would appreciate hearing that, so I told Noah I'd be his partner. Now you and Theo can spend the whole day together. You should be happy to be included."

He was exasperating. "In other words, that means you think Noah might be a better fisherman?"

"He did mention he's done a whole heck of a lot more fishing in the past four years, but that isn't the reason why I switched," he hastened to add when he saw that stubborn glint come into his daughter's eyes. "There isn't any reason to get in a snit about this. You should be thanking me for paying your fee."

"I don't want to fish Saturday. I have a hundred other things to do."

"You could win the prize. Everyone knows you're a better fisherman than I am."

She wasn't buying it. "That's not true, and you know it. Are you trying to play matchmaker? Is that why you want me to partner with Theo?"

"After the way I heard you talking to him? I don't need to do any matchmaking. You're holding your own just fine."

"Daddy, I was teasing..."

He acted as though he hadn't heard her. "Noah might be doing a little matchmaking. He told me he's never seen Theo acting like he does around you."

289

That remark got her full attention. Her father nodded, then went to the refrigerator to get some milk. He poured himself a full glass and took a long swallow.

"How does Theo act?" she asked.

"Noah says he's smiling a lot. I got the feeling that's a rarity."

"The man's on vacation. That's why he's smiling. Is your stomach bothering you? You only drink milk when you have indigestion."

"My stomach's just fine," he said impatiently, and then went right back to the subject at hand. "And when it comes to Theo, you've got a reason for everything. So explain this: How come he can't take his eyes off you? Noah noticed, and after he pointed it out to me, I took notice too." Before she could argue, he said, "Did you know that Noah works for the FBI? He wears a gun, just like Theo's. I saw it clipped to his waistband. I'm telling you, Theo has some real influential friends."

"And you know a lot of people who need help from influential friends."

Jake finished his milk and set the glass in the sink. When he turned around, she noticed in the harsh overhead light how tired he looked.

"Why don't you go home now and let Theo and me close up."

"I can see to it."

"I know you can, but the next couple of days are going to be busy. People are going to be stopping in to sign up and eat, and you know how crowded it gets in here on Thursday and

290

Friday. Go home, Daddy. Get off your feet and rest."

"You need your rest too. You've got to start working on those papers at the clinic."

"I'll have help."

"All right, then," he said. "I am tired, so I'll go on home. You shut down at one instead of two."

He leaned down and kissed her cheek. "I'll see you tomorrow."

He opened the back door, then closed it. "Oh, I forgot to tell you that Ben Nelson called looking for you. He still doesn't have any news or any suspects, but he's going to keep an eye out just in case something else bad happens. Now, I ask you, is that something you want to say to a father? He had me worried sick about you, but then I remembered Theo is staying with you. You turn your deadbolts tonight." He reopened the door and stepped out into the moonlight. "It's a comfort," he said.

"What's a comfort?"

"Knowing Theo's going to be there with you."

Michelle nodded. It was a comfort. She locked the door, flipped off the light, and went back into the bar. Theo and Noah had carried their plates over to one of the round tables and were eating their sandwiches.

One of the regulars wanted a refill. She noticed how bleary-eyed he was and asked, "Are you driving home tonight, Paulie?"

"Connie's coming by to pick me up after her shift's over at the plant. She's my designated driver tonight."

"Okay, then," she said, smiling. She poured another glass of beer, noticed how stuffy it was inside, and turned up the speed on the overhead fan. There were only five customers in The Swan. She made sure everyone was happy, then filled two tall glasses with ice water and carried them over to Noah and Theo.

Theo pulled a chair out. "Sit with us."

She handed Noah his water, then sat down between him and Theo and put Theo's glass next to his plate.

"I hope you don't mind, but I sent Daddy home, which means I have to close up the bar tonight," she said.

"It's so damned cute that you call your dad 'Daddy.' Is that a southern thing?" Noah asked.

"It's a Renard thing," she said.

Noah had just popped the last of his french fries into his mouth and was washing it down with a big gulp of water when she asked him if he wanted her to accompany him to her clinic to survey the damage.

"I've already been there. I think Theo's right. Kids didn't do it. It was a one-man operation. And whoever it was got real frustrated looking for something. Did you notice the desk? The lock was destroyed. Somebody took a long time working at that lock."

"Michelle thinks maybe it's one of Robinson's patients trying to steal his file."

"Couldn't a patient simply ask for his records?" Noah asked.

"He could get a copy of his records, but I would keep the original," Michelle answered.

292

"I doubt it was a patient. Patient charts are confidential. Everyone knows that. Whatever is in the charts stays private. And why would a patient go to such extremes tearing the place up? If he wanted his records so badly, all he had to do was break in and lift it out from those boxes. No, I don't think it was a patient, but what does Robinson say? Did he have any pain-in-the...difficult patients?"

"He hasn't returned my call yet," Michelle told him. "I'll try again in the morning. He recently moved to Phoenix, and he's probably busy getting settled."

"Why don't you give Noah his phone number and let him talk to him," Theo suggested. "People tend to sit up and take notice when the FBI calls. And on my worst day I couldn't be as abrasive as he can be. He's better at coercion."

"Yeah, right." Noah scoffed at the notion. Turning to Michelle, he said, "I've seen Theo make grown men cry. It was kind of funny actually...watching a coldhearted killer, who happens to be the head of a crime organization, blubber like a baby."

"He's exaggerating," Theo said.

"No, I'm not," Noah argued. "However, it is true that the average person doesn't know what the attorneys over in Justice do. Come to think about it, I'm not so sure I know. Besides making criminals cry, what exactly do you do, Theo?"

"Not much," he answered dryly. "We drink a lot..."

"That's a given."

"And try to think of things for you guys to do."

"I'll bet you do." Turning to Michelle, Noah added, "Those lazy Justice attorneys make the dedicated FBI agents do all the hard work."

Theo smiled. "It's called delegating. We do it so the little people won't feel left out."

The insults began to fly, and some of the outrageous things they said were hilarious. Vastly amused, she sat back and relaxed. When the subject eventually returned to her clinic, she said, "I'm not going to worry about this any longer. I've been blowing this out of proportion."

"How's that?" Noah asked.

"I was so spooked after I saw the mess, I thought I was being followed. You know that feeling you get? It's hard to explain."

"I'd pay attention to that feeling if I were you," Noah said.

"But no one was following me," she insisted. "I would have spotted him...wouldn't I?"

"Not if he's good," Noah said.

"This is a very small community. Strangers would stick out."

"Yeah? What about a man driving a van with maybe a cable company logo on the side? Would he stick out? And what about all the men and women who come here to fish? If they were dressed in fishing gear and carrying a pole, would you think they didn't belong?"

Michelle stood. "I see your point, and I appreciate your taking the time to look at the clinic, but I really believe this was just an isolated incident."

"And that belief is based on what?" Theo asked. "Wishful thinking?"

She ignored his sarcasm. "This is Bowen," she said. "If anyone had a problem with me, he'd tell me so. Now that I've had time to think about it, I didn't start jumping at shadows until after I saw the clinic. I overreacted. I will remind you," she hastened to add when he looked as though he was going to interrupt, "that nothing else has happened. You want to find a conspiracy, and there just isn't one." Turning to Noah, she said, "I do thank you for coming to Bowen."

"You don't need to thank me," Noah said. "To be honest, I only did the favor to get a favor. Theo's agreed to drive back to Biloxi with me. He's going to give a lecture for me, and I would have driven cross country to get out of that. I still have to go finish the training session, but at least I don't have to write a speech."

"When do you have to be back?"

"Monday."

"Oh." She turned away before either of them could see her disappointment.

Noah watched her walk away. "Damn, Theo, she's something else. If we were going to stay around for a while, I'd give you a run for your money. I've always been a sucker for redheads."

"You're a sucker for anything that wears a skirt."

"That's not true. Remember the Donovan case? Patty Donovan always wore skirts, and that didn't do anything for me."

Theo rolled his eyes. "Patty was a transvestite. He didn't turn anyone on."

"He had good legs. I'll give him that," Noah drawled. "So tell me something. What's happening with you and Michelle?"

"Nothing's happening."

"That's a shame."

"You never told me the topic of the lecture I'm giving," Theo said in hopes of getting Noah to change the subject. "What is it?"

Noah grinned. "Anger management."

Theo laughed. "Was this your boss's idea of a joke?"

"Sure it was," he said. "You know Morganstern. He's got a twisted sense of humor. He's making me run the training program to punish me."

"What'd you do?"

"You don't want to know." Noah paused and then said, "Morganstern could use a man like you."

"Ah, the hidden agenda comes out at last. Did Pete ask you to talk to me?"

Noah shrugged. "He might have mentioned…"

"Tell him I'm not interested."

"He likes the way your mind works."

"I'm not interested," Theo reiterated.

"You're happy where you are?"

Theo shook his head. "I'm done. All used up," he said. "I'm going back to the office, tie up loose ends, and hand in my resignation."

Noah was stunned. "You aren't kidding, are you?"

"No, I'm not kidding. It's time...past time," he corrected.

"Then what are you going to do?"

"I've got a couple of ideas."

"Does one of those ideas have red hair?"

Theo didn't answer. Before Noah could press, a man came over to the table and asked Theo if he could talk to him about a legal matter.

"Sure," Theo said. "Let's sit at the bar."

He got up, rolled his shoulders to work the kinks out, and then went behind the bar to pour himself a beer. "What can I do for you?" he asked the young man.

Five minutes later, Theo wanted to punch the man. Noah saw Theo's expression and went behind the bar to find out what was wrong. He heard Theo say, "Jake didn't suggest that you talk to me, did he?"

"No, but I heard you were helping people who had legal troubles."

"What's the problem?" Noah asked. He opened a long-neck bottle of beer, tossed the cap in the trash, and walked over to stand next to Theo.

"This is Cory," Theo said. "He's got two kids. A boy and a girl."

Noah squinted at the unpleasant-looking man. He looked more like a grungy teenager than a father of two children. Cory had long dirty blond hair that hung down in his eyes, and yellow stained teeth.

"How old are you?" Noah asked.

"I'll be twenty-two next month."

"And you've already got two kids?"

"That's right. I got divorced from Emily over six months ago because I met another woman I wanted to be with. Her name's Nora, and she and me want to get married. I've moved on, but Emily thinks I ought to keep paying child support, and that don't seem fair to me."

"So you want me to help you figure out a way you can get out of paying child support?"

"Yeah, that's right. That's what I want. I mean, they're her kids now. They're living with her, and like I said, I'm ready to move on."

The muscle in Theo's jaw flexed. Michelle was standing in the kitchen doorway, holding an empty pitcher in her hand. She'd heard the conversation and knew from the way Theo's back had stiffened that he was angry.

His voice continued to be quite mild and pleasant as he remarked to Noah, "Cory's ready to move on."

"Are *you* ready for him to move on?" Noah asked as he set his beer bottle on the counter.

"Sure am," Theo said.

Then Noah smiled. "Let me."

"You can get the door."

Michelle started forward, then stopped. Theo moved so quickly she was astonished. One second he was smiling at Noah and the next he was around the bar, had Cory by the nape of his neck and the back of his jeans, and was dragging him across the floor. Noah raced ahead and opened the door, then got out of the way so Theo could toss the man outside.

"Now, that's what I call moving on," Noah drawled as he shut the door behind him. "The little prick."

"He is that."

"You know what I wonder? How could such a butt-ugly man get two women to sleep with him?"

Theo laughed. "No accounting for taste, I guess."

The two men were walking toward the bar when the door behind them opened again and three men rushed inside. The last of the three looked like a bouncer who'd taken one too many hits in the face. The man was huge, at least six foot four, and his nose obviously had been broken several times in the past. He was frighteningly mean looking and carried a baseball bat.

"Which one of you assholes is Theo Buchanan?"

Noah had already turned. He had his eye on the baseball bat. Michelle saw him reach behind his back and unsnap the holster housing his gun.

The bar emptied. Even Paulie, who had never been known to do anything in a hurry, made it out the front door in less than five seconds.

"Michelle, go into the kitchen and shut the door," Theo said before he turned around. "I'm Theo Buchanan. Now, which one of you is Jim Carson?"

"That'd be me," the shortest of the three announced.

Theo nodded. "I've been hoping you'd stop by."

"Just who do you think you are?" Jim railed.

"I just told you who I am. Weren't you paying attention?"

"A real smartass, huh? You think you can lock up my money and fix it at my bank so I can't even get a nickel out? You think you can do that?"

"I *did* do that," Theo calmly pointed out.

Jim Carson looked like his brother. He was short, squat, with eyes that were a little too closely set in his moon-shaped face. He didn't smile like his brother, though. While Gary oozed false sincerity, Jim was the master of vulgarity. He took another threatening step toward Theo and let loose with a string of grossly obscene blasphemies.

Then he said, "You're going to be sorry you interfered in my business. Gary and I are going to shut down the mill, and then this town will lynch you."

"I'd worry about my neck if I were you. How long have you been telling your employees you're on the verge of bankruptcy? Imagine how...disappointed people will be when they find out what your annual take is and what you have squirreled away."

"Our assets are confidential information," Jim yelled. "You might know about our money, but you're an outsider trying to cause trouble, and if you tell anyone, they won't believe you. No one will."

"People tend to believe what's written in the paper, don't they?"

"What are you saying?"

"I wrote a nice little editorial that's going to be in Sunday's paper. Of course, I want it to be as accurate as possible," he added. "So, why don't I fax you over a copy of it tomorrow, and you can check it. Personally, I think it's some of my best work. I listed every cent in every account that you've made over the past five years."

"You can't do that. It's confidential." Jim was shouting now.

Theo glanced at Noah. "You know, I should have added their tax returns for the past five years too. I guess I still could."

"You're finished, Buchanan. I'm not going to let you cause any more trouble."

Jim was so angry, his brow was dripping with sweat. The man had worked himself into a lather, and it was obviously infuriating to him that Theo was unimpressed with his tantrum.

"I've only just started making trouble, Jim. When I'm finished with you and your brother, the employees are going to own the mill. It's going to happen fast too," he added. "And you will be living on the streets. That's a promise."

"You want to put that baseball bat down now?" Noah asked the giant with the nose splattered all over his homely face.

"Shit, no. I'm not putting this bat down before I use it. Isn't that right, Mr. Carson?"

"That's right, Happy."

Theo laughed. "Happy?"

"We live in a strange world," Noah replied.

"I'm supposed to break Buchanan's legs with this bat, and that's what I'm gonna do. I'm gonna hurt you too," he told Noah. "So you better stop laughing at me, because you're gonna be sorry."

Noah was now keeping a wary eye on the third man. He was almost as tall as the giant, but had a thin, wiry frame and large cauliflower ears. Both backup men looked like street fighters, but in Noah's opinion, Cauliflower was the real threat. He probably was carrying a concealed weapon. Oh, yes, he was the one who could give him real trouble, and he was apparently the surprise element Jimmy Boy had brought along in the event Happy didn't get the job done.

The bruiser was slapping the butt of the baseball bat in the palm of his hand. The smacking noise irritated Noah.

"Put the bat down," he ordered once again.

"Not before I break a couple of bones."

Noah suddenly smiled. He looked as if he'd just won the lottery. "Hey, Theo, you know what?"

"What?"

"I'd call Happy's remarks threats. Wouldn't you say they were threats? I mean, you'd know, since you're a lawyer in Justice, and I'm just a lowly little FBI agent. Those were threats. Right?"

Theo knew exactly what Noah's game was. He was letting the three men know who they were so they couldn't say they hadn't been informed when they were locked up.

"Yeah, I'd have to say they are."

"Listen, smartass," Jim said, addressing Noah, "you get in my way, and I'm going to enjoy hurting you too." He stabbed the air in front of Noah's face with his stubby finger.

Noah wasn't paying him any attention. "Maybe we ought to let one of them hit us," he suggested to Theo. "It would probably look better in court."

"I can make the case without getting hit. Unless you want to get hit."

"No, I don't want to get hit. I'm just saying…"

"You think this is a game, sonny?" Jim was bellowing now. He took yet another step forward, poked Noah in the shoulder, and said, "I'll wipe that smug smile off your face, you son of a—"

He didn't get a chance to finish the threat. Noah moved so fast, Jim didn't even have time to blink. But then again, blinking was definitely out of the question. He cried out, then froze and stared with one wide eye at Noah. The barrel of Noah's Glock was pressed snugly against his other eyelid.

"What were you going to say about my mother?" Noah asked softly.

"Nothing…nothing at all," Jim stammered.

Happy swung the bat in a wide arc while Cauliflower pivoted on his heel and reached inside his jacket.

The loud click of the shotgun as it was being pumped reverberated throughout The

Swan. The noise gained everyone's full attention.

Noah kept his gun pressed against Carson's face as he glanced behind him. Michelle was leaning against the counter with a shotgun aimed at Cauliflower. Theo moved in and grabbed the weapon from the thug's waistband. Then he looked at Michelle.

"I asked you to go to the kitchen."

"Yes, I heard you ask."

Cauliflower tried to grab his gun. "I've got a permit for that. Give it back to me."

"That's such a stupid thing to say," Theo muttered. Cauliflower lunged. Theo pivoted and using two knuckles chopped Cauliflower just below his Adam's apple. The man reeled back, and as he turned, Theo struck him on the back of his neck. Cauliflower collapsed, out cold on the floor. "I can't abide stupid people."

"I hear you," Noah said. "Jim, I'm gonna have to shoot you if Happy doesn't put that bat down real soon."

"Do it, Happy."

"But, Mr. Carson, you told me—"

"Forget what I told you. Drop the bat." He tried to back away from the gun, but Noah simply followed.

"Please put that away. I don't want you to accidentally shoot my brains out."

"That's assuming you have a brain," Noah said. "I'm not so sure about that. What were you thinking, coming in here with your hired hands? Are you so cocky you didn't worry about witnesses? Or are you too stupid to care?"

"I was mad...I wasn't thinking...I just wanted..."

He stopped stammering as soon as Noah removed the Glock. Then Jim, making up for lost time, began to blink furiously.

"Is Harry dead?" Jim asked. "If you killed Harry..."

"He's still breathing," Noah said. "Don't make me ask again, Happy. Get rid of the bat."

Happy looked decidedly unhappy as he threw the bat hard at the table next to him. Since he couldn't break any legs, he decided he wanted to break some property. Then maybe Jim Carson would still pay him. The baseball bat struck the edge of the table, bounced back, and struck Happy's foot. He let out a yelp and started hopping around as though he were playing a game of hopscotch.

Theo handed Harry's weapon to Noah and rubbed the sting out of his knuckles. "Put Jim in the chair," he added before striding to the bar. He looked at Michelle now. "Michelle, what the hell are you doing with a sawed-off shotgun? Put that down before you hurt someone." Then he got closer to her and noticed how modified the weapon was. "Where did you get this?"

"It's Daddy's."

"Okay," he said, holding his patience. "Where did Daddy get it?"

He was suddenly acting like a Justice attorney and making her feel as if she were the criminal.

"Daddy's never fired the thing. He will occasionally wave it around when he thinks there might be a bar fight."

"Answer my question."

"John Paul gave it to Daddy for protection. He taught both of us how to use it."

"You can't have this. It's illegal."

"I'll put it away."

"No, you'll give it to Noah and let him get rid of it for you." He took the weapon from her. "This sucker could take down a rhino at a hundred yards."

"Or an alligator," she remarked.

"Oh? Have there been many alligators fighting in the bar lately?"

"No, of course not, but—"

"You know how many years your dad could get for this?"

She folded her arms across her waist. "We do things different in Bowen."

"Last I heard, Bowen was part of the United States, and that means you follow the same rules. Where did your brother get hold of something like this?"

"Don't you dare think about giving my brother trouble, Theo. He's a kind, gentle, sensitive man, and I won't let you—"

He wasn't in the mood to hear a glowing testament. "Answer my question."

"I don't know where he got it. For all I know, he made the thing, and if you take this one away, John Paul will only give Daddy another one just like it."

Theo's eyelid twitched. She knew she was upsetting him, but at the moment she didn't particularly care. What was Daddy supposed to do when things got out of hand in The

Swan? Wring his hands while they tore his bar apart? Besides, her father would never shoot anyone, but the sound of the shotgun being pumped was always enough to discourage hotheads.

"That's just the way things are around here."

"Your father and your brother are breaking the law."

"The shotgun's mine," she announced then. "I made it, and I put it under the counter. Daddy doesn't even know it's there. So go ahead. Turn me in."

"It's not nice to lie to an employee of the Justice Department, sweetheart."

"I'll keep that in mind."

"And just where would your brother learn about weapons like this?"

"He doesn't like to talk about it, but he once told Daddy he was part of a specialized team in the marines."

"Specialized? No kidding."

"Now isn't the time to discuss my family, and it's really none of your business anyway."

"Oh, yes, it is."

"Why?"

He moved closer, pinning her against the counter. He leaned down until he was just an inch above her and whispered, "Don't push me."

It took him all of five seconds to realize he wasn't going to win. She couldn't be intimidated, at least by him. She stood her ground and looked him right in the eyes. As galling as it was to admit, he knew he was going to have to be the one to back down. It was a first for him, and it wasn't pleasant.

"Do you want me to call the police?" she asked.

"I'm not going to have you arrested."

Exasperated, she said, "I wasn't talking about me. I thought you might want the police to come and get the Three Stooges over there."

"What? Oh...yeah, call them, but wait a couple of minutes. I want to do some negotiating first."

Noah had put his gun away and was standing over Jim. Theo grabbed a chair, turned it to face him, and sat down.

"Have you got your phone with you?"

"What if I do?" Jim asked, antagonistic once again.

"Call your brother and tell him to get over here."

"You can't tell me what to do."

"Yes, I can," Theo said. "You're in a hell of a lot of trouble. You threatened an FBI agent and that means jail time."

"Tell it to my lawyers," Jim blustered, though his face had lost some of its color. "They'll fix it so I don't do a day behind bars."

"I don't know too many attorneys who will work pro bono. I doubt they'll do anything to help you once they hear you don't have any money to pay them."

Jim pulled out his cell phone and punched

in his brother's number. "He won't come," he told Theo. "Gary doesn't like anything unpleasant."

"Tough. You tell Gary he has ten minutes to get here, or I'll have the police pick him up at home and take him with you to jail. You boys are either going to negotiate now or sit in a cell and think about it for a couple of months. And trust me, Jim. I've got the clout to keep you there."

Gary apparently answered his phone. Jim's voice shook when he said, "You've got to get over to The Swan right away. Don't argue. Just do it. I'll explain when you get here."

He listened for a few seconds, then said, "Hell, no, it didn't go as planned. Buchanan and another fella are FBI, and they're threatening to lock both of us up." He listened for another minute, then shouted, "A bit of bad luck? You call the FBI a bit of bad luck? Stop yapping and get on over here." He slapped the phone closed and glared at Theo. "He's on his way."

Noah spotted the police car pulling into the parking lot. "Cops are here," he told Theo.

Michelle grabbed the shotgun and put it back under the counter on the bracket. "I didn't call Ben yet," she said.

Harry was still unconscious, but he was breathing. Happy was hunched over one of the tables in the corner, his head in his hands.

Noah went outside. He came in a couple of minutes later with Ben Nelson. He had obviously filled the policeman in on the particulars, because Ben barely spared Harry a glance. His gaze and his smile were on Michelle.

"Are you all right?" he asked, his concern apparent.

"I'm fine, Ben. Who called you?" she asked. "Was it Paulie?"

"No one called me. I just came by to see you."

Theo didn't like hearing that. Ben was on his way to the bar, but Theo stood, effectively blocking his path. Michelle made the introductions, though it wasn't necessary. Theo already knew who Ben was. He was the man who wanted Michelle.

Theo had never paid much attention to another man's appearance, and he really didn't know if women would consider Ben handsome or not. He had an easy smile and all of his teeth, and that was about as far as Theo went sizing him up. Ben seemed like a nice guy too. That didn't matter, though. Theo noticed the way he smiled at Michelle and took an instant dislike to him. He had to force himself not to be hostile as he shook his hand and let him know who was in charge.

Noah watched the two men with a good deal of amusement. They were posturing like roosters getting ready for a fight. It didn't take Noah any time at all to figure out why.

"I understand you're staying at Michelle's house." Ben wasn't smiling now.

"That's right. I am."

"How long do you plan to be in town, Mr. Buchanan?"

"I'm not sure how long. Why do you want to know, Chief Nelson?"

"We've got several nice motels over in St. Claire."

"Is that right?"

"Theo's leaving Monday," Michelle announced. "Aren't you?" she added, a challenging note in her voice.

"Maybe."

The noncommittal response irritated her. "He's giving a speech in Biloxi." She didn't know why she felt compelled to share that information. "So he will be leaving Monday morning."

"Maybe," Theo repeated.

The word had the same effect as the sound of a dentist's drill. She wanted to cringe. Worried she would say something she would regret if Theo uttered that word one more time, she made a hasty retreat. Grabbing the empty iced tea pitcher, she excused herself and went into the kitchen.

While Theo explained to Ben who Harry and Happy were, Noah read the thugs their rights and then used Ben's handcuffs to secure them.

"What about Jim Carson?" Ben asked. "Are you going to be pressing charges against him?"

Theo knew Jim was listening. "I sure am," he said. "But I want him to stay here until his brother arrives. I want to talk to both of them. If they don't cooperate..." He deliberately left the sentence hanging.

"I'm going to cooperate," Jim cried out.

311

Ben was a better man than Theo. He shook his hand before he left. Theo decided then that he'd acted like a jealous lover and needed to shape up.

"Thanks for your help," he called out as Ben followed Happy out the door. Noah had already shaken Harry awake and had half dragged him to the police car.

Theo glanced toward the kitchen, saw Michelle working at the sink, and then pulled out a chair and straddled it while he waited for the other Carson brother to arrive.

Michelle had decided she needed to get busy so she could take her mind off of Theo. She filled the stainless steel sink with hot water and soap, put on rubber gloves, and started scrubbing. Her father had already cleaned the kitchen, but she went over every surface again.

When she was removing her gloves, she noticed a spot of grease up on the copper overhead exhaust. She spent the next half hour taking the unit apart and cleaning every nook and cranny. Getting it back together took twice as long because she had to keep stopping to check the bar in case a customer wanted something.

On one of her trips, she saw Gary Carson come in, flanked by his attorneys.

She returned to the kitchen and scrubbed some more. Then she washed her rubber gloves—how compulsive was that? she wondered, and realized she was more revved up now than weary. What she needed, she decided, was a good, long surgery. When she was cutting, nothing got in her way. She could block the conversation swirling around her, the lame jokes, the laughter—everything but Willie Nelson because he soothed her—and she and Willie stayed in that isolated cocoon until she'd put in the last stitch. Only then did she let the world intrude.

"Get a grip," she muttered.

"Did you say something?"

Noah was standing in the doorway. He went to the sink and put three glasses on the counter.

"No, nothing," she said. "What time is it?"

"A little after one. You look tired."

She blew a strand of hair out of her eye as she dried her hands on a towel. "I'm not tired. How much longer do you think Theo will be?"

"Not long," he said. "You want me to take you home? Theo can close up."

She shook her head. "I'll wait."

Noah started to leave, then turned. "Michelle?"

"Yes?"

"Monday's a lifetime away."

CHAPTER TWENTY-SIX

As soon as Monk was back in his motel room, he called New Orleans.

Waking from a deep sleep, Dallas answered the phone, "What?"

"The surprises just keep on coming," Monk said.

"What are you talking about?"

"There's an FBI agent here with Buchanan."

"Oh my God. Give me the name."

"I don't have it yet. I heard some guys talking about him when they came out of the bar."

"So do you know what he's doing there?"

"Not yet, but it looks like they were talking about fishing."

Apprehensive, Dallas said, "Just hang tight, and I'll get back to you."

"Oh, by the way," Monk said, "I have some other information that may come in handy."

"It better be good," Dallas answered.

Monk gave an account of the Carson brothers and the two bone breakers who had gone into the bar.

"I heard one of the men tell the policeman that he wasn't going to kill Buchanan. He just wanted to hurt him. With a little planning, we might be able to use the Carsons as a scapegoat if necessary."

"Yes. Thanks."

"My pleasure," he answered sarcastically.

Monk hung up the phone, set his alarm

clock, and then closed his eyes. He fell asleep thinking about the money.

CHAPTER TWENTY-SEVEN

For the first time in her life, Michelle couldn't sleep, and it was all Theo Buchanan's fault. Everything, including the national debt, was his fault when it was the middle of the night and she was sleep-deprived because she couldn't stop thinking about him.

She tossed and turned, beat her pillows, then tossed and turned some more. Her bed looked as though a cyclone had hit. To take her mind off her lustful thoughts, she changed the sheets, then took a long, hot shower. Neither chore made her sleepy. She went downstairs then and drank warm milk—she could barely get the vile stuff down and wondered how anyone could drink milk warm when it tasted so much better cold.

Theo hadn't made a sound since he'd closed his bedroom door. He was probably sound asleep and dreaming the dreams of the innocent. The big jerk.

Michelle crept back upstairs so she wouldn't disturb him, brushed her teeth again, then opened one of her bedroom windows so she could hear the sounds of the approaching thunderstorm.

She put on a pink silk nightgown—the green cotton one felt scratchy against her shoulders—then slipped between the sheets and vowed she wasn't going to get up again. Her nightgown was bunched up around her hips. She smoothed it down, adjusted the spaghetti straps so they wouldn't droop down over her arms. There, everything was perfect. Folding her hands together over her stomach, she closed her eyes and took deep, calming breaths. She stopped when she got dizzy.

She felt a wrinkle in the bottom sheet under her ankle. *Don't think about it,* she told herself. *It's time to sleep. Relax, damn it.*

Another fifteen minutes passed and she was still wide awake. Her skin was hot, the sheets felt damp from the humidity, and she was so tired she wanted to cry.

Desperate, she started counting sheep but stopped that game as soon as she realized she was racing to get them all accounted for. Counting sheep was like chewing gum. She never chewed gum because, in a subconscious attempt to get finished, she would chew faster and faster, which of course defeated the whole notion of chewing gum in the first place.

Lord, the things a person will think about when that person is losing her ever-loving mind. She should have specialized in psychiatry, she decided. Then maybe she could figure out why she was turning looney tunes.

Television. That was it. She'd watch television. There was never anything good on TV in the middle of the night. Surely someone was selling something on one of the channels.

An infomercial was just what she needed. It was better than a sleeping pill.

She threw the sheet off, grabbed the afghan from the bottom of her bed, and dragged it across the room. The door squeaked when she opened it. Why hadn't she noticed that noise before? she wondered. Tossing the afghan onto the chair, she went out into the hallway, got down on her knees, and slowly pulled the door closed. She thought the bottom hinge was making the groaning sound and leaned close to listen as she moved the door back and forth.

That was the one, all right. She decided then to check the top hinge. She stood, grabbed the doorknob again, and moved the door back and forth while leaning in on tiptoes to listen. Sure enough, it was making a little squeaking sound too. Now where had she put that can of WD-40? She could fix this problem right this minute if she could just remember where she'd last seen that can. Wait a minute...the garage. That's where it was. She'd put it up on the shelf in the garage.

"Having trouble sleeping?"

He nearly scared her to death. She jumped, inadvertently pulled the door, and hit her head against it. "Ouch," she whispered as she let go of the handle and reached up to feel if her scalp was bleeding.

Then she turned around. She couldn't have gotten another word out if her life had depended on it. Theo stood in his doorway, casually leaning against the frame with his arms folded across his bare chest and one bare foot crossed over the other. His hair was tousled, his face needed a shave, and he looked as though he'd just been awakened from a deep sleep. He had pulled on a pair of Levi's, but hadn't bothered to zip them.

He was simply irresistible.

She stared at the narrow opening between the zipper, then realized she was staring and forced herself to look away. She settled on his chest, realized that was a mistake, and ended up staring at his feet. He had great feet.

Oh, boy, did she need help. Now his feet were turning her on. She needed therapy, intense therapy, to help her figure out how any man could make her so nuts.

He wasn't just any man, though. All along she'd known how dangerous the attraction was. It was the damned fence, she decided. If he hadn't bought the damned fence for little John Patrick, she might have been able to continue to resist him. Too late now. She let out a little groan. Theo was still a big jerk, but she'd fallen for him anyway.

She swallowed hard. He looked good enough to...don't go there. Then she looked into his eyes. She wanted him to scoop her up into his muscular arms, kiss her senseless, and carry her to bed. She wanted him to take her night-gown off and caress every inch of her body. Maybe she would toss him on the bed, take his Levi's off, and caress every inch of his body. She wanted to—

"Michelle, what are you doing? It's two-thirty in the morning."

Her fantasy came to a screeching halt. "Your door doesn't squeak."

"What?" he asked.

She shrugged, then pushed a strand of hair away from her face. "I didn't hear you because your door didn't make any noise when you opened it. How long have you been standing there?"

"Long enough to watch you play with your door."

"It squeaks."

"Yes, I know, the door squeaks."

"I'm sorry, Theo. I didn't mean to disturb you, but since you're awake..."

"Yes?"

"You want to play cards?"

He blinked. Then that slow, easy smile appeared, and she started feeling light-headed.

"No, I don't want to play cards. Do you?"

"Not really."

"Then why did you ask?"

The way he was staring at her with that penetrating gaze of his made her extremely nervous, but it was the good kind of nervous she'd felt just before he'd kissed her the night before, which meant that it was bad, because she'd never wanted the kiss to end, and what kind of convoluted sense did that make? She was losing her mind, all right. She wondered if she could schedule her patient appointments from the psychiatric ward.

"Please stop looking at me like that." Her toes curled into the carpet, and she felt her stomach doing back flips.

"Like what?"

"I don't know," she muttered. "I can't sleep. So do you want to do something until I get sleepy?"

"What did you have in mind?"

"Besides cards?" she asked nervously.

"Uh-huh."

"I could fix you a sandwich."

"No thanks."

"Pancakes," she said then. "I could fix you pancakes."

On a scale of one to ten, her anxiety was climbing past nine. Did he have any idea how much she wanted him? *Just don't think about it. Keep busy.* "I make great pancakes."

"I'm not hungry."

"What do you mean, you're not hungry? You're always hungry."

"Not tonight."

I'm drowning here, babe. Work with me. She caught her lower lip between her teeth while she frantically tried to come up with another idea.

"Television," she suddenly blurted, acting as though she'd just correctly answered the million-dollar question and Regis was handing her the check.

"What?"

"Would you like to watch television?"

"No." She felt as if he'd just snatched the lifeline out of her hands.

She sighed. "Then you think of something."

"Something we could do together? Until you get sleepy."

"Yes."

"I want to go to bed."

She didn't try to mask her disappointment. She guessed she was going to go back to counting those damn smelly sheep. "Okay. Good night, then."

He didn't go back into his bedroom, though. Pulling away from the doorway with the agility of a big, lazy, well-fed cat, he closed the distance between them in two long strides. His toes touched hers as he reached behind her and opened her bedroom door. He smelled faintly of aftershave, Dial soap, and man, and she found the combination extremely arousing. Who was she kidding? At this point, a sneeze would turn her on.

He took hold of her hand, but his grip was light. She could have easily pulled away if she'd wanted to, but she didn't. In fact, she held tight.

Then he tugged her into her bedroom. He shut the door, backed her against it, and pinned her there with his arms on either side of her face and his pelvis pressed snugly against her thighs.

The wood was cool against her back, his skin hot against her belly.

Burying his face in her hair, he whispered, "God, you smell good."

"I thought you wanted to sleep."

He kissed the base of her neck. "I never said that."

"Yes...yes, you did."

"No," he corrected. He was kissing that wonderfully sensitive spot below her ear now,

321

driving her to distraction. Her breath caught in her throat when his teeth gently closed on her earlobe.

"No?" she whispered.

"I said I wanted to go to bed. And you said..." His hands moved to cup the sides of her face. He looked into her eyes for several long seconds, and then said, "...okay."

She was a goner and she knew it. His mouth covered hers in a long, hot, passionate kiss that let her know how much he wanted her. Her lips parted, and she felt a jolt of pleasure all the way down to her toes when his tongue went in search of hers. Her arms went around his waist, and then her hands began to stroke and caress him. She could feel the hard muscles under her fingertips, and when her hips began to move restlessly against him, she felt him tremble.

The kiss went on and on until she was gripping his shoulders and shaking with desire. It was decadent the way he made her feel, and frightening too, because she had never experienced such passion before, never felt this kind of desperation to hold tight and never let go. Oh, how she loved him.

They were both panting when he lifted his head. He saw the tears glistening in her eyes and went completely still.

"Michelle. Do you want me to stop?"

She frantically shook her head. "I'll die if you do."

"We can't have that," he said gruffly.

She tugged on his jeans, trying unsuccessfully to get them past his hips.

"Slow down, sweetheart. We've got all night."

And that was the problem. She wanted more than one night. She wanted forever, but she knew that wasn't possible, and so she decided to take what he offered and cherish the moments they did have. She would love him in a way no other woman could, with her heart, her body, and her soul. And when he left her, he would never be able to forget.

They shared another long, hot, open-mouth, tongue-thrusting kiss that only made them want more. He pulled away, stepped back, and stripped out of his jeans. Her breath caught in the back of her throat. He was beautiful. And fully aroused. The sight of him overwhelmed her because he was so perfectly sculpted.

In the moonlight, his skin seemed to glisten like gold. She reached for the straps of her gown, but he stilled her hands. "Let me."

He slowly pulled her nightgown up over her head and tossed it on the floor.

"I've had such fantasies about you," he whispered. "Your body is much better than I imagined. The way you feel pressed against me...that's much better too."

"Tell me what we were doing in your fantasy, and I'll tell you mine."

"No," he whispered. "I'd rather show than tell."

His chest hair was tickling her breasts. She liked it so much, she moved against him. She could feel his arousal against her and shifted so that her hips cuddled him. It felt so good, so right to be held like this.

"In one of my fantasies, I do this."

He picked her up in his arms and carried her to the bed. He followed her down on the sheets, nudged her thighs apart, and settled between them. Then he kissed her again, lingering over the task, until she was moving restlessly against him again.

Then he rolled onto his side and touched her stomach. "And I do this." His fingers circled her belly button, then moved lower. She sucked in her breath. "Don't," she whispered.

"You don't like it?"

His fingers were magical. "Yes...yes, but if you don't stop, I'll..."

She couldn't go on. He was driving her crazy, teasing, probing, preparing her for him. His head dipped and he began to kiss the fragrant valley between her breasts.

"In my favorite fantasy, you really love this."

He kissed each breast, his tongue stroking each nipple until she was arched half off the bed. Her nails dug into his shoulders, and she kept trying to get him to move so that she could drive him out of his mind with her mouth and her tongue, but Theo wouldn't budge.

In this fantasy, he explained, she came before he did. He kissed away any resistance she might have had, and then he slowly moved down her body, kissing every inch of her stomach, teasing her belly button by gently tickling her with the tip of his tongue, and then he moved lower still between her silky thighs.

The sensations were consuming. The climax was powerful. She cried out as she clung to him and let his passion devour her.

Theo was such an amazing lover, so giving, so gentle. Then he began to torment her. He brought her to a fevered pitch a second time, but just when she was reaching the explosive brink, he stopped.

"Hold on, sweetheart. I'll be right back."

"Don't stop. Don't..."

He kissed her. "I've got to protect you."

And then he left. She closed her eyes. Her body felt as though it was on fire, yet she was chilled because his heat was gone. She began to tremble, and just as she was reaching for the covers, Theo came back to the bed and covered her body with his. It seemed he'd been gone for an eternity.

"Now, where was I?"

His restraint and control amazed her. Then she noticed the beads of perspiration on his brow. His eyes were hazy with passion, and his jaw was clenched tight, and she saw then the lengths he had gone to for her.

His hands began to stroke the passion within her once again. She fought him this time, trying to hold out until he lost his control, but he was stronger. He wasn't gentle now. She didn't want him to be. Consumed with the waves of pleasure still coursing through her body, she held him tight as he roughly parted her thighs, then lifted her hips and sank deep inside her warmth.

His head dropped down onto her shoulder. He closed his eyes in sweet surrender, and let out a loud, thoroughly arrogant groan.

Gripping her, he forced her to stay still. "I can make this last...if you...cooperate."

She smiled up at him. Lord, he was adorable. Then she moved.

"Don't...Oh, God, honey, slow down just a little..."

She moved again, more forcefully this time, arching up against him to take him deeper inside her. He couldn't hold back any longer. The need became too great. He pulled back, then thrust deep once again, then again and again and again.

Theo wanted to tell her how perfect she was, how beautiful, but he couldn't get the words out. The intensity of the feelings rocketing through his body was too overpowering. She wouldn't let him slow down. He loved her for that. He buried himself inside her, and with one final thrust and one hell of a shout, he climaxed while she held him close.

He felt as though he'd just died and been reborn. The orgasm was the most amazing thing he'd ever experienced. He'd never let himself go like this. He'd always held a part of himself back, but with Michelle, that hadn't been possible. It took long minutes for both of them to recover. He knew he had to be crushing her, but he couldn't find the strength to move away.

Michelle couldn't stop caressing him. She loved the feel of his smooth skin under her fingertips. He was all muscle and strength and yet so very gentle with her. Her fingers trailed down his spine, then slowly moved back up.

Her heart beat against her chest as though it were pounding to get out. She laughed over the absurdity of the idea.

The sound of her lusty laugh made him smile. Bracing his weight with his arms on either side of her, he lifted his head from the crook of her neck so he could look into her eyes. "What's so funny?"

"Loving you is going to be the death of me. I can see the headlines now: 'Sex kills surgeon.'"

He frowned. "That's not funny."

She wrapped her arms around his neck, leaned up and kissed him. "Yes, it is."

"You've got to stay strong because we've got nine hundred ninety-nine more to go, and I can't let you fall apart before we're finished."

"Finished doing what?"

That sparkle came into his eyes again, and she began to smile in anticipation.

"Acting out my fantasies."

She did laugh then. "A thousand?"

"Oh, yeah. At least a thousand."

"You've got quite an active imagination, Mr. Buchanan. There are places you can go to get help. They're called sex therapy clinics."

He grinned. "You were all the therapy I needed."

"I was happy I could help."

"What about you, Michelle? Didn't you ever have fantasies?"

"Yes," she admitted. "But mine weren't as creative. I kept having the same one over and over again."

He nuzzled the crook of her neck. "Tell me about it."

"It's sort of a variation on what just happened," she said softly. "But in my fantasy..."

He lifted his head again. "What?"

"I scoop you up and toss you on the bed."

Then he laughed. "I outweigh you by about two hundred pounds," he exaggerated.

"We surgeons develop incredible upper-body strength from cracking ribs and cutting through bones," she teased.

"Okay, I'm willing. If you want to pick me up..."

He stopped when she shook her head. "I'd blow a disc," she explained. "I only told you about the fantasy so you'd know..."

"What?"

"You aren't always going to be calling the shots."

"Meaning?"

"It's my turn to drive you wild."

"We'll see about that." He kissed her again, hard and fast, then got out of bed and lifted her into his arms. "I'm hot," he announced.

"Already?"

Her fingers threaded through his tousled hair, trying to restore order to the soft strands.

"Not that kind of hot, but if you keep that up..."

"Where are we going?"

"I'm sweaty hot. Let's take a shower."

She was so content and sleepy now, she would have agreed to do anything he suggested. "I'll scrub your back and you may scrub mine."

"No, I want to scrub your front, and you can—"

She put her hand over his mouth. "I get the picture."

Ten minutes later they were both squeaky clean. The water had turned cold, but that didn't squelch their passion. Feeling devilish, she leaned up on tiptoes and whispered her fantasy into his ear. She went into detail, and when she was finished, Theo was amazed he could still stand.

She pushed him back against the tile, then began to drive him out of his mind with hot, wet kisses as she slowly worked her way down his slick body.

He didn't have the strength to carry her back to bed. They haphazardly dried each other between ardent kisses. Exhausted from their lovemaking, they fell into bed. Theo rolled onto his back. She propped herself up on one elbow and traced the outline of the tiny scar from his appendectomy.

Then she leaned down and gently kissed it. His eyes were closed, but he was smiling. "Do you do that to all your patients?"

"Kiss their scars?"

"Uh-huh."

"Absolutely. I have to."

He yawned. "How come?"

"It's part of the oath I took. Kiss it and make it better."

She pulled the sheet up as she rolled onto her back and closed her eyes. She was falling into a deep sleep when Theo nudged her.

"Michelle?"

"Hmm?"

"I found your best feature."

"What is it?" she asked in a sleepy whisper.

He tugged the sheet down and put his hand on her breast. If she hadn't been so tired, she would have asked him to explain why men had such an obsession with breasts, but then she suddenly realized just where his hand was pressed and tears sprang into her eyes. How could she not love this man?

He had placed his hand over her heart.

CHAPTER TWENTY-EIGHT

Michelle didn't wake up until ten-fifteen the following morning. She stretched, then rolled over and hugged the pillow Theo had used. She closed her eyes again while she thought about the night they had shared. In the midst of her recollections, the sleep cleared from her mind and the day intruded. It was ten-fifteen, and she was supposed to have met her friends at the clinic at eight. Mary Ann was going to kill her. Was she sitting in her car waiting? No, of course not. She would have driven to the house.

Twenty minutes later, Michelle was ready

to go. Dressed in a pair of khaki shorts and a sleeveless blue blouse, she put on ankle socks and one tennis shoe. She ran down the stairs, then paused in the laundry room to lean against the washer and put the other shoe on.

She went looking for Theo. She found him in her library, sitting in her leather chair, talking on the phone. Noah was with him. He was perched on the edge of the desk. He smiled when he saw her.

"Good morning."

"Good morning," she replied.

She sat down on the sofa and bent to tie her shoelaces. Out of the corner of her eye she saw Theo hang up the phone, but she was having a little trouble looking directly at him. The memory of what they had done the night before was still acutely vivid in her mind.

It was only awkward because Noah was there, she thought.

"Sleep well?" Theo asked.

"Yes, but I was supposed to be at the clinic hours ago."

She couldn't get the knot in her shoelace untied and knew it was because she was nervous. *Take a breath,* she told herself. *You're an adult. Act like one.*

"Mary Ann—"

"Is at the clinic. Noah let her and her friend in. They came here looking for you around eight-thirty."

She finally got the knot undone and quickly tied the laces. She didn't hear Theo coming, but suddenly he was standing in front of her. His left shoelace was untied. Without even thinking about it, she reached over, tied it for him, and stood.

Theo wasn't going to let her ignore him any longer. He nudged her under her chin to get her to look at him, then leaned down and kissed her. He didn't seem to care that Noah was there. He took his time, and with very little coaxing he got her to cooperate and return the kiss.

Without making a sound, Noah got up and left the room. Theo hugged Michelle and whispered, "Want to fool around?"

"I thought we did that last night."

"It's okay. We can do it again. Besides, that was just a warm-up." She tried to wiggle out of his arms. He tightened his hold. "Michelle, you aren't embarrassed about last night, are you?"

Her gaze flew to his and she saw how worried he looked. "I'm a physician, Theo. Nothing embarrasses me."

Then she kissed him and gave it all she had. Her tongue touched his, once, then once again, and when she pulled back, she was pleased to see that I-want-to-get-you-naked look was back in his eyes.

"I have work to do," she said as she successfully disengaged herself from his embrace.

"Actually, you don't. Mary Ann told me that she and Cindy—I think that was the other woman's name—would get the files in order much faster if you stay away. I'm supposed to keep you busy."

"She did not say—"

"Yeah, she did. She said you're critical and picky. Those were her words, not mine. Your dad called to tell you John Paul moved your furniture out. He's going to fix what he can."

"He couldn't have carried my desk or my sofa by himself."

"A guy named Artie helped him. So, nothing embarrasses you?"

"Nothing," she lied.

"Then why did you look embarrassed when I kissed you good morning?"

She headed for the kitchen with Theo right on her heels. "I was thinking about Noah. I didn't want him to be embarrassed."

Theo thought that was hilarious. Noah heard the laughter and poked his head around the door. "What's so funny?"

"Nothing," Michelle said as she edged past him to get into the kitchen. She opened the refrigerator to look for a Diet Coke and did a double take. The fridge had been pretty bare the night before, but now it was packed with food and drinks. She found a Diet Coke way in the back, grabbed it, and closed the door. Then she opened the door again to make sure she hadn't imagined it, spotted the sticks of real butter, and guessed who was responsible.

"Noah doesn't know how to be embarrassed. Do you?" Theo asked his friend.

"Embarrassed about what?"

"Sex. You know what sex is, don't you?"

"Sure I do. I read all about it in a book once.

333

I'm thinking about trying it out one of these days."

They were both having a good old time teasing her. She sat down at the table and only then noticed the triple layer chocolate cake on the counter. Noah grabbed a towel and went to the stove to lift the lid on a large iron kettle. The spicy scent of gumbo immediately filled the kitchen.

"When did you have time to make this?" Noah asked. "It sure smells good."

She couldn't remember what her father had told her. Was she supposed to say she baked the cake or made the gumbo? Then Noah asked her if she wanted a slice of home-baked bread. The French loaf was sitting on waxed paper by the sink.

"Is there a card with the gumbo?"

"I didn't see one," Noah said.

"Then I made it." She smiled as she told the lie.

Theo got the milk out of the refrigerator and put it down on the table. "You were a busy woman last night. Did you bake the cake too?"

Feeling like an idiot, she asked, "Is there a card with the cake?"

"No."

"Then I guess I made that too."

"And the bread?"

"No card?" she asked, trying to maintain a straight face.

"Didn't see one."

"I just love to bake bread in the middle of the night."

Theo put a box of Frosted Flakes, a box of raisin bran, and a box of Quaker breakfast bars on the table so Michelle would have a choice. Then he got her a spoon.

"So the lady sneaking in the back door with the bread wasn't fibbing when she said you baked the bread at her house last night and forgot to bring it home?"

Michelle had gone way past feeling foolish. Where were all the stupid cards? Had her father decided to change his game plan and forgotten to mention it to her? What was she supposed to say now? If she told Theo the truth, her father would think she wasn't cooperating with his sacred cause to keep Theo in Bowen.

Daddy wasn't going to be able to accuse her of not being a game player. "That's right," she said. "Just after you fell asleep, I came downstairs, fixed the gumbo and baked the cake; then I got in the car and drove over to..."

She suddenly stopped. Theo hadn't told her the name of the woman who had dropped the bread off, and Michelle couldn't remember to whom Daddy had assigned the task. Quickly improvising, she continued, "...a friend's house and baked a couple of loaves of bread."

"Don't forget the grocery store."

"What? Oh, yes, I stopped by the grocery store."

Theo straddled the chair across from her. Stacking his arms on the back, he said, "So that's your story, huh?"

She began to smile. "Unless or until you find

a couple of 'Welcome to Bowen' cards. In that event, my story will change."

"Tell Jake I said thanks."

"Thanks for what?" she asked innocently.

"Hey, Mike, you want some gumbo?" Noah asked as he searched through the drawers looking for a ladle.

"For breakfast? I'll stick with an energy bar."

"What about you, Theo?"

"Sure," he said. "You know what goes great with gumbo? Potato chips."

"Sorry, I don't have any potato chips. They aren't good for you, anyway. Too much sodium."

"It will balance out with the sodium in the gumbo," Noah told her.

"You do too have potato chips. Two jumbo-size bags, and they're the real thing. None of that low-fat cardboard stuff. Did you forget you bought them at the grocery store last night?"

"I must have."

"You know what goes great with gumbo and chips?" Noah asked.

"What's that?" Theo asked.

"Cold beer."

"I'm on it." Theo got up and went to the refrigerator. Michelle shook her head. "Gumbo, potato chips, and beer at ten-thirty in the morning?"

"It's eleven, and we've been up for hours. Don't frown like that, honey. Let us corrupt you. Join in."

"Is she a health nut?" Noah asked.

"I think so," Theo replied. "She lives by the credo 'If it tastes good, spit it out.' "

"When you boys are having your multiple bypasses, remember this conversation."

"I talked to Dr. Robinson," Noah said then. He had found the ladle and was scooping the gumbo into two bowls. Theo already had the sack of chips and was opening it.

"And?" she prodded.

He put the bowls on the table, grabbed two tablespoons, and sat down. "He could only think of two men who gave him real trouble, and I'm running a check on both of them. An old guy named George Everett was one difficult patient. Do you know him, Mike?"

"No, I don't."

"Everett refused to pay his bill because Robinson didn't cure him of his indigestion. Everett had a drinking problem, which he also blamed on the doctor. He told Robinson he wouldn't be drinking himself drunk every night if he weren't in such terrible pain. Anyway, Robinson turned the account over to a collection agency, and that didn't sit well with Everett. He got all juiced up and called the doctor and threatened him."

"What about the other man?" Theo asked.

"The name he gave Robinson was 'John Thompson,' but I doubt that's his real name. He only saw the doctor once, and that was just a day or two before Robinson closed shop and sent his files to Mike. Thompson's a druggie from New Orleans. He drove all the way to Bowen in hopes that the physicians here would be more lax, I suppose. Anyway, he told Robinson he had this terrible back pain and needed some prescriptions for pain medication. He wanted the heavy stuff and knew just what to ask for. When Robinson refused, he told me the junkie became enraged and threatened him."

"Did he report Thompson to the police?"

Noah took a swig of beer before answering. "He should have, but he didn't because he was leaving Bowen, and he didn't want the hassle. That's what he told me, anyway."

"I'll bet Thompson tried other physicians in St. Claire," Michelle said.

"That's what I figured too," Noah said. "So I checked it out." He grinned then as he made the comment, "I really love getting doctors out of bed early in the morning. Anyway, if Thompson did go to other doctors, he used a different name. No one remembers treating him."

"In other words, a dead end."

"I think it's time for both of you to close this file," Michelle said. "And stop worrying. I'm going to clean up my clinic, put stronger locks on the doors and windows, and move on. I suggest you do the same thing."

Since neither Theo nor Noah argued with her, she assumed they were too stubborn to admit she was right.

"It's gonna rain." Theo made the prediction and then took a bite of gumbo.

"The sun's out," Noah remarked.

"Yeah, but my knee aches, so it's gonna rain. My shoulder's throbbing too."

Noah laughed. "You two are perfect for each other. A hypochondriac hooking up with a doctor. That's a match made in heaven."

"I'm not a doctor," Theo said dryly.

Noah ignored the smart-ass comment. "Mike, have you ever been to Boston?"

"No, I haven't."

"You'll like it."

She thought about what he was saying for a couple of seconds, then responded, "I'm sure, if I ever get there for a medical conference or a vacation, I'll love it."

Noah glanced back and forth between Theo and Michelle. She'd sounded defensive, but he could see the sadness in her eyes. She was giving up before she'd even gotten started, he decided. Theo's response was just as interesting. His whole body had tensed.

"So, it's two ships passing in the night?"

"Something like that," Michelle said.

"Leave it alone, Noah."

He nodded, then switched topics. "So tell me, do we still fish Saturday if it rains?"

"Fishing's better in the rain," Michelle said.

"Says who?" Noah asked.

"John Paul."

"Am I ever going to meet your brother?" Theo asked.

"I doubt it. You're leaving Monday, remember?"

It was like a sore tooth she kept rubbing. He hadn't pulled the rug out from under her.

She'd known he was going to leave. So why was she feeling so devastated?

"You'll meet her brother at The Swan Friday," Noah said. "Jake told me John Paul works as a bartender and a bouncer on weekends."

Michelle shook her head. "Daddy knows John Paul won't show up this weekend. By now, my brother knows who you both work for, so he'll stay away."

"Your brother wouldn't happen to be a wanted man, would he?" Noah asked.

"No, of course not."

"What's he got against the FBI?" Theo asked.

"You'll have to ask him that question."

"Which kind of hinges on the fact that I'll have to meet him so I can ask him the question," Theo said.

"My brother is a very private person," she said defensively. "If and when he decides he'd like to meet you, then he'll find you." She smiled as she added, "You won't see him coming. Now, if you'll excuse me, I've got work to do."

She got up from the table, tossed her empty can in the trash, and then began to gather up the dirty dishes. Theo got up to help. He was filling the sink when the doorbell rang. Noah went to answer it.

Michelle put the bowls in the sink, then turned back to the table. Theo caught her around the waist and leaned down to nuzzle her neck.

"What's going on with you?"

She wasn't sophisticated enough to play games or come up with a clever lie, and so she simply told him the truth.

"You're complicating my life."

He turned her around to face him. She backed away, but he followed her and pinned her against the sink. "You don't regret—"

"No," she whispered. "It was wonderful."

She couldn't quite look him in the eyes and focused on his chin instead so she could concentrate on what she wanted to say to him. "We're both normal adults with healthy urges, and of course it's..."

"Healthy and normal?"

"Don't tease me. These urges..."

"Yeah, I remember the urges," he said.

"We just can't keep on giving in to these..."

"Urges?" he offered when she suddenly stopped.

She found herself smiling in spite of her frustration. "You're making fun of me."

"Yeah, I am."

She pushed him back. "I'm not going to let you break my heart, Theo. Play your games with the big-city girls back home."

He laughed right in her face. "Big-city girls?"

"Will you be serious. I'm trying to tell you that we don't have a future together, so you should just leave me alone."

He cupped the sides of her face and kissed her passionately, and when he lifted his head, he saw the tears in her eyes.

"Are you going to cry on me?"

"No." The answer was emphatic.

"Good, 'cause I could have sworn I saw tears just now."

"I had no idea you could be so mean. I'm trying to tell you to stop..."

He slowly shook his head.

Her eyes widened. "No? Why not?"

His mouth brushed over hers again in a quick, no-nonsense kiss. "You're a smart girl. You figure it out."

Noah interrupted when he strolled back into the kitchen. He had a large FedEx box tucked under his arm and was carrying a huge metal pan covered with foil.

"Theo, grab the box, will you? I found it propped against the door when I opened it. There was this lady standing there with this Cajun fried chicken. She handed it to me and took off before I could thank her. She was a nervous little thing."

"Did she tell you her name?"

"Molly Beaumont," he answered. He set the pan on the table and began to unwrap the foil. "Smells good."

"Was there a card for Theo with the chicken?"

"No, she said you made the chicken, but the pan's hers and she wants it back."

Theo was sitting at the table opening the box. Noah picked up a chicken leg and took a huge bite. Then he nudged Theo. "You know what else Molly said?"

"What's that?"

"She asked me to tell Coach Buchanan,

'Hey.' Did you hear that, Theo? She called you Coach."

"Yeah, I know. Everyone in Bowen calls me Coach."

"Okay, so now I've got to wonder why," he said.

Theo wasn't paying any attention to him. He finally got the box open and let out a low whistle. "Nick came through," he said. "Play-books." He picked one up and thumbed through it.

"Football playbooks?" Noah asked with his mouth full.

"Yeah, I'll explain later. Michelle, you can ride to the clinic with Noah. He's spending the day with you."

"He doesn't need to waste his time—"

Theo cut her off. "He's going with you."

Noah nodded. "While you and your friends are organizing the files, I'll start the cleanup in your office. If there's time, I'll paint the walls."

"I'd be happy for your help, but—"

"Don't argue," Theo said.

"Okay," she agreed. "I appreciate it, Noah."

Then she turned to Theo and asked him what he was going to be doing.

"I've got a meeting with the Carsons and their attorney at one," Theo said. "I'll have to finish it by two-thirty because I promised Conrad I'd show up for practice at three. If you and Noah need a break, drop by."

"The principal offered Theo a contract," Michelle said, smiling now. "He hasn't signed it yet."

"You're making that up," Noah said.

"I think Theo's holding out for more money."

Noah was convinced the two of them were pulling his leg and was waiting to hear the punch line. "Okay," he said. "We'll stop by. What time is practice over? I've promised I'd help tend bar tonight. I should be there by five."

"I thought you were going to hook up with Mary Ann tonight," Theo reminded.

"What do you mean, you're hooking up with Mary Ann?" Michelle asked.

Noah shrugged. "She asked me if I wanted to get together later after her friend's husband picked her up, and I suggested that she stop by The Swan, and if I'm not busy—"

"She asked you to go out?" she asked, clearly surprised.

"Yes, she did. Why is that so difficult to understand? I'm a nice guy."

"It isn't difficult to understand. It's just that she's...and you're...that is, you're very..."

Noah was enjoying her discomfort. "I'm very what?"

The word "experienced" came to mind along with about a dozen others. Noah was the kind of man who had women like Mary Ann for breakfast. Michelle realized she was being judgmental and that she could be wrong. "You're..."

"Yes?" Noah prodded.

"Your friend has the hots for Noah," Theo explained.

Noah nodded. "Yeah, she does."

"Oh, for heaven's sake," she said, clearly exasperated. "Just because Mary Ann was being friendly, you immediately jump to the conclusion that she had the hots for Noah?"

Theo smiled. "I didn't jump to any conclusions. Honest. Mary Ann said, and I'm quoting here, 'Hey, Theo, I've got the hots for Noah. So is he married or what?' "

Noah nodded again. "That's about how it happened."

The sad thing was that Michelle thought Theo might be telling the truth. Mary Ann did have the annoying habit of blurting out her every thought. Michelle started laughing even as she shook her head.

"We've got to get to the clinic," she told them.

"Just a second, Michelle," Noah said as he flipped through the playbook. "Theo, look at page fifty-three. Do you remember—"

"Theodore, take that book away from your friend and get him moving now."

Calling him Theodore did the trick. He grabbed the book and got up. Noah was impressed. "She sounds like a drill sergeant," he said as he watched Michelle standing in the doorway, tapping her foot impatiently.

"She can get tough when she has to." Theo made the comment sound like a compliment.

"That's a real talent," Noah remarked.

"She gives as good as she gets. She doesn't back down. I like that. You know what else she does? Vegetables," he said as he walked through the dining room to get to the front door.

"Did you say vegetables?" Noah asked, certain he hadn't heard correctly.

"Yeah. You should see her cut vegetables with a paring knife. It's incredible. You could put it to music."

Noah followed Theo outside. "What the hell does that mean?"

"She's so...precise."

Noah laughed. "Man, oh man."

"What?"

"Have you got it bad."

CHAPTER TWENTY-NINE

Noah and Michelle didn't make it to football practice. There was simply too much work to get done at the clinic. Her friends amazed her. They got the files back in order and stacked them alphabetically in boxes, so that as soon as the new file cabinets arrived, all she had to do was drop them in the drawers. Theo drove over to the clinic to pick up Michelle, while Noah went back to his motel to shower and change before heading to The Swan to help Jake.

Michelle felt guilty that neither Theo nor Noah had gotten to fish. When she made that remark to Theo, he told her not to worry. Saturday he would be in a boat from sunup to sundown, and, anyway, the anticipation was almost as much fun as the actual event. He rattled off all the items he thought they should pack in the cooler. Like the Boy Scouts, he wanted to be prepared, and God forbid he should run out of sandwiches and beer.

He had parked the car in her driveway, and they were just getting out when Elena Miller pulled up in her little hatchback, tooting her horn to get their attention.

"Dr. Mike," she called as she ran around to the passenger side, "would you ask your young man to carry this box in?"

"What's in the box?" Michelle asked.

"Didn't you get my message? I called you from the hospital and left it on your machine."

"As you can see, I just got home, Elena," Michelle answered.

"I've had it with you doctors cluttering up my ER. This box is full of mail that was scattered all over the counters," she said, motioning with both hands to the backseat of her car. "I started with you, and next Monday I'm taking on Dr. Landusky's junk."

Michelle introduced Theo to the exasperated woman and explained that the staff secretary was trying to organize the ER.

"Why can't you have your journals sent to your clinic, Doctor? It really would help if you would just take your mail home every night. Is that too much to ask?"

"No, it isn't," Michelle said, feeling as though she were in school again. "Why didn't you just leave all this stuff in the doctors' lounge?" she asked when Theo picked up the box and she saw all the magazines.

Elena shut the door behind Theo and then got in behind the wheel. "Because I just finished cleaning out that mess," she said. "You doctors…"

She was backing the car out of the drive and didn't finish the sentence.

"I'll try to do better," Michelle called.

Placated, the woman waved as she sped down the road. Theo followed Michelle inside. "Elena reminds me of someone," he remarked as he carried the box into the library and put it on the desk. She nudged him out of the way so she could look through it. There were several journals, parcels from two pharmaceutical companies, and a pile of junk mail.

"Who?" she asked as she dropped the envelopes back into the box. There wasn't anything that required her immediate attention.

"Gene Wilder."

"She's just got a bad perm," Michelle said, laughing.

"Where's your cooler?" he asked.

"In the garage. It needs to be washed, though," she said as she headed for the steps.

"You go ahead and take your shower first while I hose it off. Then I'll clean up. And don't use all the hot water," he called after her.

He'd been a guest in her house for a couple of days, and he was already trying to tell her what to do. She shook her head as she laughed. Nice, she thought. Having him here was very, very nice.

CHAPTER THIRTY

The deep resonant boom of thunder awakened Theo. It sounded like a firecracker had gone off inside the bedroom. The bed actually shook. It was pitch black outside, but when he turned his head, he could see lightning streaking across the sky.

A hell of a storm was raging. He tried to go back to sleep, but it was too hot. The air conditioner was humming, but because the window was open a crack, the cold air was being sucked out into the storm.

Michelle was sound asleep, cuddled up against his side, one hand flat on his stomach. He gently eased her onto her back, kissed her forehead, and smiled when she tried to roll over on top of him. He was suddenly thinking about waking her up and making love to her again, but then he glanced at the glowing green numbers on the clock radio and changed his mind. It was three o'clock. Waking her was out of the question. She needed her sleep, and so did he. They'd gone to bed at ten, but they hadn't gone to sleep until midnight.

If he wanted to spend Saturday fishing, he would have to get everything else done tomorrow. He had another meeting with the Carsons and their attorneys to hammer out the details, and when he was finished, he was going to help at the clinic.

Michelle didn't want to waste the entire day Saturday fishing until Theo told her about a little side bet he'd made with Noah. Whoever caught the most fish had to pay the loser a thousand dollars.

She had been appalled by the amount of the wager—how could anyone bet that kind of money when it could be put to much better use—but as soon as Theo told her he couldn't and wouldn't call the wager off, she got with the program and became determined that he win. Boasting that she had a secret strategy, she explained that her father would take Noah to his favorite fishing spot deep in the swamp, just around the bend from John Paul's cabin. But on the other side of the bayou was an even better spot where the fish were so plentiful and friendly they would all but jump into the boat.

When he'd asked her how come she'd never told her father about her special fishing spot, she explained that she didn't want him going there alone because it was so isolated, and there were predators in the area. He'd translated the remark to mean that there were alligators in the area. She didn't deny or confirm his suspicion but took his mind off his worry by kissing him as she slowly removed his clothes. Taking his hand in hers, she'd led him to her bed. The diversion had worked like a charm.

Until now.

Maybe he'd grab that modified shotgun at The Swan and take it along. Then he remembered he was hot and wanted to close the window. He sat up, yawning loudly, and swung his legs over the side. His feet got tangled up in the sheet when he stood. He stumbled, slammed his bad knee into the bedside table, the round brass knob striking that oh-so-tender spot just below his kneecap where he was sure every nerve in his body converged, sending excruciating pain rocketing down his leg. It burned like acid. Muttering an expletive, he sat down hard on the bed and rubbed his knee.

"Theo, are you all right?" Her voice was a sleepy whisper.

"Yeah, I'm okay. I hit my knee on the table. You left the window open."

She pushed the sheet back. "I'll close it."

He gently pushed her down. "Go back to sleep. I'll get it."

She didn't argue. While he sat there rubbing the sting out of his knee, he listened to her deep, even breathing. How could anyone fall asleep that quickly? Then he thought that maybe she was exhausted because he'd worn her out making love, and he felt a little better. With a wry smile, he admitted to himself how arrogant that thought was.

He got up and limped to the window. He was pushing it down when lightning lit up the night, and he saw a man darting across the road into Michelle's front yard.

What the hell? Had he just seen what he thought he'd seen, or had he imagined it? Thunder rumbled, then another bolt of lightning flashed and he saw the man again, crouching down by the sycamore tree.

He also saw the gun. Theo was already

moving back when the shot rang out. The bullet pierced the glass, shattering it as Theo turned and dove for cover. Pain cut through his upper arm, and he thought he might have been shot. He hit the bed, grabbed Michelle as she bolted upright, and rolled with her in his arms to the floor, trying his damnedest to protect her head from striking wood. Pain shot through his arm again as he rolled off her and sprang to his feet, knocking the bedside lamp to the floor in his haste.

"Theo, what—"

"Stay down," he ordered. "And don't turn the lights on."

She was trying to comprehend what was happening. "Did lightning strike the house?"

"That was a gunshot. Someone just took a shot at me through the window."

He was up and running. If he had let Michelle go to the window, she could have been killed. It was just a piece of luck that he happened to be looking down when the sky lit up.

Sprinting toward the guest room, he shouted, "Call the police and get dressed. We've got to get out of here."

Michelle had already grabbed the phone and pulled it down next to her. She dialed 911, then put the receiver to her ear and realized the phone was dead. She didn't panic. She dropped the phone, reached for her clothes on the bureau, and ran into the hall.

"The phone's dead," she yelled. "Theo, what's happening?"

"Get dressed," he repeated. "Hurry."

He had his gun and was pressed against the wall next to the window. He sure as hell wasn't going to give the bastard an easy target this time. Edging the drapes back with the barrel of the gun, he squinted into the darkness. Another shot rang out just as the sky opened and the rain began. He saw a burst of red as the bullet left the chamber. He pulled back. He stood there, straining to hear every little sound, praying that lightning would strike again and he could see if there were any others lurking out there.

Was there just one man? God, he hoped so. If he could get one clear shot, maybe he could nail the bastard. He'd never killed anyone, never even fired the gun except in target practice, but he wasn't feeling at all shy about taking this man out.

Five seconds passed, then five more. Lightning split the sky open then, and for a heartbeat, it was as bright and clear as day.

"Hell," Theo muttered when he saw another figure darting across the road.

Michelle was in the bathroom dressing by the soft glow of the nightlight in the hall. She was shoving her feet into her tennis shoes when the nightlight went out. The bulb was too new to have burned out. Racing back into her bedroom, she saw that the clock radio dial was also dark. Either lightning had struck a power line, or someone had cut the power feeding her house. She opted for the second bleak possibility.

It was so dark without the nightlight, she couldn't see anything. The linen closet was right outside the guest room. She felt around for the handle, got the door open, and reached up on the top shelf for her flashlight. She knocked over a bottle of rubbing alcohol and a box of Band-Aids. The bottle landed hard on her instep. She kicked it into the closet to get it out of her way, found the flashlight, and then shut the door so she wouldn't bump into it.

There were Band-Aids scattered all over the floor. She slipped on one as she ran into the guest room. "The phone line's dead and the electricity's out. Theo, what is going on?"

"There are two men out in front. One's crouched down low by the tree and isn't moving. Grab my cell phone and hand it to me. We've got to get some help."

She was afraid to turn the flashlight on because the drapes were open, and whoever was outside would see the light, so she felt around on the dresser, her frustration mounting with each second.

"Where is it?" she asked. Then she heard the sound of a motor humming in the distance. She ran to the window facing the water and saw the light from the boat coming closer and closer to the dock. She couldn't tell how many were in the boat, couldn't see anything but that shimmering beacon that seemed to pulsate with a life of its own as it grew stronger and stronger.

Theo already had his jeans and shoes on and was pulling a dark T-shirt over his head and trying to keep watch at the window at the same time. Pain shot through his arm when he shoved his hand through the short sleeve, and his skin felt wet and sticky with blood. He touched the injury, felt the jagged piece of glass, and was relieved it wasn't a bullet hole. Wiping his hand on his jeans, he tugged the T-shirt down, then reached up again and plucked the shard of glass out. It burned as if a hot iron were stuck to his skin.

"There's a boat coming toward the dock," she said. "They're with the two in front, aren't they?" She felt foolish asking the question. Of course there were more of them. Who among her friends would come visiting in the middle of the night during a torrential storm? "What do they want?" she whispered.

"We'll ask them later," he said. "Where's my phone?" he demanded as he fastened the holster to his jeans, then shoved his gun into the leather pouch and closed the snap. He'd already figured out their escape route. They'd have to go out the back window, drop down onto the porch roof, and hit the ground running. With any luck, they could get to his car.

"It's not on the dresser," she said.

"Ah, hell," he muttered, for he'd suddenly remembered where he'd put it. It was sitting in the charger next to Michelle's on the desk downstairs. "I plugged it in by your phone."

"I'll go get it."

"No," he said sharply. "The steps face the back door, and if one of them is waiting there, he'll see you. Stay by the window and try to see how many get out of the boat. Has it docked yet?"

Theo kicked the door shut, then shoved the heavy dresser in front of it in hopes of slowing the men down.

"One man just got out of the boat, and he's using a flashlight. He's headed for the back-yard...no, he's going around to the front. I can't tell if there's another one."

"Open the window," he said as he picked up his car keys and shoved them into his back pocket. "We're going out that way. Let me go out first so I can catch you."

He climbed out the window, swung down, and tried to be as quiet as possible as he dropped to the porch roof. The shingles were slick from the rain, and he almost lost his footing on the sharp pitch as he landed. Bracing his legs apart, he put his arms up and waited for Michelle to jump, all the while praying that lightning wouldn't strike and give them away. If there were others in the yard or in the boat, they would see them and sound the alert.

He reached for Michelle just as he heard glass breaking downstairs. It sounded as if it was coming from the back door. The noise was immediately followed by an earsplitting sound of gunfire coming from the front of the house. The bastards were organized. They were simul-taneously rushing both entrances. They wanted to trap Theo and Michelle inside.

Michelle could hear them knocking things over downstairs. How many were there? She tucked the flashlight into the waistband of her jeans and climbed out on the ledge.

"Let's go." His voice was a low, urgent whisper.

She hesitated for a second or two, trying to focus, but then she heard the pounding of heavy footsteps on the stairs. She let go.

Theo caught her around the waist. She slipped, but he held fast until she recovered her balance. Staying close to him, she scrambled on all fours across the roof. The rain was coming down in sheets now. She could barely see her hands. She reached the edge, tested the gutter, hoping she could hang on as she swung her legs over, but the gutter was loose, and she knew it would make a racket if it fell. There were overgrown lilac bushes all along the side of her house. She put her hand over her eyes as she jumped into the center of the thicket.

Scurrying to get out of Theo's way, she ran headfirst into a thick branch. It cut her cheek, and she bit her lip to keep from crying out.

"Which way?" she whispered.

"The front. Wait here." He pulled his gun out. He edged his way to the corner of the house, ducked down, and then leaned out. The hood of his car was up, which meant they'd disabled it. He looked across the road, judging the distance to the swamp. He didn't relish getting trapped and hunted in the maze of dense vegetation, but if they could run across without being seen, then he and Michelle could make their way to the crossroads.

A car was parked further up the road. He

wouldn't have seen it if the brake lights hadn't suddenly gone on. Whoever was waiting inside had his foot on the brakes. A second later the lights went off.

Theo went back to Michelle. "We have to try to get to your boat. It's the only way out of here."

"Let's go."

They made it to the edge of the dock before they were spotted. Caught in the glare of a light shining down from the bedroom window, Theo pushed Michelle down as he turned and fired. He didn't know if he hit anything or not. The light went out, and he heard shouting.

"Give me your flashlight," he panted.

She pulled it out of her waistband. He grabbed it, held his arm out so that it wouldn't be in front of them. Pushing her down again, he tried to cover her as he whispered, "Stay still," and then flipped the light on.

The beam struck one of the bastards running toward them from the house. Michelle saw him clearly and gasped in surprise. Recognition was swift and shocking.

Theo fired twice before he was forced to turn the light off. Bullets were flying all around them, pinning them down. Theo aimed the flashlight at the other boat, turned it on, and there he was, another man, waiting for them. Squatting down low, he was looking through the scope of a high-powered rifle when Theo fired. The bullet struck the motor. He fired again as the man lunged over the side of the boat into the water.

Flipping the light off, Theo jerked her to her feet, and shouted, "Go," as gunshots sizzled and cracked in the air around them, ricocheting off the tree and the dock. Michelle slid across the dock, grabbed hold of the post to keep from falling into the water, and then frantically worked to untie their assailants' boat. Theo had already untied hers, jumped in, and was pulling on the engine cord.

She finally got the rope undone, and she pushed the boat as far away from the dock as possible. Theo was shouting at her to hurry. She jumped into her boat and fell back against Theo as he gunned the engine. A hail of bullets slapped the water around them.

Theo hunched over Michelle, trying to protect her and keep his head down at the same time. Turning the boat to the north, he shoved the lever down. The front end of the boat came out of the water, bounced back, then lurched forward. One bullet sizzled so close to his ear, he thought he felt the heat.

Looking back, he saw two men with flashlights running along the yard. Then one dove into the water. Theo figured he and Michelle had maybe a thirty-second lead to get away. He sat back on the bench and let her get up.

As soon as she lifted her head, she realized they were headed away from civilization. "You have to turn around," she told him.

"No," he answered. "It's too late to turn back. They're going to come after us. Shine the light ahead."

Michelle sat between his knees and directed the beam straight ahead. The light saved them from disaster. Another five seconds and they would have crashed into a dead tree stump sticking out of the water. Theo veered sharply to the left, then straightened the boat into a true course.

"Thank God, you grabbed your flashlight," he whispered.

"There's a sharp bend straight ahead," she told him. "Slow down and turn right. Left is another dead end."

Clasping his knee to balance herself, she turned and lifted up to look behind them. "I don't see any lights yet," she said with a wave of relief so intense it was almost painful. "Maybe they won't follow us. Maybe they'll leave us alone now that we've gotten away."

When she turned around, he pulled her back against him. "I don't think they're going to give up. I think they've just gotten started. Did you see the scope on that rifle? They're armed to the hilt. They came to hunt, and they aren't going to give up without a fight. We've got to get to a phone and get help. Show me the quickest way to get back to town."

"The bayou is like a big figure eight," she explained. "If you had headed south from my dock, you would have gone around a wide bend and would have seen The Swan. We have to backtrack."

"We'll run into them if we do."

"I know," she whispered hoarsely. She hadn't been screaming, but her throat felt raw. "There are at least twenty inlets that loop in and around. Some of them are dead ends," she warned. "And some circle back. If they know about them, they could get ahead of us and cut us off."

"Then we'll slow down, and if we see their lights, we'll take one of the channels and hide until daylight." They were approaching another bend. "Which way?" he asked.

"I'm not sure. Everything looks different at night. I think this one circles back."

"Okay, we'll go left," he said and steered the boat in that direction.

"Theo, I could be wrong."

Michelle heard the sound of a boat motor roaring in the distance. The sound was getting closer even as they sped around another tree trunk.

Theo also heard the noise. He spotted a narrow channel, slowed the engine, and turned the boat once again. There were mossy branches hanging down almost into the water. He pushed them out of the way as they passed. Once they had made another turn and he saw how narrow the channel became, he turned off the engine.

Michelle switched the flashlight off. They huddled together and turned toward the sound. It was as black as the inside of a coffin. The downpour had subsided, and a soft drizzle was falling.

The swamp pulsated with life. Theo heard something splash into the water behind them. The bullfrogs suddenly stopped croaking, and the crickets fell silent. Something was moving, though. What the hell was it? The boat struck something then. He thought it might be another tree trunk, but he couldn't be sure. The boat bobbed back, then stopped.

Michelle reached behind him, pushed a lever, and told him in a whisper to help her swing the motor up out of the water. "If we have to keep going in this channel, the blade could get caught in the mud. It gets shallow in some of these." The boat tapped the obstacle once again. "There they are," Michelle whispered.

They could see the light from the motorboat scanning the thicket like a lighthouse beacon, swinging back and forth in a wide arc, searching for them.

The light didn't find them. Michelle took a deep breath and slowly exhaled. They had just gotten over another hurdle, and she took a minute to thank God for that blessing. They weren't out of danger yet, but Theo had been right when he'd told her they could hide out until daylight and then get help. Soon there would be an end to this nightmare.

The hunters had gone on. The noise from their boat fading now. Michelle guessed that they would continue on for several more minutes before they'd turn around and backtrack, searching more thoroughly.

Theo's mind was racing. Were they professional hitters? If so, who had sent them? Could the mob have tracked him to Louisiana? Were they here to retaliate for his part in convicting so many of their leaders? Had his being here put her in danger?

Michelle heard a twig snap above her. She glanced up at the branches a scant second before she felt a weight drop on her left foot. It took every ounce of willpower she possessed not to scream. Whatever had fallen was now slithering up her leg. She froze, her hand gripping the flashlight in her lap, her finger on the switch.

"Theo, grab the oar," she whispered, trying not to move a muscle. "When I turn the light on, you've got to knock it out of the boat. Okay?"

He didn't understand. What *it?* What was she talking about? He didn't question her, though. He simply picked up the oar, held it like a baseball bat, and waited.

"I'm ready."

She flipped the switch on. Theo felt his heart lurch in his chest. He almost dropped the oar when he saw the hideous black snake. The monster's forked tongue was darting in and out, as though he were anticipating the morsel he was going to bite, his triangular flat head poised above Michelle's kneecap. He seemed to be looking into her eyes.

Time suspended as Theo swung the oar at the snake and hurled it into the water. He jumped to his feet and grabbed Michelle. "Son of a bitch," he roared. "Son of a bitch."

Michelle scrambled to her knees, her heart racing. She kept her flashlight beam trained on the snake, watching as it skimmed across the water into the bushes on the other side of the muddy bank. Then she scanned the water, reached out, and grabbed the oar that Theo had thrown out. Dropping it on the floor of the boat, she leaned back. "That was a close call."

Theo was slapping at her legs. "Did he get you?" he asked frantically.

"No, he didn't. He was probably more afraid than we were."

"What the hell was it?"

"A cottonmouth," she answered.

"Son of a...they're poisonous."

"Yes," she agreed. She grabbed his hand. "Stop hitting me."

"I just wanted to make sure there weren't any others..." He stopped when he realized how crazy he sounded.

"Any other snakes crawling up my pant leg? There aren't any. Trust me, I'd know. Try to calm down."

"How can you be so friggin' calm? That thing was on your leg."

She put her hand on his cheek. "But you got rid of it."

"Yeah, but..."

"Take a breath."

She wasn't as calm as she sounded. When he put his arms around her, he could feel her trembling. "You know what?"

"Let me guess. You hate snakes."

"How'd you know I was going to say that?"

She smiled as she pulled away from him. "I just had a feeling."

"Let's get out of here."

He put his hand into the water to see if he could push the boat away from the bank. His fingers felt as if they were being sucked into the mud.

Michelle grabbed his arm and pulled him back. "You don't want to put your hand in the water, not around here."

He didn't need to ask why. He pictured an alligator leaping up at him and shuddered over the thought. Grabbing the oar, he used it to push away. "Do you think this way cuts through?"

"I've lived here all my life and I know these waters, but in the dark, I'm still second-guessing myself. I think this one dead ends about a quarter of a mile from here. If we keep going, we could get trapped, and I don't want to walk through the swamp. It isn't safe, not at night, anyway. I think we should turn around and go back."

"That's got my vote."

"When we cross back over, let's use the oars and row across. If they're out there, they won't hear us."

She picked up the other oar and helped him get the boat turned.

"If another damned snake lands in this boat, they'll hear me, all right."

Theo changed places with Michelle and used the oars to get them to the opening of the channel. He stopped, then turned to look. "What do you think? Can we make it back to your place? If I could get to my cell phone—"

She interrupted him. "We went too far downstream. We'd have to backtrack and that's pushing our luck."

"Okay. We'll head straight across and hope there's a dock close."

He couldn't see more than ten feet ahead of him but knew it was too risky to turn the flashlight on now. Michelle climbed over the bench so she could get to the motor. She put her hand on the cord, ready to yank it if they were spotted. She was worrying about everything now. When was the last time she filled the motor with gas? She couldn't remember. What if they reached the middle and then the spotlight found them?

They were gliding across the water now. Theo's powerful arms worked the oars like an expert.

She could see the light scanning the water. "They're looking for us in the channels," she whispered.

Theo kept rowing but glanced behind him. The beam of light was crisscrossing the water, but the boat wasn't moving. It was about two hundred yards away.

"They haven't seen us yet."

"Should I turn the motor—"

"No." His voice was urgent. "Hang in there. We might make it."

A minute later, the beam turned back in their direction. Michelle didn't wait for Theo to tell her to start the motor. She pulled hard. It didn't catch the first time. Theo swung the oars in and shoved Michelle down as a bullet whizzed past his head. She yanked on the rope and cried out when the engine sputtered to life.

Theo pulled his gun from the holster, shouted for Michelle to keep her head down, just as another bullet struck the water next to them. He propped his elbow on the bench and fired his weapon.

The bastards were coming fast now. Theo was trying to shoot out the spotlight. The first shot missed, but he heard someone shout, and he hoped that meant he'd hit one of them. He squeezed the trigger again. He was on the mark this time. The bullet shattered the light, giving them maybe five, ten seconds max before one of the hitters turned his flashlight on them.

Michelle couldn't judge how close they were to the bank. She tried to reach the throttle to slow the boat down, but it was too late. The boat suddenly lurched up, out of the water, and slammed into thorny bushes. It didn't stop but bounced twice before striking a tree. The impact threw Theo into the front of the boat. He landed on his left side, slamming his knee into the aluminum. His upper arm, still throbbing from the cut from the window glass, hit the metal rim, tearing his skin and sending a jolt of pain down to his elbow.

Michelle's forehead struck the bench and she cried out as she threw her arms up to protect herself.

Theo leapt out of the boat, holstered his gun, and pulled Michelle. Dazed from the impact, she shook her head, trying to clear it as she felt around the boat for the flashlight.

"Come on," he shouted over the roar of the motor coming closer and closer.

He was lifting her when she found the flashlight. Jerking her arm free, she snatched it. Her heart was slamming against her sternum, and her head felt as though it had been split apart, the pain almost blinding as she stumbled forward.

Theo wrapped his arm around her, hauled her into his side, and, half carrying her, ran into the brush. He didn't have the faintest idea where they were headed. Completely disoriented, he ran headlong into spiny branches. He pushed through them with his right arm. He could still hear the motor roaring in the distance and was desperate to get Michelle as far away as possible before the men docked their boat.

They fought their way through the brush and the soggy undergrowth, stopping twice to listen for signs that they were being followed. Finally, breaking out of the thicket, they stumbled forward into the open.

Michelle stopped to get her second wind. She wasn't sure where they were.

"Should I risk it?" she asked as she lifted the flashlight and put her thumb on the switch. "I don't think they'll see the light if I only have it on for a second."

"Do it."

She flipped the switch, then breathed a sigh of relief. "I think I know where we are." Turning the light off, she whispered, "It's about a mile to The Swan."

They were standing on the edge of a dirt road which, to Theo, looked like a dozen others he'd driven down.

"You're sure?"

"Yes."

He clasped her hand and started running. If they could get around the bend up ahead before their pursuers reached the road, they'd be in the clear. He kept glancing over his shoulder looking for lights. The only sound was their heavy breathing and the pounding of their feet against the road.

Michelle turned on the light again, just in the nick of time, because they would have run off the road where it curved. She tripped as she turned, but Theo caught her and kept her upright without slowing down. He looked behind him again, saw the small beam of light strike the road, and increased his speed.

He was positive they hadn't seen them.

"I'm okay now," she panted. "I can run."

He let go of her, then took hold of her hand, and continued on. He could see a light twinkling like a star in the distance and headed in that direction.

The stitch in Michelle's side was burning now, and her head felt as if it were going to explode. They reached a crossroad, and Michelle doubled over, her hands clasping her knees.

"The Swan's down the road to the left," she panted. "We can call the police from there."

The road was gravel and mud. He remembered driving down this lane. As he ran, he constantly scanned the brush on either side, figuring which way they would dive if he heard someone coming.

"You doing okay?" he whispered.

"I'm good," she answered.

She felt like crying out with relief when she saw the dark building ahead of them. The feeling of euphoria was short-lived, for a scant second later, she heard the sound of a car screeching around the curve behind them.

She didn't have time to react. One second she was glancing over her shoulder to look for headlights, and the next she was flying off the road into a gully with Theo. Michelle landed hard on her backside. Theo crouched beside her and pulled his gun out, his eyes scanning the road. They were concealed by bushes and scrub.

Michelle gingerly probed the bump on her forehead, grimacing. Her mind raced. Then she remembered what she wanted to tell Theo.

She whispered his name. He put his hand over her mouth. "Shhh," he whispered close to her ear.

The car pulled up next to them. She fought the urge to recoil as she heard a thrashing noise in the bushes next to them. She realized she was holding her breath when her chest began to ache. She slowly, quietly exhaled. Her hand gripped Theo's knee. More thrashing in the underbrush, then muttering as the man walked back to the car. Gravel crunched under his shoes.

The damp air was getting to her. Her eyes suddenly began to tear and she needed to sneeze. *Please, God, not now. I can't make any noise...not yet.* She clamped her fingers over her nose and breathed through her mouth. Tears were streaming down her cheeks, and she pulled her T-shirt up over her mouth.

Theo heard the car door slam, and then the car moved on. He wasn't going to take any chances, though. He strained to hear every little sound. How many were there? He knew for certain four men had tried to ambush them. He'd seen two in the front of Michelle's house and then two who'd driven the boat to the dock. Their goal had obviously been to trap them inside the house, and he swore that as soon as they were safe and out of this jungle warfare, he would get every one of them.

He finally shifted his position to take the weight off his knees. Putting his arm around Michelle, he bent down and whispered, "They're looking for us at The Swan, and we're going to sit tight until they're gone. You still doing okay?"

She nodded against him. As soon as he turned back to watch the road, she rested her cheek against his back and closed her eyes. Her heart was slowing down now. She wanted to take advantage of the temporary breather in case they had to start running again. Who were these men, and why were they after them?

She shifted her weight from one knee to the other. She felt as though she were sitting in compost. The smell of wet, rotten, decomposing

371

leaves was thick and musty. She thought there had to be a dead animal somewhere close because she could smell the foul stench of rotting meat. She wanted to gag.

It had stopped raining. That was good, wasn't it? God, how long had they been waiting? It seemed as though an hour had passed since they'd dived into the brush, but then time had pretty much stopped from the moment the first gunshot had been fired.

She heard the car before she saw the headlights through the branches. It came roaring down the road, passed them without slowing, and sped on.

Theo chanced it and leaned out to see which way the car was headed. It slowed at the crossroad, then went straight ahead, which meant the men hadn't given up yet and were searching another back road. He tried but couldn't see the license plate.

"They'll have to give up looking for us soon," she whispered. "It will be light, and they won't want to risk being seen by early morning fishermen. Don't you think they'll give up?"

"Maybe," he allowed. "Let's go," he said then as he stood, bracing himself for the pain in his knee. He pulled her to her feet. "Stay close to the side of the road and don't turn the flashlight on."

"Okay," she agreed. "But if you hear them coming, don't throw me into a ditch again. Just tell me. My backside's going to be bruised."

He didn't sound contrite when he said, "Better a bruise than a bullet."

She sneezed. It felt good. "I know," she said.

"Can you run?"

"Can *you?*" she asked, noticing that he was favoring one leg.

"Sure. I'm just a little stiff. Let's move."

There was a single light shining from a pole near the opening to the parking lot. Theo wasn't taking any chances. He pulled Michelle over into the brush and edged around The Swan to the back door. He couldn't see anything moving inside. The back door was metal, so Theo began to backtrack to one of the front windows, looking down at the ground now for a sturdy rock.

"I'll have to climb in through the window," he said as he picked up a jagged rock.

"What are you doing?"

"I'm gonna break the glass."

"No," she whispered. "I know where Daddy hides his spare key."

Theo dropped the rock and walked over to the door. She turned the flashlight on and reached up over the door and picked up the key from the ledge.

"That's a real clever hiding place," he said.

"Don't be sarcastic. No one would think of breaking in Daddy's bar."

"Why wouldn't they?"

"John Paul would go after them, and they all know it. Daddy could leave the doors unlocked if he wanted to."

It took her two tries to get the key in the lock because her hands were shaking. Aftermath, she thought. Her body was finally reacting to the terror she and Theo had lived through.

Theo went inside first, squinting into the darkness, then, keeping Michelle behind him, he told her in a whisper to lock the door. He heard the sound of the deadbolt slipping into place. The refrigerator began to hum and vibrate. The phone, he remembered, was in the main room at the end of the bar, just outside of the storage room. He thought he heard a sound, maybe a squeaky floorboard.

"Stay here," he whispered as he pulled his gun out and cautiously walked into the bar.

The light from the parking lot cast a gray shadow on the tables and the floor. It was still dark in the corners, though. Theo went behind the bar. His eyes had adjusted to the dim light, his gaze now fully directed on the half-opened door to the storage area. It was a perfect place for a man to hide. Would they have left a man behind? No, that didn't make any sense to Theo, but he still continued to watch the door as he crept along.

At the center of the bar, he stopped, and then reached underneath the counter to search for Jake's shotgun. He wouldn't miss his target with that sucker, he thought as his hand touched the butt of the shotgun. Lifting it off the bracket, he carefully pulled it out.

Theo was turning away from the counter when he felt the tiniest brush of air on the back of his neck. He knew without turning around or hearing a sound that someone was coming up behind him and coming fast.

CHAPTER THIRTY-ONE

Michelle, run," Theo shouted. He dropped the shotgun on the counter, then pivoted, his Glock cocked and ready.

He couldn't see the man's face; it was too dark. The huge shadow karate-chopped Theo's wrist, but he held tight to the gun. Then the shadow grabbed Theo's arm and twisted it back with one hand as the other was coming up fast to nail him under the chin.

Theo ducked, but not fast enough. The shadow's knuckles grazed his chin, snapping his head back. Searing pain shot through his jaw. Theo put every ounce of power he had in his left fist and punched the attacker in the gut. He knew then he was in real trouble. His fist felt as though he'd just struck a cement block, and he thought he might have broken his hand.

Where had the son of a bitch come from? Had he already gotten to Michelle? Enraged, Theo hit again. With the speed of a jackhammer, the man swung his foot up to kick Theo's knee.

Michelle turned on the fluorescent lights and shouted, "John Paul! No! Let him go."

The two adversaries were now engaged in a bear hug, each trying to use his strength to break the other's back. When John Paul heard his sister's shout, he let go. Theo didn't. He tried to hit him again, hoping to smash his face, but John Paul easily blocked the punch with as much effort as it would take to swat a pesky mosquito away. In the process, his hand struck a bottle of whiskey, sending it careening into the other bottles lined up on the shelf against the wall behind the bar.

Both men took a step back at the same time, sizing each other up. Michelle got between them, glancing from one angry expression to the other, and then decided Theo was the one more out of control. She put her hand on his chest, told him to take a deep breath, and held him until he came to his senses and did as she asked.

Theo took a long hard look at the man. John Paul looked like a savage. Dressed in a pair of army green shorts, boots, and a T-shirt, he was muscular enough to be the Jolly Green Giant. Only there wasn't anything jolly about him. The bowie knife sheathed in the lining of his boot and the steely, pissed-off look in his eyes indicated he still wanted to break every bone in Theo's body. No, he definitely wasn't the Jolly Green Giant. Bad comparison, Theo thought as he continued to pant for breath from the exertion and the fear that maybe Michelle had been hurt. Her brother could star in a warlock movie. His hair was almost long enough, and he had the scars—one on his cheek and another one on his thigh—to make Theo think he was a throwback to times gone by.

"Theo, I'd like you to meet my brother, John Paul." Feeling it was safe now to let go of him, she turned to her brother. "John Paul, this is—"

Her brother cut her off. "I know who he is."

Theo blinked. "You know who I am?"

"That's right," John Paul said.

John Paul had never backed away from a fight in his life, and when Theo took a step toward him, he took an immediate step forward. Michelle was squeezed between them.

"If you knew who I was, why did you jump me?" Theo growled.

"Yes, why did you?" Michelle wanted to know, craning her neck back so she could look into her brother's eyes. "That was rude, John Paul."

His sister always knew just what to say to make him laugh. It took effort to maintain his angry expression. Rude. Hell, yes, he supposed it had been rude.

He folded his arms across his chest. "I couldn't let him take the shotgun," he explained to Michelle. "He might be the kind to spook easy and shoot someone, or maybe even shoot himself in the foot."

Theo wasn't placated. He took another step forward. "You were trying to kick me in my bad knee, weren't you?"

John Paul smiled. "Always go for the weakest point," he said. "You were favoring your leg, so I figured..."

"You knew I was a friend of your sister's, and you were still going to break my kneecap?"

"I wasn't going to break it," he countered. "I was just going to make you go down."

"You could have hurt him," Michelle said.

"Michelle, I don't need you to defend me," Theo muttered. His masculinity was taking a beating, and he had had all he was going to take of Mad Max.

"If I had wanted to hurt him, I would have. I could have killed him, but I didn't."

"The hell you could," Theo said, as he dropped the gun in the holster.

"I could have snapped your neck, but I resisted the impulse."

It was then, as Michelle was turning to tell Theo to stop baiting her brother, that she noticed the blood on his arm. She turned the bar light on and stepped closer to Theo. In the light she could see a sliver of glass imbedded in the deep cut. "When did this happen? You're going to need stitches." She didn't give him time to explain. Whirling around, she went after her brother. She poked him in his chest and demanded, "Did you do that? What were you thinking?"

Theo smiled. He could have put an end to her tirade by speaking up and telling her that her brother hadn't caused the injury, but he was getting a real kick out of watching John Paul squirm. Her brother was backing away from her as she read him the riot act. His expression, Theo thought with a good deal of smug satisfaction, was laughable. The guy looked as if he didn't know what to do. When she was finished blistering him with her guilt trip, her brother appeared to be a little contrite. Not much, but a little.

In the harsh light, Theo could see a bit of a resemblance between brother and sister. Both had high cheekbones and blue eyes of the identical color, but that was where the resemblance ended. Michelle was beautiful. She had a gentle, loving disposition. John Paul didn't.

Theo childishly wanted to keep on hating the man, but he knew he couldn't because he could see in John Paul's eyes that he loved Michelle, and Theo figured he was just like any other big brother, doing whatever it took to protect her.

His magnanimous gesture to give the guy a break was short-lived. John Paul glared at him and demanded, "My sister looks like she's been dragged through the mud. What the hell have you been up to?"

Michelle turned his attention then. "You're going to have to tell Daddy you broke his best whiskey bottle," she told her brother. "Now, clean it up while I call Ben."

She pushed Theo out of her way to get to the phone. She called the police station and asked the operator to put her through to Ben Nelson's home.

Theo told John Paul to turn the light off. Surprisingly he did as he was told, then Theo explained what had happened. John Paul didn't show any reaction.

When Theo ended his account of the attack, John Paul asked, "You think they'll come back? Is that why you don't want the light on?"

"They probably won't, but I'm not taking any chances. We could get trapped in here."

"No, we couldn't," John Paul argued. "Besides, I'd hear them coming."

"Yeah? You'd hear them even if they were creeping up on us?"

John Paul nodded. "Yeah, I would."

"You think you're Superman?"

Her brother grinned. "Pretty much. I'd love it if they tried to come in. It would give me the opportunity to kill a couple of them."

"There's nothing more fun than a shoot-out," Theo said, his voice reeking with sarcasm, "but not with your sister here."

"Yeah, I know."

Theo was beginning to feel the effects of the fight. His jaw hurt and his arm was throbbing. He opened the cooler, took out two cold long-neck bottles of beer, and though he wanted to hit John Paul over the head with one of them, he figured that would be a waste of good beer and handed it to him instead.

John Paul didn't thank him, but then Theo didn't expect him to. He opened his and took a long drink.

Theo heard Michelle talking to Ben and interrupted. "Tell him to meet us at the house."

She asked Ben to hold on and told Theo they needed to get to the hospital.

He decided his arm was way down the list of priorities. "No," he said firmly. "We're going to your house first."

"God, you're stubborn," she whispered, but she gave in.

Theo wanted to get off his feet so his knee would stop aching. He went over to one of the tables, sat down, then pulled another chair out and propped his foot up on it.

John Paul followed him, and stood beside him, towering over him.

"Sit down," Theo said.

John Paul circled the table, pulled a chair out, and sat. He began to ask questions, wanting more details. Theo took another swig of his beer and then explained once again from beginning to end what had happened, only leaving out the part that he had been in Michelle's bed. He didn't think her brother would appreciate hearing that.

John Paul homed in on what Theo hadn't told him. "Why were you closing the window in Mike's room?"

"It was open."

"Theo? Do you know what make the car was?" Michelle called out.

"A gray Toyota...new," he answered.

"They're probably long gone by now," John Paul remarked.

Theo agreed. He was watching Michelle now, and John Paul patiently waited for him to turn back around so he could tell him he was going to have to beat the hell out of him because he knew damn well that Theo had been in Michelle's bed. He didn't care that his sister could make her own choices, and he didn't care that it wasn't his business. She was his little sister, and Theo, John Paul decided, had taken advantage of her.

"My sister's a gifted surgeon," John Paul said with a snarl.

"I know."

"She's spent most of her life getting her training."

"What are you trying to say?"

"She hasn't had much training with men... doesn't know what pricks they can be."

"She's an adult."

"She's naïve."

"Who's naïve?" Michelle asked as she hurried to the table.

"Never mind," her brother said as he continued to glare at Theo. He was angry with Michelle too, he realized, for not only had she allowed herself to become vulnerable by getting involved with an outsider, but damned if she hadn't chosen a government man. That was almost unforgivable.

"Mike, you and I are going to have to have a talk."

She ignored the anger radiating in her brother's voice. "Ben's getting dressed and will meet us at the house in about ten minutes. He's also sending out a couple of police cars to try to find the Toyota. I told him I thought there were three or four men, maybe more."

"At least four," Theo said.

"Do you know where Daddy keeps the Tylenol?" she asked her brother.

"Above the sink in the kitchen. You want me to get it?"

"I'll do it. Theo, we should go directly to the hospital," she said as she walked away.

"Stitches can wait."

Michelle came back with a bottle of Tylenol and two glasses of water. Tucked under her arm were two bags of frozen vegetables. She set the Tylenol on the table with the glasses and held up the bags.

"Peas or carrots?"

Theo was unscrewing the childproof bottle of Tylenol. "Carrots."

She crunched the bag in her hands to break up the frozen chunks then put the bag on Theo's knee.

"Better?"

"Yeah, thanks."

She lifted the bag of peas to the top of her forehead. Theo immediately let go of the bottle and pulled Michelle onto his lap.

"You hurt yourself? Here, let me see."

The concern in his voice made her feel a little weepy. She took a breath and said, "It's nothing. Just a little bump. Honestly, it's no big—"

"Shhh," he whispered as he gently pushed her hand away and tilted her head down so he could see the injury in the dim light.

The more John Paul observed, the more depressed he became. He knew from the tender way Theo was touching Mike that the man obviously cared about her, and it was too late to do anything about it. A Fed. How could she have fallen for a Fed?

"Damn," he muttered.

Michelle and Theo ignored him. "You didn't cut your scalp."

"I told you it wasn't anything."

"You've got a hell of a bump."

"It's okay."

He was gently brushing her hair away from

her face. John Paul's disgust was becoming unbearable.

"Mike, get off his lap and sit in a chair."

"I don't think your brother likes me," Theo said with a smile. Because he knew John Paul was glaring at him, he kissed her forehead. "When did you hit your head? Was it when the snake fell on you?"

She slipped off his lap and sat in the chair next to him.

"What snake?" John Paul asked.

"A cottonmouth fell out of a tree," she explained to her brother.

Theo opened the bottle of Tylenol. Michelle put her hand out, and he dropped two capsules into her palm as she said, "Theo, we have to get to the hospital and find that package."

"What are you talking about? What package?" Theo asked.

Michelle decided she needed to start at the beginning. Propping her elbow on the table, she placed the bag of peas against her forehead and said, "I recognized one of them."

"And you're just now telling me?" He jerked upright, sending the bag of carrots flying. John Paul caught the bag in midair, then reached over and slammed it down on Theo's knee.

She cringed because the shout made her head hurt more. "The man who was running toward us while we were trying to get to my boat...he's the man I recognized. You turned the flashlight on his face, remember? He was the messenger from the Speedy Messenger Service.

He came up to me while I was sitting in the bleachers at the stadium watching you work with the football team…"

"I saw the guy at the stadium, but I didn't see his face. He was wearing that cap. You're talking about the guy I shot at?"

"Yes."

"Did you kill him?" John Paul wanted to know.

Theo's mind was racing. "No," he answered impatiently. "I missed. Michelle, I still don't understand why you waited so long to tell me that you knew one of them."

"When did I have time to tell you? While they were shooting at us and chasing us? Or when we were hiding in the swamp and you wouldn't let me talk?"

"You're absolutely certain it was the same man?"

"Yes," she said emphatically. "You know what's really odd? When I was talking to him at the stadium, I had this feeling I'd seen him before, but then I thought I had probably run into him at the hospital. We're always getting deliveries there."

"Did you recognize any of the others? What about the guy in the boat?"

"I didn't see his face," she answered. "He jumped into the water when you shot at him."

"Did you kill *him?*" John Paul asked.

"No, I missed."

John Paul looked incredulous. "Why do you carry a gun if you don't know how to use it?"

"I do know how to use it," he snapped defensively. "I'll be happy to demonstrate."

"He might have winged him," Michelle said hopefully, then recognized the irony. She was supposed to be dedicated to saving lives, not destroying them. Getting shot at had certainly turned her moral code upside down.

"Yeah, right," John Paul grunted with disgust. "How far away was this guy?"

"We were getting fired at from both directions," she said. "And Theo was busy trying to shield me and shoot at the same time."

John Paul ignored her explanation. "Why do you carry a gun?" he asked.

"Because I've been ordered to carry one. I get a lot of death threats."

"I can see that," John Paul said.

"Will you stop fighting with one another? We're in a mess here. Theo, I think I know what's going on now. The man, or men, who tore up my clinic were looking for a package. The guy who came up to me at the stadium said another employee of Speedy Messenger had delivered the wrong one to me, and he was trying to get it back. I called the staff secretary and told her to look for it and give it to him. I sent him to the hospital, but never followed up to see if he got the package," she said. "Remember Elena dropped that box of mail off earlier? I think the men who came to my house last night thought it was there. But I went through the box, and there was no special delivery in it. My guess is that they didn't find it at the hospital yesterday and they thought she brought it to me last night."

"There's only one way they could have known Elena was going to drop anything off," John Paul said.

"They tapped into her phone line," Theo said. "Damn, why didn't I check?"

"I'll find it," John Paul offered.

"Do you know what to look for?"

Her brother looked offended. "Of course."

Theo thought for a second and then said, "When you find it, leave it alone."

"Why?" Michelle asked.

"Because I don't want them to know we're aware of it. We might want to give them some false information."

"Tell me exactly what the guy said to you," John Paul said, and Theo noticed he wasn't quite as antagonistic now.

"He said there was a mix-up at the delivery service," Michelle said. "Frank—that's the name he gave me—told me that another messenger named Eddie inadvertently switched labels on two packages he picked up. Whatever I got by mistake is obviously what they're after."

Theo shook his head. "And you know it was a mix-up because...?" He didn't wait for the light to dawn. "Nothing is true until it's proven, and we aren't going to believe the package was misdirected until we open it and look inside."

She nodded. "Because the man shooting at us could have been lying."

"Jeez, Mike. Use your head," John Paul said.

"My head aches, John Paul." Upset with herself because she'd been so slow, she sighed. "Of course he was lying."

"Not necessarily," Theo qualified.

"You just said…" she snapped.

Theo smiled. "He could have been telling the truth. It could be a misdirected package. When we find it, we'll see what it is. Until then…"

"I understand," she said wearily.

"You remember telling me you had the feeling someone was following you? I think you were right. Whoever he is…he's good. I never spotted him, and I was looking."

"Maybe they were watching the house," Michelle suggested.

"What do you think about all this?" John Paul asked Theo.

"I don't know," he admitted. "When we find that package, we'll know what we're up against."

"You're going home with me, Mike. I can protect you."

"Are you saying I can't?" Theo asked, angry now.

"When I shoot, I shoot to kill. I don't miss."

Theo was ready to punch him again, but Michelle put a stop to the hostility.

"Excuse me, gentlemen," she snapped. "I can and will protect myself. John Paul, I'm going to the hospital with Theo."

"Mike—"

"That's the way it's going to be."

"She'll be okay with me," Theo said, and was surprised when John Paul didn't argue. Rubbing his brow, Theo added, "Noah's in New Orleans. I'll want him to stay there and do a couple of things before he drives back to Bowen."

"Noah is—" Michelle began, thinking to explain.

"I know who he is. FBI." John Paul snapped the words out, his disdain apparent.

"So, in the meantime," Theo continued as though neither one of them had interrupted his train of thought, "you keep your dad close."

Michelle dropped the bag of peas on the table. "You think they'll go after Daddy?"

"I'm just covering every possibility I can think of until I have time to figure out what the next move should be."

Theo finished his beer and set the bottle on the table. "We should get going."

Michelle asked, "John Paul, will you get the pickup started? Daddy hasn't driven it in over a week now. He told me something's wrong with the starter, and he hasn't had time to get it fixed."

"I'll get it started."

Exhaustion was finally catching up with Michelle. She slowly stood. "Then let's get going."

Theo handed her the bag of carrots to put back in the freezer as he stood and tested his knee by slowly putting weight on it. The ice pack had helped. His knee didn't buckle, and it wasn't throbbing much at all now.

Michelle held the bag of peas against her forehead as she headed to the kitchen.

"We have to stop by the house first," Theo reiterated.

"Because Ben will be waiting for us? I could call him—"

"No," Theo said. "Because I want to pick up my cell phone, and I need more bullets."

He knew what was coming before John Paul opened his mouth.

"What do you need more bullets for?"

"I'm almost out."

"Seems like a waste to me."

Michelle had had it with her brother. Turning around, she said, "Don't shoot him, Theo. I know you want to because my brother can be a real pain in the backside. But I love him, so don't do it."

Theo winked at her.

John Paul scoffed, "I'm not worried."

"You should be," Michelle said.

"Why?" John Paul asked. "If he shoots, he'll miss."

CHAPTER THIRTY-TWO

While Michelle stood by the car talking to Ben, Theo went inside her house. He left his shoes by the door so he wouldn't track in mud, then ran upstairs, stripped out of his clothes, and took a quick hot shower. He was relieved he didn't find any ticks or leeches. He was back outside ten minutes later, carrying both Michelle's and his cell phones and her charger. He had already reloaded his gun and stuck an extra magazine in his pocket.

"Ready to go?" he asked Michelle.

"John Paul got your car started," she told him as she got inside. "Keys are in the ignition."

"Where is your brother?"

She nodded toward the side of the house. John Paul was sprinting toward the pickup he'd left parked on the road.

Theo intercepted him and handed him Michelle's cell phone and charger.

"I don't want that." There was a look of repulsion on John Paul's face as he stared at the phone.

"I have to be able to get hold of you. Take it."

"I don't—"

Theo wasn't in the mood to argue. "What are Michelle and I supposed to do if we need you? Send up a prayer?"

John Paul relented. He grabbed the phone and charger and headed for the pickup. He heard his sister call, "You take care of Daddy, John Paul. Don't let anything happen to him. And you be careful too. You aren't invincible."

Theo got in the car and was closing the door when Ben shouted and came running.

"I think we just got a lucky break," Ben said.

"What's that?"

"Dispatch just called. There's a detective from New Orleans waiting to talk to me. Says it's urgent."

"Do you know what the detective wants? No way New Orleans could have found out what happened last night. Not enough time."

"I'm on my way back to the station to find out, but I've got a feeling this," he said, waving toward Michelle's house, "and the detective from New Orleans are connected. They might know something that could help us."

"Call me at the hospital as soon as you know anything," he said.

It didn't take them long to get to the hospital. Michelle led the way through the back corridor into the emergency room. She hadn't looked at herself in a mirror, and it wasn't until she noticed the staff staring at her that she realized she should have taken time to clean up. She thought she probably smelled awful too. Megan, the young, newly certified nurse working the emergency room, did a double take.

"You look like you fell in a garbage truck," she said. "What the heck happened to you?"

"Fell in a garbage truck."

Another nurse named Frances looked up from behind the nurses' station. She was also young, but had earned the nickname "Grannie" because she acted like a ninety-year-old. Michelle told her she needed a tray prepared for stitches.

Frances got up and hurried around the counter. Her rubber shoes squeaked with each step she took.

"You stay here, Theo," Michelle said. "I'm going to go into the doctors' lounge and take a shower."

"I'm going with you. It's quiet there, isn't it?"

"Yes."

"Good. I've got to call Noah."

Megan was wide-eyed and gawking as they walked past her. Michelle noticed her full attention was directed on Theo now.

Michelle led the way into the spacious lounge. There were lockers against one wall, a sofa and coffee table on the opposite side of the room, a couple of recliners, and a desk. Just inside the door was a narrow table with a coffee urn and plastic cups. In the corner sat a refrigerator.

A narrow hallway led to two doors. While Michelle was getting clean clothes out of her locker, Theo opened both doors to see what was inside. Each was a fully equipped bathroom with a shower.

"Nice setup," he remarked as she passed him on her way into the bath. Grabbing a container of bottled water out of the refrigerator, he sat down at the desk and dialed Noah's cell phone. A second later he was listening to Noah telling him to leave a message. He had a pretty good idea where Noah was, but he would have to wait until Michelle finished showering to get the phone number.

Next, he dialed the hospital operator and asked her to page Elena Miller. He heard the sound of papers rustling in the background, then the operator told him that Elena wasn't on duty yet. Although she refused to give Theo the woman's home number, she finally agreed to dial it for him. Elena answered on the second ring, and after identifying himself, Theo asked her to describe the messenger who had come by the hospital to pick up the package on Wednesday and to tell him what the man had said.

Elena couldn't wait to tell Theo all about the rude man. "He had the gall to shout at me," she said.

Theo made notes on a notepad he found on the desk and asked her several questions. When he was finished, he hung up, then looked up the phone number of the Speedy Messenger Service in New Orleans in the yellow pages he found in the bottom desk drawer and called them. Three people later, he got to the supervisor. The man sounded frazzled and didn't want to cooperate until Theo threatened to send over a couple of policemen to get the information. The supervisor was suddenly happy to help. He explained that all the deliveries were kept in the computer. He typed in Michelle Renard's name and told Theo when and where the package was delivered.

"I want to know who sent it," Theo said.

"Benchley, Tarrance, and Paulson," the supervisor replied. "The package was signed for at the St. Claire Hospital at five-fifteen according to my records. You want me to send you a copy?"

"That won't be necessary," Theo said.

By the time Michelle had showered and washed her hair, she felt pretty good. She thought she looked like hell, but she felt good, and right now, that was all she cared about. She got dressed, combed her hair, wincing when she accidentally hit her tender scalp. Tucking the strands behind her ears, she decided to let it dry on its own. She was walking toward Theo, pulling the drawstring tight on her pants and tying it, as he turned to her.

"Did you talk to Noah?" she asked.

"Not yet," he answered. "I did talk to the supervisor at Speedy. Guess what?"

"There's no Frank or Eddie, right? God, I feel like such an idiot."

"No, there isn't any Frank or Eddie, but why would you feel like an idiot? There was absolutely no reason for you to be suspicious."

"Theo, I'm telling you, I've seen that man before. I assumed I had run into him at the hospital, but that obviously isn't the case. So where did I see him?"

"It will come to you," he said. "Try not to force it, and when you're thinking about something else, that's when you'll remember. You know what else the supervisor told me?"

Michelle crossed the room to the sofa, sat down, and bent over to tie her shoelaces.

"Tell me," she said.

"The package was sent from Benchley, Tarrance, and Paulson."

"Addressed to me?"

"Yes," he answered. "I called the firm, but no one is going to tell me anything over the phone, so I'm sending Noah over there. Oh, and I also talked to Elena Miller. She was on a tirade."

Michelle nodded. "Elena's always on a tirade about something. What did she say?"

"The messenger was hostile."

"We already know that."

"When she couldn't locate the package for him, she said he started shouting at her. He threatened her too. She was so furious she was going to call the messenger service and report him, but she got busy and forgot about it."

She stood and walked over to the desk. Noticing the way he was staring at her, she asked, "What's the matter?"

"I just noticed how tired you look."

"I'm okay."

"I'm worried about you. You look like you're about to fall over."

"I'm fine," she insisted.

She didn't look fine. Her complexion was pale and she was tense. She needed to take a couple of minutes to chill out, he thought. Her nervous energy was going to run out, and then she would crash.

"Come here."

"Theo, we have to get moving. I've got to stitch your arm and find that package."

"The stitches and the package can wait a few more minutes. Take a deep breath and try to unwind. You want something to drink? A cola or something?"

"No, thanks."

"Come here."

"I am here."

"Closer."

She took a step to the side of the desk. "Theo..."

"Closer."

The man was irresistible. She knew she shouldn't allow him to sidetrack her. They both had too much to do. Folding her arms across her chest, she frowned at him. "Now isn't the time to fool around."

He pulled her onto his lap. "Why do you think I want to fool around?"

His hand had moved to the back of her neck, and he was slowly pulling her toward him.

"I don't know...it's just a feeling I have that you might want to kiss me," she said as she placed her hands on his shoulders.

"The thought never entered my mind. We can't fool around now, sweetheart. We've got too much to do."

He was nibbling on her neck. She closed her eyes and tilted her head to the side so he could kiss her earlobe.

"Then I must have misread the signals," she whispered.

"Must have," he agreed a scant second before his mouth captured hers for a long, scorching kiss. His tongue slid inside her warm mouth, and, oh, God, the slow, lazy penetration drove her wild. He teased and tantalized until she was trembling and gripping his shoulders in a silent demand for more.

Theo had meant only to give her a quick kiss, but once his mouth touched hers, he simply couldn't resist. He knew he had to stop before things got completely out of hand, and yet he continued to kiss her until she pulled back.

"We can't do this." She was panting now and

sounded dazed. "We just can't." Her forehead dropped on his. "This has to stop, Theo."

"Yeah, okay," he said gruffly as he tried to get his heartbeat to slow down.

She kissed his forehead, then moved lower to the bridge of his nose. "This is a hospital, for the love of God."

She kissed him on the mouth. And just when he was beginning to gain the upper hand, she tore her mouth away and whispered, "I work here. I can't go around kissing people all the time."

And damned if she didn't kiss him again. Theo could feel his control slipping. He abruptly pulled back and lifted her off his lap.

She leaned against the desk in case her legs gave out. Lord, could he kiss, and, oh, how she loved the taste of him. Disheartened, she realized she loved everything about him. His calm, take-charge attitude...his self-confidence. He was so comfortable in his own skin, so sure of himself. When he was afraid, he didn't hide it the way her brother did. He was so secure he didn't care what other people thought.

Michelle admired that trait most of all.

She took a deep breath and headed for the ER. Pushing the swinging door open with the flat of her hand, she went into the hallway. Theo was right behind her.

"You've got the sexiest walk," he told her.

"Didn't you read the sign?"

"What sign?"

"No flirting in the hospital."

He relented. "Okay," he agreed. "We'll start searching for the package in the emergency room first," he said, suddenly all business again. "I noticed on our way in that it wasn't busy, so now is the perfect time. I'm going to get some of the staff to help."

"I'm going to sew you back together first."

"No, Michelle, I want—"

She turned around and walked backwards as she said, "Theo, I'm in charge here. Deal with it."

The shower had revitalized her, but she knew the burst of energy she was feeling was going to be short and the lack of sleep would eventually catch up with her. For that reason she wanted to get the more important task finished. Theo came first whether he wanted to or not.

She was also feeling relaxed and sure of herself again. She was on safe ground at the hospital and knew that she and Theo could let their guard down here. No one would be shooting at them. There was safety in numbers. She thought it might be a good idea if they slept at the hospital and was going to suggest it when Theo turned her attention.

"Slow down," he demanded. "Who do I talk to about getting personnel to start looking?"

"Those people have jobs to do."

"This is a priority."

"You could call the administrator. He's usually here by eight, and it's almost that now, but he's not going to cooperate with you. He doesn't like anything disrupting routine."

"Tough," he said. "He'll cooperate. You're practically running. Slow down," he said once again.

"You're dragging your feet. Are you afraid of a couple of stitches?" The possibility made her smile. "Scared I'll hurt you?"

"No, I just don't like needles."

"I don't either," she said. "I faint every time I see one."

"That's not funny, Michelle."

She thought it was and laughed. Frances, the nurse of the perpetual frown, was standing outside one of the exam areas. She pulled the drape back. "Everything's ready, Doctor."

Michelle patted the exam table while the nurse raised the head so Theo could lean back. He sat down, his attention on Michelle now as she put on a pair of sterile gloves. The nurse distracted him when she came at him with a pair of scissors and took hold of his T-shirt. He reached over and pulled the sleeve up over his shoulder. While she swabbed the skin around the cut with a strong-smelling disinfectant, he picked up his cell phone and started dialing.

"You can't use that cell phone in the hospital," Frances told him, and tried to snatch the phone out of his hand.

He wanted to say, "Back off, lady," but he didn't. He turned the phone off and put it on the exam table next to him. "Get me a phone I can use."

He must have sounded hostile. Though it didn't seem possible, Frances's frown intensified. "He's an irritable one, isn't he, Doctor?"

Michelle was working at the corner with her back to Theo, but he knew she was smiling. He could hear it in her voice when she said, "He needs a nap."

"I need a phone."

Frances finished cleaning the area and left. Theo assumed she'd gone to get him a phone. Then Michelle walked over to him with her hand behind her back. He took exception to the fact that she was treating him like a ten-year-old, hiding the syringe so he wouldn't see the needle.

Exasperated, he said, "Make this quick. We've got things to do."

He didn't flinch as she injected the lidocaine. "This should be numb in a minute. Would you like to lie down?"

"Would it make your job easier or quicker if I did?"

"No."

"Then I'm fine. Go ahead and start."

Frances had returned with a clipboard and papers. She'd obviously heard Theo tell Michelle to get started.

"Young man, you shouldn't rush the doctor. That's how mistakes are made."

Young man? Hell, he had to be older than she was. "Where's a phone?"

"Relax, Theo," Michelle said as she motioned for Frances to move the tray closer to her side. "I'm not going to hurry." Then she smiled and whispered, "Someone told me that if you want something done right..."

"What?"

"You have to be slow and easy. It's the only way."

In spite of his irritability, he had to smile. He wanted to kiss her, but he knew the nurse from *X-Files* would probably try to deck him if he did.

"Frances, are you married?"

"Yes, I am. Why do you ask?"

"I was thinking Michelle should hook you up with her brother, John Paul. You two have a lot in common."

"Doctor, we don't have paperwork on this patient," she said curtly.

"Where's my phone?" Theo asked.

"He'll fill out the forms after I'm finished," Michelle said.

"That isn't proper procedure."

"I'm gonna count to five. If I don't have a phone in my hand by the time I'm finished, I'm getting off this table..." Theo warned.

"Frances, please bring Theo a phone."

"There's one on the wall," she pointed out.

"But he can't reach it, can he?" Michelle sounded testy now.

"Very well, Doctor."

Frances delegated the task to Megan, who was leaning over the nurses' station flirting with a paramedic.

The phone was an old-fashioned desk model. Megan unclipped the wall phone outlet, snapped the plug in, and handed the phone to Theo. "You have to dial nine to get outside."

Michelle had finished cleaning the wound and was ready to begin stitching. "Quit squirming," she told him. "Are you trying to get Noah again?"

"I want to talk to the administrator first and get us some help. If we have to tear this place apart, that's what we're going to do. I want to find that package."

"I'm the one who has to look...maybe you and one other person could help. If you have everyone searching, I won't know where they looked and where they didn't. Let me look around the ER and the surgical floor before you call in reinforcements."

"Why just those two areas?"

"Because any mail I don't pick up down here is sent up to surgical. All the surgeons have cubicles upstairs, and that's where they drop our mail."

"She's right," Megan said. "I've taken lots of mail up. I go upstairs at least twice a day. I try to be helpful." Then she added, "There's a really cute tech up there. I've been trying get him to notice me. I'll help you, Dr. Mike. Nothing much is happening in the ER, and Frances will page me if she needs me."

"Thanks, Megan."

"No problem. What am I helping you do?"

"Find a package that was delivered by the Speedy Messenger Service."

"Oh, we get lots of packages."

"Michelle, honey, are you almost finished?" Theo asked.

"Wooo! He just called you honey," Megan crooned.

"Megan, you're in my light."

"Sorry, Doctor." As she stepped back, her gaze bounced from Theo to Michelle and back again. "So what's the deal?" she asked in a whisper.

"Why don't you start searching through the desks and cabinets down here while Michelle finishes this," Theo ordered.

"Yes, sir."

"Be thorough," Michelle said without looking up.

The second Megan pulled the curtain closed, Michelle whispered, "You shouldn't have called me honey."

"Did I undermine your authority?"

"No. It's just that..."

"What?"

"Megan's sweet, but she tells everything, and I can only imagine what the gossip will be tomorrow. They'll have me barefoot and pregnant."

He tilted his head. "The pregnant part...that's a nice image."

She rolled her eyes. "For heaven's sake."

He smiled. "A woman who could breeze through a snake crawling up her leg can handle a little gossip. You're tougher than you look."

She focused on the task at hand. "One more stitch and I'm finished. When did you have your last tetanus shot?"

He didn't miss a heartbeat. "Yesterday."

"So you hate shots too, huh? You're getting one."

He reached across to touch her cheek. "You get flustered when I tease you, and you get embarrassed with compliments. You don't know what to do with them, do you?"

"Finished," she announced. "You're back together again, Humpty-Dumpty. Don't get up yet," she quickly added when he moved. "I'm finished. You're not."

"What does that mean?"

"Bandage and shot."

"How many stitches?"

"Six."

The curtain parted as Michelle was removing her gloves. Megan interrupted. "Dr. Mike, there's a detective from New Orleans wanting to talk to you and your boyfriend."

"He's a patient," Michelle snapped, and too late realized she shouldn't have said anything. She'd sounded defensive, which, of course, only fueled Megan's overactive imagination.

Megan pulled the curtain back. "This is Detective Harris," she said.

The woman was tall, strikingly attractive, with an oval face and piercing eyes. As she strode forward, Michelle could see the lines at the corners of her eyes and around her mouth. Dressed in a pair of black pants, sensible black shoes, and a pale blue blouse, she moved toward Theo. When she extended her hand to shake his, Michelle noticed the badge and gun clipped to her belt.

Harris didn't waste time on preliminaries. "I want to hear exactly what happened last night. Chief Nelson filled me in on what went down, but I want to hear your version."

"Where is Ben?" Michelle asked.

"He went back to your house to finish sweeping the crime scene." She gave Michelle a cursory once-over before continuing. "I'll take whatever he bags back to the lab in New Orleans."

Theo studied Harris while she talked to Michelle. The detective was like a thousand other police officers he'd known. There was a weariness about her as though she'd been exhausted most of her life. Her attitude was brittle and hard.

"How long have you been with the department?" he asked.

"Four years in homicide," she responded impatiently. "Three years with vice before the transfer."

Ah. Vice. That explained it. "So what brought you to Bowen?"

"If you don't mind, I'll ask the questions."

"Sure," he said agreeably. "Just as soon as you answer mine."

Her lip curled in what Theo thought might have been an attempt at a smile. "If Nelson hadn't already told me, I would have guessed you were an attorney."

Theo didn't respond to the comment. He simply waited for her to answer his question. She tried to outstare and intimidate him, but she lost on both counts.

With a sigh, she answered, "I got a tip...a good, reliable, inside tip that a hitter I've been trailing for three long years is setting up here. I was told he's in Bowen to do a job, and,

I swear to God, I'm going to get him this time."

"Who is he?"

"A ghost. At least, that's what some of the guys in homicide call him, because he vanishes into thin air every time I get close. According to my informant, he's calling himself Monk these days. I've put him with two murders in New Orleans in the past year. We're pretty sure he killed a teenager in Metairie, and we think the girl's father paid for the hit so he could collect insurance, but we can't prove it."

"How do you know it was Monk?" Theo asked.

"He left his calling card. He always does," she explained. "My informant is close to Monk, knows his routine. He told me that Monk leaves a long-stemmed red rose as proof that he did the job. He always makes the murders look like accidents or suicide, and in every case I've been involved in, someone benefits from the death."

"A father had his child killed so he could get money?" Michelle rubbed her arms as though to ward off a chill. That a father would do such a monstrous thing was staggering. She felt sick to her stomach. That poor child.

"The rose was missing from the girl's bedroom," Harris continued. "But there was one petal, still uncurled, half under the dresser. On another case, the crime unit found a thorn stuck in the bedspread. Monk does most of his work at night when his victims are sleeping."

"Who was the victim in the second case you mentioned?" Theo asked.

"An old man, a wealthy grandfather whose only relative had a heavy drug problem."

"From what you've told me about this man," Theo said, "it doesn't seem his style to work with others. He sounds like a loner."

"Until now, he has acted alone, but my gut's telling me he was at the doctor's house last night."

"If he was involved," Michelle said, "then he must be after the package. Maybe there's something inside that will incriminate him or the person who hired him."

"What package?" Harris asked sharply. She looked as if she was about to pounce on Michelle for withholding information.

Michelle explained, and when she was finished, the detective couldn't hide her excitement.

"You're telling me you can ID one of them? You saw his face and you're certain he's the man who came up to you at the stadium?"

"Yes."

"My God, wouldn't that be a piece of luck if the man you saw was Monk. No one's seen him before, but now with a description..."

"I'd like to talk to your informant," Theo said.

She shook her head. "You think I have his phone number? It doesn't work that way. He calls me when he feels like it, and he always uses a pay phone. We've traced the calls, but a car never gets there in time. He's as elusive as the ghost."

"Okay," Theo said. "What about your file on Monk?"

"What about it?"

"I want to see it."

She ignored his request. "We've got to find that package," she said to Michelle. "No hint of what might be inside?"

"Not yet."

"I'm going to get Monk this time. I swear it on my mother's grave. He's so close I can almost smell him."

"I want to see your file," Theo repeated. This time he made sure she understood he wasn't asking. He was demanding.

She gave him an icy stare without responding.

Michelle hurried to diffuse the antagonism. "We'll help you any way that we can, Detective."

Harris was still looking at Theo as she answered. "The best way to help is to stay out of my way. I'm running this operation. Is that understood?"

When Theo didn't answer, she cleared her throat nervously. "I'll put a net around the area and start squeezing. You take the doctor home and stay there. If you hear or see anything suspect, you call me."

She pulled out two cards and handed one to Theo and gave the other one to Michelle. "You can always get me on my cell phone."

It didn't take a law degree to know Harris wasn't going to cooperate. She was playing close to the vest, and in retaliation, Theo didn't feel the need to share the information he'd collected with her.

"I'm going to want to see your file, Detective, and I'm going to want to see what's inside that package," he snapped. He wasn't going to take no for an answer.

"You can see what's in the package," she said. "And if it's something unrelated to Monk, then you can investigate to your heart's content."

"And if there is information connecting Monk?" Michelle asked.

"Then I'm calling the shots. This is my investigation, and I'm not about to let the Feds mess it up. I've spent three long years chasing Monk's shadow, and I've got too much invested to let the FBI interfere. It's not going to happen."

Her contempt was palpable. The unfriendly rivalry between the Bureau and local law enforcement agencies was deep-rooted and a hell of a nuisance, as far as Theo was concerned. He wasn't in the mood to be diplomatic or play games.

"You're worried the FBI will take your case?" Michelle asked.

"Damn right, I'm worried. Three years," she repeated. "I'm going to get Monk, and when I do, I'm not going to hand him over to you," she told Theo.

"Hey, I'm an attorney with the Justice Department. I don't care what you do with him, unless he's one of the shooters who tried to kill Michelle and me last night. If that's the case, then you and I are going to have to come to an understanding."

She shook her head and said, "The police chief told me you are on vacation...that you

410

came here to fish. So go fish and let me do my job."

"Look, I understand why you want the collar, but—"

"What?" she demanded before he could finish.

"I'm in, like it or not. You think I'm going to sit around and wait? Maybe I didn't make myself clear. He tried to kill us."

Harris was irate. "I'm not letting you screw up this investigation."

Theo wasn't about to get involved in a shouting match. Forcing himself to speak in a level voice, he asked, "How many times do I have to say it before you understand? You're not stopping me."

"The hell I'm—"

He cut her off. "I can stop you, though, and we both know it. One phone call. That's all it would take."

He wasn't bluffing. When it came to push and shove, he had the muscle. She didn't. Simple as that.

Harris decided on a more prudent approach. "Okay, we'll share information. I'll send you copies of what I've got on Monk as soon as I get back to the station. And I'll let you see what's inside the package."

"Assuming we can find it," Michelle interjected.

"We have to find it," she snapped.

"Now, I want something," Harris said.

"What?"

"I want forty-eight hours before you start

interfering or call in your troops. I guarantee I'll have Monk behind bars before then. If he's working with the men who came after you and the doctor, I'll get them too."

"You're pretty sure of yourself. What aren't you telling me, Detective? Do you know where Monk is now?"

"Forty-eight hours," she insisted.

He didn't waste any time thinking about it. "No."

"Twenty-four hours, then," she demanded. "That's reasonable."

Her neck was getting red from anger, but Theo didn't give a damn if he was making her life difficult or not.

"No."

"What the hell do you want? Give me something. My men are closing the net now, and we've all worked too damn long to let you take over. Let us get him. Three long years—"

"Yeah, I know. Three years," he said. "Okay. I'll give you twelve hours, but not one minute more. If you haven't made any arrests by then, I'm acting."

She checked her watch. "It's almost nine o'clock now. Twelve hours...yeah, I can live with that. You take the doctor home and stay there with her until nine tonight." Turning to Michelle, she said, "Let's get moving. Where do we start looking for that package?"

Michelle saw Frances motioning to her. She was holding the phone up. "It's either down here somewhere or upstairs on the surgical wing. Will you excuse me? I've got a phone call." She didn't wait for permission. As she hurried to the counter, she called out, "Megan, why don't you and Detective Harris go on up to the surgical floor and start looking. I'll be up in a minute to help. Frances, you can go ahead and bandage Mr. Buchanan and give him a tetanus shot."

She picked up the phone and moved back to get out of Megan's path.

"This way, Detective," Megan said, leading her toward the elevator.

Michelle wasn't on the phone long. She came back to Theo and said, "Dr. Landusky found out I was in the hospital and asked me to check a patient for him. Has the numbing worn off? I could give you something if you're hurting."

"I'm okay."

"See to that paperwork, Doctor," Frances said before she left them alone.

Theo was watching the elevator. As soon as the doors closed, he picked up the phone and asked Michelle to give him Mary Ann's home phone number.

She rattled off the number. "Why do you want to talk to Mary Ann?"

"I don't."

Michelle's friend answered on the third ring. She sounded sleepy. Theo didn't waste time chatting. "Let me talk to Noah."

Michelle's mouth dropped open. "He went back to New Orleans with Mary Ann?"

She had her answer a second later when Theo said, "Get out of her bed and go in the other room so we can talk."

Noah yawned loudly into the phone. "This better be good."

"It is," he promised.

"Yeah, all right. Hold on a minute."

Michelle heard her name being paged and went back to the counter to pick up the phone. A nurse wanted her to check a chart before she gave the patient medication. Michelle hung up just as Theo was ending his conversation.

She heard him say, "After you check it out, get back here. Thanks, Noah."

The second he hung up the phone, Michelle asked, "What are you doing? I heard you promise the detective you would give her twelve hours and not do anything until then."

"Uh-huh."

"You did say twelve hours?"

"Yes, I did," he agreed. "So you know what that must mean."

"What?"

"I lied."

CHAPTER THIRTY-THREE

They were searching the wrong cubicle. Michelle went past her desk and found Detective Harris and Megan sorting through Dr. Landusky's things.

"Have you already searched my cubicle?" she asked Megan.

"I thought this was where you worked,"

Megan said. She was sitting on the floor next to the desk, going through folders.

"Mine's next door."

"Gee, I'm sorry, Dr. Mike. All this time, since I started working here, I thought you were a slob because I thought this was your workspace. Every time I came up here, you were sitting at this desk dictating or writing in one of the charts."

"I used Dr. Landusky's cubicle because that's where the nurses and the staff secretaries put his charts, and I covered his practice while he was on vacation."

"But, I've been dropping your stuff off here."

"We'd better keep going, then," Harris said. "Maybe it was dropped here by mistake."

Since Detective Harris was searching the desk, Michelle got down on her knees and began to go through the pile against the wall. "I don't know how Landusky can work like this."

"He's always behind on his charts," Megan volunteered.

"Will you concentrate on the task at hand?" Harris demanded. She sounded like a schoolteacher reprimanding two errant students.

"I can talk and look at the same time," Megan assured her.

"Keep looking," Harris urged.

"Could this be it?" Megan asked a few seconds later. She handed a small yellow envelope to Michelle.

"No," Michelle answered. "It has to have the Speedy Messenger Service label on it."

"What about this one?" Megan asked.

Once again, she passed a package to Michelle. Harris glanced over her shoulder and waited for Michelle to answer.

The package was a legal-sized, padded manila envelope. Michelle read the name of a law firm in the upper corner just above the label and caught her breath.

"I think this could be it," she said as she handed the envelope to the detective.

Harris acted as though she'd just been given an explosive. She gingerly tested the weight, then slowly turned the package over. The detective took time and care pulling the tab across the top. There was another manila envelope inside. Harris sliced it open with a letter opener.

Holding the envelope by one edge, she looked around the desk. "This will work," she said as she picked up a large binder clip from one of the shelves. "I don't want to touch the papers inside and mess up any prints."

"I could get you some gloves," Megan offered.

Harris smiled. "Thanks, but this should work."

Michelle leaned back against the wall, a pile of folders in her lap. She watched as the detective used the clip to clasp the corner of one of the sheets and lift it halfway out.

Megan knocked over a stack of newspapers and charts when she got up on her knees. Michelle helped her restack the pile in the corner.

"What does it say?" Michelle asked the detective.

Harris looked disappointed. "It's some kind of an audit or a financial statement. No names on this page, just initials next to what I think are transactions. Lots and lots of numbers," she added.

"What about the other papers?"

"Looks like there's around twelve pages, maybe more, but some of them are stapled together behind this sheet," she said. Shaking her head, she added, "Too risky to try to pull out."

She was slowly pushing the paper back into the envelope. "I've got to rush this to the lab. Once they've gone over the pages, then I'll get someone to help me figure out what all these numbers mean."

It was a huge letdown not knowing what any of it meant. Michelle moved the folders and got up as Harris walked to the elevator and pushed the button. "Thanks for your help," she said. "I'll keep you apprised."

"You promised Theo you'd let him see the contents of that package," Michelle reminded her.

The elevator door opened. Harris stepped inside and punched the button. As the door was closing, she flashed Michelle a smile and said, "I'll let him see the papers in twelve hours and not a minute before."

Michelle stood with her hands on her hips, shaking her head as the door closed. Megan came up behind her.

"What did you expect to find in that envelope?" she asked.

"Answers."

"When things settle down, will you tell me what's going on?"

"Sure," Michelle agreed. "*If* I ever find out what's going on, I'll be happy to fill you in."

"Your boyfriend's an attorney. He'll probably know what those numbers mean, and you know he's not going to let that detective get past him without looking. I'm going to take the stairs down to ER. I don't want to miss the fireworks."

Michelle had one more patient to check; then she would be finished. "Tell Theo I'll only be a minute," she called out as she turned and headed to CCU.

Detective Harris wasn't about to take the chance of running into Buchanan. She got off the elevator on the second floor and took the stairs to the first. Following the exit signs, she found a side door and slipped out without anyone seeing her. She circled the outside of the hospital and was running toward the parking lot with the envelope clutched to her chest when she heard screeching tires behind her. Harris swung around just as the gray Toyota bore down on her.

CHAPTER THIRTY-FOUR

The detective wasn't answering her cell phone, and Theo was furious. He tried twice, and each time he was transferred to voice mail. His messages were to the point. He wanted that package, and he wanted it now. He also left a message for her at her precinct and was just hanging up the phone when Michelle got off the elevator. Even though Theo had heard one version from Megan of what had transpired, he made Michelle go over it again as he followed her into the doctors' lounge to pick up her clothes.

"But you didn't see the papers?"

"No," she answered. "She wasn't about to let me touch them. She was worried about messing up fingerprints."

"The hell she was," he snapped. "She was playing you," he said. "She's determined to keep me out of her investigation."

"For twelve hours anyway," she said.

She had shoved her clothes and shoes into a plastic bag and was now standing at the door. Theo was reaching for the phone. "I guess it's time to get tough," he muttered.

"Theo?"

He finally looked at her. "Yes?"

"I'm beat. I've got to get some sleep, and so do you. Can we please go home?"

"Yeah, okay."

"Give the woman twelve hours," she said. "You did promise." She yawned. "I know she doesn't want to cooperate with you and that infuriates you, but I think you should give her a little slack. She has put in three years."

"I don't care if she's put in fifteen," he countered. "I'm not backing away."

He was getting riled up. By the time they reached the car, he was threatening to take the detective's badge. Michelle let him vent his frustration without interrupting. When he was finished, she asked, "Feel better now?"

"Yeah, I do."

He handed her his phone. "Call your dad and tell him we're coming over."

"Could we stop by my house first so I can get a change of clothes?"

"Sure."

While she dialed, he turned the corner and entered Bowen. Now that he knew his way around, it didn't seem all that complicated, although he still believed the town could use a couple of signs.

No one answered at her father's house. Since he wouldn't use an answering machine, she couldn't leave a message. Remembering that John Paul had her cell phone, she dialed the number and waited.

"Yeah?"

"Is that any way to answer a phone?" Michelle asked.

"Oh, it's you," her brother said. "You okay?"

"Yes, but Theo and I are coming over. Where's Daddy?"

"Right beside me. We're on our way over to your house. Dad heard what happened last night and wants to see you to make sure you're okay."

"Tell him I'm fine."

"I already did, but he still wants to see for himself."

He abruptly disconnected his phone before she had a chance to speak to her father. She pushed the end button and handed the phone back to Theo.

John Paul and Jake pulled into the drive behind them. After Michelle calmed her father down, she packed some clothes and toiletries and they headed out. John Paul suggested they leave the rental car in the driveway and ride with him and Michelle's father so that if anyone came looking, they would see the car and assume Theo and Michelle were inside. Theo wasn't in a mood to argue with him.

The pickup needed new shocks. Michelle sat on Theo's lap by the window and had to duck down every time her brother sped over a bump. As they were crossing the junction, Daddy remarked, "You both have to be tuckered out, what with those terrible men shooting at you and chasing you half the night."

Big Daddy Jake had a sprawling home. From the front it looked like a tract house on a cement slab. John Paul pulled the truck around to the back, and Theo could then see the windows on a second level facing the water. There was also another room, obviously built on as an afterthought, jutting out on the back. Like Michelle, her father also had a big screened porch overlooking the water.

There were three boats, all small, tied to the dock.

Daddy didn't like air-conditioning. He had a couple of window units, but neither was turned on. The floors were old, worn hardwood, the boards warped in the living room. Braided oval rugs were strewn about the floor. It wasn't stuffy inside, though. The overhead ceiling fan made a clicking sound with each turn and helped carry in a breeze from the water.

Sunlight spilled in through the windows, casting a bright light on the old furniture. Theo carried Michelle's bag and followed her down a long hallway. He could see Jake's big double bed through the open doorway at the end of the hall. Michelle opened the door on the left and went inside.

There were two single beds with a nightstand between them. The window faced the front yard. It was stuffy and hot, but thankfully there was another air conditioner in the window. Michelle turned it on high, kicked off her shoes, and sat on the side of the bed covered in a blue-and-white quilt. Daddy didn't care about coordinating colors. The other bed had a red-and-yellow-striped quilt on it. Michelle took her socks off and fell back against the pillow. She was sound asleep in less than a minute.

Theo quietly shut the door behind him and went back into the living room.

An hour later, Daddy's booming laughter woke Michelle. She got up and was walking to the bathroom when Theo came around the corner.

"Did we wake you?" he asked.

She shook her head and backed up so he could get by, but he followed her until he had her pressed against the wall. Then he kissed her.

"That's the way to start a new day. Kissing a beautiful woman," he said, and went back into the living room.

She looked at herself in the mirror and was appalled. Time to bring out the makeup, she decided, and start acting like a woman. He'd called her beautiful? She thought then that Theo needed to wear his glasses all the time.

In a half hour, she was as good as she was going to get. She wished she'd packed a skirt, but she hadn't, and her only choices were a pair of navy shorts or jeans. Since it was hot, she opted for the shorts. There wasn't any choice for tops. She'd packed a pale yellow blouse with a little too much spandex.

Barefoot, she padded down the hallway with her makeup bag and put it on the dresser in the bedroom. Theo came in to get his glasses. He was talking on the phone as he walked. He gave her a quick once-over, his gaze lingering on her legs, and she heard him ask the person on the other end to repeat what he had just said.

"I got it. Yeah, her dad got the certified letter about an hour ago. No, Michelle doesn't know. I'll let Jake tell her."

"Who was that?" she asked.

"Ben. He's still waiting for the crime scene report."

"What is it you want Daddy to tell me?"

"Good news," he promised.

"Were there people here earlier? I thought I heard the door opening and closing and lots of strange voices."

"A couple of your dad's friends brought over the food from your house. There are four pies on the kitchen table," he added with a grin.

"But no cards, right?"

"Mike, I want to talk to you," her father called.

"I'm coming, Daddy."

She and Theo walked into the living room together. She saw the photo album on the table and whispered, "Uh-oh. Daddy's melancholy."

"He looks happy to me."

"He's melancholy. He only gets the family album out when he's feeling blue."

John Paul was sprawled out on the sofa. His hands were stacked on his chest and his eyes were closed.

Jake was sitting at a big round oak table in the country kitchen, which opened to the living room.

"Now aren't you sorry you didn't go to the funeral?" he asked his son.

John Paul didn't open his eyes when he answered. "No."

"You should be," Jake said. "Your cousin wasn't the sourpuss you thought she was."

"I never said she was a sourpuss. I said—"

His father quickly stopped him. "I remember what you said, but I don't want you repeating it in front of company. Besides, I know you've got to be feeling contrite now."

John Paul didn't have anything to say about that, unless a grunt qualified as a response.

"Your cousin was mindful of family after all. Mike, come and sit at the table. I've got something important to tell you. Theo, you sit down too. I want you to see some pictures."

Theo pulled out a chair for Michelle, then sat beside her. Jake took hold of Michelle's hand and looked her in the eyes. "Brace yourself, sugar. This is gonna be a shock."

"Who died?"

Her father blinked. "No one died. It's your cousin Catherine Bodine."

"The dead one," John Paul called out.

"Of course she's dead. We've only got one cousin in the family on your mama's side." Jake shook his head.

"What about her?" Michelle asked.

"She left us money. A heap of money," he stressed, raising his eyebrows.

Michelle didn't believe him. "Oh, Daddy, that's got to be a mistake. You're telling me Catherine left us money? No, she wouldn't."

"I just told you she did," her father countered. "I know it's hard to believe, and it's a shock, just like I warned you it would be, but it's true. She left us money."

"Why would she leave us anything? She hated us."

"Don't talk like that," he chided. Pulling his handkerchief from his pocket, he wiped his eyes. "Your cousin was a wonderful woman."

"That's called rewriting history," John Paul muttered.

Still the doubting Thomas, Michelle shook her head. "There has to be a mistake."

"No, sugar, there isn't any mistake. Aren't you curious to know how much money she gave us?"

"Sure," she said, wondering what kind of joke Catherine had played. From what she'd heard about her cousin from her brothers, the woman had a cruel streak.

"Your dear cousin left each one of us one hundred thousand dollars."

Michelle's mouth dropped open. "One hundred..."

"Thousand dollars," her father finished for her. "I just got off the phone with Remy. I called your brother to tell him about his cousin's generosity, and his reaction was just like yours and John Paul's. I raised three cynical children."

Michelle was having a difficult time processing the shocking news. "Catherine Bodine...gave...one hundred..."

John Paul laughed. "You're sputtering, little sister."

"You hush now, John Paul," his father ordered. In a softer voice, he said to Michelle, "You see, sugar? Catherine didn't hate us. She just didn't have much use for us is all. She was...different, and we were a reminder of hard times."

Michelle suddenly realized Theo wouldn't have any idea who they were talking about. "My cousin was around seven or eight when her mother married a very wealthy man named

Bodine. They moved to New Orleans and pretty much severed ties with us. I never met Catherine," she admitted, "or spoke to her on the phone. I can't believe she would leave us anything."

"Catherine's mother was my wife's sister," Jake explained. "Her name was June, but we all called her Junie. She wasn't married when she found herself in the family way. Back then, having a child out of wedlock caused quite a stir, but folks forgot about it as time passed. Her father never forgot or forgave her, though. He tossed her out on her ear is what he did. Now, Ellie and I were newly married, so Junie moved in with us. When the baby came, the two of them stayed on. It was crowded, but we all made do," he added. "Then Junie met that rich fella, got married, and moved away. Junie passed on when Catherine was eleven. I wasn't going to let that child forget she had family in Bowen who loved her, so I made it a point to call her up at least once a month and visit with her. She never had much to say, though, and I did a lot of bragging about my three so she'd know her cousins. Catherine was real impressed when she found out Mike was going to be a doctor. She was proud of you, sugar. She just never said so."

"Catherine didn't even invite you to her wedding," Michelle reminded her father. "And I know that must have hurt your feelings."

"No, it didn't. Besides, it was a tiny affair in the courthouse. She told me so herself."

Michelle had her elbow propped on the table and was twirling a lock of hair around her finger in an absentminded fashion while she thought about the windfall. The money was a godsend. There was more than enough to fix up the clinic and hire a nurse.

Her father was smiling as he watched her. "There you go again, twisting your hair." Turning to Theo, he said, "When she was a little tiny thing, she'd wrap her hair around her fingers and suck her thumb until she fell asleep. I can't remember the number of times Remy or I had to untangle the knots she made."

Michelle let go of her hair and folded her hands. "I'm feeling guilty," she said, "because I can't think of one nice thing to say about Catherine, and I've already figured out how I'm going to spend some of her money."

Her father pushed the thick family album with a black-and-red-checked cover toward Theo. Theo opened it and began to look at the photos while Jake pointed out who was who. Michelle excused herself to get a Diet Coke and carried one back to the table for Theo. He'd put his glasses on and looked quite scholarly.

Putting her hand on his shoulder, she asked, "Are you hungry?"

"Yeah, sure," he answered as he turned another page.

"Daddy, Theo doesn't want to look at our family photos."

"Yes, I do."

She reached over Theo's shoulder, put her can of Diet Coke on a coaster next to Theo's, then straightened and turned to her brother. "John Paul, fix Theo and me something to eat."

"Like that's gonna happen," he chuckled.

She walked over to the sofa and sat down on his stomach. He knew what she was going to do and braced himself.

"I'm sleeping," he snapped. "Leave me the hell alone."

She ignored his grumbling and pulled on his hair as she leaned back against the cushions. "Can you believe Catherine left us so much money?"

"No."

"It's mind-boggling."

"Uh-huh."

"Open your eyes," she demanded.

He sighed loudly, then did as she asked. "What?"

"Can you think of anything nice to say about her?"

"Sure I can. She was a selfish, obsessive, compulsive, greedy—"

Michelle pinched him. "Say something nice about her."

"She's dead. That's kind of nice."

"Shame on you. Are you hungry?"

"No."

"Yes, you are. You're always hungry. Come help me."

He grabbed her arm when she tried to stand. "When is Theo leaving?"

The question came out of nowhere, catching her off guard. "Monday," she whispered. "He leaves with his friend, Noah, Monday morning."

Even she could hear the sadness in her voice. She didn't try to be cavalier or pretend she didn't care, because she couldn't fool her brother. John Paul knew her better than anyone in the whole world, and he had always been able to see through her defenses. She never lied or played games with him.

"You were stupid," he whispered.

She nodded. "Yes."

"You shouldn't have allowed yourself to become so vulnerable."

"I know."

"Then why didn't you protect yourself? He's an outsider."

"I didn't see it coming. What can I say? It just...happened."

"So?"

"So what?"

"So are you gonna fall apart when he leaves?"

"No," she whispered. Then she said it again more forcefully. "No."

"We'll see."

Theo wasn't paying any attention to Michelle or John Paul. He had just turned a page in the album and was looking at a faded photo of a beautiful young woman. She was posed standing under a tree, holding a bouquet of daisies in her hand. The woman wore an ankle-length, light-colored organza dress with a ribbon streaming down from her waist. Her short, curly hair framed an angelic face. The photo was black-and-white, but Theo guessed her hair was red and her eyes were blue. If the clothes and the haircut had been more contemporary, he would have thought he was looking at Michelle.

"That's my Ellie," Jake said. "She's pretty, isn't she?"

"Yes, sir, she is."

"I look at my three, and I see Ellie in all of them. Remy got her laugh, John Paul got her love of the outdoors, and Michelle got her heart."

Theo nodded. John Paul was following Michelle into the kitchen, but when he heard his father mention his mother, he paused to look over Theo's shoulder. Then Theo turned the page, and John Paul moved on. There was a photo of Remy and John Paul when they were little boys and a girl standing between them. The boys looked as though they'd been rolling around in mud and were happy about it. Their grins were ornery. The girl wasn't smiling and had outgrown the dress she was wearing.

"That's Catherine," Jake told him. "She always had to wear a dress, no matter what the occasion. That one was one of her favorites because it had lace on it. I remember she would nag her mama to stitch this or that seam back together. Catherine had a healthy appetite."

Theo kept turning the pages. Catherine's mother must have sent photos after she'd moved, because there were at least twenty of her daughter. In each photo the girl was wearing a dress, but the quality had improved. In one, the child stood in front of a Christmas tree holding two identical dolls in her arms. He turned another page and saw Catherine in a different dress holding two stuffed bears.

Jake chuckled when he saw the photo. "Catherine always had to have two of every-thing," he explained. "Some folks, once they've been poor, when they come into money, no matter how young or old they are, well, they just can't have enough. Do you know what I'm talking about?"

"Yes," Theo answered. "People who lived through the Depression were always storing up for the next one."

"That's right. Catherine was just like that. The Depression was just a history lesson to her, but she acted like she'd lived through one. She was worried she'd run out, I suppose, so if she liked a doll or a bear, she made her mama buy her another one just like it in case some-thing happened to the first one. She did the same thing with clothes. Once Junie had money to spend, she made sure her daughter had the finest of everything and she catered to her every whim. Ellie thought Junie was spoiling her out of guilt because she wasn't married when she had her.

"I thought she'd outgrow the need to hoard things, but she didn't. Come to find out, it got worse. She started doing some mighty strange things. She even put in a second phone line. When I asked her why, she said it was in case the first line broke. Said she didn't want to have to wait on the phone repair people."

Michelle interrupted when she came back to the table. "John Paul's warming up the gumbo," she said.

Theo was turning the pages back and forth. He looked at the photo of Catherine dressed in an obvious hand-me-down that was too small for her growing body, then flipped back to the photo of Catherine dressed like a princess, clutching the two identical dolls.

"The poor thing started putting on the weight after she married," Jake remarked.

"How would you know that?" Michelle asked. "She never let you come and see her."

"Her housekeeper told me," he said. "Rosa Vincetti and I would chat every now and again when she answered the phone. She's a real nice woman. Very timid, but sweet as can be. She gave me a recipe for homemade pasta, but I haven't tried it out yet. She also told me she was getting alarmed by Catherine's weight. Worried her heart would blow up on her, she said."

"Catherine was—" Michelle began.

"Weird," John Paul shouted from the kitchen.

"And you're not?" Michelle countered.

"Hell, I'm normal compared to her."

"Daddy, how did you find out we were getting money?" Michelle asked.

"You still don't believe me?" Jake asked.

"I didn't say that."

"You're still not convinced, though, are you?" Jake pushed the chair back and stood. "I got a certified letter to prove it. It came about an hour ago."

Jake went to the kitchen counter, lifted the lid on the elephant-shaped cookie jar where he kept all his important papers, and pulled out the envelope.

Michelle was sitting next to Theo now, looking through the album. There was a photo of her mother holding a baby in her lap. With the tip of her finger, she touched her mother's face.

"That's Remy when he was a baby."

Two pages later, he was looking at photos of Michelle and laughing. In every photo there was something sticking up or out. Her hair, her shirt, her tongue.

"I was adorable, wasn't I?"

He laughed. "Definitely adorable."

Jake dropped the envelope in front of Michelle. "Here's your proof, Dr. Smarty-pants."

Michelle just shook her head and smiled. "Daddy has lots of cute nicknames for me."

Theo was laughing when he glanced over and saw the name of the law firm in the upper left-hand corner of the envelope. "That's it," he whispered. "That's it," he repeated and slapped the table.

"What's it?"

"The connection. It's the same law firm. Son of a..." Turning, he grabbed the letter out of Jake's hand. "Do you mind?"

"Go ahead," Jake said.

"But you haven't explained..." Michelle started.

Theo put his hand on hers. "In a minute. Okay? Where are my glasses?"

"You're wearing them."

"Oh, right. Man, it's falling into place."

Jake and Michelle both stared at him while he read the letter. When he finished, he pushed his chair back and stood. "I've got to go to New Orleans."

Michelle picked up the letter and quickly read it. According to Catherine's instructions, her attorney, Phillip Benchley, was hereby informing each of the beneficiaries of the total sum of the estate and the amount of each bequest. The Renard family was to receive four hundred thousand dollars to be divided equally among Jake and his three children. Rosa Maria Vincetti would receive one hundred fifty thousand dollars for her years of loyal service to Catherine. John Russell, Catherine's husband, would receive one hundred dollars, and the remainder of the vast estate would be given to the Epston bird sanctuary.

"Her husband gets only a hundred dollars?" she asked, astonished.

"They might not have had a happy marriage," Jake remarked.

"No kidding," John Paul offered from the kitchen door.

"Rosa sure didn't like him," Jake added. "I think it's nice that Catherine didn't forget to leave her housekeeper something. She took good care of her."

"John must have signed a prenuptial agreement for Catherine to control her own money," Michelle said.

"He'll still try to contest it," Theo said. "What does the man do for a living?"

"He's a lawyer," Jake told him. "He works for one of the big banks in New Orleans. I've never actually talked to the man, and I think that's a crying shame. Mike and I didn't even get a chance to speak to him at the funeral, did we, sugar?"

"No, Daddy, we didn't. But that was my fault. I had to get back to the hospital, and you had to drive me."

Theo's cell phone rang and interrupted the conversation. Noah was on the line.

"Where are you?" Theo asked.

"I just reached St. Claire," Noah answered.

"Drive to Jake's house. Do you know the way?"

"Yeah. I'll be there in ten minutes."

"What did you find out?" Theo walked through the kitchen and onto the screened porch. He pulled the door shut behind him.

Michelle assumed he wanted privacy and decided to set the table. John Paul was leaning against the counter, glaring at her.

"What's the matter?" she asked as she opened the drawer and got out the place mats.

"You're gonna let another FBI agent inside this house?"

"Yes, I am," she said. "Don't give me attitude, John Paul. I'm not in the mood. You're going to be polite to Noah."

"You think so?"

"I know so. Daddy? John Paul..."

She didn't have to go any further. Her brother shook his head in exasperation and then smiled. "You're still telling on me, aren't you, brat?"

She smiled back. "It still works, doesn't it? Thank you, John Paul."

"I didn't say..."

"You didn't have to. You're going to try to remember how to be nice."

She went back to the table and put the place mats down. Weary, she sat down and propped her head on her hands. She kept thinking about the hundred thousand dollars, and her guilt was intensifying. Why would such a mean-spirited woman do such a kind thing? And what else had Catherine sent her that was of such interest to the police and the men who would kill to get hold of it?

Daddy was sitting next to her, going through the album again.

"Poor Catherine," Michelle said. "She didn't have many friends. At the funeral...there weren't many people. The only person who shed a tear was her housekeeper. Remember, Daddy? She was crying for Catherine, but no one else was. I feel bad about that."

She was remembering the pitiful little procession walking through the cemetery. Rosa was carrying rosary beads and crying. John walked behind the priest and kept glancing back at Daddy and her. Since neither one of them had ever met the man, she assumed he was wondering who they were. Another man looked back too. He was walking beside John, and he...

"Oh, my God, that's the man...that was him," she cried out as she jumped up. In her excitement to tell Theo what she had remembered, she'd knocked the chair over. She impatiently picked it up, then ran through the kitchen. Theo was coming inside. He ended the phone call as she ran into him. Grabbing her, he stepped back onto the porch.

"What's the matter?"

"I remember where I saw that man before... remember, I told you he looked familiar? It's the same guy." Her words were tripping over each other.

"Slow down," he said, "and start over."

"The delivery man who talked to me at the stadium. I told you he looked familiar, and I thought I must have run into him at the hospital, but that wasn't it. He was at Catherine's funeral. He was talking with John, and he walked beside him at the cemetery."

Daddy hadn't heard the conversation. He also was thinking about Catherine's generosity and thinking that Ellie was smiling now because her niece had done such a nice thing for her family. She'd always worried about the selfish streak in Catherine, but now Catherine had redeemed herself.

He heard Michelle mention John's name and called out, "I'm thinking I ought to get on the phone and ring up Catherine's husband."

"Oh, Daddy, don't do that," Michelle said.

"No," Theo ordered sharply at the same time.

"Why not?" Daddy asked. He turned in his chair and looked at Theo. "I ought to tell him thank you for the money. It's the right thing to do. He was Catherine's husband, and he had to approve it."

Michelle was shaking her head as Theo

was walking toward her father. "Sir, I don't want you to call him. Promise me you won't."

"Give me a reason, then," Daddy said. "And I'll promise. Make it a good one."

"Okay," Theo said. His voice was calm as he continued, "He tried to kill your daughter."

CHAPTER THIRTY-FIVE

Daddy took the news much better than John Paul did. Michelle's brother wanted to get in the pickup, hunt down the bastard, and blow his head off. He wasn't in the mood to listen to reason, and he didn't give a hoot about the law.

"If you know he's the man behind this, then take him out before he has another chance to kill her," he demanded.

Theo wasn't fazed by John Paul's fury. "I can't prove it yet. It's all circumstantial," he explained. "Which is why I have to go to New Orleans."

John Paul looked as if he wanted to hit Theo. Michelle got between the two men and tried to make her brother calm down.

The doorbell rang, interrupting the argument. While Daddy went to let Noah in, Theo said, "We hang tight."

"What the hell does that mean?"

"It means you can't shoot anyone."

Theo turned to Michelle. "Promise me you

won't leave The Swan until I get back. No ifs or buts about it. I don't want to be worrying about you..."

"Okay," she said. She patted his chest and stepped closer. "You be careful too."

"If there's any trouble, you do what Noah tells you to do. John Paul, you watch your father's back. Got that?"

Her brother stopped arguing and gave an abrupt nod. Noah was standing by the front door talking to Daddy. The FBI agent hadn't bothered to shave and looked scruffy in torn jeans and a faded blue shirt. She went to greet him. She could certainly understand Mary Ann's interest. There was an element of danger about the man that made women want to run from him and try to rehabilitate him at the same time.

Those blue eyes penetrated as he said, "I heard you had a busy night dodging bullets."

She couldn't resist. "I heard you had a busy night too."

"Yes, I did. Your friend told me to tell you 'hey.' I think that means 'hi,' " he said, grinning. "I sure didn't have much fun this morning, though. You'd figure a man on vacation should be able to sleep in. Where's Theo?" he asked.

"He is on the porch with John Paul. Through the kitchen," she said.

Noah headed that way, but she stopped him when she said, "Will you please do me a favor?"

"Sure," he said. "What is it?"

"Put up with my brother."

Noah laughed. "I can get along with anyone."
"Want to bet?"

It was too bad she hadn't wagered money because she would have won. Less than three minutes had passed when the shouting started. Her brother was doing most of the yelling, but Noah was keeping up.

Theo came into the kitchen with Noah's car keys. Michelle winced when she heard her brother call Noah a grossly obscene name.

Theo heard it too. Grinning, he said, "I knew they'd get along."

Her eyes widened. "You call that getting along?"

"You don't hear any gunshots, do you? Noah likes your brother."

Then she heard her brother threaten Noah. His vocabulary was not only colorful, but creative. After that, Noah threatened John Paul in his own rather colorful and creative way. His threat would ensure John Paul would never father children.

"Oh, I can tell he likes him a lot."

"The two of them have a great deal in common. What'd I do with my glasses?"

"They're on the table. Exactly what could they have in common?"

"They're both mean as snakes," he said as he picked up the glasses and folded them.

"Noah's not mean. He smiles all the time."

"Yes, he does," he agreed. "And that's what makes him more dangerous. You don't see it coming until it's too late. Some of the stories I've heard about him from my brother

441

are chilling, which is why Noah's going to be watching out for you."

He draped his arm around her shoulders and pulled her along to the front door.

"You haven't told me why you need to go to New Orleans."

"I'm going to check out some things," he said, which really wasn't an answer to her question.

He leaned down and kissed her. It was a quick brush of his mouth against hers, and it was thoroughly unsatisfying in her opinion. He must have thought so, because after he let go of her and opened the door, he roughly pulled her into his arms and kissed her again. This one was vastly different.

Smiling, he pulled the door closed behind him. Michelle stood by the window watching until Theo had driven away. He had John Paul on his guard looking out for Daddy, and Noah was supposed to baby-sit her. Who was going to watch out for Theo? She shook her head. No worry, she told herself. Detective Harris would make the arrests any minute now.

What more could happen?

CHAPTER THIRTY-SIX

The Sowing Club had gathered in John's motel room in St. Claire. John was going through the papers, making certain the entire printout was there, while Dallas, Cameron, and Preston silently waited. He finally finished, looked up, and laughed.

"The bitch even included a copy of the letter she wrote to me," he said.

"I'm still making a protest," Preston said. "The way we got those papers back was too risky."

"Does that matter now? We're in the clear."

Dallas disagreed. "Not until we've gotten rid of Buchanan and the doctor. And we've got to do it tonight, thanks to yet another one of Cameron's screwups."

"Look, I panicked. Okay? I saw Buchanan looking out the window, and I thought I could get him, so I shot at him."

"We had decided to go in easy," Preston reminded him.

"I was desperate to get him...for the good of the club," Cameron stammered. "Besides, Buchanan doesn't know I shot at him, and it stands to reason that he would assume someone's after him. Dallas, you did the background check. You're the one who told us the guy has gotten death threats."

Preston nodded. "No time to waste. We have to kill them tonight."

"I wonder if the doctor has remembered where she's seen Cameron," Dallas said.

None of them looked at Cameron as they thought about that.

"I told you I was sick of waiting," Cameron said.

"You had no right..." Preston began.

John put his hand up. "Let it go," he said. "It's done and Cameron regrets his mistakes. Isn't that right?" he asked.

It wasn't what he said but how he said it, with such feigned kindness, that made Cameron see what was happening.

"John's right," Dallas said. "Cameron has been our friend for too many years to let a couple of mistakes ruin anything. Forgive and forget. Right, Preston?"

Preston smiled. "Yeah, okay. Want a drink, Cam?"

He shook his head. He could feel the bile rising in his throat. "I should pack up and head back to New Orleans...unless you've changed your mind, John, and want me to stay and help."

"Help with what?"

"Buchanan and the doctor. You're going to go after them tonight, aren't you?"

"Yes," John said. "But both of them have seen your face, so you can't stay around. We've gone over this, Cameron. Go home and wait. I'll call you after it's finished, and we'll go out and celebrate."

"The doctor saw you at the funeral too. How come you're staying here?"

"To coordinate," he said.

Cameron stood. "Where's Monk?" he asked, squelching the mounting fear inside him.

"Out buying some equipment. Why do you want to know?"

Cameron shrugged. "Is he going to help you get Buchanan?"

"Yes," Dallas answered.

"What about the FBI agent, the man named Clayborne."

"Let us worry about him," John said smoothly. "You better get going now."

"Don't worry," Dallas said. "Everything's going to be fine."

Cameron went outside and pulled the door closed. Because he thought one of them might be watching him through the crack in the drapes, he strolled to the corner as though he wasn't in any particular hurry. He turned toward his room and then started running. When he reached the door, he pulled out his gun, cocked it, and rushed inside.

He half expected to find Monk waiting for him, but the room was empty. He gagged, so great was his relief. He threw his clothes into his overnight bag, grabbed his car keys, and ran to his car. Desperate to get away, he slammed his foot down on the accelerator. The car fishtailed out of the parking lot.

John had told him to go home and wait. That's where it was going to happen, he decided. Would his dear friends come after him, or would they send Monk to kill him? Either way, Cameron knew he was a dead man. He pulled onto the highway, checking the rearview mirror every other second to make sure he wasn't being followed by Monk now. There

445

were no cars behind him. Cameron finally allowed himself to exhale, letting out a long, loud breath. His hands were clammy and shaking. He struggled to hold them steady on the steering wheel, and then he began to cry.

He had to go to his apartment because he had money stashed under one of the floorboards, and he would need it when he left town. He had time, he told himself. They would need Monk to help them with Buchanan. Yes, he had time.

Cameron was quivering so badly now he knew the only thing that would calm him down and help him think was a drink. He pulled off the highway at the next exit and started looking for a bar.

CHAPTER THIRTY-SEVEN

Phillip Benchley was not a happy camper. The attorney had just stepped onto the first tee of the back nine at the prestigious New Orleans Country Club when he was summoned to the clubhouse to meet with an attorney from the U.S. Department of Justice.

Impatient but polite, he announced, "My friends are waiting," as he walked into the locker room and sat down on a bench to retie his black-and-white saddle golf shoes. "I would appreciate it if you would make this quick."

Theo introduced himself. The second Benchley heard that the case he wanted to discuss involved John Russell, his manner improved and he actually smiled.

"You're investigating John Russell? Oh, I'd love it if you could get that prick. The sheer arrogance of the man is unbelievable. When Catherine Russell called me and asked me to change her will, it took all I had not to cheer. She never should have married that man. Never," he repeated. "Now, tell me, what can I do to help you nail him?"

"You told FBI agent Noah Clayborne that you sent Dr. Michelle Renard a package from Catherine. Isn't that right?"

Benchley nodded. "Yes, I did, but, as I explained to him, if you're wanting to know what was inside, you'll have to ask the doctor. Catherine gave me a sealed envelope and instructed me not to open it."

"The envelope was taken away before Michelle could look at it," he said. "Catherine didn't give you any hint of what was inside? Anything about a financial statement or an audit? Anything at all?" Theo asked.

"No, but I'll tell you this. Whatever it was must have been explosive, because Catherine assured me that once John knew about it, he wouldn't dare contest the will. She was very sure about that."

"He signed a prenup?"

"Yes, he did, but John's an attorney and he's smart. He wouldn't have let that much money slip through his fingers. He would have taken it to court."

"How come you waited six weeks from the time of her death to read the will?"

"You've been doing your research. Again, I was following Catherine's instructions." He smiled as he added, "She was a bit vindictive, and she told me to wait so that John's bills would pile up. He lived the high life, was indiscreet, and used her trust money to buy his mistresses presents. When Catherine found out about his adultery, she called me and told me she was changing the will."

"Did you attend the funeral?"

"I went to the mass," he said. "But I didn't go to the cemetery."

"Michelle said there was only a handful of mourners. Did you know any of them?"

"I knew the housekeeper, Rosa Vincetti. I met her when I came to the house to discuss the changes in the will."

"What about John's coworkers or friends?"

"A couple of men and women from the trust department where he works were there. I talked to one man, and he introduced me to the others, but I don't remember their names."

"What about John's friends?"

"Let me think," he said. "I remember there was a woman standing in the back of the church. She told me she was Catherine's interior designer but that she had also redecorated John's office. As I was leaving the church, she chased me and handed me one of her cards. I thought that was most inappropriate, and as soon as I got back to the office, I threw the card away. The only other person I remember seeing was Cameron Lynch. He's a close friend of John's."

"Tell me about him."

"He's a stockbroker," Benchley said. "A very successful broker," he stressed. "I had heard of him, but I'd never met him until the day of the funeral. I remember thinking that he was an alcoholic. It wasn't a charitable thought, granted, but he smelled like booze, and his eyes were bloodshot. I'm certain he was hungover. He also had that look about him—you know what I mean, the gray skin, red nose, puffy eyes, indicating he had been a heavy drinker for some time. Cameron stayed close to John and sat in the pew with him like he was family."

"Did John speak to you?"

"Are you kidding? He looked right through me, and I must say, I did get a chuckle out of that. The man despises me, and that couldn't make me happier."

Theo was almost finished. He asked a couple more questions, then thanked Benchley for his help and left. The attorney had thoughtfully called his secretary and gotten the addresses Theo needed.

He had at least two more stops before he could head back to Bowen.

Theo needed to make sure Cameron Lynch was the man Michelle and he had seen the night before. He drove to the brokerage firm and went into the lobby. He had already come up with a good lie to tell the receptionist so she would find a photo for him, but that wasn't necessary. As soon as he walked through the doors, he saw an eight-by-ten color photo of Cameron Lynch on the wall.

Theo came to a dead stop. There was a grouping displaying all the brokers in the firm. Cameron was in the middle. Theo glanced at the receptionist. She was talking into her headset but smiling at him. Theo smiled back. Then he lifted the photo off the wall, turned around, and walked out.

He needed help with the next stop. He called Captain Welles, the man who had introduced him at the awards ceremony, and asked him for assistance. Then he drove to Cameron Lynch's apartment, located in a sleazy neighborhood adjacent to the newly refurbished warehouse district. He parked his car down the street and waited for two detectives from the captain's precinct to arrive.

The two men pulled up behind him fifteen minutes later. Detective Underwood, the senior of the two, shook Theo's hand.

"The captain told us you're the man who got The Count. It's an honor to meet you."

Then Detective Basham stepped forward. "I heard your speech at the banquet."

Theo had removed the photo from the frame. He handed it to Underwood and said, "This is the man I want."

"The captain said we're taking Cameron Lynch in for attempted murder and that you've got a witness," Basham said.

"I'm one of the witnesses. Lynch tried to kill a friend of mine and me."

"We did a sweep of the neighborhood, and his car isn't here," Underwood said.

"So how do you want us to do this?" Basham

asked. "Captain said you had special instructions."

"Assume he's armed and dangerous," Theo said. "When you cuff him, read him his rights and take him in, but don't book him yet. I want him locked in an interrogation room so I can talk to him. I don't want his name in the computer, not yet anyway."

"We'll stake out the place. You want to wait with us?"

"No, I've got another stop to make, but as soon as you have him, call me on my cell phone or at a bar in Bowen named The Swan. Hopefully, you won't have to wait long. I think he's on his way home."

It seemed logical. Lynch wouldn't want to stay in Bowen, not after he'd been spotted, and he wouldn't know that Theo had made the connection. Theo wrote down his number and handed it to the detective, then reiterated that he wanted to be called, no matter what time, the second they had Lynch.

"Yes, sir, we'll call," Basham promised.

"Wait a minute," Theo said as the two men walked away. He picked up his notepad, flipped through the pages until he found what he was looking for, and then asked if either one of them could give him directions to the address Benchley had given him.

Underwood told him the quickest route to take and then remarked, "That's a bad-ass neighborhood. Be careful."

Theo drove through the heart of New Orleans, slowly negotiating his way through the narrow streets. He was sure he'd gotten lost, but once he turned the car around, he spotted the street he was looking for. Two blocks later he found the address. He parked the car, then picked up his phone and called Noah.

"Find out anything?" Noah asked.

Theo told him about Cameron Lynch. "Ask Ben Nelson to look for a '92 blue Ford Taurus." He gave him the license number and told him to tell Ben that if he found the car, to proceed with extreme caution.

"You think he can handle it?" Noah asked.

"Yes," Theo answered. "He knows what he's doing. Just make sure he knows Lynch is one of the shooters. I want that bastard locked up and isolated until I can interrogate him."

"I doubt that Lynch is still hanging around Bowen. He's got to know you can ID him."

"I don't think he's there either," Theo said. "I'm hoping he's on his way home. What's Michelle doing?"

"She's a funny woman," he said. "She fell asleep sitting at the table."

"She had a long night."

"So did you," Noah pointed out. "Anyway, she's getting ready to go to The Swan with Jake and me...and his laugh-a-minute son. Have you heard from Detective Harris yet?"

"No, I haven't, and I've left her three messages. The first two were sort of polite, the third wasn't."

"While I was in New Orleans this morning, I went over to her precinct like you asked," Noah said. "I talked to her captain."

"Did you get a copy of the file on Monk?"

"No," he answered. "The captain told me Harris was out on an investigation. He wouldn't give me any indication of where she might be. He made it clear he didn't want me interfering. The twelve hours will be up soon. When are you heading back to Bowen?"

"I've got one more stop, and then I'm on my way."

"I've got to go," Noah said. "Michelle's calling me."

Theo grabbed his notepad and glasses and stared at the tiny ranch house in front of him. The little patch of yard was meticulously cared for with flowers lining either side of the sidewalk leading up to the door. The house needed paint, and the wood around the windows was rotten. Termites, he thought as he walked to the door. The fact that the yard was well-tended and the house ignored suggested to him that the occupant took care of what she could afford.

He rang the bell and waited. Out of the corner of his eye, he saw the curtain move in the front window. He rang the bell again.

A woman called out through the door. "What do you want?"

"I'm looking for Rosa Vincetti."

"Are you police?" the woman asked.

"No," he answered. "I'm a friend of Jake Renard."

The woman opened the door a crack with the security chain in place. "I'm Rosa," she said. "What do you want?"

She was obviously frightened. He should have taken the time to shave. "Jake Renard told me that he often talked to you on the phone when he called Catherine."

"Yes," she said. "Mr. Renard loved Catherine."

Theo couldn't see the woman's face. She was hiding behind the door. There was a light flickering behind her. He thought it might be a candle burning.

"You aren't with the police?" she asked again.

"No, I'm an attorney," he explained.

Rosa shut the door, slipped the chain back, and then opened it again. She stepped back so Theo could come inside. Theo stayed on the porch. Concerned she would panic when she saw his gun, he explained quickly why he had to carry the weapon. And when he finished, he once again assured her he wasn't a policeman, and he hadn't driven to her house to cause her any trouble.

Rosa was a surprise. She was much younger than he'd expected, around fifty he judged, and almost as tall as he was. Streaks of gray highlighted her dark hair. Heavy brows framed midnight black eyes. There were tears in those eyes now as she once again motioned for him to come inside.

"My name is Theo Buchanan," he said as he walked into her living room.

She was already nodding. "I know who you are. I prayed to God, and He sent you to me."

He didn't know what to say to that, and so he simply nodded. "Please sit," she said and pointed to a gray brocade sofa, "and tell me why you have come here."

Theo waited until she had taken her seat across from him. An oval glass table was between them. Theo leaned forward with his arms on his knees and told Rosa how he had met Michelle Renard. He was trying to put her at ease and help her understand his relationship to the Renard family. Rosa listened intently.

She obviously was a deeply religious woman. Signs of her faith adorned every surface in her home. Against the wall behind her was a long sofa table that had been converted into an altar with a lace runner on top. At one end, two votive candles burned, and at the other end was a framed picture of the Blessed Mother. Black rosary beads were draped over the frame.

Theo explained what had happened the night before and how he and Michelle had been ambushed. "Catherine sent Michelle a package," he said.

She nodded. "Yes, I know."

He kept his excitement hidden. His guess had been right.

"I believe the men who came after Michelle and me were trying to get that package," he said. "They weren't successful," he added. "The police have it now."

Rosa stiffened. "Did you have a chance to read the papers?" she asked.

"Not yet," he said. "However, I'm sure that John Russell is behind this, and I want to get him. To do that, I'm going to need your help."

"He's an evil man," she whispered. "He will go to hell when he dies. He killed her, you know."

She said it almost casually, as though the startling news had been in the papers for weeks.

"He killed Catherine?"

"Yes, he did. I don't have any proof," she hastened to add. "But in my heart I know he did it. The ambulance people who came to the house...one of them told me she choked to death on caramels." She was shaking her head. "I knew the truth then."

"How did you know?"

"She wouldn't eat caramels. She had a loose bridge and she constantly fretted that it would break. She would never leave the house to go to a dentist, so she was extremely careful. Mr. Russell brought her a box of chocolates every night, and then he left to be with his whores, but Catherine only ate the soft candies. She never would have touched a caramel."

She made the sign of the cross and folded her hands as though in prayer. "You must find proof and arrest John Russell. It would be a sin to let such an evil man get away with murder. You must do this for Catherine and me."

Theo nodded. "I'm going to try," he promised. "Catherine found out about John's affairs, didn't she? That was the reason she left him only a hundred dollars in her will."

"Yes, she heard him on the phone. He called her terrible names when he was talking to his mistress. She cried for days," she added. "And then one night she heard him talking to a man about a deposit he had made in an account outside of the United States. She heard him tell the man not to worry, that no one would know because all the records were in his computer at home."

Theo began to make notes as Rosa fed him the information she'd been given by Catherine.

"How did she break into his files? How did she come up with the right password?"

"John gave it to her," Rosa said. "Of course, he didn't know it at the time. She listened to his phone conversations, and twice she heard him refer to the Sowing Club. The next day, after he had gone to work and I had sent the maid to the grocery store, I helped her go down to the library. She typed in the words but was denied access. The spelling, you see, was incorrect. Catherine was a very smart woman," she added. "The second time she typed in the correct spelling, and the files opened up to her."

"So it's *sowing,* as in sowing wild oats, instead of *sewing,* as in stitching clothes?"

"Yes," she said. "That's what Catherine told me."

"Did she tell you what was in those files?"

"She said her husband was doing illegal things with money."

He rubbed his jaw. "Why did she instruct her attorney to wait until after her death to send copies of the files? Why didn't she just have John arrested?"

"You don't understand."

"Help me understand," he urged.

"Catherine had many fine qualities, but she was also a very controlling woman. She wanted things done just so, and she wanted her husband to respect his marriage vows." She shook her head as she added, "She wouldn't let him go, but after she died, she wouldn't let any other woman have him. She was going to use the papers she'd given Mr. Benchley to make him..."

"Toe the line?" Theo asked.

"Yes."

"Did you meet any of John's friends?"

She shook her head. "He never invited anyone to the house. I think he was keeping Catherine isolated. He was ashamed of her, but even after she took to her bed and stayed in her room, he still didn't have friends to the house."

Theo closed his notepad. "May I ask you a personal question?"

"What is it?"

"Why are you so afraid of the police?"

She looked down at her hands. "My son got into trouble last year. The police...they came to the house in the middle of the night and dragged him out of his bed. He was taken to jail, and I was very afraid for him. Catherine called her attorney, and he gave her the name of someone else who could help my boy."

"A criminal attorney?"

"I think so," she said. "My son is out on probation now, but every night when he doesn't come home, I think he's been taken away again. He runs with bad people, and I pray to God every night that He will look out for him. He's a good boy," she whispered. "But he's a follower and does whatever those bad people tell him to do."

"What kind of trouble did he get into?"

"Drugs," she said, and then she crossed herself again. "He was taking money from people and giving them drugs. He's stopped that," she hastened to add. "He promised me and he stopped."

Theo nodded. "I understand," he said. "I don't want to make things more difficult for you, but there's something I need, Rosa...and you have it, don't you?"

CHAPTER THIRTY-EIGHT

God love Catherine Russell and her obsession with having two of everything. Theo had banked on her compulsion when he'd gone to see Rosa. Catherine hadn't let him down. She had indeed made another copy of the files and given them to Rosa for safekeeping.

Theo hadn't expected to hear that Rosa believed John had killed his wife, but then he realized he shouldn't have been surprised at all. The man was capable of anything.

The copies of all the papers Catherine had sent to Michelle were on the seat beside him.

Theo knew he'd need a couple of hours to break the codes. He hadn't done more than glance through them when he was with Rosa, but he understood enough to know he could nail the son of a bitch for tax evasion, extortion, fraud, insider trading, and more. Detective Harris had told Michelle that the sheet she'd pulled from the envelope looked like a financial statement, and she had been right about that. The other papers were filled with the breakdown of each transaction. All of them, Theo was sure, were illegal, and as he drove toward Bowen, he added up all the charges he could file. There was enough to put Russell behind bars for the rest of his life. Theo was going to add the charge of attempted murder—he was certain John was one of the shooters the night before—but he couldn't prove it...yet. He also wanted justice for Catherine, and he needed time to figure out how to get the evidence he would need to prove the woman had been murdered.

Had John killed her, or had he hired it out? Was that why Detective Harris was in Bowen? She'd told Theo she had an inside tip that a hit man was in town. Had Monk killed Catherine, and was he now helping John get incriminating evidence back?

Where the hell was Cameron Lynch? Underwood had promised to call him the second they picked up Lynch. He was the key, Theo had decided. If he could turn him, he could get all of them.

He thought about the transactions listed in the papers again. There was a letter in brackets beside each entry, indicating the person responsible for that contribution. There was a *C*, most likely Cameron Lynch. *J* was for John Russell, but who were *P* and *D?* The Sowing Club. What a cute name for their crooked little group. Four men who had illegally accumulated millions of dollars.

"Two down and two to go," he said.

Then he laughed. Catherine had also made a copy of the letter she'd written to John, and Theo pictured how her husband must have reacted when he read the letter and found out what she had done.

Oh, Catherine. You were such a devious woman.

CHAPTER THIRTY-NINE

The Swan was packed. The crowd, mostly fishermen, was so dense and loud, Michelle could feel the floor trembling under her feet. She and Noah worked behind the bar, filling drink orders. Noah made the job easy. No matter what alcoholic beverage anyone ordered, he served a draft of beer. The only other choice he allowed was a soft drink.

John Paul managed crowd control and bussed tables from the supper traffic, while Daddy sat at the end of the bar by the kitchen door with his Big Chief tablet and a ballpoint pen. He'd cleaned out an old metal

461

tackle box and was using it as his safe for the tournament money so it wouldn't get mixed up with the cash taken in at the bar. All the latecomers who wanted to sign up for the tournament formed a line that reached to the parking lot. Each man paid his fee in cash— Daddy wouldn't take checks or credit cards— signed his name in the tablet, and was then given a ticket with a registration number on it. The fishermen would hand in the ticket at five o'clock tomorrow morning and receive a tag. Anyone who tried to sneak out earlier to get a head start would automatically be disqualified by not receiving a tag.

There were quite a few outsiders from neighboring parishes. Preston and Monk easily blended in. Like at least half the crowd, they wore ball caps and jeans and guzzled beer while they stood by the jukebox, pretending to be waiting for an empty table.

They acted as though they were having a good old time. Preston struck up a conversation with three men nursing beers at a nearby table. He told them a fishing story about the big one that got away. Monk joined in by showing off a couple of lures he'd purchased at the tackle shop down the road. He wore an oversized fisherman's vest to conceal his gun. Unlike Preston, he wasn't willing to go into the bar unarmed with an FBI agent less than twenty feet away.

Preston was better at chitchat than Monk. They both laughed and drank, even flirted with a couple of available women who hit on them,

462

but never did they let Michelle out of their line of sight while they waited for Theo Buchanan to walk through the door.

John, Dallas, and Preston had made the decision that it would be safer and easier if they hit both Michelle and Theo at the same time. The plan was to lure them outside, then take them at gunpoint into the swamp and kill them. Cameron was out of the picture. Monk had already been instructed to follow him back to New Orleans after he finished his job in Bowen. Although Monk usually decided the method, in this case Dallas explained that they would need a quick death certificate to withdraw their money from the Sowing account. Since everyone at his firm knew how distraught and depressed Cameron was over his pending divorce, Dallas thought Monk should use Cameron's gun to kill him and leave a suicide note behind.

Monk was no longer willing to work on credit. After all, the stakes were higher now. When John protested that there was no way they could get the money in cash so quickly, Monk decided to negotiate. He knew all about their dirty dealings and the money they had waiting for them, so instead of his fee, he offered to help them out this time for Cameron's cut of the funds. As far as John and Preston and Dallas were concerned, time was critical. They had to agree to his terms.

So where was Theo Buchanan? Had it not been three deep at the bar, Preston would have tried to strike up a conversation with Michelle or her father. He'd ask her who her fishing partner was—he'd seen Buchanan's name next to hers on the sign-up sheet—and then casually inquire where Buchanan was.

It was too loud and crowded to talk to her now. Preston would have to wait until the traffic thinned out a little. He figured that most of the fishermen would head home by ten because they had to be back at The Swan with their boats and fishing gear at five A.M. The tournament would officially begin at five-fifteen.

John and Dallas were in a rental car at a crossroad a half a mile away. They were waiting for Preston to call them. The longer they waited, the more anxious and trigger-happy they became. What the hell were Monk and Preston doing?

John opened a bottle of water and took a drink. "No matter what, we do this tonight. I don't care who gets in the way. If we have to kill everyone in that bar, then, by God, that's what we'll do. We've got the firepower, and I want this finished. Why hasn't Preston called?"

"You saw the cars in the lot. He's waiting for his opportunity," Dallas said.

At almost nine o'clock, the bar was still teeming. The jukebox was blaring—Elvis was singing about his blue suede shoes—and the customers had to raise their voices to be heard over the music. Had Michelle not been at the end of the bar by the phone serving customers, she wouldn't have heard it ringing.

She put the receiver against one ear and held her hand over her other ear so she could hear the caller. She still had trouble understanding and walked into the storage room. Cherry Waterson was on the line, calling from the hospital. The woman was hysterical. Michelle couldn't make any sense out of what she was saying and finally demanded that she put a nurse on the line.

Thirty seconds later, after giving the nurse orders, Michelle hung up the phone and ran to Noah. "We have to go to the hospital now."

Noah didn't need to hear the details. The look on Michelle's face told him it was serious. He dropped the bar towel, whistled, and motioned to John Paul. They followed Michelle into the kitchen.

"What's the problem?" her brother asked.

"I need your car keys," Noah said.

"John Patrick got in the way of a dart. It's imbedded in his chest," she blurted as she unlocked the back door and opened it. "Gotta go."

John Paul tossed Noah the keys.

Michelle grabbed Noah's phone and was calling radiology as she walked. Noah shouted to John Paul just as he closed the door, "Call Theo. He's on his way here. Tell him where we're going."

Preston had pushed his way through the throng and was now hovering close to Jake Renard, pretending to study the sign-up sheet tacked to the wall. He strained to hear every word as John Paul told his father what had

465

happened. The second he heard that Michelle was on her way to the hospital and that John Paul was going to call Theo and tell him to meet Michelle there, Preston set his glass down on the bar and headed for the door.

Across the room, one of the old men was telling Monk a fishing story. He'd invited Monk to join him and his friends at the table, but Monk stayed where he was so that he could watch the parking lot through the front window.

"I sit all day at a computer," he said. "What were you saying about that speckled trout?"

The old man shook his head because Monk obviously hadn't been listening, and then once again launched into his story from the beginning. Monk nodded a couple of times so that he would appear interested. When he saw Noah and Michelle get into an old pickup, he immediately headed for the door. The old man shouted something to him, but Monk ignored him and kept going. His hand was in his vest pocket.

Out in the parking lot, Preston was walking to his car with his head down in case Michelle or the FBI agent happened to be looking back. Monk caught up with him.

"Where are they going in such a hurry?"

"To the hospital," Preston answered. "And Buchanan's on his way. If Clayborne drops the doctor off, then we can get Buchanan and her there. It shouldn't be crowded this time of night. Most surgeons operate early in the morning."

John changed the plan. When Preston called him and told him the news, he said, "Dallas and I will wait in the car in the hospital parking lot and grab Buchanan when he arrives. If he gets there ahead of us, Dallas will go in and lure him out. You and Monk go in and keep tabs on the doctor. When she's alone, you grab her and meet us like we planned."

"Screw that," Preston shouted. "I heard her brother say she's going to operate on some kid. I think we should do her there. We'll get the FBI agent too if he hangs around."

John gritted his teeth. "Are you out of your mind? Do you know how many people will be in there with her? For God's sake, use your head. We want to make this look like a professional hit on Buchanan, remember? And we want the police and the FBI to think the doctor got hit because she was with him."

"What about Clayborne?"

John considered the question for several seconds and then said, "If the agent gets in the way, you're going to have to kill him too."

"My God, if anyone could hear us..." Dallas raged.

"Shut up," John snarled. Then he continued his conversation with Preston. "What kind of car is the doctor driving?"

"An old red pickup truck."

John punched the end button and dropped the phone in his lap as Dallas muttered, "Slow down. The hospital is right around the corner."

He realized he was speeding and slowed

the rental car. "What was Preston arguing with you about?" Dallas asked.

"He wanted to go in shooting."

"How did this get so screwed up? You're talking about killing two, maybe three people, and I'm going along with it."

"We don't have any choice."

"The hell we don't. We could pack our bags and fly to the Caymans. We could get the money now, split it three ways, and then disappear."

"We have to have Cameron's death certificate to get the money."

"Monk could get it to us."

"How come you're feeling guilty about killing strangers, but you aren't having any trouble with killing Cameron?"

"He became a dangerous liability."

"Exactly," John said. "And so have Buchanan and his friends. Let's finish this tonight."

"I think we should call the whole thing off."

"No," John shouted.

"It's out of control," Dallas shouted back. "And it's all your fault, you bastard."

John's hand gripped his gun. He had the nearly overwhelming urge to put the barrel against Dallas's temple and pull the trigger. He took a deep breath instead.

"Don't you dare fall apart on me," he said. "Look, there's Preston's car. He and Monk must already be inside."

"The parking lot's almost empty. That's good."

John was craning his neck to see the doctors' lot. Then he smiled. "There's the pickup truck."

"Clayborne obviously didn't drop her off and go back to The Swan. He's inside with her."

"Then he's in the game."

"Pull in next to that purple van behind the line of trees."

John swung the car into the spot, pushed the button to bring the window down, and turned the motor off.

Dallas reached into the backseat for a black windbreaker and put it on. The pocket contained a small semiautomatic.

"I'm trying to go over every possibility in my head," Dallas said. "Buchanan and the doctor shouldn't be difficult. Clayborne's going to be the tough one. He's trained, and he'll be looking for trouble. If it goes bad and Preston and Monk and I have to hit them inside, he'll go down shooting, and he'll try to take us with him."

"Then you'll take him out first. Remember, the element of surprise will be on your side. He won't see it coming."

"But he'll...anticipate."

"You're going to be able to lure Buchanan outside."

"I'm just saying that if something goes wrong then—"

"Look," John said impatiently. "Monk will be thinking the same thing you are. You and he can maybe get Clayborne between you. Preston can get Buchanan."

"You prick. You should go in with us."

"The doctor knows who I am. It's too risky. She could be standing in the hallway and spot me right away. No, I'll wait here."

Dallas reached over and snatched the key out of the ignition. John was highly insulted. "Do you think I'm going to run out on you?"

"If you hear shooting, you just might."

John put his hands up. "Fine. Take the keys, but keep them where you can get to them quickly."

John saw a car coming down the drive, and even though the trees hid them from view, he still ducked down. The car drove on. They had a perfect vantage point. The ER entrance was right in front of them. Buchanan would either park his car in the visitors' lot or pull in and park next to the doctor's truck in the adjacent lot. Either way, he wouldn't see Dallas or John.

"If I have to go in after him...it could blow up in my face," Dallas worried.

"Think about the money," John whispered, his voice as smooth as satin. "Just think about the money."

Slumping down in their seats, they silently waited.

CHAPTER FORTY

Theo had made one more detour before he drove to the hospital. He stopped at a Pak Mail store, made copies of the papers Rosa had given him, and then, using the store phone, he called his superior in Boston and told him what had happened. As he was talking to him, he had one of the store's employees fax the papers to his boss.

Then he called the local FBI branch, got their fax number, and sent copies to their office as well. And because he was tired and feeling a little paranoid, he faxed a set to his home.

By the time he reached the outskirts of St. Claire, the signal on his cell phone was fading. The battery was almost out of juice. He wanted to call Ben and ask him to meet him at the hospital so he could give him copies too, his intent to include the chief in the investigation. Theo decided he would have to wait and call him from the hospital. While he waited at a stoplight, he stacked the papers and put them into the glove compartment.

Now that he felt he had covered all the bases—his boss was going to fax a copy to a friend at the IRS—Theo once again went over the conversation he'd had with Rosa Vincetti. The poor woman was terrified of the police, and based on her past experience, he certainly didn't blame her. They had broken down her door in the middle of the night and, with their guns drawn, had rushed

471

through her home, dragged her son out of his bed, handcuffed him, and taken him away. Ever since that night, Rosa had been living in terror that it would happen again.

"Did Catherine know about your fear of the police?" he'd asked.

"Yes, she did," she'd answered. "I told her everything. We were very close, like sisters. She depended on me."

Then, as Theo was leaving, Rosa told him she kept expecting to read about John's arrest in the papers because Catherine had told her that the copies she'd made of her husband's secret files would put him in prison for the rest of his life.

"What were you supposed to do with your copies?" he asked.

"I don't know. She told me to keep them in a safe place. I've been praying...and waiting."

"Waiting for what?"

"God to tell me what to do," she answered.

After assuring her that the papers were safe with him, he'd thanked her and left.

He was just a couple of blocks away from the hospital when he glanced at the digital clock on the dashboard. Nine-fifteen. Time flies when you're having fun, he thought. No wonder his stomach was growling, and he was yawning every other minute. He hadn't had anything to eat or drink all day. He needed food and caffeine. Maybe after he checked on Michelle and talked to Noah, he could grab something in the hospital cafeteria.

He drove along the hospital drive, noticed there weren't any cars under the canopy outside the emergency entrance, pulled up just beyond the No Parking sign, and parked the car in the slanted slots reserved for police.

A male nurse was coming out of the entrance as Theo was going in. "Hey, buddy, you can't park your car there. You'll get ticketed."

"FBI vehicle," Theo called back.

"Damn," John muttered when he saw Buchanan park his car next to the building and go inside.

Dallas opened the car door. "Call Preston and Monk. Have them meet me in the stairwell, north side. I want to synchronize this just in case Buchanan gives me trouble."

As Dallas slammed the door and took off running, John made the call. After he disconnected, he reached into the backseat and pulled his laptop into the front. Then he opened the glove compartment, got out the other set of keys he'd requested when he'd rented the car, and put the car key in the ignition.

Dallas was only just now beginning to distrust him. John smiled as he thought about that. All of them—even cynical, burned-out Cameron—for all their illegal wheeling and dealing, were naïve when it came to understanding John's capabilities. They actually believed that he couldn't get the money without them. What was even more amusing to him was the fact that his worker bees thought he would share the fortune. Ah, trust. What a wonderful weapon.

He leaned back and waited. It was a beautiful sultry night. Maybe it all would work out and he wouldn't have to go to his contingency plan. Preston was acting like a hothead now, though. John was pretty sure Preston wouldn't be able to stop himself from shooting someone. It would go bad then. Maybe all of them would die.

Wouldn't that be a stroke of luck.

Theo was going to take the stairs to the second floor, but as he was crossing the hallway to get to the stairwell door, Elliott Waterson shouted at him.

"Coach? My parents are upstairs."

The teenager was standing inside the elevator, holding the door open. He obviously thought that Theo had come to sit with Cherry and Daryl while John Patrick was in surgery.

Theo joined him. "How are you holding up, Elliott?"

The teenager began to cry. He looked like he'd been through a war. His eyes were swollen, his nose was red, and there was a sad and haunted look about him.

His head bowed, he whispered, "Did you hear what I did to my little brother?" He began to sob then. "I hurt him, Coach. I hurt him bad."

"I'm sure it was an accident, Elliott."

Theo knew that Michelle had rushed to the hospital and that the patient was John Patrick, the little boy who wanted him to shoot Lois, but when Michelle's brother had called, he hadn't given any details about the extent of the injury or how it had happened. Still, Theo knew Elliott would never intentionally hurt his brother. Elliott was a decent kid and came from a loving, close-knit family.

"I know you didn't mean to hurt John Patrick."

"But it's my fault and now he's gonna die."

Elliott nearly knocked Theo over when he threw himself against him. He was sobbing uncontrollably now, his face buried in Theo's shoulder. Elliott was a big, strapping boy who outweighed Theo by at least thirty pounds, but he was still a kid who needed to be comforted.

"Let's go find your mother," Theo suggested.

Barely coherent, Elliott stammered, "I never should have... I didn't mean to..."

Theo's heart ached for him. He put his arm around him and patted. "It's going to be okay." It wasn't a promise; it was a prayer. "You've got to have hope, Elliott."

He realized then that the elevator wasn't moving. He stretched his other arm around the teenager so he could reach the button.

"Tell me what happened."

"Mom told me not to get him the dartboard. She said he was too little and he could cut himself on those sharp darts, but John Patrick really wanted it for his birthday present, so I got it for him anyway. Mom was really mad at me," he stammered. "I should have taken it back...but I didn't. I hung the board with some rope off the big tree in the front yard. I put it down low so John Patrick could use it, and when it started to get dark and he got tired of playing with it and climbed up in the tree like he likes to do, I picked up the darts and I started throwing them. I got back real far, and I was really hurling them."

Theo winced. He knew what was coming. Elliott was too distraught to go on. The elevator doors opened, and Theo pulled him along as he stepped out.

Noah was leaning against the wall facing the elevators. When he saw Elliott with Theo, he immediately went down the hall to get the boy's parents.

"John Patrick jumped down out of the tree just as I hurled a dart," Elliott sobbed. "I got him in the chest, maybe his heart... I don't know, but he didn't cry. He just looked so surprised. I was screaming 'no' and running to him 'cause I knew what he was going to do. He tried to pull the dart out...but it didn't come out...just the fuzzy end...and he closed his eyes and went down on the ground. He...just...crumbled. I thought he was dead. Daddy saw it happen too. He had just gotten out of the van and was going up the steps. John Patrick's gonna die, isn't he, Coach? I know he is."

Theo didn't know what to say that could possibly console the boy. He cleared his throat and then said decisively, "Come on. Let's go find your mother."

There were signs on the wall directly ahead of him across from the elevator. Surgery was to the left down a long hallway. Noah had gone right, and Theo pulled Elliott along as he turned to follow. Noah stepped out of an open door and moved out of the way as Cherry and Daryl came hurrying toward Theo.

When Elliott saw his mother, he let go of Theo and ran to her. She put her arms around him and hugged him.

"I'm so sorry to hear about John Patrick," Theo said to Daryl.

The father looked as though he had aged ten years since they'd met. "I know, I know."

"He's such a little boy," Cherry cried.

"But he's strong," Daryl told her. "He's going to make it."

"How long has he been in surgery?" Theo asked.

"A half hour now," he answered.

"Any word yet? A progress report?"

Elliott had let go of his mother and was now standing beside her, holding her hand. Cherry looked dazed.

Daryl answered the question. "Dr. Mike sent a nurse in a few minutes ago to tell us it's going well. Did you hear that, Elliott?" he asked. "You had just gone downstairs to look for the minister when that nurse came in. Dr. Mike said that John Patrick's guardian angel was looking out for him because the arrow missed hitting an artery. The nurse was guessing it would be another hour at least before the operation is finished."

"They may have to give my boy a transfusion," Cherry said.

"So we were thinking we ought to go down to the lab and give them some of our blood," Daryl said, "in case John Patrick needs it."

"They're not going to take your blood, Daryl," Cherry said. "Not with your recent surgery."

"I'm going to ask them all the same."

"I'm going to give my blood too," Elliott said. He stepped away from his mother, straightened, and wiped his eyes with the backs of his hands.

"Where are your other boys?" Theo asked.

"Down in the cafeteria," Cherry said. "I should check on them. Henry must be getting fretful. It's past his bedtime, and I didn't think to bring his little blanket he likes to hold up against his nose when he sucks his thumb." She started crying.

Daryl put his arm around her. "Henry's just fine. The reverend's wife is going to take the little ones home and put them to bed," he explained to Theo. "They should be here any minute, so let's get going to the lab, Cherry. I want to get back here before the doctor comes out."

Daryl was agitated. Theo understood the father's need to do something, anything, to help his child. Waiting would have driven Theo crazy, and he couldn't even begin to imagine the anguish John Patrick's parents were going through.

"Maybe one of us ought to stay here," Cherry said as the elevator doors opened.

"I'll be here," Theo said. "I'll page you if anything happens."

Noah had hung back, but as soon as the elevator doors closed, he walked over to Theo. "The mother looks like she's in shock."

"How bad was it? Do you know?"

"It looked bad, but I honestly don't know. It got crazy here. I was watching Mike through the window. She was standing at the sink scrubbing her hands and arms and looking at the X rays another doctor was holding up for her. There were nurses and doctors and technicians rushing back and forth. Everyone seemed to be shouting orders, everyone but Mike. She was as calm and cool as a summer breeze." His voice was filled with admiration. "She sure knows how to handle herself in a crisis. I guess that's why she became a surgeon."

Theo nodded. "She was that way last night when the bullets were flying all around us."

"Speaking of bullets flying, did you get everything done in New Orleans?"

"Oh, yes," Theo said. "You're not going to believe what I found out."

He then told Noah about the Sowing Club and the millions of dollars tucked away in a Cayman Islands account. When he was finished taking Noah through the steps that had led him to Cameron and Rosa, he added, "I want to get John Russell, but I have a feeling there's more to his crimes than what's in those records. As soon as the detectives pick up Cameron Lynch, I'll talk to him. He'll tell me what I want to know."

"From what Nick's told me about your powers of persuasion, I don't doubt you'll get him to talk. I want to look at those papers."

"I left copies in the glove compartment of your car."

"Was that smart?"

Theo smiled. "Didn't I mention copies went out to my boss, the IRS, the FBI, and my home?"

"No, you didn't mention that. You said the initials next to those transactions were *J, C, P,* and *D,*" Noah said. "Too bad John didn't put their full names."

"Maybe Catherine did. Maybe there was an explanation with the papers she sent Michelle."

"John Russell is obviously *J,* and Cameron Lynch is *C.* So who are *P* and *D?*"

"That's the riddle, and I bet I'll have the answer soon. Detectives Underwood and Basham have a couple of other detectives running all over New Orleans talking to some of John's associates. It won't be long before we have the names."

"Maybe Detective Harris knows who they are. Has she called yet?"

"No."

Noah shook his head. "Guess she isn't a woman of her word. It's been over twelve hours, and didn't she promise to give you a copy of the file then?"

"She'll probably be furious when she finds out I got a copy from Rosa."

"But you're not going to tell her."

"Hell, no," he said. "I'm not sharing information with her. I'm going to let Underwood and Basham make the collars and take the credit."

He heard his name being paged over the speaker, saw the phone on the wall directly across from the elevator, and walked over to answer it. As soon as he identified himself, the operator put him on hold. Two seconds later, Detective Underwood came on the line.

The conversation was very informative. Then Theo said, "Sure, I'll be waiting. Let me know." He hung up and turned to Noah. "*Preston* and *Dallas*."

"Yeah? That was quick."

"One of the detectives got the names from John's ex-girlfriend. A woman named Lindsey. She was trying to get in John's house, said she'd left some clothes. She told him she had met Cameron but never the others. She'd heard John talking on the phone, though, and remembered the names *Preston* and *Dallas* because they called often."

"No last names?"

"Not yet. And guess what? Another man called once looking for Dallas. His name was Monk. She remembered the phone call because John was so deferential to him, like he almost was afraid of him."

"Interesting," Noah said. "Did Lindsey ever talk to him or any of the others?"

"No," Theo answered. "She wasn't allowed to answer the phone, said John told her he didn't want people to know he was shacking up with her so soon after his wife's death. She also told the detective they were supposed to get married, but John came home a couple of nights ago, told her to pack up and get out. He wasn't nice about it."

"Which is why she's so chatty now?"

"Exactly. I figure they'll have Preston and Dallas under wraps before midnight."

"Could be sooner," Noah said. "How did Detective Underwood find you?"

"I told him I'd be on my cell phone or at The Swan. John Paul or Jake must have told him I was at the hospital."

"So all we have to do is hang tight a little longer. It'll be over soon."

Theo yawned loudly and rubbed the back of his neck. "I need some caffeine."

"There's some coffee in the waiting room."

"Good," he said. "I'm going to check on Michelle first. Can I go inside there?" he asked, tilting his head toward the wide double doors with the sign above stating in bold red letters, "No Admittance."

"Sure you can. I did. You can look through the window and see Mike. She's in the operating room on the left around the corner where it dead ends. Just don't let anyone see you. The nurses tend to shout. I'm going to make a couple of phone calls," he added as he turned and headed down the hallway to the waiting room. "Want me to bring you some coffee?"

"No," Theo answered. "I'll get my own." He had his palm on the door, ready to push, when he suddenly stopped and turned around. "Hey, Noah, you know what's really odd?"

"What's that?"

"The channels Catherine used...sending the files to an unsuspecting relative she'd never met."

"John Paul told me she was an odd duck."

"She was."

"So maybe that's your answer."

"Yeah. Maybe," he said, but he wasn't convinced.

He pushed the door and stepped into the forbidden area, feeling a little like a kid sneaking into an R-rated movie. He half expected someone to start shouting at him or grab him by the collar and toss him out.

He was inside a wide hallway with several sets of swinging doors and an elevator. Turning into a hall to the left, he went around the corner. There was a gurney against the wall where the hallway dead ended, and to the right was the surgical suite Michelle was using.

It was at least twenty degrees colder here. He could hear music as he walked closer, and he recognized the voice. Good old Willie Nelson, Michelle's favorite. Theo felt a stirring of a memory too elusive to catch hold of. There was something familiar about the smell and the song and the cold. Maybe it was because of his own surgery.

He looked in through the square window and was surprised at how small the room was. It was crowded with people. He counted six, including the guy sitting behind the patient's head checking dials on the machines next to him. He couldn't see John Patrick, a nurse blocked his view, but he got a glimpse of Michelle's forehead when the nurse handed her an instrument and she turned slightly. As he watched her, he could feel the tension easing away. He began to relax, took a deep breath, and realized he was suddenly feeling good because she was close.

"Man, I do have it bad," he whispered as he turned and walked back through the swinging doors. Was he becoming obsessive about Michelle? No, of course not, but the world did seem a little brighter, and definitely better, when he was with her.

Now, Catherine was the epitome of an obsessive personality. That thought led him right back to the riddle he'd been trying to solve. Rosa had told him that Catherine had wanted to use the files as a threat to control John's behavior while she was alive. Why hadn't Catherine simply directed her attorney to give the papers to the police after her death? Was she worried that Benchley wouldn't follow through, or had Rosa's distrust of the authorities rubbed off on her?

Theo could understand why Catherine chose Michelle. Catherine knew how smart her cousin was. Every time Jake called her, he did a lot of boasting, and Catherine, knowing what Michelle had already accomplished in her life, surely knew that her cousin would understand what all the numbers and transactions meant. Catherine might not have thought that Jake would figure it out—his good-old-boy façade fooled a lot of people into believing he wasn't as intelligent as Theo knew he was. Catherine wouldn't have known that about him, but she certainly would have known how persistent he could be, because he never gave up on her. He called her once a month to check on her, refusing to be put off by her cold, indifferent manner. Catherine probably assumed that Jake would make certain Michelle gave the papers her full attention and got them to the right people.

But she'd circumvented the police and given her second copy to Rosa. Now, why would she do that?

The answer was suddenly glaringly obvious. Because she knew that Rosa would never go to the police. And that meant...

"Son of a bitch," he whispered.

He was berating himself for taking so long to figure it out. *Sorry, Catherine. I'm dense, okay?*

He couldn't wait to tell Noah. Shoving the swinging door open, he ran into the hall, and in his haste, he bumped into one of the supply carts, sending it careening into the opposite wall. A stack of towels fell on his feet as he grabbed the cart to keep it from falling over. Squatting down, he was scooping up the towels in his arms when he heard the bing of the elevator followed by the swooshing sound the doors made when they opened.

Detective Harris stepped out of the alcove that led to the elevator. She turned away from him and headed toward the waiting room.

She wasn't wearing sensible shoes today. She was moving fast, the way most overworked policemen instinctively do because they are always behind, and her heels clicked against the linoleum floor like castanets.

Theo walked forward as he called out to her. "Hey, Detective, are you looking for me?"

She had almost reached the waiting room. Startled, she whirled around as she shoved her hand into her pocket, and then smiled. "Where did you come from?"

Noah stepped into the hall behind Harris as she hurried toward Theo.

"Surgery," he answered. "I'll be right with you. I've just one quick call to make." He turned to the wall phone next to him, picked it up, dialed the operator, and spoke in a low voice. Then he hung up and smiled again.

"How'd you know I was here?"

"I'm a detective. I know how to find people." Then she laughed. "A man at The Swan told me you were here and Admitting told me you were on this floor. It didn't take much investigative work. I'm a little late. It's been more than twelve hours, but I got detained. I did keep my word, though."

"I didn't think you'd show. I'm impressed."

"I've got copies of the papers from that package, which I'm letting you read out of the goodness of my heart," she said. "Just remember, it's my investigation," she added quickly.

"I won't touch it," he promised. "So where are the files on Monk?"

"I guess you didn't believe me when I said I'd spent three years chasing the ghost. I've got two huge cardboard file boxes in the trunk. It's going to take you a couple of weeks to go through all of it."

"You trying to make me sorry I asked for them?"

"Of course." She visibly shivered. "God, it's cold up here. It's like a tomb. So what do you want to do?" she asked. "Transfer the boxes to your car now, or do you want me to drop them off someplace?"

"We could transfer them now. I could start looking through them tonight."

"Whatever you want."

"Did you make any arrests yet?"

Her eyes narrowed slightly. The question obviously irritated her. "Not yet," she said sharply. "He got away. He does it to me every damned time. Vanishes into thin air. We tracked him to a motel in St. Claire. We surrounded it, and then we closed in. His car was there, parked right in front of his door, but he was gone. He had to leave fast, though. He didn't have time to pack his equipment or his clothes before he took off. I'm hoping my people will get lucky this time and find a print. They're working on it now."

"Think I could drive over and take a look?"

"Sure, as along as you don't interfere."

"I already promised I wouldn't."

"Okay," she said. "You can look. It's the St. Claire Motel, on Fourth and Summit."

She pushed the button for the elevator and waited. Looking up, she saw the number four was lit. They waited side by side for several seconds. She punched the button again.

Impatient now, she said, "Let's take the stairs. It's quicker, and I want to get back to New Orleans."

"Hot date?"

"How'd you know?"

"Just a guess. It's gonna be late by the time you drive back."

She glanced up at the numbers again. The light was still on four. "New Orleans doesn't sleep. The Quarter will be buzzing when I get there." Theo stepped away from her as she said, "Let's go."

Turning to take the lead, she suddenly stopped. Noah was standing in front of her, his hands clasped behind his back.

"Hello there," he said cheerfully.

"There you are," Theo said. "I'd like to introduce you to Detective Harris. Detective, this is Noah Clayborne," he said as he put his hand on her shoulder. "Noah works for the FBI, but he's also a good friend."

Theo stepped behind her as Noah said, "It's a pleasure to meet you, Detective. I was just..."

Theo took another step back. "Hey, Dallas," he said.

She instinctively turned. Even as she did, she realized what had just happened. Her eyes widened and she jerked back, but it was too late. Theo shoved her into the elevator doors, face-first, making it impossible for her to fire the gun he knew she had hidden in her pocket.

Noah stepped forward, forced her arm back and up into an unnatural position, then struck her wrist hard to get her to let go of the weapon. The gun dropped to the floor, and Theo kicked it away.

"Where are your friends?" Theo demanded. He slackened his hold so he could force her to turn around. She took advantage, and cursing, she whirled and tried to slam her knee into Noah's groin.

"Is that nice?" he asked as he dodged the knee. "Where are your friends?" He repeated Theo's question in a much more unfriendly tone.

She wasn't talking. Her lips pinched tight, her jaw clenched, she glared at Noah with loathing.

Theo looked up at the elevator numbers again. Still locked on four. "They're in the stairwells," he said. "They must have blocked the elevator so I'd have to take the steps. They may not know you're here."

"Do they?" Noah asked Dallas. His hand was around her neck, his thumb pressing into her flesh as he held her off the floor against the elevator.

She turned to the left and screamed at the top of her lungs, "Preston!" And then swinging to the right, "Monk! Now!"

Theo's fist silenced her. Her eyes closed instantly, and when Noah let go of her, she collapsed to the floor, unconscious. Noah tilted his head toward the hallway and whispered, "Get ready," as he quickly patted Dallas down for weapons. He found the Glock in its holster and removed it. He shoved her onto her back and was about to search for another weapon in an ankle strap under her slacks, when he heard the faint squeak of a door opening. He pointed toward the waiting room, indicating to Theo that that was where the sound had come from.

Theo had heard it. He nodded and took a step closer. Noah found the ankle strap, lifted the gun, and shoved it into the waistband of his jeans. He went back to the pockets in her jacket, pulled out four magazines, and stood. He moved quickly, silently to Theo's back. He shoved two of the magazines into Theo's back pockets, then handed him Harris's Glock so that he would have a weapon in each hand. Barrels pointed to the ceiling, they waited, hidden by the recess in front of the elevator doors.

Theo heard the soft click of a door closing. It came from the exit just beyond the waiting room. Monk. Then another click, at the opposite end of the hall by the OR doors. Preston had to be the man at the other end of the hall. Where was John? Was he in the elevator? Or was he in the stairwell?

He strained to hear footsteps. Nothing. Not a sound. Were they waiting for Noah and him to step out into the hall?

His heart was pounding in his ears; his breathing was harsh.

"Ambush," Noah whispered. "Let them come to us."

Theo shook his head. He didn't care that he was trapped. He couldn't wait. Wouldn't. The elevator was still locked on the fourth floor.

There were two men waiting to blow them away, but these men wouldn't wait long, and if Michelle or one of the nurses came out to talk to the Watersons, they'd kill her.

"Michelle." He whispered her name. Noah nodded, letting him know he understood.

Theo tucked one of his guns under his arm, reached down, and grabbed one of Dallas's shoes. Then he threw it into the hallway. Preston immediately opened fire. Three shots. Then silence again.

They both heard the wail of sirens getting closer and closer. "Police?" Noah asked.

Theo nodded, letting him know he'd told the operator to call them, then whispered, "Can't wait," because he knew that Preston and Monk and John had also heard the sound. They might think the noise was from an ambulance, but they would still want to move quickly to get the job done. No, they wouldn't wait much longer. Theo took a step toward the hallway. Noah nudged him.

"Back to back," he whispered. "Only way we do it. Move out together. On three?"

Their guns up, they each took a deep breath. Noah turned his back to Theo's and whispered, "One."

Out of the corner of his eye, Theo saw Dallas move. She was swinging up onto her knees. She'd reached the gun Theo had kicked aside and was taking aim at Noah.

Theo fired. The blast shook the elevator doors. The bullet struck Harris in the hollow just below her throat. Eyes wide in disbelief, she fell back. Her eyes closed a second later, and she was dead. Her head dropped to her chest as she slumped against the elevator doors.

Noah barely spared her a glance before continuing his countdown. "Two…" He turned again, his shoulders touching Theo's now.

"Let's do it," Theo whispered.

"Go!"

Theo and Noah rushed into the hallway. Each found his target, homed in, and fired.

Noah winged Monk, but the killer didn't slow down. He got the door open and dove into the stairwell. Noah kept going, running now, safe in the knowledge that Theo was protecting his back just as he was protecting his. When he got to the door, he flattened himself against the wall, reached in, and fired again. Monk was waiting for him. He fired at the same time. His bullet tore a groove in the door as Noah jumped back. A hail of bullets followed until the wall across from the door was riddled with holes, and plaster bits flew out in every direction. The air was gray from plaster dust.

The noise was deafening. The blasts echoed in his ears, but he thought he heard a woman scream. He couldn't be sure. Noah glanced over his shoulder, saw Theo running, his guns firing again and again as the man he was chasing ducked behind the OR doors.

Go to the right. Go right. Away from Michelle. Theo surged forward, through the doors. He dropped to the floor, rolled, praying to God that Preston was trying to get to the exit.

The Glock in his left hand was empty. He couldn't waste time reloading. The doors leading to ICU were swinging. Preston was there, waiting, Theo was certain. He scrambled to get to his feet, saw a blur streak past the window, and knew he had to get around the corner and out of the line of fire.

He made it, but only just barely. A bullet missed his face by an inch. A nurse ran out of the OR, screaming.

"Get back," he shouted as he ejected the empty magazine from the gun, grabbed another one from his back pocket, and snapped it in place. The nurse disappeared into the OR as he pressed his back against the wall and waited. He could hear Willie singing.

His shoulder rubbed the wall as he edged closer to the corner. He accidentally hit the light switch, and just as the song ended, the hallway went dark. The light spilling through the window of the OR was sufficient for him to see. Where had Preston gone? Had he already gotten a hostage? Or had he found another way out? He'd have to come this way, wouldn't he?

Where the hell were the police? Never around when you need them, he thought. *Come on, Ben. Get your ass in here. Save the day.*

You're not getting past me, Preston. No way. Stay inside, Michelle. Don't come out until this is over. He remembered the gurney and moved back until his foot touched it. He hooked his leg around the metal bar and pulled the gurney close to the corner.

Come on. Come on. Make your move.

Michelle had just put in the last stitch and was waiting for that beautiful first cough after the anesthesiologist had removed the tube. The child had come through the surgery like a champion. Barring any complications, John Patrick would be climbing his favorite tree again within a month. Providing, of course, that his mother would let him out of her sight.

"Come on, sweetie. Cough for me," she whispered.

She heard a tiny little groan followed by a dry cough a second later. "Good to go," the anesthesiologist said. He pulled his mask down and grinned. "This is one lucky boy."

"Great job," she told the team.

Suddenly, gunshots rang out in the hallway. Chaos followed. One of the nurses screamed and ran to the door to find out what was happening, ignoring both Michelle's and Landusky's shouts to come back. Then Michelle heard Theo shout to the woman to get back.

"It's Theo. Is he hurt?" Michelle demanded.

"I don't know. What in God's name is going on?"

No one had an answer. Their concern was for the patient now. John Patrick was breathing on his own, the sound nice and clear. Landusky quickly helped Michelle roll the table over against the wall by the doors. A nurse moved the IV stand. She put it to the side, and then she and another nurse leaned over the boy to protect him from harm if anyone rushed into the OR firing a weapon. Landusky had the same idea. He stood behind John Patrick's head, cupped his hands on either side of the boy's face, and hunched over him. The others squatted down behind the foot of the table and waited. A technician put her hands over her ears and was silently crying.

Michelle had already grabbed the heavy fire extinguisher, holding it like a baseball bat. She stood to the side of the door but far enough away so that if the shooter slammed the door against the wall, it wouldn't block her. Then she turned the lights off and waited. She wouldn't allow herself to think about Theo. She had only one thought now and that was to keep the gunman out of the OR.

"If anyone fires a gun in here, the whole floor could blow up," Landusky whispered. "The oxygen tanks and the—"

"Shhh," she whispered. She and everyone else in the OR were well aware of the danger.

She pressed forward to listen. What was that soft whirring noise? It sounded like a centrifuge spinning. Oh, God, her Willie Nelson tape was automatically rewinding. When it reached the beginning, it would start playing again. The recorder was on top of a table against the wall on the other side of the doors. A sterile sheet covered it.

She wanted to shout to Theo. She couldn't, of course. *Let him be okay. If he's hurt...if he's bleeding while I'm hiding behind this door... Don't.*

Don't think about it. Where was Noah? Why wasn't he helping Theo? Was he out there too? *Theo, where are you?*

Theo hunched behind the gurney. He was ready. He sensed rather than heard the man coming, and Theo kicked the gurney with all his might as Preston sprinted around the corner. He was firing into the center of the corridor. The gurney crashed into him, but it didn't slow him down. He easily blocked the gurney with his arm, then threw his weight into it and sent it hurling into Theo, slamming him back against the wall.

Theo went down hard. As Preston was trying to shove the gurney out of his way so he could get a clear shot, Theo rolled under the table and fired. The bullet struck Preston in the left thigh. And that didn't seem to slow him down either. His empty magazine clattered to the floor, and he was snapping another one into the weapon as Theo, roaring like a bear on the attack, lifted the gurney with his shoulder, grabbed it with one hand, and used it as a battering ram, forcing Preston back. Theo shot through the pad falling from the gurney. Preston pivoted and the bullet creased the top of his shoulder.

The bastard didn't even flinch. What the hell was it going to take to bring him down? As Preston was diving around the corner, Theo aimed and fired again. Click. Nothing happened. The magazine was empty. He reached behind him to grab the second one Noah had shoved into his pocket, loaded it in the gun, then dove as Preston opened fire on him.

One bullet skimmed Theo's forehead. How many bullets did he have left? Theo wondered. If he was lucky, maybe two. Three was pushing it. He felt a flash of searing pain in his arm as he dove again to get out of the line of fire.

The gurney lay on its side. Thank God, he thought as he scrambled to get behind it.

Preston lunged to get Theo in his sights, but Theo lashed out with his foot and nailed him in his knee. And still he didn't go down. He staggered back, firing into the ceiling.

The doors around the corner suddenly exploded. Preston didn't look behind him to see who was coming. He was just a couple of feet away from a darkened room, saw the swinging doors, and knew it was time to get the hell out. He rushed into the OR, hoping there was another way out on the other side.

Preston stopped and squinted into the dark, listening as he edged away from the doors. He turned toward Michelle, the barrel of his gun pointed in her direction.

She could hear him panting. He was too close. Another step and he'd bump into her. She knew she'd have to step back to get a good swing at him. But he'd hear it, she thought.

Why wasn't he moving? Did he know she was there? Just one step forward.

She needed a distraction. Something...anything to get him to turn away from her so she could strike. Willie Nelson came to her rescue. "To all the girls I've loved before..." The instant the song started, Preston whirled around and fired again and again at the tape recorder. Michelle swung the extinguisher, slamming it into his jaw.

"Hit the lights," she shouted as he staggered backward into the hallway. She went after him, struck him again on the side of the head. The second blow seemed to do the trick. He went flying back and landed with a thud against the wall.

Michelle stopped. Theo sprang in front of her as Preston was bringing his gun up. Theo fired and hit him in the abdomen.

He was using his back to push Michelle into the OR and out of danger.

Preston fell to his knees as Noah ran toward him shouting, "Drop the gun."

Preston turned toward Noah and took aim. He never got to pull the trigger. Noah fired. One bullet through the temple. Preston pitched forward facedown on the floor. A pool of black blood rapidly formed a puddle around him.

Michelle nudged Theo forward to get him out of the way of the doors as she called out, "It's clear. Get the patient to recovery."

Theo leaned against the wall, then slowly slid down into a sitting position as Noah squatted next to Preston and lifted the gun from his hand.

Everyone started shouting and talking at once then. Theo closed his eyes and took a deep breath. He could hear the squeak of the rollers as the nurses pushed John Patrick's bed out and around Preston.

Michelle knelt down beside Theo. She'd peeled her gloves off and was gently probing the cut below his eye.

"I'm too old for this," he muttered.

"You okay?" Noah asked as he reholstered his gun.

"Yes. Did you get the one she called Monk?"

"No."

"No?" he shouted. He was trying to dodge Michelle's hand so he could see Noah.

"I don't know how he did it, but he got away. I know I winged him," Noah said. "All the exits are blocked, and they're making a sweep of each floor, but he's long gone."

"You can't know that."

"A patient up on four was looking out his window and saw a man run across a bed of flowers up the hill. The patient said he was bent over."

"What about John Russell? Any sign of him?" Theo asked.

"No," Noah answered.

"You tore your stitches," Michelle said.

"What?"

She'd whispered the news and it sounded like a scolding. He was looking at Noah, wondering what the white streaks were on his face when she'd interrupted. He finally looked at her face. And when he saw the tears streaming down her cheeks, he was astonished. She wasn't so tough after all. Not with him, anyway.

"I didn't do it on purpose, sweetheart."

He tried to wipe a tear from her cheek. She pushed his hand away. "I'm going to have to sew you back together again." She was trembling now like an alcoholic who'd gone too long without a drink. "Look at my hands. They're shaking."

"Then we're gonna wait before you pick up a needle and go to work on me."

"You threw yourself in front of me so he'd shoot you. That was very heroic, you big jerk. You could have been killed."

He wouldn't let her push him away this time. Cupping her face with his hands, he whispered, "I love you too."

CHAPTER FORTY-ONE

Always have a contingency plan. When two police cars came zooming down the drive to the hospital with their lights flashing and their sirens blaring, John knew it was time to leave. He ducked down in his seat—an unnecessary precaution, but instinctive all the same—and turned the ignition on. He waited a couple of seconds, until he saw the policemen running into the hospital. Then he slowly backed the car out of the parking spot, turned, and eased out of the lot.

He didn't really care if his friends were dead or alive. Why would he? His plans weren't going to be affected, no matter what the outcome.

Even if the police took them alive and they told them everything they knew, it would be too late. And if by some miracle one or two of them escaped, well, that just didn't matter either. John had enough time to get the money from the Sowing Club account transferred to the account in Switzerland he'd set up years ago. He had his laptop with him—he found it curious that Dallas hadn't questioned him as to why he'd brought it along—and all he had to do was to get to a phone line, type a few commands on his computer, and he would be set for life.

Getting away quickly was all he cared about now. Within the next few minutes, one of those policemen might come running outside and try to block the main entrance leading into the hospital drive.

"Hmmm," he whispered. There might already be a police car there now. Too risky to chance being stopped, John decided. He backed the car into the lot again, turned around, and then drove at a snail's pace down the tarred service road behind the hospital.

And that was when he spotted Monk hobbling up the hill toward the street. One hand was clutching his side. Had he been shot? It looked as though he had.

John chuckled. The opportunity was simply too good to pass up. No one was around. No one would see. He owed Monk a considerable amount of money. "Hmmm," he whispered again. *Do it,* his mind screamed. *Do it now.*

He seized the moment. Turning the car sharply, he drove over the curb, then pressed his foot down on the accelerator. Monk heard him coming and turned. When he saw John, he stopped and waited.

He thinks I'm going to pick him up. He increased his speed as he got closer. The expression on Monk's face when he realized what was going to happen was hilarious. He looked positively shocked.

John miscalculated, though. He thought Monk would dive to the left and turned the wheel ever so slightly so he could hit him straight on, but Monk leapt the other way, and the car only brushed him as it sped past.

He didn't dare risk backing up and trying again. "Oh, well, you do what you can," he said as he hit the curb and bounced into the street. Cutting through a run-down neighborhood, he reached the main street six blocks away from the hospital and knew then he was safe.

He picked up his cell phone, dialed the pilot he'd hired months ago, and told him he would arrive at the municipal airport in forty-five minutes. He turned left at the stoplight and headed in the opposite direction from New Orleans. He'd never be able to go back, of course. Even though he had a new identity—the passport was in the case with his computer—he knew he would never return to the United States.

No great loss, he thought. After all, he had millions of dollars to keep him happy. John wasn't one to gloat, but he did just that now. He had, after all, gotten away with murder.

CHAPTER FORTY-TWO

Michelle finished writing orders and then went into recovery to look in on John Patrick. The nurse had led his parents in, and Daryl and Cherry stood holding hands by their son's bedside. Elliott was outside the door, too upset to do more than peek in at his brother.

"The worst is over," Daryl said. Then he looked at Michelle. "You've been through the wringer tonight too, haven't you? The police blocked off the steps and the elevators, and we knew something terrible was going on, but we didn't know how bad it was."

"I'm glad we didn't know," Cherry said as she dabbed at the corners of her eyes with a tissue.

"We could hear the gunshots. Everyone in the hospital could hear them, but we knew you wouldn't let anything happen to John Patrick."

"Dr. Landusky will be here through the night," she said. "But if you'd rather I stay—"

Daryl wouldn't let her finish. "You did your part, and we don't know how we're ever going to repay you. You go on home."

Michelle took the steps down to the emergency room to get Theo. The notion of sleeping for a week sounded glorious. She wondered if he was as tired as she was. She had already stitched his arm again, but he was waiting in the ER, sitting on an exam table with an ice pack on his knee while he talked on the phone.

He hung up as she walked in. "Detectives Underwood and Basham picked up Cameron Lynch. He was in the mood to talk," he added. "First thing he said after they read him his rights was that he wasn't going to take the fall for murdering John's wife. He called it a mercy killing."

"And that made it okay?" she asked, shaking her head.

"I don't know what kind of spin he's putting on it," Theo said. "The bottom line is that he was motivated by money."

He reached out and pulled her into his side and held her around her waist. He needed to have her close, to touch her. There was a moment upstairs when he had thought he was going to lose her, and he knew he would never ever forget that terror.

He kissed her on the side of her neck. A nurse was standing at the counter watching. He didn't care, and from the way Michelle leaned into him, he knew she didn't care either.

Noah walked into the ER then.

"What have you got all over your face?" Michelle asked.

He went to the mirror above the sink to look. "Plaster chips and dust I guess," he said as he turned the water on and grabbed a towel.

Theo told him about Cameron while Noah washed his face. "John's already moved the money out of the Cayman account. He did it with his computer."

"Where'd he transfer it?" Noah asked.

"Don't know yet, but Underwood has people

working on it. It's an interesting group," he commented.

"The Sowing Club? What's interesting about four deviants?" Noah asked. He wiped his face dry with the towel and dropped it into the sink. Then he turned around, folded his arms across his chest, and waited for Theo to explain.

"When John first set the account up, he told his friends that all four of them would have to go to the bank to get any money out. It was a safeguard, he'd explained, but that obviously wasn't the truth. He played them from the beginning, and Dallas and Preston and Cameron were fools to keep on trusting him after he manipulated them into helping hire the hit on his wife."

"Why did he need their cooperation?"

"Dallas was the connection to Monk," Theo said. "I'm not sure why he wanted to involve the other two. They had all the bases covered. John worked the banking end. He was a lawyer and a VP in the trust department. Cameron used his brokerage firm to screw clients out of their retirement money, Dallas was police, and Preston worked in the D.A.'s office and took care of any problems with the law.

"Dallas was actually telling the truth about the ghost. She did keep a file on him and all his past deeds, just to cover herself. Underwood has the file now. He said Monk killed a young girl a while back and that the father hired him to do the job. There's enough evidence to arrest the father, and they've got detectives picking him up now."

"I hope he rots in prison," Michelle said.

Theo nodded. "Underwood thinks Monk has flair." He lifted the ice pack and put it on the table behind him.

"What did he mean by 'flair'?" Michelle asked. She saw Theo grimace as he lifted his leg. She grabbed the ice pack and put it back on his knee.

"He always places a rose near the victim, usually on the bed, because he prefers killing them at night."

"So Detective Harris wasn't lying about that," Michelle said.

"She was smart," Theo said. "She stuck close to the truth as much as possible so she wouldn't get tripped up on lies."

"How did you know Harris was one of them?" Michelle asked.

"When Noah was in New Orleans, I had him check her out," he said. "I thought it was odd that her captain wouldn't tell Noah anything about the case she was working on. Noah's used to dealing with antagonistic detectives who don't want the FBI working with them, so he assumed the captain was being evasive on purpose. I thought maybe the captain didn't know what Harris was up to, but I didn't take that any further. I just filed it away and moved on."

"I should have taken the time to talk to some of the other detectives," Noah said. "To find out how they felt about working with her."

"They probably would have closed ranks on you," Theo said.

"I still don't understand how you put it together, Theo," Michelle said.

"Catherine told me," he said. "She was a smart woman, so I finally realized why she'd made it so complicated. She didn't have the attorney give the papers to the police because she knew one of the members of the Sowing Club was a detective. She gave the second backup copy to Rosa because she knew the housekeeper would never go to the police. I honestly don't know what she thought Rosa would do, though. Maybe mail the files... I don't know."

He yawned then and said, "Anyway, I'd narrowed it down to Preston and Dallas, knew one of them was a policeman, and then Harris showed up wearing a jacket when it was blistering hot and muggy outside. When she stepped into the hall and turned, her back was to me and I saw her reach behind and unsnap the strap on her gun, but she kept the other hand in her pocket. I figured she was carrying extra firepower."

"I sure would like to know where John Russell is hiding," Noah said.

Theo nodded. "We'll get him eventually." Then he yawned. "Let's go home."

"I'm ready," she agreed.

"Noah's going to sleep in your guest room," he said. "Just as a precaution."

"You don't think that John or Monk—"

He didn't let her finish. "No, but I'll sleep easier, and so will you."

They headed for the exit. Theo looped his arm around Michelle's shoulder as they walked along.

"I've got to stop at the motel and pick up some things," Noah said. "How's that kid doing, Mike? Give me some good news."

"He's going to be fine," she answered. "It wasn't as bad as it looked."

"Are you still chafed you let Monk get away?" Theo asked.

"I couldn't be in two places at once," he replied. "I knew I had to get back and save your sorry ass, and the police had the stairwells blocked off. I figured they'd get him."

"I saved your sorry ass," Theo corrected.

"The hell you did. Where are my car keys?"

"I left them in the car."

"Noah, how do you know you shot Monk?" she asked. "Did you see him fall?"

"No, he didn't go down," he explained. "But there was blood on the door and on the stairs. I either got him in the hip or the side. He went up to the roof, crossed over, then down the fire escape." He turned to leave. "I'll see you later."

"Could you wait a minute and make sure I can get the pickup started?" Michelle asked.

She was glad she'd asked, because Noah had to hot-wire it to get it going. Theo insisted on driving and didn't seem to have any trouble using his right leg to work the clutch.

"I'm going to sleep until noon," she said.

"You can't. You've got to get up and go fishing."

Michelle groaned. "I'm staying home."

"You've got to go with me. You're my partner."

"We don't have a boat, remember? Mine's buried in the shrubs somewhere, and we wouldn't have a chance of winning without one. The best fishing spots are deep in the swamp."

"Your dad made John Paul loan us one of his. It's already docked behind The Swan."

She didn't like hearing that. "I want to stay in bed, but I'll leave the decision to you. You're company, after all." She moved closer, put her hand on his thigh, and tried to sound sultry when she whispered, "I'll do whatever you want."

"That's a tough one," he drawled. "Let's see. I could either get up before dawn—and I really like doing that—and sit in a boat all day long worrying about snakes falling on my head while I'm sweating through my clothes and slapping at mosquitoes, or..."

"Yes?" she said, smiling now.

"I could spend the day in bed fooling around with a beautiful, naked lady. Yeah, that's a tough one, all right."

"Who said anything about me being naked?"

He gave her a look that made her heart race. "Honey, that's a given."

"Oh, boy."

"You're blushing. After everything we've—"

She put her hand over his mouth. "I remember what we did."

She suddenly realized he'd made a wrong turn. "Where are you going?"

"McDonald's. I'm starving."

"We have plenty of food at home."

"A cheeseburger will hold me until we get home."

"Okay, that's fine with me."

A minute later he understood why she was suddenly being so cooperative. She knew McDonald's was closed. By the time they got home, he was in too much of a hurry to get her undressed to think about food. She wanted to shower, and that was fine with him, as long as he could get in the shower with her.

They fell into bed together and made love again. He pressed her down into the mattress, held her hands prisoner above her head, and told her all the loving words he needed to say and she needed to hear.

Then it was her turn. "Say it," he whispered.

She wanted to be practical. "When you get home and get back into your routine—"

"Say it," he demanded.

"You'll look back on this as a...fling."

"Are we going to have our first fight?"

"No, I'm just..."

"Say it."

Tears welled up in her eyes. "We've only known each other..."

"Say it."

"I love you," she whispered.

He was so pleased he kissed her; then he rolled onto his side and pulled her up against him. She cried all over his chest. He knew why. She thought he would return to Boston and go on with his life...without her.

He would have gotten angry if he hadn't remembered that the woman he loved didn't know squat about men. He waited until she was finished crying and was hiccupping.

Stroking her back, he said, "I dated Rebecca for a year before she moved in. We lived together for another year before we got married, and you know what?"

She lifted her head so she could see his face. "What?"

"I didn't know her as well as I already know you. Life's too short, Michelle. I want to be with you. I want to grow old with you."

She desperately wanted to believe him. She knew he was telling the truth, but she was also convinced that, once he returned to his job in Boston and his friends and family, he would realize he belonged there.

"Marry me, Michelle."

"You have to go back to Boston. If you feel the way you do now in six months, then ask me again."

"I can't stay away from you that long."

"I want you to be sensible about this. Six months," she repeated.

He pushed her on her back and rolled on top of her, bracing his weight with his arms. God, how he loved her. Even when she was being stubborn.

He stopped arguing. He had other things on his mind now. He began to nuzzle her as he nudged her thighs apart.

"You win, sweetheart. Six months."

CHAPTER FORTY-THREE

He lasted three long miserable weeks. Then he called the movers, put his boats up for sale, packed the trunk of his car, and drove to Bowen. He stopped by The Swan first, shook Jake's hand, and formally asked for permission to marry his daughter.

Then he went home. To Michelle. He knocked on the door, and when she answered, he pulled her into his arms and told her, in no uncertain terms, that he had no intention of staying away from the woman he loved for six months. He was there to stay, and she was going to have to deal with it.

She wasn't arguing with him—she was too busy trying to kiss him—but Theo was on a roll and couldn't stop. He told her he would open an office in Bowen and give the sleazy attorneys in St. Claire some competition, that he would also do some government work in New Orleans a couple of days a week—Justice wasn't going to let him go—and that he had enough money invested to keep their heads well above water.

He could actually retire now, thanks to his sister, Jordan. He and the others in the family had invested in her company, and she had made them a small fortune. And one last thing, he added as he dodged her hands, he had already called Conrad and informed him that he would be signing the coaching contract.

Then he kissed her and told her how much he loved her.

"I came to Bowen in search of what I had lost. I wanted to feel that passion and energy again. Now I feel alive. My life is here with you, Michelle. I'm home."

Tears streamed down her face. "I love you, Theo."

He hugged her tight. "If you *ever* send me away again, I swear I'll do something so embarrassing, you'll never live it down. The people in Bowen will be telling our grand-children about it."

"I'm a doctor," she reminded him. "Nothing embarrasses me."

"Yeah? So then if I call the hospital while you're making rounds, you won't be embarrassed when I have the operator page Dr. Smarty-pants?"

She pulled back so she could look into his eyes. "You wouldn't..."

"Try me."

"I'll never send you away again. I promise."

The tension eased out of his shoulders and he relaxed. "I want you to go with me to my brother's wedding next weekend. It's in Iowa. I want you to meet my family, and they'll all be there. Okay, sweetheart?"

"Theo, are you sure—"

"I'm sure," he said emphatically. "You can get Landusky to cover for you, can't you? Your dad told me you still haven't taken a vacation."

"When did you talk to Daddy?"

"I stopped by The Swan on my way here. Will you marry me, Michelle?"

"Yes." As simple as that. The joy she felt was overwhelming, and she began to cry.

"I asked your dad for permission to marry you."

"That was sweet."

"He cried."

She got teary-eyed again. Then he made her laugh. "John Paul cried too."

"He'll get used to you."

"The whole town's going to be celebrating. Everyone's been trying to help you catch a man."

"What?"

He grinned. "That's why there weren't any 'Welcome to Bowen' cards with all that food. How come you didn't figure it out? Everyone knew we belonged together, everyone but you."

Before she could get upset over the conspiracy, he kissed her again. Then he checked the time.

"Gotta go, sweetheart. I don't want to be late for practice."

She stood on the porch watching as he drove away. Then she sighed. She had a wedding to plan. She thought about all the things she would need to get done and decided that if she rushed, she could throw it together in six months. That was doable. Yes, six months.

They were married in three.

The wedding was elegant. The reception was a blowout. Michelle's brothers, Remy and John Paul, were groomsmen, and Theo's sisters, Jordan and Sydney, were bridesmaids.

His brother Nick was Theo's best man, and Mary Ann was Michelle's maid of honor.

The bride was radiant, but terribly nervous as she held on to her daddy's arm on that long walk down the center aisle of the church. When the groom stepped forward, looking so devastatingly handsome in his tuxedo, and winked at her, she began to relax.

Daddy had wanted to rent a fancy ballroom in one of the expensive New Orleans hotels, but Theo and Michelle wouldn't hear of it. They wanted the reception to take place at The Swan.

Since they wouldn't compromise, Daddy gave in and decided then to use a little bit of his inheritance from Catherine to spruce the place up. He left the swan on top of the building alone because he felt the wing hanging down gave the place a little added charm, but he paved the parking lot, rented a big white tent, and filled it with flowers and tables covered in white linen cloths.

He hired a band too, but at the last minute Theo's brother Zachary had to fill in for the drummer, Elton Spinner, who had flown the coop as soon as he heard how many law enforcement officers would be attending the affair. It seemed that Elton still had that warrant hanging over his head.

Theo stood next to his brother Nick, watching Michelle dance with their father. Laurant, Nick's bride, was dancing with little John Patrick; Noah and Mary Ann were glued to each other as they swayed to the music, while

515

Daddy twirled Theo's mother around and around.

"Any word yet on John Russell? Or Monk?" Nick asked. "Noah told me they're following every lead..."

"They're closing in. It won't be long before they get both of them."

"That's an optimistic outlook."

"Hey, it's my wedding day. I'm allowed to be optimistic."

Nick changed the subject to a more pleasant one. "Noah and Jake won that tournament?"

"Yeah, they did. They donated the cash to the football team. All the players are getting new cleats, and Jake's trying to figure out a way he can advertise The Swan on the side of the shoes."

Nick smiled. "So, now you're a football coach on top of everything else, huh?"

Theo couldn't take his gaze off his beautiful bride long enough to look at his brother. "Yeah, I am. Go figure."

Nick laughed. "It's gonna be nice having a doctor in the family. So tell me," he said, elbowing his brother to get his attention.

"What?"

"How'd that happen?"

"How'd what happen?"

"How'd you end up being a coach?"

Theo grinned. "There was this kid..."

CHAPTER FORTY-FOUR

It was another glorious night in paradise. The air was crisp and clean; the sky was filled with stars shining down on the golden city.

Dressed in a silk robe and suede slippers, John stood on the terrace of his palatial penthouse apartment, looking out at the night. Life didn't get any better than this. He took a drink of the warm brandy in the crystal snifter and sighed with contentment. The sweet fragrances of the night swirled around him.

This was utopia. He had a new life, a new identity, and so much money he would never have to touch the principal. He could live like a king on the interest alone. And that was more glorious to him than his surroundings.

Behind him, he heard the rustle of clothing and knew the woman was getting dressed. She called out to him. He glanced back just as she blew him a kiss and walked out the door. This one, he thought, had been better than any of the others, and he knew he would have her again. She was so creative in bed, so brashly uninhibited. Perhaps he would call her tomorrow, but then he remembered the blond he had scheduled to entertain him. What was her name? He couldn't remember. He did remember how she had intrigued him. She reminded him a little of Dallas, and perhaps that was why he wanted her. A remembrance of the past. The Sowing Club. It seemed a lifetime ago, yet it had only been a little over six months since he'd climbed into that plane. Dallas and Preston were dead. He'd read about them in the paper, and he often found himself wondering exactly how they had died. Had Buchanan killed them, or had the other one shot them? What was his name? Clayborne. Yes, that was it.

Ironic, he thought, that the weakest member of the club had survived. Poor, poor Cameron. John knew how claustrophobic he was. How was he enjoying prison life, he wondered, and then he smiled. Had his mind snapped yet?

Monk was probably dead. John had seen the blood on his shirt. He wouldn't have risked getting medical aid, and John thought he probably crawled into a hole somewhere like a wounded animal, hiding while he died.

He finished his brandy and put the glass on the table. Yawning, he walked through the living room and down the hall. The woman had worn him out, and tomorrow was going to be a busy day. He wanted to get up early so that he could be on his yacht by nine. He would do his last-minute packing for his cruise in the morning.

He opened the bedroom door, stepped inside, and turned on the light. He could smell the woman's perfume. He smiled again. No, life didn't get any better than this.

Turning toward the bed, he lazily stretched his arms out and then untied his robe. He took a step forward, then leapt back. "No!" he cried. "No!"

There in the center of the satin sheets lay a long-stemmed red rose.

APACK

3102

10/1

V